too many…

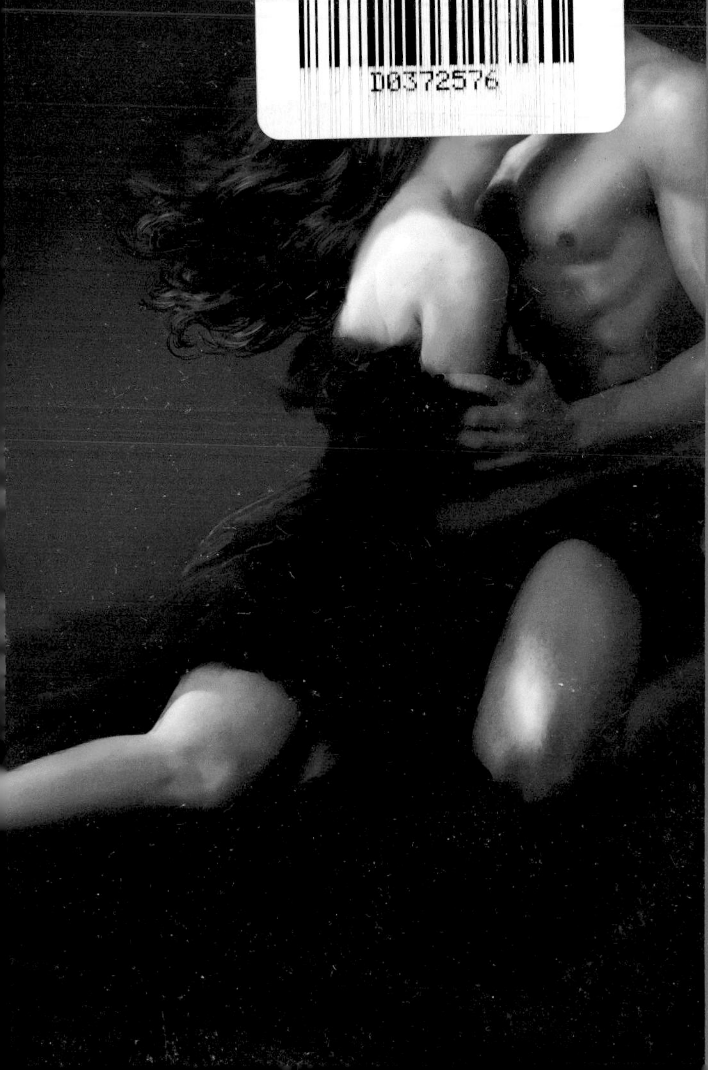

"Promise me something."

He stopped, but he did not look at her. "What's that?"

"If you must marry—and I can see you are quite determined to do so—promise me you'll marry only for love."

"I am sure that if I choose to marry a woman of good character and if we share mutual respect and fondness, love will surely follow."

"Either that," she said with a dry chuckle, "or you'll bore each other to death."

"Your view of love and mine are obviously different, Lady Julia. Good night."

Once again Aidan moved to leave, but to his astonishment, she reached out to stop him. He froze and closed his eyes, arousal stirring again. He fought it, hating her because she could still evoke with the touch of her hand what had already destroyed his honor and his reputation.

"Marriage without love is hell, Aidan," she said. "Don't go into that hell. Promise me you won't."

He didn't reply, for there was nothing to say. Desire was flooding through him, and love and marriage were the last things on his mind.

By Laura Lee Guhrke

SCANDAL OF THE YEAR
WEDDING OF THE SEASON
WITH SEDUCTION IN MIND
SECRET DESIRES OF A GENTLEMAN
THE WICKED WAYS OF A DUKE
AND THEN HE KISSED HER
SHE'S NO PRINCESS
THE MARRIAGE BED
HIS EVERY KISS
GUILTY PLEASURES

Laura Lee Guhrke

Scandal of the Year

ABANDONED AT THE ALTAR

AVON
An Imprint of HarperCollinsPublishers

AVON BOOKS
An Imprint of HarperCollins*Publishers*
10 East 53rd Street
New York, New York 10022–5299

Copyright © 2011 by Laura Lee Guhrke
Excerpt from *What I Did For a Duke* copyright © 2011 by Julie Anne Long
ISBN 978-0-06-196316-2
www.avonromance.com

First Avon Books paperback printing: February 2011

Avon Trademark Reg. U.S. Pat. Off. and in Other Countries, Marca Registrada, Hecho en U.S.A.
HarperCollins® is a registered trademark of HarperCollins Publishers.

Printed in the U.S.A.

10 9 8 7 6 5 4 3 2

*For the talented fellow authors who helped me so much
during the writing of this book:
Elizabeth Boyle, Gayle Callen, and Kathryn Smith.
I can't tell you how much your friendship,
support, and enthusiasm mean to me.*

Thank you.

Out of the night that covers me,
Black as the Pit from pole to pole,
I thank whatever gods may be
For my unconquerable soul.

In the fell clutch of circumstance
I have not winced nor cried aloud.
Under the bludgeonings of chance
My head is bloody, but unbowed.

Beyond this place of wrath and tears
Looms but the Horror of the shade,
And yet the menace of the years
Finds, and shall find, me unafraid.

It matters not how strait the gate,
How charged with punishments the scroll,
I am the master of my fate:
I am the captain of my soul.

"Invictus"
William Ernest Henley, 1875

Prologue

From the London society newspaper *Talk of the Town*, Friday, October 9, 1903:

YARDLEY DIVORCE HEARING
CONVENES TODAY!

Will the baroness publicly admit to her adultery? Or will she deny it to save herself from further disgrace?

The London courtroom was packed to the rafters, and Julia could feel the avid stares of the curious crowd boring into her back as she walked up the aisle to stand before the president of the divorce court.

Plenty of reporters were there, of course, pencils in hand, scribbling down the lurid details that would appear in the evening papers.

Yardley was there, too, arms folded, remote and inhuman—just as usual, in other words. Julia did not acknowledge his presence. Without turning her head, she spared him only the briefest sideways glance as she passed the table where he sat.

She knew several members of her family and some of her friends were present as well, but she did not look back to find their faces in the crowd. She couldn't, not now, not yet, not until it was over.

When Sir Birrell cast his stern, reproving eye upon her, Julia felt no pang of conscience for what she had done or what she was about to do. When he asked her if the accusation of her husband was true, she took a deep breath and lifted her chin to an angle she hoped was as unrepentant as she felt. Casting aside the fear that had haunted her for the twelve long, loveless years of her marriage, she turned to look into Yardley's cold black eyes.

"Yes," she said, her voice ringing out like a bell of liberty, filled with such adamant conviction that she almost believed herself. "On the afternoon of August 21, 1903, I had intimate relations of a sexual nature with Aidan Carr, the Duke of Trathen."

The court erupted. Sir Birrell pounded his gavel, demanding order, and when it had been regained, he declared Yardley's petition granted. A decree of divorce would be issued immediately and would be declared final in six months. Julia's knees sagged beneath her in relief, and the desperation and despair that had haunted her since the day of her wedding began to ease away. A slave when she came into the court, she turned to leave it knowing that at last she would be free.

It was then that she saw Aidan at the back of the courtroom, standing by the door. His presence surprised her, for as named co-respondent, he had already submitted a written statement and had sworn to its validity before this court a short while ago. He had no need to linger here, and by remaining, he was only giving the ravenous scandal sheets more meat to savor.

As she looked at him, her mind flashed back to the first time she'd ever seen him, standing by that brook in Dorset twelve years earlier, and though it seemed a lifetime ago, he hadn't changed much during the intervening years. He was as gravely handsome at twenty-nine as he'd been at seventeen.

She could read nothing in his expression as he studied her. Several tendrils of his unruly brown hair curled over his straight brown brows, and below them, his hazel eyes were steady and unblinking as they looked into hers. His stare was hard, searching, but with no glimmer of doubt. As she approached where he stood by the door, his chin went up a notch, and the lines of Henley's "Invictus" echoed through her mind.

It hurt to look at him now, in the aftermath of what she had wrought. He'd been publicly humiliated, his reputation stained. He would not be permanently damaged, but Julia knew that wasn't the point. She had done far worse than stain his reputation. She had compromised his honor and stolen his self-respect. For the first time, guilt pressed upon her, a weight against her chest and a shadow on her soul, but she could not find it in her heart to regret what she had done.

As she drew closer, his lips tightened, but he spoke no word to her. He did not turn his head to watch her as she passed. He stood as a soldier stands to post, without moving, his wide shoulders stiff and proud, reminding her that although she was now free, she was not the only one who had paid the price for her freedom.

Chapter One

London
May 1904

The Duke of Trathen needed to find a wife. The
problem was that when it came to picking
the right woman for the job, His Grace was
having a serious run of bad luck.

One might think that for a man of his station, choosing a bride would be a relatively straightforward business. Dukes were a rare commodity, highly sought in
the marriage mart, so it wasn't as if he lacked a substantial slate of candidates from which to choose. Nor
were dukes hampered by anything as inconvenient as
love. Alliance was a perfectly acceptable reason for
matrimony among those of the aristocracy, and Aidan
Thomas Carr was a man who could trace his aristo-
cratic lineage to the days of Queen Elizabeth.

The eleventh Duke of Trathen, Aidan was in possession of half a dozen lesser titles as well. He was also one of the wealthiest men in Britain, with substantial lands and investments. He had an astute head for business, had a keen interest in politics, and was considered by many among the fair sex to be quite a handsome fellow.

This stellar résumé notwithstanding, the Duke of Trathen was a jilted man, having been abandoned at the altar not once, but twice. He was a bit skittish about making a third attempt, but every duke had a duty to his family and his heritage to marry well, produce sons, and pass everything on to the next generation, and Aidan was a man who would never ignore his duty.

When the time arrived for the Marquess of Kayne's annual May Day Ball, the most prominent charity event of the London season, the Duke of Trathen was among the attendees. He was not particularly fond of dancing, he hated these crowded charity affairs, and given the endless gossip about him these days, he would have preferred to spend the spring as he had spent the winter—at his favorite estate in Cornwall—but he could not afford that luxury. He was now thirty years old, time was going by, and a man could meet many potential marriage partners at a charity ball.

When he'd begun his search for a duchess three years earlier, he'd never dreamed it would be this difficult. He had decided, quite logically, that twenty-seven was a good age at which to wed, and he had set about finding his duchess. Four months later, he'd met

Lady Beatrix Danbury, a girl who was not only beautiful, with honey-blond hair and big, soft brown eyes, but also charming and intelligent. The daughter of an earl, she'd been groomed all her life for the duties of a high-ranking peeress. Aidan had thought their interests coincided, and their affection mutual. Not an overmastering passion, perhaps, but he had never been the sort of man to be carried away by passion, a fact that had seemed acceptable to Beatrix. By Christmas of that year, they had become engaged, but less than two months before the wedding, she'd thrown him over for her childhood sweetheart, the Duke of Sunderland.

Aidan's heart, though bruised, was not broken. After spending six months in Cornwall, he'd launched his second search for a suitable duchess, and by the end of the season, he had decided upon Lady Rosalind Drummond, the eldest daughter of a Scottish marquess.

But then had come that inexplicable and disastrous episode with Lady Yardley. By the time the story of their afternoon tryst hit the society pages, Aidan was already on his way to Scotland to face his fiancée, but he could offer Rosalind no defense. Hell, he couldn't offer so much as an explanation.

He didn't even *like* Lady Yardley. Just how he had ended up naked in bed with that woman, her enraged husband standing over them both, was still vague in his mind, but he did know that the catastrophe had been preceded by a picnic, an inordinate quantity of champagne, and his own foolish determination to prove he could resist the seductive baroness no matter what.

Along with some hazy, hotly erotic memories, he re-membered little else of the incident that had brought public humiliation raining down upon him, and to this day, he could not understand what it was about that woman that had evoked such promiscuous and unac-ceptable behavior in him.

Regardless of how it had come about, he'd had to face the consequences, including a second broken en-gagement. Another winter at his Cornish estate, the ar-rival of another London season, and now he was back in town to begin again his search for a suitable bride, but having been twice jilted, as well as humiliated and disgraced, Aidan found himself unable to summon much enthusiasm about the process.

Still, with his worthless cousin as his sole heir, Aidan knew he could not afford the luxury of waiting much longer to marry. To secure his estates and the empire he had built, he needed a duchess by his side and strong, healthy sons in his nursery.

Which was why he was here, Aidan reminded him-self. Setting aside pointless remembrances of past romantic contretemps, he returned his attention to the glittering ballroom before him. As he did so, he reached for one of the glasses on the tray held by a nearby footman, but he made a sound of exaspera-tion when he realized the glass held champagne rather than punch. He'd discovered long ago that alcohol was rather a dangerous substance where he was concerned, and he usually limited himself to no more than a single glass of wine on any social occasion. The fact that he'd broken that rule in Lady Yardley's company last summer was only one of many things about that day that still baffled him. Aidan contemplated the glass in his hand for a moment, then prudently set it back on the tray and resumed his study of the many young ladies scattered about the ballroom of Lord Kayne's Park Lane residence.

Many were dancing, and they flitted across his line of vision like so many gauzy pastel butterflies. The first young lady in the room to catch his eye, however, was not dancing. Instead, Lady Frances Mowbray was standing quite near him with a group of her friends. Before meeting Beatrix, he had considered Lady Frances, but Mowbray's penchant for deep-stakes gambling and inability to afford it meant he would be paying his father-in-law's debts endlessly. He'd rather not.

His gaze shifted to one of her companions, Minnie Goulet, a pretty American girl. Not part of the old New York Knickerbocker set, Miss Goulet was very much new money. Aidan, with neither the need nor the desire to marry for money, and the patriotism to prefer a British wife, moved on.

Miss Patricia Hopworth? Not as pretty as Miss Goulet, to be sure, but agreeable enough. Her background was impeccable, and from what he could recall, she had a sweet disposition—

"Heavens, Trathen," a cheerful feminine voice broke into his thoughts, "what are you doing tucked back here alone? The first ball of the season you have deigned to attend, and here you are skulking in a corner?"

Aidan turned to find Lady Vale standing nearby, shaking her head at him. "Countess," he greeted with a bow. "I am not skulking," he added, impelled to correct her choice of words. "I am observing."

"I see." She gave him a thoughtful glance as she moved closer to his side, but she said nothing more, seeming content to stand beside him and watch the couples swirling across the floor. It was not until the waltz ended that she spoke again.

"Ah," she said as if making a sudden discovery, "so Felicia *was* dancing. I thought perhaps she might have gone to the refreshment room for a glass of punch." There was another pause, and Lady Vale gave a delicate laugh. "You are perhaps not acquainted with my youngest daughter?" When he shook his head, Lady Vale waved her fan toward another part of the room. "She is standing beside that enormous vase of lilacs over there."

Aidan's gaze followed Lady Vale's gesture to a petite girl in a pink frock standing by a vase of lavender lilacs. She was lovely, with gold hair, porcelain skin, and dark, almond-shaped eyes, but there was something about her prettiness that made her seem rather like a doll, for he fancied a certain vapidity in her expression. Still, meeting the girl could do no harm, especially since her mother seemed quite willing to arrange it.

He turned toward the countess, but before he could request an introduction to Lady Felicia, his attention was diverted by another feminine figure, one he immediately recognized.

Good God, he thought, appalled, what was that woman doing here?

That was how he usually thought of Lady Yardley—as *that woman*. Legal precedent enabled her to retain her husband's title, her Christian name was Julia, and her friends called her Julie, but in Aidan's mind, she was *that woman*, or when he was in a less charitable frame of mind, *that plague on mankind*.

The color of her gown suited her, he supposed—a crimson dress for a scarlet woman. Cut with a generous expanse of décolleté, caught at the shoulders by the tiniest of cap sleeves, and made of silk charmeuse, the gown displayed her shape without regard for modesty. She'd gained a bit of weight, he noted, his gaze skimming over her. The curves of her body were more generous than before, her breasts fuller, her hips wider, and it aggravated Aidan beyond belief that though many details of that afternoon still eluded him, he could recall perfectly just how her body had looked without any clothes.

Lady Vale, perceiving that his attention had gone astray, turned to see what had caught his eye, but though he sensed the countess's gaze on him, he could not seem to tear his own from the woman in the doorway.

Other memories of Lady Yardley went through his mind, vague, illicit flashes—his hands unbuttoning her white dress and pulling it down her shoulders, her breasts in his hands, her body on top of his.

All of a sudden, the ballroom seemed suffocatingly

hot. Aidan drew a deep breath and ran a finger around the inside of his collar, knowing he ought to leave the room before she noticed him, but he could not seem to move.

Her heart-shaped face seemed the same, though perhaps not quite so drawn as before. He was too far away to see the color of her eyes, but he already knew they were the same shade of lavender as the lilacs that adorned the room, but the shadows that had been beneath those eyes last summer were gone now. Her hair was piled atop her head in the Gibson fashion, displaying her long, slender neck to perfection, but Aidan's mind could not escape the image of her riotous raven-black tresses tumbling down around her bare white shoulders amid a snowy mound of white sheets, an image that did not make the room feel any cooler.

Diamonds sparkled at her throat, drawing his attention. *Had he kissed her there?* he wondered, his gaze riveted to the creamy expanse of skin above her breasts. The heat that immediately began spreading through his body gave him the answer to that question. Even now, he thought with chagrin, even two dozen feet away from her and three quarters of a year from that fateful day, he could still imagine the texture of her skin, like warm satin against his mouth.

The waltz ended, the last notes faded away, and Aidan came to his senses with a start, realizing how quiet the room had become. Then he heard the murmurs begin, a ripple of discreet whispers. He could imagine what people were saying—reminders that her husband's divorce petition had become final last month, tittering jokes about their mutual presence here, speculation as to whether he intended to resume his amour with her.

Beside him, Lady Vale murmured a rather frosty farewell and departed, having drawn the obvious conclusion from his scrutiny of the other woman. A quick glance around confirmed that she was not the only one who had done so. Many curious gazes were sliding back and forth between him and the scandalous divorcee.

Leave, he told himself, now, before any gossip could begin that coupled their names. Yet, even as that thought passed through his mind, he could not find the will to move. Instead, like a moth drawn to a destructive flame, he returned his attention to the woman in the doorway, and he discovered it was now too late to escape her notice even if he chose to do so, for she'd seen him. She acknowledged him with a nod, then she waited, watching him, a faint smile curving one corner of her rouged lips.

He could still make his feelings clear to everyone present. All he had to do was give her the cut direct. By turning his back on her without an acknowledging bow, he would put a stop to any ridiculous speculation that they might once again be lovers.

The wise thing to do, he knew, but he couldn't do it. He could not compound his lapse of gentlemanly conduct nine months ago by being ungentlemanly now. The fact that her husband had divorced her was his fault as well as hers. He bowed to her, the slightest bow good manners could allow, then he turned away from her and the erotic images that hovered just at the edge of his conscious mind.

He kept his head high as he made his way amid the crowd to the open French doors leading onto the terrace. He stepped outside and moved to stand at the carved marble railing, where he stared out into the darkness of Kayne's gardens and breathed deeply of the spring air to cool his blood. With that woman near him again, anything might happen, and Aidan was glad that this time around, he'd chosen to forgo the champagne.

Julia sighed as she watched Aidan leave the ballroom amid the whispers and stares. *He hasn't changed a bit*, she thought in frustration. Still so stiff and so proud, still considering women who were all wrong for him, and still just too damned nice for his own good. He should have cut her a moment ago, for it was obvious why he was at this ball, and acknowledging her did him no favors in that quarter.

Guilt nudged at her, the same guilt that she'd felt the last time she'd seen him. It was a feeling she was unaccustomed to and one she did not like, and she wondered if perhaps she should have stayed in France. She shrugged her shoulders several times as if to shrug off that niggling guilt and reminded herself that one had to face the music sometime. Besides, she hadn't gone to all this trouble freeing herself from Yardley so that she could hide away somewhere. She'd done enough hiding in her life already. Unlike Aidan, she didn't mind being stared at and whispered about. She didn't mind losing her reputation. She'd never given a damn what society thought. Aidan did, he minded terribly, and that was the difference between them.

"Julie!"

The voice of the Marchioness of Kayne broke into her reverie, and she turned her attention to the slender blond in sapphire silk approaching her.

Julia evaded the other woman's outstretched hands and took an uneasy glance around. "Are you sure you should welcome me so enthusiastically, Maria? I don't want you to suffer any guilt by association."

"Stuff." With that scoffing rejoinder, Maria grasped Julia's gloved hands in her own and pressed a kiss to each of her cheeks. "Showing my support in public is crucial if we're to rebuild your reputation."

"I appreciate your trying to rebuild the walls of Jericho, darling, but I fear it's a lost cause." She squeezed her friend's hands with affection, then released them to take a glass of champagne from the tray held by the footman nearby.

"If it can be done for Lady Shrewsbury, it can be done for you," Maria pointed out. "You have powerful friends, you know. I just wish I had known you had arrived in town. Where are you staying? With Danbury?"

This reference to Julia's cousin, the Earl of Danbury, caused her to give an affirmative nod. "Aunt Eugenia is beside herself, worrying about how it will look to have the black sheep divorcee of the family staying with them, but Paul, bless him, overruled his mother, and I am firmly ensconced in Berkeley Square."

"Excellent. Why didn't you tell me you were coming to my ball tonight?"

With those words, Julia was struck by a ghastly possibility, one that contradicted all her own information. "Yardley's not here, is he?" she asked, glancing around.

"Heavens, no! You think I'd offer that man a voucher to a charity ball of mine? Never! Not even for the hospitals."

They both laughed at that, but then Maria's face took on a more somber expression. "I heard Yardley's not in town, but many people don't come for the season until after Whitsuntide. He might come then."

"I doubt it," she answered, relieved that her information about her former husband's impending holiday seemed to be accurate after all. "He's not a sociable man, as you may have noticed, and besides, I heard he's off to Africa. On safari, I'm told. Sorry I didn't tell you I was coming tonight," she added, desperate to change the subject. "I know crashing a ball is the height of bad taste, but I didn't want my name appearing on the printed guest list." She gave her friend an impudent wink. "Hospitals need all the funds they can get, and if people knew I was coming, London society might develop a mass epidemic of the sniffles."

"Nonsense!" Maria turned, hooking her arm through Julia's to pull her more firmly into the room. "I told you, your friends are working hard on your behalf. That's why I wish you'd written ahead, so I could reassure you. The stand we're taking is that you and Yardley had an open arrangement, you both knew the score, and it was quite bad form for him to come storming into that cottage the way he did."

Julia couldn't help a laugh. "So his sin is that he opened us both to scandal by barging in on my love nest with Trathen, queering the pitch and then going public with the story? The absurdities of English etiquette! It's all right for couples living apart to commit infidelity upon each other, but one simply must be discreet about it!"

"I know, it seems silly, but it's the only way to frame the situation. Yardley has enemies, you know, some of them powerful men willing to condemn him. You'd have more sympathy, of course, if—" She stopped, but Julia knew what she'd almost said.

"If I'd given my husband a son or two before having affairs?" Julia's hand tightened around the stem of her champagne glass, but with an effort, she kept her voice light. "Simply not possible, darling. I'd have had to throw myself off a cliff."

"Oh, Julie!" Maria stared at her in wide-eyed horror. "Don't say things like that! You don't mean it."

She did mean it, but she didn't argue the point. After all, her former life was not the sort of thing one talked about, particularly at parties. "Maria, dearest, don't look so stricken!" she said, forcing a laugh. "It's all over, I'm free of that beastly man, and it doesn't matter to me in the least that I am not received at court or welcomed in the high circles because he divorced me. I've always preferred the bohemians anyway. Although," she added, feeling another pang of conscience, "it's different for the rest of the family. I do wish they didn't have to suffer by association."

"We're doing what we can to change that. Your friends are standing by you, and now that Danbury has thrown his support behind you as well by having you to stay, even better."

"Don't have any illusions my cousin did this for me," Julia said, laughing, striving to keep her carefree air intact. "Paul's welcoming me back with open arms because he's in desperate need of meaningful conversation. His wife has gone back to the States, his brother Geoff is at Oxford, and our cousin Beatrix is in Egypt. He's all alone with his mother in that house, and having only my Aunt Eugenia for company would drive any sane man off his chump."

"We both know that's not his reason," Maria demurred with a smile. "But try not to worry about your reputation or your family suffering for it. You'll soon have some invitations, more and more of them as time goes on. I am seeing to that."

Julia was quite touched, well aware of the precarious social precipice onto which her friend was stepping. "Dear Maria, I don't want to reflect badly on you. You've spent over ten years building your place in society. I don't want to spoil things for you."

"You won't. Though I am merely the daughter of a chef, and though I once owned a shop and engaged in trade, my mother was gentry, so I have a tiny bit of acceptable blood in my veins. In the eyes of some, I will never be accepted, of course. But I have four healthy sons to my credit, and my husband is both rich and powerful, so my place is reasonably secure. I am happy to help you any way I can. Kayne endorses my decision, by the way, and offers his help and support as well."

"I fear we'll need it. My family seems to have become a favorite topic of gossip the past few years. Paul's wife taking such a long time to come back to England makes Paul a target. And that whole business of Beatrix throwing over Trathen to elope with the Duke of Sunderland caused quite a stir as well." She paused, noting the furtive stares in her direction, then added, "Still, I've managed to steal their thunder, haven't I? I fear I'm the scandal of the year, perhaps even the decade."

Maria put a hand on her arm, her blue eyes filled with sympathy. "I wish there was more I could do."

"Don't you dare feel sorry for me! I don't mind all this for myself. I knew what I was doing. But for my family's sake, I thank you." She gave her friend a rueful smile. "I don't suppose you could work another miracle and find Trathen a wife, could you? A good one who'd make him happy?"

"Well, it won't be Lady Rosalind. She's engaged to Lord Creighton now."

Julia was glad of that. Lady Rosalind was a doe-eyed schemer with a mercenary heart, and the fact that she'd had to settle for a wealthy marquess instead of an even wealthier duke didn't tweak Julia's conscience one bit. Aidan was a different matter. She shrugged her shoulders again, trying to banish that nagging guilt. What was done was done. No undoing it now, and she wouldn't even if she could.

Still, when she thought of Aidan's eyes filled with self-condemnation, Julia found it hard to take comfort in her fait accompli.

Chapter Two

Aidan went for a walk in the gardens of Park Lane, and when he started back toward Kayne House some thirty minutes later, he felt his blood had cooled sufficiently that he could return to the ball.

Aware that being anywhere near Lady Yardley was dangerous to both his peace of mind and his reputation, he intended to keep well away from that woman for the remainder of the evening, but as he started toward the terrace, his intentions were forgotten at the sight of her slim figure sitting on the wide steps. Light from the ballroom spilled over her, thin ribbons of cigarette smoke swirled over her head, and the crimson silk of her gown pooled at her feet.

The moment he saw her, images of that August afternoon came roaring back, but he worked not to show any sign of it. "Lady Yardley," he said, and glanced at the cigarette in her fingers as he approached the steps. "Still smoking, I see."

She smiled a little. "I'm trying to give it up, if that raises me in your estimation." Her nose wrinkled ruefully at his unchanged expression. "Obviously it doesn't."

"I bid you good evening." For the second time tonight, he bowed to her, but as he started to ascend the steps to the ballroom, her voice stopped him.

"I was waiting for you here because I wanted to thank you."

He stopped, curious. "For what do you thank me?" he asked, even as he knew it was probably a mistake to inquire.

With her free hand, she reached for the glass of champagne perched on the step above the one where she sat. Then, turning, she leaned back against the carved stone balustrade of the stair railing and faced him, lifting her glass in salute. "Thank you for not giving me the cut direct earlier. Given the last time we saw each other, I thought you might."

He stiffened. "Contrary to some of my past behavior, I am still a gentleman." But even as he spoke, his gaze was lowering to the shadowy cleft between her breasts, and he feared that when it came to Lady Yardley, he was in fact hopelessly depraved. "At least I strive to be," he muttered, and forced his gaze back to her upturned face.

She was looking at him in a thoughtful way he didn't quite understand. "No striving necessary. You couldn't stop being a gentleman if you tried."

He gave a short, unamused laugh. "That's ironic, coming from you. The last time I was in your company, my gentlemanly side took quite a holiday."

She took a pull on her cigarette and tilted her head farther back to exhale the smoke overhead. "And you've been condemning yourself for it ever since, I daresay."

"Don't worry," he reassured her at once. "I have plenty of condemnation for you as well."

"As you should. I suspect, however, that you are reserving most of the blame for yourself."

"Can I be expected to do otherwise, having compromised a lady?"

She smiled, a dazzling flash of white in the moonlight. "Only you would think tumbling a willing and experienced woman was compromising her. That, and the fact that you can still refer to me as a lady, prove my point. But you need to stop being so damned chivalrous." She paused, her smile faded, and she added in a softer voice, "It makes you quite vulnerable, you know."

"Vulnerable?" he echoed, surprised by the word.

"To women who are all wrong for you."

He stiffened. "If you mean yourself, Lady Yardley, and that tiresome business last year, I can assure you—"

"I wasn't referring to myself," she interrupted. "I meant Rosalind. And Felicia Vale, too, of course. Yes," she added, "I saw you looking at her when I arrived, but you're wasting your time considering her. The girl's dim as a firefly."

This confirmation of his own suspicion had the curious effect of making him want to argue the point. "Nonsense. There is nothing wrong with Lady Felicia's intelligence."

"Hmm . . . it's obvious you haven't met her yet. She talks just like a mouse." As she spoke, her voice rose to an unbearably high, painful pitch. "Just like a teeny-tiny, itty-bitty mouse. Squeak, squeak, squeak." She paused to take a sip of champagne, then added in a normal voice, "She'll drive you mad in half an hour."

Aidan felt compelled to defend the poor girl against this criticism. "Even if what you say is true, a high voice does not imply stupidity."

He might have been talking to the wind. "Lady Felicia would be a terrible duchess. Especially for a brainy chap like you, with your interest in history, science, and politics."

"I haven't an interest in politics," he answered tersely. "Not anymore. It was suggested by certain colleagues that I not take my seat in the House of Lords for the good of the party. Tories and scandals do not mix."

"I'm sorry. I . . ." She paused and took another sip of champagne. "I didn't know that."

He looked away. "It doesn't matter," he lied.

"Even so," she went on, "with Lady Felicia, you couldn't even discuss politics. I doubt the poor girl knows which party is which."

"That's absurd. Her father's in the House. She must have some appreciation of—" He broke off, realizing too late he was becoming entangled in an argument with a woman whose opinion did not matter to him about a girl he did not know. He drew a deep breath.

"Forgive me," he said, pasting on a mask of cool, puzzled disinterest, "but what is the purpose of your rather ruthless assessment of Lady Felicia's intelligence?"

"Isn't it obvious? You're back on the hunt."

"And if I am, what has it to do with you?"

"Nothing at all. Still," she added irrepressibly, "you might want to reconsider your strategy. Appearing at public balls could prove to be more trouble than it's worth."

"I met your cousin Beatrix at a public ball."

"In St. Ives. London during the season is a different kettle of fish, as you are well aware. You'll be drowning in invitations by the end of the week, most of them from matchmaking mamas in the lower ranks who want to move up the social ladder."

"Given the curtailing of invitations from my own set because of my association with you, Lady Yardley," he shot back, "I am forced to widen my circle of acquaintance."

She bit her lip. "That won't last forever, not for you. One season. Perhaps two."

"Possibly, but I don't have the luxury of sitting back and waiting for my reputation to be restored. And I don't recall soliciting your views on the subject. And I have a title," he added, attempting a haughty, dampening tone without the least hope it would have any effect. "Would you mind terribly if I asked you to address me by it?"

She flashed him a grin. "I don't mind at all if you *ask*," she responded, as unimpressed by this attempt at ducal hauteur as he'd suspected she would be. "I can't promise to comply, though. Addressing everyone in the proper way is so predictable, and I do hate being predictable."

"I'm delighted to hear it," he countered. "No doubt you will surprise me then, and refrain from offering me any more of your pert opinions."

She held up her hand, waving it in an airy gesture toward the ballroom. "Oh, don't mind me. Go back inside, though I don't know what you expect to gain. Most of the unmarried women here are ladies you've already considered and rejected, or debutantes who are too young for you anyway."

She might have a point, but he refused to concede it. A man in search of a wife had to start somewhere. Folding his arms, he said, "Is there a point to any of this?"

"I suppose I'm warning you," she said slowly. "Don't allow yourself to be trapped or entangled with some girl whose character you know nothing about. It could happen if you're not careful."

"You mean because I allowed myself to be manipulated by you, I can be manipulated by any woman, is that it?"

If he hoped his words would sting, he was disappointed. She shrugged, his comment sliding off her back like water off a duck. "We all have our weaknesses, petal. Yours is your fine, upstanding character."

"How in heaven's name is that a weakness?"

"It makes you particularly susceptible to women who would do anything to secure a man of your position."

"Are you basing this conclusion on your own past ability to manipulate me, or are you just deeply cynical about your own sex?"

"I'm not cynical," she denied. "Just realistic. Most women are prohibited from earning their way in the world, and making a good marriage ensures their future and that of their children. You're a duke. You're also rich and successful, and despite our little tête-à-tête, you still wield a great deal of power. And you're so good-looking, too, without a scrap of conceit about it. What more could a girl ask for?"

He set his jaw. "Yes, that's me," he said with a hint of bitterness. "Every girl's dream."

Her head tilted to one side and she skimmed a considering glance over him. "You are, you know," she said, returning her gaze to his face. "You're just the sort of man girls dream about, and their ambitious parents, too. Snaring a duke, even if he is a bit tarnished, would be the coup de grâce for any family. Hell, thousands of women would marry you for your money alone."

"I would not be inclined to a girl of that sort."

"Rosalind Drummond was just that sort! I daresay if Creighton hadn't come along so soon, you'd have been able to win her back by the end of the season. Felicia Vale is just the same, though she hasn't Rosalind's brains. Neither of them is worthy of you. Honestly," she added with a hint of impatience, "what is it about melting brown eyes that makes your judgment go utterly awry?"

"That's nonsense!"

"Is it? Don't tell me Felicia's eyes weren't tempting you to ask Lady Vale for an introduction."

God, he thought in horror, was he that shallow? The idea didn't bear thinking about. "You don't have brown eyes," he pointed out, "and history proves that when it comes to you, my judgment is not awry, it's nonexistent. And since we are on the subject of my taste in women, Beatrix—if I understand you correctly—is just another mercenary woman who lied to me."

"Trix? No, she's not mercenary in the least, but . . ." Julia paused, considering. "But yes, in a way, she did lie to you."

"She's your own cousin. Yet you deem her dishonest?"

"There are different kinds of lies. Don't misunderstand me. I love Trix like a sister, and I don't think she's ever uttered a deliberate lie in her life. But when I introduced her to you at the St. Ives Ball, she was still feeling the pangs of heartache over Sunderland going off to Egypt, not to mention terrible grief and loss over the death of her father. She was at the lowest point of her life, and then you came along, just the right balm to soothe her wounded feminine pride and protect her from an uncertain future, the perfect hero charging in to save her. She convinced herself that she could be happy with you, but it was a lie, because the only man who's ever made her happy is Sunderland. As for you,

you took one look into Trix's big, sad eyes, and you were captivated. But that's all."

"All? How do you know I wasn't madly in love with her?"

Her answer was simple, direct, and brutal. "Because when Sunderland came back and she broke her engagement to you, you didn't fight to keep her."

"God," he choked, "you do give your opinions honestly, don't you, Baroness?"

"You asked," she said, and shrugged, taking a sip of champagne and another pull on her cigarette. "I just wish you'd be equally honest about yourself when it comes to matters of romance. You're a lot like Trix, you know. Honorable and good and trying so hard to always do the right thing, the dutiful thing. Striving all your life to live up to everyone's expectations and trying to believe virtue is its own reward."

"So it is."

She made a sound of derision. "You like to think it is. That's why you accepted my invitation for a picnic that day. You wanted to prove to yourself you could resist me, and you wanted to pat yourself on the back for your virtuous nature afterward."

He inhaled sharply, damning both her perspicacity and his own arrogance. "Well, I was appropriately punished for my conceit in that regard, wasn't I?"

Her mouth took on a sulky curve. "You did what you secretly wanted to do. You'd be happier if you'd be honest enough with yourself to admit that under all the gentlemanly honor you revere, you long for adventure and excitement and a taste now and then of the forbidden fruit."

"Getting drunk and sleeping with a married woman and being publicly humiliated for it is the sort of adventure I could well do without! You talk as if what happened was merely some delicious, harmless little romp in the country, but it wasn't. You used me," he accused in a hard, tight voice, angry with her and even more angry with himself. "You wanted a divorce, and the only way you could obtain it was by taking a new lover and arranging for Yardley to discover your adultery. For reasons I cannot fathom, you chose me to be your pawn."

She didn't deny it. She didn't try to defend herself. She said nothing, and her silence only fueled his anger.

"I have to admire your talent for strategy," he went on. "Yardley had overlooked your previous lovers, but how could he overlook it when he found you actually in bed with another man? And then, just to be doubly sure, you gave the whole sordid story to the gutter press, causing a scandal so blatant Yardley had no choice but to set you aside. You played me, and you played him, moving us around like pieces on a chessboard. You, madam, are a female Iago!"

Hurt shimmered across her face, and his shame deepened. He looked away. "I'm sorry," he apologized tightly, and worked to force his emotions back into governable order before he looked at her again. "That was uncalled for."

"No, it wasn't." She lifted her cigarette, then changed

her mind and crushed it out on the step below the one where she sat. "Why apologize for telling the truth? I did and I am all of which you accused me."

"Why did you do it? I can appreciate that your marriage was unhappy, but breaking it caused pain and humiliation not only to you and me, but also to two innocent people. Doesn't that bother you? Don't you care?"

She jerked, her chin lifting with the same defiance he'd seen her display that day in the divorce court. "My husband was a bastard," she said, her pale violet eyes glittering like gray steel in the dim light, and her voice was so hard and cold it chilled him. "I loathed that man to the very core, and I cannot work up even a tiny pang of conscience over any pain or humiliation he suffered. I'm sorry about Lady Rosalind, though I know her well enough to know she's probably not worth my regret, or yours, either. And she seems to have recovered nicely from the experience, for she's engaged again, I hear. So, no, to answer your question, I don't care. I would do it all over again."

He stared at her, shaking his head in disbelief at her icy disdain and lack of remorse. "What did your husband do to make you hate him so?"

"What did he do?" she echoed, and with mercurial suddenness, her face changed. The cold glint in her eyes vanished as if it had never been, and her disdain gave way to amusement. "Fucked the chambermaids, of course," she said lightly, laughing as if it was all a joke. "Don't they all?"

"Many do," he was forced to agree, concluding that Yardley was one of them, but he didn't see what was amusing about it. "But not all."

"Well, you won't," she said, and waved her hand toward the ballroom. "Go. Stop wasting your time with me. Go find your duchess."

He hesitated, feeling as if there was more to be said, but he decided they'd both said quite enough already. He turned away.

"But promise me something," she said as he started past her up the steps.

He stopped, but he did not look at her. "What's that?"

"Why anyone would want to marry at all baffles me, I confess, and my advice would be not to bother. But if you must marry—and I can see you are quite determined to do so—promise me you'll marry for love and no other reason, someone worthy of you who would make you happy. Believe it or not, I want you to be happy, for I do like you, you know. I always have."

He was inclined to doubt that, and her desire for his happiness seemed a bit late in the day to be genuine, but he didn't argue the point. "I am sure that if I marry a woman whose background and interests match my own, and if we share fondness and affection, genuine love will surely follow."

"Either that," she said dryly, "or you'll bore each other to death. I wouldn't call that love."

"Your view of love and mine are obviously different, Lady Yardley. Good night."

Once again he moved to leave, but to his astonishment, she reached out and actually put a hand on his leg to stop him. He froze and closed his eyes, arousal stirring inside him at her touch. He fought it, hating that she could still evoke with the touch of her hand what had already destroyed his honor and hurt his reputation, hating that she could move him like a chess piece, controlling in him what he could not seem to control in himself.

"An unhappy marriage is hell, Aidan," she said, her fingers curled around his shin. "I should know. Promise me you won't do what I did."

He didn't reply, for there was nothing to say. He was a duke, and he had a duty to marry, with love or without it. Slowly, he pulled away from her touch and went back inside without giving her the promise she'd asked for. He never made promises he wasn't sure he could keep.

It still hurt to see him, Julia realized as she watched him go, even seven months after that day in court. He hated her now. She couldn't blame him, of course, but it hurt just the same.

In the wake of his departure, his words lingered, echoing in the cool spring air.

Yes, that's me. Every girl's dream.

She'd heard the bitter, sarcastic tinge in those words, and that hurt, too. She leaned back, picturing him as he'd stood before her just moments ago, seeing again his splendid square jaw, the tawny glints in his dark brown hair, the wide set of his shoulders. She thought of his impeccably tailored black evening suit and snowy white linen shirt, remembering just what his body looked like without them—the chiseled muscles of his chest and abdomen, his tapered waist and long, strong legs. It was a body honed by the playing fields of Eton, the rowing oars of Oxford, and the tennis championships at St. Ives and Wimbledon, a body any woman ought to be able to appreciate and take pleasure in, but that day at her cottage she'd been unable to do so. Pleasure of that sort had long ago been stripped from her.

That had nothing to do with Aidan. He was every girl's dream even if he couldn't see it. He was also a gentleman down to his bones, the sort who believed in the old school tie, playing the game, and always doing the right thing, no matter what it cost him. But he also had a bit of the devil in him, a darker side that wanted the forbidden. He'd always wanted her, and from their very first meeting thirteen years ago, she'd known it. When given the chance, she'd exploited that knowledge for her own purposes with perfect finesse.

A female Iago.

His description stung, but it was apt. If Shakespeare's Iago could be played as a soul in hell, driven, dark, and desperate, willing to do anything, willing to use anyone, in order to escape from that hell, then yes, she had been Iago, the consummate manipulator, perfect in her part from start to finish.

God help her.

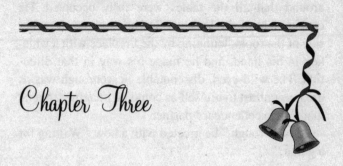

Chapter Three

The moment Aidan returned to the ballroom, he realized he could not remain there. He could not smile, and request introductions, and dance with young ladies, not when desire for that woman was flooding through his body, along with a generous amount of anger and frustration. Nor could he simply go home. At this hour of the evening, the ball was an absolute crush. It would take him an hour just to have his carriage brought around.

He crossed to the other side of the ballroom, ignoring any speculative glances he received along the way, and walked out, heading down the corridor to the card room. It was also a smoking room, but the haze of smoke seemed a tolerable option to him at present. He suspected even Lady Yardley wouldn't have the brass to come into a bastion reserved exclusively for gentlemen. Besides, cards were an excellent diversion.

He paused in the doorway, noting with a glance around that all the tables were fully occupied. He caught sight of the Duke of Scarborough on the other side of the room, lounging by the fireplace with a whiskey in his hand, and he made his way in that direction. The wild-eyed, disreputable Scarborough was as great a contrast to himself as could be imagined, but he made an excellent card partner.

"Scarborough," he greeted with a bow. "Waiting for a game?"

"I am." The other man lifted his glass, took a hefty swallow, and grimaced. "Thank God there's cards. It's the only way to get through one of these beastly things."

"Beastly things?" Aidan smiled. "You mean a public ball?"

"I mean any ball at all. I believe if I have to attend another one of these affairs, I'll go mad. And it's only May."

He took another drink and scowled. "It's a hellish business, Trathen, being in charge of a debutante."

This reference to the other man's American ward gave Aidan pause. He'd seen the girl out driving with her mother and Scarborough in Hyde Park a few days earlier, and Miss Annabel Wheaton, if he recalled correctly, was a pretty woman, demure and sweet-looking, with chestnut-brown hair. He wondered what color her eyes might be, but then Julia's words about his preference for dark eyes came back to him, and he gave an exasperated sigh.

Damn that woman and her knowledge of his tastes.

Shoving her out of his mind, he glanced over the various tables. "Are you looking to put together a whist game?"

"I'd prefer auction bridge, if I can find a partner with even a decent understanding of the strategy."

"Ouch," Aidan murmured dryly. "That hurts, Scarborough."

"Sorry, I didn't mean that the way it sounded," the other man assured him, laughing as he touched his free hand to his forehead. "I wasn't impugning your knowledge of cards. On the contrary, you are one of the few men in London who comprehends the concept of bidding hands and leading the proper cards."

"Then would you be interested in partnering with me for a few hands?"

"I'd adore it, but you know how I run, old chap. Deep stakes. Very reckless, I know, but there it is."

Aidan shrugged, not minding a high-stakes game at this particular moment. "I can afford it, and besides, twenty-five percent of the winnings are donated to the London hospitals."

"Still, extravagant gambling isn't your cup of tea, really, is it?"

"Perhaps you don't know me as well as you think you do."

One of Scarborough's devilish black brows lifted in surprise. "Fair enough," he murmured, and clapped him on the shoulder. "Let's do a good turn for the hospitals by fleecing some of these idiotic young dandies out of their quarterly allowance, shall we?"

* * *

Cards provided Aidan with plenty of distraction for the remainder of the evening, but in the days that followed the May Day Ball, Lady Yardley proved harder to dismiss from his mind.

Upon waking, the sight of his bed linens evoked the image of her naked in bed beside him at her cottage. The sight of a motorcar in the street as he traveled back and forth to his offices in the Strand made him think of her Mercedes and the wild way she drove it. Any white dress recalled to his mind the way she'd looked coming out of the water that afternoon at Gwithian Cove, her wet muslin frock clinging to her body like a second skin. He'd worked so hard to put the events of that day behind him, yet now, after one encounter with her, it seemed as if his efforts all had been for naught.

Aidan looked away from the work on his desk to stare out the window of his office, seeing past the wet spring day, past that day in the divorce court, past the hot August afternoon at her cottage, all the way back to the beginning, to the summer he was seventeen and the footbridge in Dorset where he'd first met her.

In fact, he could bring to mind every time he'd seen her over the years. The ball at St. Ives where he'd danced with her cousin because she was married. The house party at Lord Marlowe's villa where she'd played bawdy ragtime on the piano and he'd tried to keep his wits about him. The day before their picnic when she'd waved at him across the High Street in St. Ives and he'd crossed the street to speak to her even though he'd sensed he was making a huge mistake. The picnic, and watching her come out of the water, naked under that wet, white muslin dress.

All these incidents were vivid in his mind, so vivid that they might have happened hours rather than months and years ago. But he didn't really know the reason for such clarity.

Lady Yardley was beautiful, yes, but she was also brash, impudent, and immoral. She danced until dawn and smoked like a chimney and had never shown the least regard for her husband, her marriage vows, or the conventions of society. Yet, despite the fact that she seemed to possess all the traits in a woman he most disliked, despite the months or years that passed between their chance encounters, he could never seem to quite forget her. Why?

It doesn't matter, he told himself, and with an effort, he returned his attention to the business that had brought him into his offices this afternoon. He was supposed to meet with Lord Marlowe in three days to complete the negotiations for Trathen Mills to supply the paper to Marlowe Publishing during the coming year. Marlowe had sent over a counteroffer in response to his bid, and he needed to review it, but Aidan had barely reached for the viscount's proposal before his door opened and his secretary came bustling in.

There really was no other way to describe it. Mr. Charles Lambert was an energetic, bespectacled young man with a keen, intelligent face rather reminiscent of a greyhound. His sleeves were always rolled back, a pencil was always tucked behind his right ear, and a clipboard with paper was as much of an accessory to his daily apparel as a parasol was to a young lady's walking ensemble.

"I've sorted the afternoon post, Your Grace," Lambert announced as he approached the desk, his ever-present clipboard tucked under one arm, Aidan's appointment book under the other, and an enormous bundle of papers in his hands. "It's a bit more than usual," he added as he set the pile of correspondence on the desk. "Invitations, mostly."

"Due to my appearance at the May Day Ball, no doubt."

"I expect so, sir."

Aidan might be forever shunned in royal circles and never again received at court, and perhaps there were fewer invitations from the higher echelons and more from the lower ones among the stack on his desk, but the quantity of invitations confirmed that he was still an eligible *parti*, despite the blot on his copybook.

Lady Yardley had been right that many women would desire him for things that had nothing to do with his mind and character and everything to do with his position and money. And possibly, he acknowledged with a hint of distaste, with his appearance. He'd always known that. Such women might very well lie or maneuver their way into his affections, without caring two straws about him.

He'd never been a cynical man, and he didn't want to make a cynical match. He didn't expect overwhelming passion, which inevitably died once it was sated, but neither did he want the sort of marriage most peers had—mutual distaste, discreet love affairs, and separate lives. And he refused to be like his own father. The previous Duke of Trathen had made love to nearly every woman he knew, and though Aidan believed in tradition, that was a tradition he had no intention of carrying on.

He hoped to do better, to make a contented match with a compatible partner, but though he had launched this boost in his social life with that hope in view, he was now finding it hard to be enthusiastic about the process.

Staring at the stack of invitations his secretary had just brought him, he was suddenly tempted to change his mind, forgo marriage altogether, and let his cousin Reggie inherit the whole blinking show. That would make Aunt Caroline happy, no doubt, but Aidan knew he couldn't do it. His cousin would do his best to bankrupt the estates left in his care. No, Aidan had a duty to find a wife and he could not shirk it.

Promise me you'll marry for love and no other reason.

Aidan made a sound of aggravation. He had to put that woman back in the past where she belonged.

"Sir?"

"Hmm? What?" He looked up to find his secretary watching him with a puzzled expression, waiting to carry on with the matter at hand. "Sorry, Mr. Lambert," he said with a shake of his head. "Where were we?"

"Today's correspondence, sir."

"Ah, yes, thank you." He gestured to the chair opposite his desk, and the secretary sat down, placing his clipboard on his lap and opening Aidan's appointment book before reaching for the first invitation.

"Lord Danbury wishes to know if you are free for tennis on Thursday morning."

The invitation surprised him. Given his ill-fated entanglements with both of Paul Danbury's female cousins, he and the other man had the tendency to avoid each other these days, but perhaps this invitation to play tennis was an attempt by Paul to heal the breach. "Am I free Thursday morning?" he asked his secretary.

Lambert nodded, scanning that day's page of appointments. "You have no commitments that morning, so I believe you would have time for tennis." He glanced at the note again. "His Lordship warns you that he's been honing his serve, so if you accept his invitation, be prepared to lose."

Aidan grinned, liking the challenge. "Tell him I accept, and that I'm impressed he's improved his serve because it certainly needed improvement. Also tell him all the practice in the world won't help him because my backhand shall dispatch any serve he sends my way as it always does."

The secretary, who was not in the least athletic, did not quite understand this sort of bragging and insulting badinage between men about their superior skill at sport, but he scribbled the dictation on his clipboard, noted the engagement in Aidan's appointment book, and lifted the next letter from the stack. "Lord Marlowe wishes to confirm your receipt of his latest proposal, and if so, he suggests Thursday afternoon in his offices for the final negotiations, if that would be convenient." The secretary looked up. "You are free from half past two until five o'clock."

"Confirm with the viscount's secretary that we are in receipt of the proposal and that his time for an appointment would be acceptable, Mr. Lambert."

After another notation, the secretary moved on to the next item. "Lord Vale wishes to know if you would honor him by sharing his box with him and his family at Covent Garden Thursday night."

He hesitated, for although Lady Yardley might be a provocative minx, she was also a very accomplished judge of character. And he, too, had suspected Vale's youngest daughter to be somewhat lacking in brain matter. On the other hand, it wasn't fair to judge the girl so precipitously, and Lady Yardley could be having him on for mischievous reasons of her own. "Tell Vale I'd be delighted to call upon him and his family in their box during intermission."

"Yes, sir. First or second?"

Aidan blinked. "I beg your pardon?"

"I believe it's a Wagnerian opera on Thursday, sir. That means two intermissions. You might prefer the second one, since you also have an invitation to dinner for Thursday evening." He pulled the next invitation from the pile. "The Duke of Scarborough has asked you to dine with him; his ward, Miss Annabel Wheaton; and her mother, Mrs. Henrietta Chumley, at the Savoy. Half past seven. You could accept if you called at Lord Vale's box for the second intermission rather than the first."

Aidan shook his head. "No. I shall have to return to Grosvenor Square at some point and change into evening clothes before the opera, and I hate rushing back and forth across town. Express my regrets to Scarborough and tell him I should be delighted to dine with him another night."

Lambert nodded in confirmation as he made notes. "It's probably for the best anyway, sir," the secretary added, running his finger along the page of Aidan's appointment book. "Your schedule is now quite full for Thursday. Tennis in the morning, an appointment with your boot maker at eleven and your tailor at half past, then lunch at the Clarendon with Lord and Lady Malvers, the meeting with Lord Marlowe, and tea at the Savoy with Lord and Lady Worthing, and then the opera. You'll be exhausted, sir, by the time the day's done. Why do you always commit yourself to so many engagements during the season?"

Unfortunately, this sort of frenetic social activity was going to be his life for the next three months because it was the most efficient means of finding a wife, something he wouldn't have to be doing now if he'd been able to resist a certain dark-haired beauty nine months ago.

"I have my duty, Mr. Lambert," he said with a sigh.

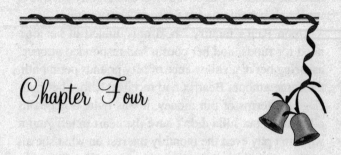

Chapter Four

Julia was in England to rebuild her life after razing it to the ground, and that meant facing the consequences of her past. One of those consequences was a pile of debt and no way to pay it. With his wealthy American wife's return to the States, Paul's only source of income was Danbury Downs, and covering Julia's enormous debts would cause him and his family a great deal of hardship. She'd given them so much grief already; she didn't want to cause any more.

One morning a week after the May Day Ball, Paul took her aside and inquired as to her finances. She couldn't bear to tell him just how far in debt she was, for it would enrage her cousin to learn Yardley hadn't paid her a shilling of support during the last six years of her marriage, and there was no point in doing that. Besides, he'd be so disappointed in her if he knew she hadn't altered her spending habits one iota in consequence of

Yardley's parsimony. He would feel compelled to lecture her about her extravagance, and rightly so, and it would all become such a tiresome conversation.

Upon Paul's inquiry, she'd only hinted at her dire need for funds, and her cousin had responded at once, assuring her of an allowance of fifty pounds per month, the same amount Beatrix had received before her marriage. In terms of pin money, it was quite a generous allowance, but Julia didn't have the heart to tell Paul it wouldn't pay even the monthly interest on what she already owed. Still, she accepted her cousin's offer without a murmur, and knew she had to find another way to pay her debts.

After breakfast, she gathered all her overdue bills and sat down at the secretaire in her room with quill, ink, and paper, determined to find a solution to her financial woes, but she was well aware that she had very few options.

Her dowry had been handed over to Yardley on their wedding day. Only seventeen at that time, she hadn't had the wits to insist upon prenuptial settlements for herself, and her parents had seen marriage to a peer, any peer, as their rebellious daughter's only chance to make good. The modest amount she'd inherited upon the deaths of her parents had gone to payment of the death duties, and her entailed family home was passed to a cousin of her father's, leaving her little in the way of property.

Her cottage in Cornwall, an inheritance from her grandmother, was one of the few possessions she had left, but it was entailed within the family, so she couldn't sell it even if she wanted to. And she didn't want to. Dovecotes was her haven, her refuge, and the closest thing she had to a home of her own.

She could sell the Mercedes, which was the only other thing of real value that she owned, but at the thought of parting with her beloved motorcar, Julia's very soul rebelled. She'd originally acquired it as a means of escape, using it to flee as quickly as possible whenever her husband had been inclined to arrive on the scene and make trouble. She didn't need it for that purpose any longer, of course, but it meant more to her than just a means of escape. It was a symbol of her liberty, and whenever she drove it, with the wind in her hair and the sound of the engine in her ears, she felt free. No, she decided, not the Mercedes.

She supposed she could take up a profession. Julia considered the women she knew who had at some point earned their living. Lady Marlowe and Lady Avermore, longtime friends of their family, were both writers, and writing was certainly a respectable occupation, one many in the aristocracy embarked upon. Still, Julia knew she couldn't write to save herself. Amusing, rambling, grammatically hopeless letters to friends, she could manage, but stories or poetry? Mess about with plots and themes and rhyme and meter? No. She hadn't the talent or discipline for such an occupation.

Art? Her cousin Beatrix had explored that possibility shortly after breaking her engagement to Aidan, and oh, the to-do that had ensued from the family!

Julia would prefer not to cause her relations any further anxiety, but it hardly mattered anyway, for unlike her cousin, Julia had no artistic talent. She was accomplished at the piano, but taking up a post as the piano player in a music hall would hardly be the sort of respectable occupation she was looking for.

She tapped her quill thoughtfully against her desk. Lucy, she supposed, might have some ideas. Her friend Lucy, now Lady Weston, owned an employment agency. But, even so, what sort of position could Lucy obtain for her? She couldn't operate a typewriting machine. She was too chatty to be a telephone operator. She could see herself intervening in the conversations she heard, offering opinions and advice and being sacked for her trouble. Governess? God, no. Who'd hire a notorious divorcee for that?

Trade? She paused, considering. Maria, before becoming the Marchioness of Kayne, had owned a bakery. Vivian Marlowe was the famous dressmaker Vivienne, with a very posh shop in New Bond Street. But opening a shop required money, the lack of which was Julia's exact problem. And truthfully, would she be able to go to a shop and open for business every day? Mess about with tradesmen's books and hire shopgirls and make them work and sack them if they didn't? It sounded terribly tedious. Julia knew her own character well, and she feared she had far too frivolous a nature to be an accomplished woman of business.

She sighed, tossing down her quill, feeling hopelessly inadequate. She longed for a cigarette, but she hadn't smoked since the May Day Ball, and giving in to that temptation after only a week of abstinence would not help either her self-esteem or her pocketbook. Instead, she plunked her elbows on the desk, cupped her chin in her hands, and stared at the mountain of bills before her, trying to think of a solution. Just what was a gregarious social butterfly with a ruined reputation qualified to do?

Only one thing, really. Julia found that realization terribly depressing. The last thing she wanted was to become some man's mistress, which to her way of thinking wasn't much different from being married. Though not as absolute as marriage, it was still a form of enslavement. Even more important, she didn't have the stomach for it. She'd deliberately cultivated a scandalous reputation, but it was a sham. Since marrying Yardley, there had been only one man she'd ever considered as a lover. Only one.

Whenever she thought of how she'd been that day with Aidan, when she thought of the wanton things she'd done, she was still rather shocked by how she'd managed to be so seductive on the surface, so bold and so sensual, when underneath, she'd felt such desperation and panic.

The door opened, and Julia came out of her reverie with a start. She looked up as her maid, Giselle, entered the room, bringing Spike, Julia's beloved pet bulldog, with her on a leather leash. The moment the animal caught sight of his mistress, he bounded across the room, pulling the leash out of Giselle's hand in his enthusiastic efforts. Too fat now to jump all the way into Julia's lap, he contented himself with laying his forepaws on her thigh and wriggling his tailless backside in an ecstatic greeting.

"Hullo, boy," she said, rubbing his broad, wrinkled head with affection. "Been walking, have you?"

"Non," Giselle's dry voice answered on the dog's behalf. "He has not been for a walk, madame. The hall boy, he tried, but . . ."

Giselle shrugged her substantial shoulders and Julia gave another sigh, this one a sigh of disappointment at the fact that her beloved pet was terrorizing the men of Paul's household. Again.

"Did he bite Smithison, Giselle?"

Lips pressed grimly together, Giselle shook her head. *"Non,* the boy, he is quick. But it was very close. One day, madame . . ."

She let her voice trail ominously away, and Julia nodded. "I know, I know. I simply must do something about it. But what? I cannot discipline Spike for being a watchdog with an aversion to men when that is the reason I bought him in the first place."

Giselle, a middle-aged, hardheaded, practical Frenchwoman, waved one hand in the air, dismissing that objection. "Yardley is gone, madame. And the dog, he is intelligent. He will learn to behave, but you must train him to be with the gentlemen, discipline him when he growls at them."

Julia, who found disciplining Spike for his fear of men almost as depressing as the stack of bills on her desk, decided both she and her dog needed a diversion from discipline altogether. "Poor boy didn't get a walk today," she murmured, rubbing Spike behind the ears. "Shall we go then, hmm? Up to New Bond Street? We'll pay a call on Vivian at her shop. No evil men to bother you there, sweetums, I promise."

Giselle sighed, and Julia was well aware that this expression of disappointment was over her mistress's terrible tendency to procrastinate, but she ignored it. "Giselle, fetch my hat."

An hour later Julia was leading Spike into Vivienne, London's most fashionable dressmaking establishment, an utterly feminine conclave of white, black, and pale pink. Julia had been friends with Vivian Marlowe since childhood, and after she'd given her name and handed over the bulldog to a dressmaker's assistant, she'd waited only two minutes in the black-and-white tiled foyer of the showroom before a delighted voice called down to her from the mezzanine above. "Julie!"

She looked up, laughing as her friend, a tall, slender, exuberant redhead, came tripping down the curving staircase of marble and wrought iron to greet her.

"Hullo, Viv," she said as her friend reached the bottom of the stairs, evaded an assistant who was crossing the room with an armload of fabrics, and came running to sweep her up in a hug.

"I had no idea you were back! What do you need? An evening gown? An afternoon dress? Lingerie?"

"I'd love all of those, but I can't buy anything today."

Vivian pulled back, frowning at Julia's walking suit,

a periwinkle-blue tailor-made that was over a year out of fashion. "Look at this jacket!" she groaned, fingering the enormous leg-o'-mutton sleeves. "These scream of last spring! I haven't a single one in my new collection. It's all fitted sleeves and flared cuffs this year."

Julia gave a sigh, painfully aware that she was quite out of date, but also aware that her desperate straits made buying anything new impossible. "Oh, Viv, don't tempt me! I just can't afford any new clothes nowadays. I'm stone broke, darling. Paul's giving me an allowance, but I have to pay debts with it. Tragic, I know."

Vivian made a sound of impatience. "You think I care if you pay me? We've known each other since birth! Besides, I adore having you arrive anywhere in London wearing one of my models. I always obtain more business as a result."

Julia made a face. "Only because I'm so notorious."

"Well, you do have a talent for creating sensation wherever you go," Vivian conceded. "But sensation wouldn't help me a bit if you didn't have the panache to carry off my designs. What about a new afternoon ensemble? You can parade around the Row every day telling everyone how wonderful my spring collection is, and I shall gain at least half a dozen new clients."

Julia laughed and relented. "All right, all right. You've twisted my arm."

Vivian cast another glance over her. "I like that you've gained a bit of weight," she said, hooking her arm through Julia's and guiding her to a nearby settee of black-and-white striped velvet. "When I last saw you at Pixy Cove, you were so terribly thin, dearest."

Vivian gestured for her to sit, then glanced around and beckoned to one of the tall, sylphlike assistants standing about the room. "Miss Wellesley," she said as the girl approached, "I want you to display the spring afternoon toilettes for Lady Yardley, if you please. Ask Miss Lovell to assist you."

The girl strutted off with the rather insolent, catlike stride all living mannequins seemed to possess, and Vivian settled herself beside Julia on the settee. "So, I'm dying to know how it was to relax at the spas of Biarritz over the winter, now that you've cut the chains of matrimony and are a free woman."

"Divine," she confessed. "I cannot deny it. But really, Viv," she added with a hint of surprise, "why all this talk of chains? When did you develop such an aversion to marriage?"

Her friend shrugged. "I don't know that I would use the word *aversion*. But I am thirty-two, remember. I've been on the shelf for quite some time." She opened her arms in a sweeping gesture of her surroundings. "Besides, with all this, when would I have time for a husband and children?"

"I suppose you're right. But you're not judging the entire institution of matrimony based on my horrible experience, are you? Yardley isn't . . ." Julia felt her throat closing up at the mention of her former husband, and she swallowed hard, working to regain her voice. "Not all men are like Yardley."

"True, but nonetheless, I don't think I shall risk it. Given the opportunity, would you ever marry again?"

"God, no!" she said, appalled by the very idea.

"You see?" Vivian laughed. "We haven't changed since childhood. We're still in agreement about nearly everything."

"Ma'am?"

Both women looked up as Miss Wellesley approached, and it was clear something untoward had happened, for the mannequin had not changed into one of the afternoon gowns she was supposed to be modeling for Julia, and her usual expression of sophisticated boredom had been replaced by unmistakable panic. She leaned down to whisper in Vivian's ear, and as the dressmaker listened, her auburn brows lifted in surprise.

"She loathes the chiffon, you say? Loathes it?"

At Miss Wellesley's frantic nod, Vivian sighed. "Just like a princess to have more money than taste," she murmured and turned to Julia. "Her Royal Highness, the Princess of Montenegro, does not like the blue silk chiffon I am recommending for her ball gown, though it is perfect for her figure. She is demanding my immediate presence in the fitting rooms. Do you mind if I leave you for a moment?"

"Go, go," Julia said, laughing, waving a hand toward the fitting rooms in the back of the shop. "It doesn't do to keep a princess waiting!"

"I'll be back. In the meantime, I shall have Miss Wellesley carry on with those afternoon ensembles for you." She glanced at the mannequin, who immediately departed. "I'll also have some fabrics brought out for you to look at," Vivian added over her shoulder as she started after her employee. "I've a lovely lilac mousseline de soie I think would be divine for you."

Vivian departed, and to occupy herself while she waited, Julia reached for the most recent edition of *La Mode Illustrée* from the table, but she had barely opened the fashion magazine before an excited feminine voice came within earshot, a voice that squeaked happily along as its owner came closer to where Julia sat.

"Of course I couldn't believe Papa would actually dare to invite him. He so hates to push, you know, and Trathen is a duke, after all."

Julia lifted her head at the mention of Aidan, curious. She cocked her head, straining to hear that one voice amid the eddy of feminine conversation in the room. It wasn't all that difficult. Lady Felicia Vale had a voice that carried.

"But Mama absolutely insisted Papa issue the invitation," the girl went on, causing Julia to hunker down beneath her enormous hat, hoping not to be identified as the girl came closer to where she sat. "The duke, she said, had displayed great interest in making my acquaintance. Of course, I thought Mama was exaggerating, as she so often does, you know. But you could have knocked me over with a feather when the reply from the duke's secretary came this morning!"

Julia made a sound of exasperation, then instantly bit her lip, for she didn't want to be noticed.

"I almost fainted when Mama read his reply aloud," Felicia went on. "I was so overcome! Even now, my heart flutters and trembles, Cora, to know that I shall meet my hero at last."

Julia rolled her eyes. Really, the man was hopeless. She'd already warned him about Felicia. What on earth was he doing, consenting to spend time with that girl? Did he have no sense?

"You're not teasing me?" Felicia's companion asked, sounding understandably skeptical. "Trathen is truly sitting in your papa's box tomorrow night?"

"Well, not precisely," the girl was forced to concede. "He has deigned to call upon us at intermission."

That information eased Julia's exasperation with Aidan a little at the knowledge that he hadn't committed to an entire evening in the girl's company. He had that much sense, at least.

"But I," Felicia went on, a surprisingly steely hint entering her voice, "have every intention of seeing that he remains for the remainder of the evening."

An image of Aidan trying to escape as Felicia Vale clutched his coattails popped into her head, and Julia had to smother her shout of laughter by covering her mouth with her hand. She simply must finagle Paul's box for the evening so she could observe the encounter through opera glasses. That, she thought, with silent laughter, would be a far more entertaining performance than anything on the Covent Garden stage.

Aidan, as everyone in society knew, was a smashing good tennis player. He'd been captain of the Oxford team, twice made the quarterfinals at Wimbledon, and had defeated the Earl of Danbury in the St. Ives Tournament. At the time, Paul had good-naturedly vowed revenge as they'd shaken hands over the net, but it was two years later, three days after issuing his latest challenge to play, that he got that revenge by defeating Aidan in straight sets.

"Yes!" Paul cried as the ball, untouched by Aidan's lunging attempt at a volley, bounced off the grass of the court just inside the chalk line, and went out of bounds.

Aidan, carried by momentum, was unable to recover his footing. He stumbled a few steps and went down hard onto his knees, watching in chagrin as the ball bounced away along the turf of the Hyde Park Tennis Club. When it stopped, he turned and looked at his friend, who was grinning at him over the top of the net like a boy on Christmas morning.

"I warned you I'd been practicing my serve."

Aidan knew Paul's serve, good as it had become, wasn't the only reason he'd just been trounced. Thoughts of Paul's devilish cousin hadn't helped his game.

He rubbed his wrist across his forehead to dab away the sweat, and stood up. He walked to the net, shifted his racquet to his left hand, and stuck out his right for the customary handshake. "Congratulations, my friend. Well played."

"I don't think I've ever defeated you in straight sets before," Paul said as he accepted the handshake, but then he frowned at Aidan over the net. "I say, you're not ill, are you?"

"Ill? Of course not. Just having trouble concentrating, that's all." He pulled his racquet from under his arm and gestured to the building nearby that contained baths and changing rooms. "Shall we?"

The two men walked together. "Do you have plans for the Whitsuntide holiday?" Aidan asked as they entered the changing rooms. "If not, we ought to be able to play quite a bit. With everyone in the country for the holiday, London should be empty. We wouldn't even have to reserve a court."

"I appreciate the invitation," Paul replied, taking a towel from the attendant. "But I'm off home for the holiday. My mother and I are having a house party at Danbury Downs. Dozens of people have been invited—" He stopped, then cleared his throat, looking pained. "You're welcome to come," he added awkwardly. "I would have invited you already, but . . ." He paused again, took a deep breath, and said, "Julie's home from Europe."

"Yes, I know," Aidan said, also taking a towel before turning to his locker, and felt impelled to fill in the sudden silence. "Surely you didn't ask me to tennis just to tell me Lady Yardley was in town, did you?" he asked, working to imbue his voice with just the right amount of amused indifference.

"Not precisely. I just thought this might be a good time to try and smooth things over between our families." He paused. "I wouldn't blame you if you told me to go to the devil."

That genuinely astonished him. "Why should I? None of what happened was your fault."

"Still, you haven't had much luck in your relations with the Danburys, and as head of the family, I can't help feeling badly about it. I've been wanting to tell you that for quite some time, but it just hasn't seemed like the right moment. I mean, first Trix, then Julie." He paused and grimaced. "Sorry. Hell, this is awkward."

Aidan saved him any further distress. "Paul, that business with Beatrix is all water under the bridge, and I wish her nothing but happiness. As for Lady Yardley . . ." He paused to take a deep breath. "She and I are indifferent acquaintances. Despite . . . certain events, we are nothing more than that."

"I see." Paul paused, then added unexpectedly, "Yardley's a rotter. Always was."

Aidan had already concluded that much, but he didn't find the confirmation particularly comforting. "Enjoy your house party. Perhaps when you return to town, we can arrange a rematch? Be warned, though," he added when Paul agreed to his suggestion with a nod, "I intend to extract revenge for today."

"If you can." Paul laughed. "You'll have to regain your ability to concentrate."

Aidan set his jaw. "From this moment on," he vowed, more for his own benefit than Paul's, "that shall not be a problem."

During the remainder of the day, Aidan was forced to use all his considerable self-discipline to keep Lady Yardley in the past where she belonged.

He had a bathe at the tennis club, changed into a

fresh shirt and dark blue morning suit, and went on with his day. He called at his boot maker, and then his tailor, and whenever a thought of that woman entered his head, he shoved it out again at once.

By the time he lunched at the Clarendon with Lord and Lady Malvers, Aidan felt as if he was beginning to regain his equilibrium. Thankfully, Malvers and his wife were unacquainted with Lady Yardley, and there were no associations that could connect her to them in Aidan's mind. The consequence was a most agreeable luncheon.

Afterward, he met with Marlowe, and he found their business negotiations distracting enough to prevent any memories associated with that woman from entering his brain. The two men were able to come to an agreement favorable to both parties.

By the end of the afternoon, Aidan had managed to regain much of the equanimity he'd worked so hard to acquire during the past nine months. But the moment he entered the tearoom of the Savoy to join Lord and Lady Worthing for tea, his efforts went to the wall, for seated at one of the tables was the woman he'd been trying so hard to forget.

Aidan froze, his gaze riveted to where she sat with a group of friends having tea. She was wearing an enormous straw hat topped with masses of white ostrich feathers, but beneath its wide brim, there was no mistaking Lady Yardley's delicate features and violet eyes.

Someone coughed behind him, and he turned to find people waiting to enter the tearoom. He moved out of the doorway, and as a waiter led him past her table to where his own party was seated, he did not look at her. He crossed the Savoy's tearoom, greeted Lord and Lady Worthing, and sat down. He made desultory small talk, read over the menu, and ordered tea, and the entire time, he did not so much as glance in that woman's direction, but though he didn't look at her, one question kept running through his mind, the same question that had tormented him for months.

What on earth had possessed him to go on that picnic with her? He'd asked himself that question innumerable times, but for the first time, an answer echoed back to him.

Under that gentlemanly honor you revere so much, you long for adventure and excitement and a taste of the forbidden fruit.

It was true, he realized, and it galled him to know she could see in him things he could not see in himself. At the time, he'd told himself all the reasons calling upon her at her cottage, picnicking with her, and being alone with her were inappropriate, foolish, and just plain wrong, but those reminders hadn't stopped him from going. When she'd offered him a second glass of champagne, he'd reminded himself of why he never had a second glass, and then he'd drunk it. And then he'd drunk another, and another, and though he didn't remember much after they'd uncorked the second bottle, he vividly remembered the lust that had flooded through his body and burned away any sense of honor he'd ever had.

Aidan slid a glance at her, but when he did, he didn't picture her as she was here, in a frothy tea gown of pale blue silk, sipping tea at the Savoy amid crystal chandeliers, plush carpets, and potted palms. No, he saw her in a wet dress of white muslin, walking out of the water and across the sand toward him.

She lifted her teacup, but in his mind her fingers weren't curled around a piece of delicate china. Instead, they were gliding down the damp skin at the base of her throat.

Arousal flickered up inside him.

Aidan looked away, murmured something polite about the weather, and wondered if he'd only been deluding himself all these months. He began to fear that despite all it had cost him, the desire he'd always felt for her could once again consume him. And if he let that happen again, what price would he pay for it?

Violently, he stood up, earning himself astonished stares from his companions. "Forgive me," he said at once, and he knew he ought to sit back down, but he just could not remain here another moment. He mumbled something about a sudden headache, excused himself from Lord and Lady Worthing, and left the Savoy.

Damn that woman, he thought, as he started down the sidewalk. Damn her for still being tempting as hell.

He was here for the season to find a suitable duchess, not lust after a notorious divorcee, but he knew as long as they both remained in town, he would feel this every time he saw her if he didn't find a way to stop it.

He walked back along the Embankment to his offices. Lambert had already departed for the day, but, thankfully, his secretary had left a stack of contracts and bid proposals on his desk for his review.

Aidan took off his jacket, rolled up his sleeves, and sat down at his desk. Work, he knew from past experience, was not an antidote to that woman, but it was a distraction, and for now, that would have to be enough.

It was well past dark by the time his carriage made the slow crawl from the City back to Mayfair, and when he reached his home in Grosvenor Square, all he wanted was to have a bite of supper and go to bed. As he walked up his front steps, his butler was already opening the door to him.

"Good evening, sir. We did not expect you home quite so soon."

He found that remark rather puzzling, but he was too tired to inquire further. "Good evening, Covington," he answered, handing over his hat and cloak. "Have Mrs. Bowles prepare a light supper for me, would you? I'll await it in my study."

The butler nodded, handed Aidan's things to a footman, and bustled off to comply with his master's instructions. Aidan crossed the foyer in the opposite direction and went down the corridor that led to his study.

Because the corridor was unlit, no light spilled into the room, making its interior pitch black, but memory guided his steps to his favorite chair. He settled into its comfortable leather confines, then reached beside him for the electrical cord of the lamp on the table. He slid his palm along the cord until he found the switch. Rolling the wheel forward with his thumb, he opened his eyes as electric light poured from beneath the amber glass lampshade to illuminate not only the burled maple table and his own leather chair, but also the matching chair across from him.

There, lounging back in a plum-colored evening gown and long white gloves, diamonds round her throat and an amused smile on her lips, was the woman he'd been trying to forget all day, all week, all year—the same woman, in fact, he'd been trying to forget since he was seventeen years old.

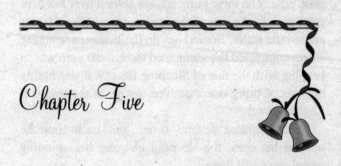

Chapter Five

Dorset, 1891

The first time Aidan ever saw Julia, he thought he'd stepped out of a forest in Dorset and into a storybook.

He'd finished his final term at Eton, and he was enjoying a much-needed summer holiday before going on to Oxford for the autumn. On a glorious afternoon in July, he was taking a walk through the woods when he caught sight of a beautiful girl lying as if asleep on a footbridge over a meandering brook. The sight was so much like a storybook illustration, he stopped in astonishment.

Dressed in a blue velvet gown, her eyes closed, her face relaxed in repose, and her hands clasped beneath one cheek, she made him think at once of Sleeping Beauty, if one could imagine the heroine of that particular fable with hair of raven black rather than angelic gold. The long, curly tresses spilled over her bent arms and off the side of the bridge, where the ends just grazed the water. Behind her on the bridge, a spinning wheel completed the scene, and though the item was in keeping with the tale of Sleeping Beauty, it was hardly the sort of thing one stumbled across in the midst of English woods.

Aidan blinked several times, but each time he opened his eyes, the sleeping girl and her spinning wheel were still there.

She made a charming, if incongruous, picture lying there, dappled by the sunlight that filtered down between the weeping willows. Aidan wasn't a fanciful man or a macabre one, but if the bridge were changed to a glass coffin, the picture of Princess Aurora would be complete. The only thing lacking, he thought, was the prince to kiss her.

But that moment, she seemed to awaken without that sort of heroic assistance, and when she spoke, his impression of the sweet, dulcet heroine waiting to be awakened by a kiss was utterly and completely shattered.

"Oh, bloody hell!" she cried, sitting up, swinging her legs over the side—her bare legs, he realized as her hem caught on the edge of the bridge, bunching her skirts up around her knees. Her toes hit the water with a splash, and Aidan lifted his gaze, forcing himself to look at her face rather than her legs.

"What the devil comes next?" she muttered in vexation. "I'll muff this, I know I will, and then I'll be sunk." Grinding her teeth, she pressed a palm to her forehead. "Sunk like a damned ship. What am I going to do?"

With her words, the spell was broken, for no fairy-tale heroine would make use of such language. But the girl did seem to be in some sort of distress, and Aidan stepped forward.

"Good afternoon," he said, emerging from amid the trees. "Are you in need of assistance?"

She gave a gasp at the sound of his voice and looked up. "Damn and blast!" she cried, pressing a hand to her chest. "How you startled me!"

He stopped at the foot of the bridge, and as he studied her face, his initial impression faded even more, for now that Sleeping Beauty had awakened, he was more inclined to think of street urchins than storybook heroines. Her heart-shaped face was lovely, but in a rakish sort of way, with big, violet-blue eyes, sooty lashes, and a pointed chin. Her hair tumbled around her shoulders, not in perfect, picture-book waves but a riot of rebellious curls.

"I'm terribly sorry," he apologized, giving her a bow. "I didn't mean to startle you. My only excuse is that I was a bit shocked myself. I thought for a moment you were Sleeping Beauty."

Her frown transformed at once into a grin, revealing a pair of dimples and a streak of impudence. "That's the idea."

He frowned, puzzled by this cryptic reply, but

before he could ask what she meant, she reached into the pocket of her skirt and spoke again. "That is," she said, pulling out several folded sheets of paper, "if I can manage to remember my lines."

She unfolded the papers and scanned the top sheet, and as she did so, her legs swayed idly back and forth, her toes skimming the water, and Aidan froze, suddenly riveted.

In the entire seventeen years of his life, he'd never observed a woman's bare legs. As a young boy, he and some of his friends had stumbled upon a group of girls their own age bathing naked, but since they'd all been about nine years old at the time, that hardly counted. During the years since, he'd caught occasional glimpses of stocking-clad ankles when gusts of wind sent the skirts of young ladies whipping up. He'd even been given a view of the shadowy contours of a courtesan's body not long ago, in the dim light of a brothel after a somewhat disillusioning first coupling. But he'd never before been given a view like this—a view of shapely calves, delicate ankles, and slender feet boldly displayed in broad daylight. Adolescent lust began coursing through his body in the space of two heartbeats, a sudden, powerful wave that disconcerted him, embarrassed him, and robbed him of the ability to think or even breathe.

She wiggled her toes in the water, pretty pink and white toes that splashed the surface, and he began to feel a bit desperate, not sure if he'd be able to hide or suppress what was rapidly overtaking him. Ever since he could remember, Aidan had taken great pride in having a well-disciplined body and mind, of always being in complete control of himself and any situation. But this unaccountable slip of a girl was testing his notions of self-discipline in a way he'd never had to overcome before.

Striving to think of things like honor and good breeding and gentlemanly codes of conduct, he tore his gaze away from her naked legs and forced himself to remember what they'd been discussing. "Lines? Are you in a play, then?"

"Heavens, no!" she answered at once, looking up from her sheet of paper. "I go about the forest in my blue velvet gown all the time. And my spinning wheel? I cart it along everywhere I go."

He grinned at that. She certainly was a saucy creature.

She laughed, watching him. "There!" she cried, sounding triumphant. "A smile. I was beginning to think you had no sense of humor. I mean, any other bloke who'd run across this situation would have been laughing long before now, in disbelief, if nothing else."

"Forgive me. I didn't realize a woman in distress was something to smile about," he said with a polite bow.

"Oh, don't!" she cried, sounding vexed and frowning again. "Don't turn all stiff and formal on me, not now, not when we've begun to be friends."

He doubted he and this wild girl could ever find the common ground to be friends. She seemed to be some sort of actress, and he was a duke, and the only friendship that could come from that sort of situation was a rather unsavory one. Still, it would be unseemly to express that thought aloud. "So," he said instead, "you are an actress?"

"No, no, but I am in a play." She caught his puzzled look and laughed. "It's just a skit, really, to raise money for the orphanage fund. All the events today are for the orphanage."

"Ah," he said, a bit more enlightened. "So there's a fete on?"

"This afternoon." She waved the sheaf of papers in her hand again. "I have only a bit of time left to learn my lines, so I decided to find a nice quiet spot and see if I can memorize enough to keep from making an utter fool of myself today. I fear it's hopeless, though, for I've left it too late."

Aidan, who never made a fool of himself if he could avoid it, and who never left anything until the last minute, felt impelled to point out the obvious. "Wouldn't it have been wise to spend more time preparing for your part?"

"Well, yes," she conceded with another grin, "but why do today what one can put off until tomorrow?"

"You don't seem to be taking your role very seriously."

"Petal, I don't take anything seriously." She cast him a shrewd glance. "You, I'll wager, have the opposite problem. Do you drink?"

He blinked, taken rather aback by this seemingly irrelevant question. "No," he answered with a decided shake of his head. "I don't. Why do you ask?"

"You should drink, at least a little. You're wound a bit tight. A drink now and again would loosen you up."

"It did, I'm afraid. With disastrous results."

"Really?" she exclaimed with lively curiosity. "What happened?"

"I don't know. I was sixteen. I, along with my friends, raided my father's wine cellar, and we drank his entire stock of French champagnes."

"Oh my." She chuckled. "I'm beginning to like you."

"The next thing I remember was waking up in a room at the local inn without any idea how I got there. It was morning, and I don't remember much of anything about the night before, but from the accounts of my friends, it seems I let all my father's dogs out of the kennels, rode horseback into the village, serenaded the vicar around three o'clock in the morning, and tried to seduce the innkeeper's daughter—" He stopped, astonished he was telling such embarrassing things to a complete stranger. "It was stupid."

"So why did you do it?"

The question made him grimace. "I don't know."

"Of course you know. You did it because you wanted to." She tilted her head to one side, studying him thoughtfully. "You're one of those dutiful sons, I'll wager, the sort who never causes his parents any anxiety, who always does the right thing, obeys the rules, works hard, is determined to make good."

He stared at her, shocked by this seemingly haphazard but astute guesswork. "What are you, miss? A Gypsy fortune-teller?"

"That's not fortune-telling. It's common sense. And experience."

"Your own experience?"

"Heavens, no! I've been rebelling since birth. My parents, I fear, have nearly given up on me. But my cousin Trix is like you—all about duty and responsibility. Ugh. It's so tiresome being good all the time. One of these days, she's going to burst out, break free, go on a tear, and then . . . whew, who knows what will happen?"

"And what about you?" he asked. "Being a rebel carries consequences, does it not?"

Her expression darkened a little and she looked away. "So it does," she murmured. "And I'm about to pay the piper, I'm afraid. But," she added, looking at him again, her face lighting with a dazzling, unexpected smile that made him think of the sun shining out between storm clouds, "we're not talking about me and my beastly past. We're talking about you and your desire to rebel against authority."

That mention of her past made him curious, but he was reluctant to pry, and besides, he felt compelled to protest her words about him. "I don't wish to rebel."

"You already did. And probably had a hell of a good time in the process, even if you can't remember most of it. Why not just admit you wanted to do it?" She shook her head. "No wonder you're wound so tight, if you can't even admit you wanted to carouse and have a bit of fun. And why shouldn't you? You're young, you're handsome, you're obviously wealthy, if your clothes are anything to go by. Why not enjoy yourself?"

He thought of his father, who'd done enough carousing for both of them. The late duke had caused both his wife and son a great deal of pain in the process, and the last thing Aidan wanted to do was be like that.

"If you went on a tear more often," she added, "you'd be less of a prig. Happier, too."

He frowned, not liking this assessment of his character at all. "You offer your advice to strangers very freely, miss."

"You think it's cheek? It is, rather, but if you knew me better, you wouldn't be surprised." She looked at him with an expression of mock apology, but there was an unmistakable glint of mischief in her violet-blue eyes. "I'm very cheeky. My greatest flaw, I fear."

"That," he countered with a nod to the paper in her hand, "or procrastination, perhaps."

"Now you're teasing! But I can't contradict you, for I do procrastinate, which is why I'm in the suds today. I fear I shall truly embarrass myself in front of my fiancé, and his mother, too. She wrote the skit, and if I bungle it, I shall fall even more in her estimation, though I'm not sure that's possible."

"You are engaged to be married?"

She wrinkled her pert nose at him. "Your surprise is hardly flattering, sir."

He wasn't surprised by her engagement, but by his own disappointment at the news of it, a disappointment that was all out of proportion to the situation. He didn't even know this girl, and from what he could discern so far, she was not his sort at all. In fact, he'd never met anyone quite like her. Being disappointed made no sense, and he tried to dismiss it. "My congratulations," he said instead.

"Don't congratulate me yet." She gave him a wink. "If I do make an utter fool of myself this afternoon, my fiancé might jilt me at the altar."

The careless, offhand way she spoke of a circumstance most people would deem calamitous seemed quite odd to him, but it would be rude to inquire about such an intimate topic. "I should be on my way," he said instead, "so you can be alone to study your part."

"Perhaps it would be better if you stayed."

Against his will, his gaze slid down over her knees and along her bare shins to her toes idly skimming circles on the water. "I don't think so."

"You could read the lines with me, which would help me enormously."

He set his jaw. "It wouldn't be proper. There's no chaperone."

"Well, it isn't as if we'd be doing anything naughty! And I fear you're too much of a gentleman to even attempt to take advantage of me. Rather a pity, that," she added with a glance over him. "You're terribly good-looking."

He realized, much to his chagrin, that he was blushing. Not because of the compliment, but because images of "being naughty" with her were going through his mind.

She perceived his embarrassment, though he hoped not the reason for it. "La, la," she said, laughing, "see how the boy blushes!"

"You, miss," he said stiffly, "are a flirt and a tease."

She didn't seem in the least offended by his reproof. But after a moment of silence, her amusement faded and she said in all seriousness, "You don't like to be teased, do you?"

"No. Nor do I like to be flirted with by a girl about to marry someone else."

"Flirtation is harmless. You should try it sometime. Although," she amended, "perhaps that wouldn't be wise. A handsome prince shouldn't flirt, I suppose. Too much risk to the hearts of girls in the kingdom."

He didn't know how to respond to such nonsense. "Thank you for the compliment," he said, taking refuge in good manners, "but I'm not a prince. Merely a duke." He bowed. "Aidan Carr, Duke of Trathen, at your service."

"A duke?" She laughed merrily, not seeming the least bit impressed by his rank. "Well, I was right then, for a duke's very close to a prince, isn't it? I'm so glad we met. Sleeping Beauty does need a prince, although you seem to have woken me without even giving me a kiss." She sighed. "I feel thoroughly let down."

He had no talent for flirtation, and he decided it was wise not to try. "You hardly need me for that role. Your fiancé," he added as she gave him a puzzled stare. "Isn't he your prince?"

Something he couldn't quite fathom came into her face, something that was like a shadow. It made him uneasy. "Oh yes," she agreed, an odd inflection in her voice, "he's my prince."

"You say that as if he isn't."

She shook her head and laughed again, dispelling his uneasiness. "He isn't a prince, not really, nor even a duke. Merely a baron."

"A baron?" He eyed the urchin before him with doubt. "Your fiancé is a baron?"

She drew herself up as if affronted, but she was smiling. "What, do you think I'm not good enough to marry a peer?"

"I didn't mean it that way—" He stopped and gave a sigh. "Sorry."

"It's all right. You're quite right about me, you know," she added softly, her smile twisting a little. "I may be the niece of an earl and the daughter of a squire, but despite what my parents want for me, I'm not the sort of girl who ought to marry an aristocrat. I'm more pixy than peeress, I fear."

As if to prove the truth of that, she proceeded to shock him yet again. Turning on the bridge, she hitched her heavy skirt a bit higher, crossed her legs beneath her, and pulled a rolled cigarette and a match from the pocket of her gown.

He stared at her, surprised, though he supposed he shouldn't be surprised by anything at this point. "You smoke," he said flatly.

"He disapproves!" she said, her dark brows drawing together in what he suspected was an imitation of his own expression at this moment. "The girl is so uncivilized! She swears. She smokes. She goes about barefoot. Deuce take it, she even whistles!"

Pursing her lips, she gave him a few bars of "Ta-ra-ra-boom-de-ay," then her impudent manner once again fell away and she assumed a crestfallen air. "You do disapprove of me. I'm hurt," she added with a sniff. "Brokenhearted. I shall go off now and pine for you until the end of my days."

She looked so comically tragic, he almost smiled, but then she put the cigarette between her lips and struck the match on the weathered wood of the bridge, and any inclination he had to smile vanished. "Why do you engage in such a vile habit?" he asked, suddenly angry.

It was her turn to stare. Over the lit match in her hand, her vivid eyes widened in surprise at his sudden outburst. He was rather surprised himself, for he was angry with her for smoking, and he didn't even know why he felt that way, or why he'd been so forthright in expressing it. Whatever behavior this girl chose to engage in, it wasn't his affair.

"Heaven bless the man, we're not in someone's drawing room," she muttered around the cigarette between her lips. She lit it, then tossed the match into the water and exhaled a stream of smoke overhead. "No velvet draperies that the overworked maids shall have to shake out later," she added, took another pull on the cigarette, and blew a perfect smoke ring in his direction. "Why shouldn't I smoke?"

He moved aside and the wispy ring sailed past him,

disintegrating on the summer breeze. "It leaves an unpleasant odor on clothes as well as drapes and cushions," he pointed out.

"Well, yes, I suppose it does, but it's not as if one cigarette makes much difference there. Simply everyone smokes nowadays." She made an up-and-down gesture at him with the lit cigarette. "Present company excepted, obviously. But unless you live like a hermit, you're bound to smell like tobacco most of the time anyway, so what does my little cigarette matter to the scent of your clothes?"

"Women should not smoke. It isn't decorous."

"Decorous?" She burst out laughing. "I've never been decorous in my life."

"It's vile," he repeated stubbornly. "And some doctors fear it has an adverse effect upon the lungs. Bad enough that men engage in it, but for women to do so is even worse."

"How puritanical you are! You don't smoke, you don't drink, and you're filled with moral rectitude and propriety." She frowned. "I don't think the handsome prince ought to be like that."

"And I don't think a baron would want his wife to smoke."

Her violet eyes met his, and there was a cool, metallic flash of defiance in their depths as she took another pull on the cigarette and exhaled the smoke. "I already told you, I've been defying authority all my life. I'm about to make a respectable marriage and atone for all my sins, but I shall have my petty rebellions all the same. No other way to keep my sanity."

"Your fiancé might cry off if he found out."

"He already knows." There was such hardness in her piquant face that he was startled, but when she spoke, her voice was quite cheerful. "But he's determined to have me despite all my flaws."

"But that's a good thing." He paused. "Isn't it?"

"Of course!" She tossed her cigarette into the stream and reached for the velvet slippers beside her. "Well, handsome prince, I'd best be off," she said as she put them on. "It's almost curtain time, and if I'm late, they'll be thinking I've done a funk. If you want to come and watch me ruin the show, we've set up the stage on the village green. Admission one shilling." With that, she stood up, lifted her spinning wheel into her arms, and turned away, whistling as she started down the other side of the bridge.

"Wait!" he called after her. "I don't even know your name."

"Julie." She laughed, turning around to look at him even as she kept walking away. "At least that's what my friends call me."

"Friends? But we aren't friends. We're barely acquainted."

"We shall be friends though. I'm quite determined."

"Why should you be?"

"Because you don't like me, that's why."

He shook his head, bemused. "Even if that were true, it makes no sense."

"Yes, it does. I hate not being liked. Besides . . ." She paused to glance over her shoulder to see where her backward steps were taking her, then she returned her intense gaze to him and went on, "I like you, despite your snooty manner and your morality and your hopelessly old-fashioned ideas. We shall be friends one day. You might as well resign yourself to it now," she added before he could protest that he was not snooty, "for you haven't a hope of resisting me. Cheerio."

She shifted the spinning wheel to one arm, pressed the palm of her free hand to her lips and blew him a smacking kiss, then turned her back and walked away.

Aidan watched her go, telling himself he ought to be relieved by her departure. She did things no young lady ought to do. She said things that caught him off-guard, nonsensical things to which he could think of no intelligent response and shrewd things that made him uncomfortable. She was flippant and brazen and rebellious, and even though she was engaged to be married, she had no scruples about flirting with men.

Still, despite all that, as she vanished from sight amid the trees, he felt something that wasn't relief at all, but regret. He'd never before encountered a storybook heroine, and he knew he'd probably never see this one again.

It would be ten years before circumstances proved him wrong.

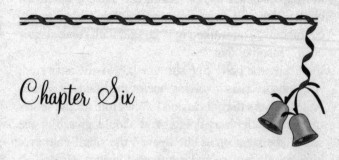

Chapter Six

*Y*ou again!" Startled, he jumped to his feet, staring in dismay at the woman in his study, a woman he couldn't seem to avoid no matter how he tried. "What the devil are you doing here?"

She eased back the ermine wrap that was slung round her shoulders, revealing a disconcerting amount of décolleté to his view. "I might ask you the same question."

Aidan was in no mood for riddles. He folded his arms and glared down at her. "How did you enter my home without my butler knowing about it?"

"Well, I didn't break in, if that's what you're thinking." She gestured to her evening gown. "Climb through a first floor window in this ensemble? Heavens, no! I opened the door and walked in. No one seemed to notice. Really, Aidan," she added, shaking her head as if in amazement, "it doesn't seem like you to have such an inferior butler. He must be a new man."

Covington was new, but he had no intention of admitting that fact to her. She might have a talent for observation and deduction, but he didn't have to encourage it. "You walked in?" he said with some skepticism. "Just like that?"

"I rang the bell." She shrugged. "No one answered. A domestic crisis involving one of the maids, it seems. At least that's the conclusion I drew from all the shouting your butler was doing. You should give him the sack," she went on as she opened the small gold evening bag on her lap and rummaged inside. "He doesn't ensure that your doors are latched at night. That's madness here in London. Why, anyone could just walk in, abscond with some of that lovely Tass silver you've got displayed in your foyer, and be back out the door in two shakes of a lamb's tail."

She paused long enough to pull out a slim, enameled case and extract a cigarette and a match, but before he could raise an objection to her smoking, she went on, "He abuses the lower servants, Aidan. He was berating that poor maid of yours loudly enough that I could hear his insults before I'd even reached your front door! Evidently, she missed a bit of soot when she was polishing the fireplace fender or some such nonsense, and he had the poor girl in tears over it." She paused, and a queer, frozen brittleness came into her face. "She's terrified of him."

Aidan frowned, not liking her implications about his butler, liking even less what he saw in her face. But then she looked up at him and smiled again, and the brittleness dissolved into her usual cheerful impudence. "Mind if I smoke?"

"I do mind, as a matter of fact. You know how I feel about it. And I thought you said you were trying to stop this particular vice."

"I am trying, but it isn't going very well." She sighed and shot him an apologetic look. "I've no willpower at all, I'm afraid."

"Try harder," he said, unfolding his arms and leaning down to yank the cigarette and the match out of her hands. He tossed the offending items into the fireplace. "Women should not smoke. It's—"

"Not decorous, yes, I know," she interrupted. "You said that the first time we ever met."

It surprised him that she still remembered their very first conversation, but then every time he saw her, she seemed able to surprise him, shock him, and keep him off-balance. It was very trying.

"You haven't changed since then, by the way," she told him. "Your notions about what women should do are as antiquated now as they were when we were seventeen. But really, Aidan, when have I ever done what I should?"

"Never," he acknowledged with a sigh.

"Besides, I don't think my smoking habit, shameless as it is, ought to be your greatest concern at this moment. You've something far more important to worry about, I fear."

"And what is that?"

"The time, darling! It's after ten." She sighed, looking at him and shaking her head. "And you're not even dressed for the opera."

"Opera?" Realization dawned, followed by dismay. "Lady Felicia. Damn and blast, I completely forgot."

She laughed. "Lady Felicia does have that effect on men."

He cast her an impatient glance as he pulled out his pocket watch, not nearly as amused as she seemed to be. He confirmed the time, his dismay growing. "I've already missed the first intermission."

"Don't worry, petal. You shall arrive in plenty of time to make the second one. That is," she added, rising to follow him as he put his watch away and started for the door, "if your valet is more efficient than your butler. If so, you'll be able to change clothes and be at Covent Garden just in time. Still, if I were you, I wouldn't rush it, not to be in Lady Felicia's company. You already have a ticket, I hope?"

He stopped and turned to find her so close that she almost cannoned into him. Instinctively, he put his hands on her arms to steady them both. The moment he did, he felt her silky skin against his palms and jerked his hands down, but it was already too late. With just that brief contact, arousal began flooding his body.

He took a deep breath, trying to think. "I don't need a ticket. I have a box, something I'm surprised you don't know, since you seem to know everything else about me. And since we're on the subject, how do you know I'm supposed to be attending the opera and meeting Lady Felicia? Never mind," he added as she opened her mouth to explain. "I don't want to know."

He turned and started for the stairs, but then he remembered what she'd said about Covington, and he paused to give the bellpull at the foot of the stairs a hard yank. As he waited for his summons to be answered, Julia did not depart. Instead, she paused by the front door as the parlor maid, Ellis, came running from the back of the house.

The moment Aidan saw the servant's face, Julia's concern was confirmed. The maid's lip was cut and her cheek was swollen, and it was clear she'd been backhanded, hard. When she looked at him, he saw that her eyes were red-rimmed from weeping, and there was a painful resignation in her expression that told him she fully expected to be dismissed from her post as the one to blame. Rage began seeping into Aidan's bones, and he wondered if Scotland Yard would do anything to punish a duke if he beat his soon-to-be former butler to a bloody pulp.

The maid ducked her head and dipped a curtsy, lowering her gaze to the floor. "You rang the bell, sir?"

"I did, Miss Ellis. Tell Mrs. Bowles to cancel the supper I requested, and have my carriage brought around. And have a footman inform Covington that I wish to see him in my rooms at once."

Her shoulders drooped, her resignation deepening into despair. "Yes, sir," she whispered, and started to depart, but he stopped her.

"Ellis?" When she paused, he said gently, "Tell

Bowles I said to make an ice poultice for you. And don't be uneasy, my girl. You won't be sacked, and he won't strike you again. He'll be gone before I leave this evening. I promise you."

The poor girl's knees almost caved beneath her and she gave a sob of relief.

"I will inform Mrs. Ward of this situation before I depart," he went on. "As housekeeper, she will be in charge until a new butler is engaged. You may go."

"Yes, sir. Thank you, sir." She curtsied again and departed, practically stumbling over her own feet in her haste to carry out his instructions.

When she was gone, he glanced at Julia and found her watching him. She started to speak, then stopped and swallowed hard. It was several moments before she tried again. "You're a good man, Aidan," she said at last.

He looked away, embarrassed yet strangely pleased, though he didn't feel he deserved praise for his action. No true gentleman would continue to employ a butler who abused the lower servants, or any other woman for that matter. "Why the devil are you still here?" he said in a gruff voice as he started up the stairs. "I thought you said you had plans this evening?"

"I'm going, I'm going," she assured him as she opened the front door. "I don't want to miss the Ride of the Valkyries. It's my favorite part."

"You're going to Covent Garden, too?" He stopped again and turned on the landing to look at her. "Of course you are," he muttered, answering his own question. "Why should my luck change now?"

She smiled that dazzling smile of hers. "Want to share a cab?"

Despite everything, he could feel an answering smile tugging at the corners of his own mouth. He turned away before she could see it, for he didn't want to encourage her.

"I saw that," she called after him as he continued up the stairs.

He grinned. He couldn't help it. She really was the most outrageous woman. She always had been.

The second intermission had just begun when Julia returned to Covent Garden. Paul and Eugenia were attending the opera with her, but only Paul was in the Danbury box when she entered it.

Paul, fair-haired and brown-eyed like their mutual cousin Beatrix, stood by the rail, staring down at the crowd below and drinking a glass of champagne. "All alone?" she asked as she crossed to his side.

He turned to her as she joined him at the rail, visibly relieved. "Mum saw that the Marlowe family is here, and she went to have a visit with them during intermission. Where on earth have you been? I thought you were only slipping out for some fresh air, but you've been gone over an hour."

"I encountered some people I knew, and we started talking, and the minutes just flew by. I didn't realize how much time had passed until other people began streaming outside and I realized it was the second intermission."

Julia was able to utter this slew of lies without a

blush. A lifetime of being rebellious and twelve years of marriage to Yardley had given her a perfectly honed ability to lie whenever she deemed it necessary.

Paul accepted the story without even asking whom she'd encountered outside. "Well, thank heaven you're back. Mother insisted upon whispering to me all during the second act because she didn't have you to talk to instead."

"Driving you a bit batty, was she?" Julia asked with sympathy as she set her evening bag on her seat and draped her stole over the crimson velvet back.

"Rather. Why you women insist upon watching people through your opera glasses and gossiping, instead of watching the performance, is beyond my understanding."

"Darling Paul, no one—except you, perhaps—goes to the opera for what's on stage. The audience is the interesting part." She chuckled as she glanced across the way and located Vale's box. Squinting, she could make out a feminine figure in pale green standing by the railing, but she was too far away to see who it was, and in any case, there seemed to be no one else in Vale's box at present. Aidan, who'd had to change into evening clothes, hadn't yet arrived.

Julia bent down to retrieve her opera glasses from the pocket attached to the short wall in front of her seat, for when he did appear, she wanted to be ready. She adored comedy, and watching Aidan, so polite and proper, attempt to escape Lady Felicia was sure to be deuced amusing. She'd been looking forward to it ever since visiting Vivienne the day before, and she'd been so disappointed when the first intermission had come and gone with no sign of him, so disappointed in fact that she'd had to go looking for him.

"Anyway," Paul went on, "I forbid you to leave your seat again until this is over, Julie. That way, Mum will resume chatting with you about who's here and with whom, and who's wearing which jewels, and I can enjoy the music."

"I shall be happy to be your buffer, Paul. It's the least I can do, after the way you've so staunchly stood by me."

"Of course I'll stand by you. We all will. Family, you know. I just wish I'd been able to rid you of that blackguard years ago."

"I know." She squeezed his arm affectionately. "But there was nothing you could have done, and it's over now. I'm just sorry the family has to endure the humiliation of it all."

"No need to be sorry. I suppose any woman married to Yardley would eventually be driven into the arms of another man."

That made her almost want to smile. Paul was such a pet. He actually believed it had all been accidental and romantic.

"Who'd have dreamed Yardley would kick up such a fuss over you having an affair? But still, Julie . . . Aidan?" He paused and shook his head, looking at her, bemused. "You could have knocked me down with a feather—all of us, really—when the story came out.

We didn't think the two of you even liked each other, and with Trix having been engaged to him, and all that—" He stopped and cleared his throat. "Yes, well, I'm babbling. Point is, having you home again has been a godsend. You've been back less than a week, and already my life is so much more pleasant."

"I'm glad." She hesitated, then said, "Is there no chance you and Susanna could—"

"No," he cut her off before she could finish asking about his wife's possible return to England from America. "She has informed me she intends to stay in Newport indefinitely."

Julia sighed and sank down onto her chair. "I do wish you two would work things out."

"We can't." His face was frozen, his body stiff as he sat down beside her. "It's not possible."

"I'm sorry."

"Yes, well, love's rotten." He tried to smile. "When it's over."

"Yes," she agreed, "but it's wonderful while it lasts."

She looked down over the rail, but in her mind's eye, she didn't see the boxes across the way with their crimson velvet seats and their gilded moldings and lavishly dressed patrons. Instead, she saw the lodge on her father's estate and the man who had leased it, a dozen years older than she, a man with long hair and Dangerous Ideas. "I was in love once."

"You were?" Paul's voice was full of astonishment. "I never knew that. Who was he? Not Yardley, surely!"

She shook her head. "Not Yardley."

"Who, then?"

She didn't answer for a moment. She was thinking back to that moment when she'd first laid eyes on Stephen Graham. A handsome man, handsome in the dreamy, wild, brooding poet's way that had appealed so much to her girlish heart. She hadn't known, not in that first moment, that he wrote the most beautiful poetry she'd ever read in her life. She hadn't known she would risk everything simply to be with him and the price she would pay for it. But in that first shared glance, before she'd even known his name, she had already known what it was like to love and be loved. What had Stephen called it in a poem? The divine sting of happiness.

"He was no one important," she said, answering Paul's question. "We used to meet in secret." She paused. "It was wonderful."

"What happened?"

"Papa found out and put a stop to it, forbade me to marry him, and sent him away."

"Deuced bad luck," Paul murmured. "Why couldn't you have fallen in love with someone acceptable to Uncle Percy?"

"Me?" she quipped, forcing lightness into the moment. "Do something acceptable? Heaven forbid."

Paul laughed at that. "You do have a tendency to swim against the tide. You always have."

"We were going to elope," she confided. "He left, and I followed him to Scotland a few weeks later, but when I got to Peebles, he was dead. Scarlet fever, his people told me. Part of me died with him. Papa and

Mama came after me and dragged me home, and they insisted on marrying me off to someone else before I caused a scandal that couldn't be hushed up."

"That's how you ended up marrying Yardley. Our lot all knew when you became engaged that something wasn't right. Your parents were pushing for the match, but you didn't seem to want it much. We never understood why you agreed."

"It would have been like me to rebel at that, too, you think?"

"Well . . ." Paul shot her a look of apology. "Yes."

She smiled ruefully. "I wanted to make good for all my past mistakes. Yardley was . . . I suppose I thought he was my penance."

"A high price for falling in love," Paul remarked. "Do you ever regret it? Falling in love, I mean?"

She smiled. "Never."

"No. Neither do I." He smiled, a melancholy smile. "Susanna's not coming back."

She nodded gently, not surprised. "I gathered that."

"I went to Newport last autumn, thinking to try and win her back, but . . ." He shook his head. "She wasn't having any of that. She never did like England much."

"So why don't you divorce her? You'd certainly have cause."

"I know, but why bother? It isn't as if I want to marry anyone else. I don't."

"Neither do I." She laughed. "We should form a society."

He laughed. But then his laughter faded, and he

looked at her thoughtfully. "Do you ever think you'll fall in love again?"

Julia considered, and then, slowly and with great care, she put love in the past, burying it beside the grief and fear that had followed in its wake. Loving Stephen had been her heaven, and Yardley had been the price she paid for sneaking past that particular set of pearly gates. Now, she just wanted to live unencumbered, with no need to run, nothing to cause her to brood, and nothing to weigh her down, not even love. She was free, and she wanted nothing from life but to enjoy that freedom.

"No," she said quietly. "I wouldn't. Once was enough for me."

"Me too. Hell, we're a cynical pair, aren't we?"

"I'm not cynical!" she protested. "I believe in love and marriage. I do." She paused and winked. "For everybody else."

He laughed. He opened his mouth to reply, but then the gong sounded once, indicating intermission was half over, and Julia suddenly remembered the performance she'd really come to see. "Oh, bother!" she cried, unfolding her opera glasses. "I'm missing all the fun."

"Fun? What do you mean?"

"I wanted to see—" She broke off, perching the glasses on her nose as she located Lord Vale's box, and whatever she'd been about to say was forgotten at the sight of Aidan standing with the girl in the green dress. The girl's back was to her, but Julia didn't need to see Felicia's face to know her identity. She could discern that particular information from Aidan's blank, almost dazed expression.

She burst out laughing. She couldn't help it, for she could almost hear Felicia squeaking away, even from here. If this were a *Punch* cartoon, the imaginary bubble over Aidan's head would have borne the caption: *Is intermission over yet?*

Poor fellow, but she had tried to warn him. She laughed again, but she decided the next time she saw him, she wouldn't crow about having been right. Well, not too much anyway.

"What do you find so amusing?" Paul asked, leaning closer to her, looking out at the crowd.

She pulled the opera glasses down and grinned at her cousin. "I thought you didn't care about observing people and gossiping."

Caught, he looked away, a bit shamefaced. "Just asking."

She returned her attention to the scene across the way, and it was too delicious not to share. "I'm watching Trathen," she confessed. "He's in Lord Vale's box, having a visit, and Lady Felicia has commandeered him. Oh, the look on his face. It's priceless."

Paul groaned. "Poor chap. That girl cornered me for two hours at a ball last month. She would not stop talking. I finally had to be rude in order to get away."

"Trathen's in the same boat, I fear. No doubt she'll trap him into sitting with her somehow, and the next ninety minutes will be agony for the man. Go rescue him, Paul. Do. He'll be ever so grateful. And it never hurts to have a duke's gratitude."

"Perhaps, but is that wise? Even if he consented to come sit with us, it wouldn't be a good idea. People would see him with you and think—"

"Chérie!"

She and Paul both turned as a slender, dark-haired man entered the box, a man Julia recognized at once.

"René!" she cried with delight, jumping up. "By all that's wonderful."

She folded her opera glasses and tucked them back into the pocket in front of her seat, then moved to greet the young, debonair Frenchman as he came toward her with outstretched hands. She took them in hers, accepting a kiss on each cheek. "I had no idea you were in England."

"I arrived from Paris only yesterday. I am down below, talking to friends and thinking this German opera is so very dull, but then I look up and see you, and the evening becomes much brighter."

When he glanced past her, Julia turned. "Paul," she said as her cousin moved to her side, "you remember René DuBois, don't you? From the motor races at Scarborough two years ago?"

Paul, who remembered René perfectly and didn't like him in the least, gave a polite smile. "Of course. Evening, DuBois."

René bowed, not seeming to mind this rather stiff English greeting. *"Bonne nuit."*

Julia, sensing the tension, waved a hand in Paul's direction. "Go after poor Trathen before Felicia gets her hooks into him. You don't need to bring him here. Invent some excuse and take him to Marlowe's box.

He knows all of them, and even if they've no empty seats, Marlowe would be happy to pull him outside and talk business with him. In fact," she added, struck by a sudden idea, "the more I think about it, the more I like this plan. Go, Paul. The poor man's in desperate need of rescuing. See to it, will you?"

"All right," Paul acceded with a sigh, giving in to the inevitable, "but what about afterward? Marlowe's bound to invite him to his supper party at the Savoy, and we'll be there, too."

That was exactly the point. She wanted to talk to Aidan about the idea that had just come to her, and supper would be a perfect opportunity. "For heaven's sake, Paul, we're all mature adults. Surely we can all be in the same room together for an evening, can't we?"

"For the sake of all our reputations, you and Trathen really ought to avoid each other as much as possible."

"It's not a formal dinner, so I shall ask Marlowe's wife to put his sister Phoebe beside Trathen, which should steer gossip in that direction and away from me. And," she added, putting her arm through that of the Frenchman beside her, "we'll bring René to make doubly sure. You'll come, René, won't you?"

"I should be delighted."

"Julie! You can't go about inviting people to other people's supper parties!"

"Nonsense, Paul. The Marlowes won't mind. I think we'll be quite a merry party tonight, don't you?"

Paul gave a resigned sigh as he started off on his errand. "Sometimes, cousin," he said over his shoulder as he walked to the door, "I do not understand your devilish sense of humor. You're doing this just to crow."

Julia watched him go, not bothering to correct his assumption. While teasing Trathen was always an almost irresistible temptation, and the episode with Felicia gave her plenty of ammunition in that regard, that wasn't why she was arranging for him to join them at supper. She wanted to ask him for a favor, and with that being the case, teasing him about Lady Felicia would not be wise.

Chapter Seven

Never before had Aidan appreciated just how long twenty minutes could be.

"And when Mama told me that a very special guest would be joining us during intermission as a surprise for my first season, why, I was just so excited," Lady Felicia gushed, making him appreciate Julia's skill as a mimic.

He'd arrived at Covent Garden ten minutes past the start of the second intermission, but he'd barely had time to greet his host and hostess before he'd been introduced to their daughter, and the remaining minutes were dragging by in interminable fashion. Lady Felicia, however, was prattling along at top speed.

"And although I knew it was meant to be a surprise, I just had to ask who the special guest was. Mama kept refusing to tell me, of course. I mean, it wouldn't be a surprise, otherwise, would it? But that fact didn't stop me. I'm very determined when I want something," she added with a giggle. "So I just kept asking and asking, and Mama—who never could keep a secret—finally relented enough to give me a hint. And what she said, you'll never guess."

There was a pause, indicating that despite her prediction, he was expected to make the attempt. At this moment, however, Aidan just couldn't work up the enthusiasm to do so. He merely raised his eyebrows.

That small gesture proved to be sufficient encouragement. "Mama told me that at long last, I would be able to meet my hero."

She gave him a smile that, had she never before spoken a word, might have been quite captivating. Unfortunately for both of them, her beauty had ceased to captivate him the moment she began to talk, and when she gave him a melting look with those lovely, dark, almond-shaped eyes, he felt not the least stirring of attraction, thereby disproving Julia's silly accusation that he was particularly susceptible to brown eyes. Nonetheless, he had just been given a compliment, and he was required to respond accordingly. "You flatter me, Lady Felicia," he murmured, "and I do thank you for it, but I hardly think I am worthy of the description of hero."

"Oh, but you are, Your Grace! We had occasion to meet once before, though I'm sure you don't remember it."

Aidan, who didn't, cast a quick but desperate glance at the door, wondering if he really had to stay the entire time for etiquette to be satisfied. But even as he thought that, he knew anything less was unworthy of a gentleman. He glanced around the box for an alternative to Lady Felicia's nonstop stream of chatter. His gaze paused on the girl's parents, hoping to see a way of bringing them into conversation, but their backs were to him and their daughter as they talked with other guests, making it clear he was on his own.

"It was eight years ago," Felicia said, and Aidan was forced to return his attention to her. "I was only a girl then, of course, and I was riding with my governess in Hyde Park when suddenly my horse bolted. It frightened me out of my wits, for I couldn't rein the mare in. I tried and tried, but I've always been rather delicate, certainly no match for a big, strong horse." She paused with a tinkling laugh. "Well, there we were, headed straight for the Serpentine, when you came racing alongside, caught me up, and pulled me right onto your saddle! I was so overcome, being swept up in your strong arms like that, that I fainted dead away. When I awoke, I was lying in the grass, with my governess kneeling beside me, rubbing my wrists, and you standing guard so protectively to keep the crowd away."

Now that she was reminding him of it, Aidan did remember the incident in question, though he'd never learned the girl's name, and his version was perhaps not quite as romantic as hers. About eleven or twelve at the time, she'd urged her plodding mare from a trot to a canter and then panicked at the increased speed, dropping her reins and screaming for help. He'd come alongside, attempting to guide her, but she'd been too frightened and hysterical to follow his instructions, and in the end, he'd given up on instruction and hauled her onto his horse. In his recollection of the events, she hadn't fainted, and he'd returned her to her governess in a perfectly lucid state, tipped his hat, and gone on his way. He did not, of course, point out these minor discrepancies between their versions. That would have been rude.

"You departed before I could thank you for your assistance, Your Grace, but I shall never forget your chivalry." She clasped her gloved hands together, gazing at him with a reverence all out of proportion to the situation. "You will always be my hero." The last two words came out in a rapturous squeak.

Looking at the girl's worshipful face, Aidan thought of Julia's assessment from the other night, and he felt a hint of irritation. He was no hero.

As if to prove it, a recollection of pulling apart Julia's dress flashed through his mind, demonstrating that he shouldn't be any girl's white-knight fantasy.

"I'm sure I did what any man would have done in the circumstances," he murmured, and before she could heap any more undeserved praise upon him, the gong sounded a second time, indicating only five minutes remained before curtain, and Aidan hoped he had now fulfilled his obligation and could depart for home.

He opened his mouth to murmur a farewell and something vague about another social obligation somewhere, but Lady Felicia had a sharper mind than Julia had given her credit for. Sensing that he was about to bid her good night, she spoke first. "You must sit with us for the final act, Your Grace."

She moved as if to actually put her arm through his and drag him to a chair, but before he was forced to choose between acceding to Lady Felicia's ghastly invitation or issuing a peremptory refusal that would hurt her feelings, another voice entered the conversation.

"Trathen, I thought I saw you over here!"

Aidan turned toward the Earl of Danbury, who was just entering Vale's box, giving the other man a look of both relief and gratitude.

Paul stopped to shake hands with Lord Vale and compliment Lady Vale on her smashing gown before coming to him and the girl by his side. "Lady Felicia, how lovely you look, but then you always do. Trathen, you devil, managing to find the prettiest girl at any event, but really, your absentmindedness these days . . ." He paused, shaking his head as if in exasperation as he slanted Aidan a meaningful glance. "You promised Marlowe you'd go by his box sometime during the first intermission to discuss business matters, and you never arrived. Not that I blame you for forgetting," he added with another smile at the girl, "given the distractions here this evening."

Aidan took his cue at once. "Right, business. I did forget. Can't imagine how I could have done such a thing."

"I was with Marlowe when he spied you over here, and he sent me to ask if you'd mind terribly coming now? He's leaving tomorrow apparently—wants to spend a few days at Marlowe Park before my house party at Whitsuntide. If you don't talk to him now, you may not have another chance."

"I obviously can't allow that to happen." He turned, hoping he looked regretful. "Lady Felicia, you must forgive me. Business before pleasure, I fear."

Her lip jutted out a bit mutinously, but she really had no means of circumventing that particular argument. "Of course."

Aidan thanked his hosts, bid them farewell, and allowed Paul to usher him out the door. "Thank you, Paul," he said as the two men walked along the curved corridor toward Viscount Marlowe's box.

"Thank Julie. She's the one who asked me to come to your aid." He proceeded to explain, and though Aidan suspected Julia of having a bit of fun at his expense, he couldn't argue that he rather deserved a bit of teasing about Felicia.

Though he hadn't received a formal invitation from Marlowe to join them, he was too glad to be away from Vale's box to quibble about the impropriety of it. Fortunately, Marlowe tended to be casual in such matters and was amused to learn he'd been the means of rescuing Aidan from the clutches of a grasping debutante. The viscount provided him with a seat in their box and invited him to supper at the Savoy afterward. Aidan, who found the Marlowe family quite enjoyable company, chose to accept.

Paul returned to his own seat, and Aidan barely had time to greet Marlowe's mother, wife, and two sisters before the lights dimmed and the curtain went up. He took the seat offered to him beside Marlowe's sister Phoebe, giving her a smile as he sat down, then he leaned back in his seat with a heartfelt sigh of relief. He didn't care much for Wagnerian opera, but the lurid refrain of a Valkyrie was a vast improvement over Felicia's chirps and squeaks.

He feared tonight was a perfect example of what he had to look forward to in the coming months. Rounds of parties he wasn't interested in attending, awkward introductions, interfering parents, prying eyes, gossip columns, and tiresome, often downright silly conversations with hundreds of women, all in the hope of finding just one he could envision spending his life with, a woman who was both attractive to him and appropriate to be a duchess. Then, of course, he'd actually need to have the luck—absent of late—to get her to the altar.

Beside him, Phoebe Marlowe shifted in her chair, making him slide a considering sideways glance at her. Phoebe was an attractive woman, certainly, with cherubic cheeks, dark brown hair, and blue eyes. She also had brains and a sense of humor. But when he tried to see himself married to her, he couldn't quite envision the picture. He liked Phoebe, but he'd first met her at the house party where Beatrix had broken their engagement, and the associations were a bit awkward. That episode had been a difficult and embarrassing one and something he'd rather not have a constant reminder of for the rest of his life. And his liking for Phoebe was a lukewarm one at best, one that had not deepened upon closer acquaintance. Phoebe, he suspected, had similar feelings. And yet, did it matter? He was looking for a suitable duchess, Phoebe was certainly qualified for that role, and yet, the idea of marrying for suitability now left him cold. Why?

Either that, or you'll bore each other to death . . . you crave the forbidden fruit.

As Julia's words echoed through his mind, Aidan's gaze lifted to the Danbury box on the other side of the theater and he reached into the breast pocket of his evening jacket for his opera glasses.

She was smiling, her head tilted to one side as a man Aidan had never seen before whispered something in her ear. Whatever it was, it made her laugh. He wondered if the man was her latest lover, and anger surged through him, anger that only deepened as he realized its cause. He was jealous.

Appalled, he studied her laughing face and wondered what the hell was wrong with him. Like himself, the other man was only one in a long line of her conquests. He knew she wasn't worth his concern, and her love affairs were none of his business. Yet, even as he reminded himself of these things, jealousy continued to wash over him in a hot, smothering wave.

Aidan lowered the opera glasses and tilted back his head, staring at the gold-and-white ceiling of the Royal Opera House, angry with himself for these savage, primal feelings he could not seem to control. He had always wanted her, ever since that day on the footbridge when he was seventeen, and despite everything, he still wanted her. No matter how much time passed, no matter what he did or tried to do, he could not seem to eradicate his desire for her.

He knew he had to find a way. They would surely see each other again and again throughout the season, and he had to rid himself of this insatiable need for her before it could further damage his reputation, hamper his goals, and taint his honor.

But what was the antidote to a woman who seemed able to awaken his deepest carnal appetites against his will? He might have thought bedding her was the answer, but he'd already done that, and it hadn't changed a thing.

On the other hand, he reflected, did that afternoon at her cottage really count in that regard? There was a great deal about that afternoon he didn't remember. Perhaps that was why he couldn't get past this. Perhaps it was time to try filling in the blank spaces of his memory instead of trying to suppress it or forget it. Perhaps that was how he could finally conquer it.

Aidan straightened in his seat, lifted the opera glasses again, and studied her, letting anything he could remember about that afternoon enter his mind.

The white dress was the first thing he thought of. He remembered that, God knew, for the image of her in it soaking wet with nothing underneath was burned on his brain for all time. There had been buttons down the front, pearl buttons, and although the fabric had been damp, the buttons had slipped free of their holes with ease. No doubt that was why she'd chosen it, and why she'd chosen to wear no undergarments beneath it. Everything—the dress, the water, the lack of underclothes—had been meant to make the seduction as easy as possible.

He'd pulled the dress down her shoulders, but he hadn't done that at the cove. No, they'd been in the kitchen of her cottage by that time, though he couldn't recall walking back from the beach below.

Through the opera glasses, he watched her lean back in her seat and close her eyes as she listened to the music. The move gave him a splendid view of her exposed throat and décolleté, evoking the memory of how he had trailed kisses along her throat and across her bare shoulder.

He'd put his hands on her arms at some point—to push her away or bring her closer? He didn't know what his intent might have been, but did know that he'd cupped her breasts in his hands, and any vague idea he might have had about pushing her away had gone to the wall.

He remembered her hand raking through his hair, pulling his head down to her breast, and how her skin had been warm and soft with the delicate scent of lilacs. He remembered his hands on her buttocks and the hot, aching tension building in his body as he'd pulled her closer. He was feeling it again now, watching her across the theater.

What had happened next? He stared at her across the theater, striving to remember. Had he taken her right there, standing up, her legs wrapped around his hips? Or had he carried her upstairs to her room first? What had happened next? *Damn it*, he thought, his gaze riveted on her, *what was next?*

On the stage below, the Valkyrie soprano hit the high-C. Julia opened her eyes and straightened in her seat as if to resume watching the performance, but then she paused, turning her head to look straight at him. Caught, he jerked the glasses down and leaned back, awash in arousal and frustration.

He didn't remember anything more, but what did it matter? His honor had already been proved a sham by that point, and envisioning the various ways in which the actual coupling had taken place would only inflame the passion he was trying to extinguish.

His mind went further back, to their very first meeting and her bare legs dangling over the side of a bridge with her pretty toes skimming the water. Did it all come down to that? Surely he hadn't thrown caution to the wind, compromised his reputation, and made himself a cad just to fulfill a silly adolescent fantasy.

He refused to believe it was that simple, or that he was that facile, yet she was the only woman who had ever tempted him beyond reason and beyond honor.

Why her? he wondered, thoroughly exasperated with himself. Perhaps she'd been right to say he harbored a secret longing for what he could not have, but there were many women among his acquaintance who could be considered the "forbidden fruit," as she'd put it, and yet he was not like his father—he didn't lust after every woman he met. So what was it about this particular woman that made her so hard to resist?

Aidan glanced at the bewitching woman across the way, and decided it was damned well time he found out.

Julia was restless. She paced about the crimson and gold interior of one of the Savoy's elegant sitting rooms as Marlowe's other guests milled about in a much more leisurely fashion, engaging in small talk as they waited for supper to be served in the private dining room beyond. Only one guest had not yet arrived, and though Marlowe had confirmed Aidan would be coming, Julia kept glancing at the door, a bit aggravated. Aidan was never unpunctual. What was taking him so long?

She wanted to talk with him about the idea she'd had earlier, and this supper party seemed a perfect opportunity, but she knew he had very little reason to talk with her, and the more time that passed without his arrival, the more nervous she became. She wandered about, unable to sit down for more than two minutes at a time, she tapped her fingers against her champagne glass and her foot against the floor, and though René tried several times to engage her in conversation, she was too distracted to respond with anything more than a few murmured monosyllables.

With only ten minutes remaining until supper would be served, he finally arrived, but Julia wanted to speak to him out of earshot of anyone else, and she was forced to wait a little longer while he greeted his hosts and was introduced to René.

When he moved to the refreshment table across the room, she saw her chance at last, but as she came up beside him, he gave her nothing more than an indifferent glance, and her nervousness grew. She strove to keep it hidden, taking refuge in teasing him as she watched him pour himself a glass of port.

"Port, Aidan?" she said, giving him an impudent look. "Is that wise?"

"In your company, probably not," he answered dryly. "But I do sometimes drink, as you are well aware. I simply make it a rule to limit myself to one glass. In that sense, port serves me well since I dislike it. And," he added, grimacing as he took a sip, "after the events of earlier this evening, God knows I need a drink."

She laughed, but before she could reply, he held up his free hand, palm toward her in a gesture of surrender. "You were right about Felicia Vale. Absolutely right. That is why you made a beeline for me just now, isn't it? So you could gloat?"

"Well, no, actually, but now that you mention it . . ." She paused, grinning. "Told you so."

A hint of wry amusement curved the corners of his mouth. "No doubt you have a very strong pair of opera glasses, and saw the entire episode?"

She didn't even try to deny it. "Every delicious moment."

"That poor girl. I shall dance a waltz with her to compensate for your heartless way of entertaining yourself at her expense."

"No you won't. Even your sense of chivalry doesn't extend that far."

Unexpectedly, he chuckled. "I daresay you're right."

"But I didn't make a beeline for you, as you put it, so that I could tease you about Felicia. I want to talk with you about something else. That is, I want to ask you something." She paused and glanced around. "But I don't want anyone else to overhear."

"I don't know if that's wise," he murmured. "The private conversations I have with you never seem to turn out well."

She had rather the opposite point of view, for one of their private conversations had turned out to be her salvation, but it would not be wise to say so, not when she was about to surpass all her previous gall and ask him for help. "I understand your reluctance, and you have every right, but this is important, Aidan," she said quietly. "Could you give me a moment?"

Her suddenly serious tone surprised him, she could tell, but he nodded. "Of course."

At that moment, Sir George and Lady Debenham approached the refreshment table, and Aidan moved with her to an unoccupied part of the room, but when he gestured to a pair of facing chairs near the fireplace with a questioning glance at her, she shook her head. She was nervous enough already, and if she were sitting down, she'd probably start wriggling in her chair. "I'd prefer to stand, if you don't mind."

"Certainly." He paused for a sip of port. "What did you wish to discuss?"

She took a deep breath and plunged in. "I am in need

of an occupation, and I thought you might be able to help me."

"An occupation?" he echoed, a puzzled frown knitting his brows. "What do you mean?"

"I . . . umm . . . I need money, you see."

His frown deepened. "But surely Paul—"

"Paul can't help me, and I wouldn't ask him to. He's giving me a very generous allowance in pin money, but that's not much good because . . ." She paused, for this was much harder than she'd thought it would be. She hated talking of unpleasant subjects, and she really hated putting herself in a bad light to someone whose opinion she respected, but there was nothing for it. Aidan, at least, already thought the worst of her, so what she was about to say wouldn't surprise him. "I'm in debt. Quite heavily in debt."

"I see."

Just that, two murmured words, and she felt defensive all of a sudden. "It's not gambling, if that's what you're thinking. Or clothes, although I do spend a lot on clothes, I know. Some of it is the Mercedes, too. It was an expensive trinket, I daresay, but I had reasons for purchasing it, reasons which—"

"Julia," he interrupted, "I didn't ask you for an explanation of how you spend your money. I'm just trying to clarify what it is you want of me. Are you asking me for employment?"

She looked into those steady hazel eyes, but she could read nothing in their murky depths. Nor could she detect from his polite impassivity what he might be

thinking. "Well . . . yes. I mean, possibly. I mean—"
She paused again, cursing herself for stammering like
a schoolgirl all of a sudden. It took gall for her to ask
him for help after what she'd done, and if their posi-
tions were reversed, she'd probably tell him to go to
hell. Though she knew Aidan wouldn't say such a thing
to any woman, that knowledge didn't soothe her jan-
gled nerves.

She took a deep breath, reminded herself of how
limited her options were, and tried again. "You are a
man of considerable business acumen, and you have
many investment holdings. I was thinking . . . hoping
you might have some post available that I could . . .
umm . . . do, or at least a suggestion of how I might
earn the money to pay my debts. That is," she added
with a forced laugh, "if you can think of anything I'm
remotely qualified to do."

He didn't reply. Instead, his gaze skimmed over her
in a slow, assessing perusal that seemed to miss nothing and perhaps remember a great deal. Under this
scrutiny, Julia suddenly felt warm and flushed, and she
had an inexplicable desire to bolt for the door. By the
time his eyes once again met hers, she felt as if a dozen
butterflies were fluttering around inside her. In his
eyes, there was no spark of desire that she could discern; his gaze was cool, objective, almost disinterested.
Strangely, that made her feel more vulnerable than any
hot look of desire would have done, more naked than
she'd been that afternoon in Cornwall. Suddenly, she
was the one in desperate need of a drink.

"If this were a melodrama," he said as she lifted her glass of champagne to her lips, "I would make you my mistress."

Julia froze, the glass poised just below her parted lips, and her heart slammed against her ribs. Desperate, she grasped for her most effective weapon, the witty remark, and pasted on a careless smile. "What's it pay?" she quipped, and took a swallow of champagne.

As expected, he laughed, but that didn't diffuse her increasing tension. There was something new in the air, a change in the way he was looking at her, in the way he was speaking to her. It seemed more impersonal and distant than what she was accustomed to with him, and she didn't like it. It made her feel even more off-balance.

She forced herself back to the matter at hand. "In all seriousness, I do need employment of some sort. Honorable employment. I want . . ." She paused, trying to find a way to explain without being asked any probing, inconvenient questions. "I want to do something useful with my life."

He raised one eyebrow, looking so skeptical of her sudden earnestness, she couldn't help laughing a little. "I know, I know, I've been such a lily of the field most of my life, but I want to change that. I was hoping you could suggest how I might do so."

He was silent for a moment, and she knew he was considering any possible ulterior motives she might have. "I might have some ideas for you," he said at last. "Come see me tomorrow. Nine o'clock," he added. "Be punctual."

She suppressed her sigh of relief. "Nine? Heavens, Aidan, the birds aren't even awake at nine. Oh, all right," she added as he gave her a look that dared her to keep objecting. "Nine o'clock tomorrow. But," she added, feeling the need to make things absolutely clear, "if that bit about being your mistress wasn't a joke, let me set you straight and say no in advance."

"No need to refuse me, Baroness, for I would never consider making you my mistress, and I wouldn't dream of proposing such an arrangement."

Such an unequivocal reply surprised her a little, she had to admit. Not that she was unduly conceited, but Aidan had always been rather susceptible to her charms—she'd known that from the first time they'd ever met, so it wasn't unreasonable of her to be a bit taken aback by his statement. And though he had ample reason to avoid becoming entangled with her again, it stung a little that he was so uninterested in the prospect. "Why not?" she couldn't resist asking. "Because you're too much of a gentleman to take a mistress?"

"No," he answered and started to move past her. "Because I already have one. Now, if you will excuse me?"

He bowed to her and walked away without waiting for an answer, which was a good thing, since she could not, for the life of her, think of a witty comeback to that.

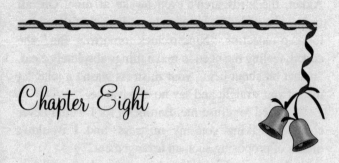

Chapter Eight

*J*ulia was not a punctual person, and not always a reliable one. Part of this was due to years of ducking and dodging and running away from Yardley, which had necessitated a lack of reliability in her social commitments and a believable set of excuses to go with it. And part was due, she would have been the first to admit, to her innate procrastination, her love of late night parties, and her hatred for early rising, all of which she had been able to indulge freely during the past six months without fear or worry.

Her family, who loved her and understood all this, were quite accustomed to her lack of punctuality; her friends found her amusing enough to overlook that particular flaw. Aidan, however, was an entirely different kettle of fish, and so, upon arriving home after supper at the Savoy, she instructed Giselle to awaken her at half past six.

Despite such firm resolve, when the maid arrived

in obedience to the emphatic instructions issued three hours earlier, Julia groaned, rolled over, and went back to sleep. When Giselle reentered her room thirty minutes later with morning tea and a compelling reminder that she had a very important meeting in the City two hours hence, Julia made the hazy rationale that she could always charm away any irritation that ensued from her lateness on any occasion, and drifted back into the very pleasant dream she'd been having about an absurd little Vivienne hat.

Another half hour passed, and her maid returned. Noting that her mistress was still asleep, Giselle, who knew Julia's foibles quite well, took the course of action most likely to yield the necessary result. She leaned down to murmur in her mistress's ear, and when Julia heard the words *Duke of Trathen*, her eyes opened as if she'd just been plunked down in an ice bath. Any dreams of absurd little hats and charming excuses went right out of her head.

"Heavens!" she cried, flinging back the sheets and sitting up, wide awake. "Giselle, what time is it?"

"Half past seven, madame." The maid, who was holding open a violet silk peignoir for her to slip into, added, "You have no time to bathe, but I have hot water waiting on the washstand."

"Such a good thing I did not smoke cigarettes last night," Julia murmured, waving aside the robe as she ran to the washstand. "Aidan hates the smell of smoke, and I've no time to wash my hair."

The mere mention of cigarettes made her crave one, but the image of Aidan's disapproving face as she'd pulled her case out the night before in his study was enough to banish her craving, at least for now.

Giselle vanished into the dressing room, and Julia slipped off her nightgown. She shoved the braid of her hair over her shoulder, poured steaming water into the washbasin, grabbed the square of French-milled lilac soap that sat in a little dish on the marble-topped washstand, and began a quick but serviceable bath, beginning with her face and working her way down.

"How long shall it take to arrive in the City, Giselle, do you think?" she called, soaping beneath her arms.

The maid emerged from the dressing room, carrying a tailor-made coat and skirt of pale gray, one of Julia's less lavish white shirtwaists, and a pile of snowy white undergarments. "One hour."

"An hour? Traffic in London is that awful nowadays? Oh, dear, I'm sunk like a ship."

"Perhaps less than an hour," the maid conceded grudgingly, setting the clothes on the bed, before coming to help her rinse away the soap and dry off. "But it does not do to be always late, madame."

"I know, I know, I'm terrible. Come, Giselle, help me dress. I'll do my hair while you go down and find me a taxi."

She and the maid worked frantically to dress her in the many layers of garments required of a lady, then Giselle departed. Julia unraveled her braid, then twisted her black curls at the back of her head, making use of many hairpins and a few impatient oaths. She donned an enormous hat of gray felt with a wide brim and heaps of ribbons and feathers that would conceal her rather crooked efforts with her hair, then she thrust her feet into black kid walking shoes, caught up a pair of white gloves, and raced for the stairs, hoping Giselle had succeeded in her task, for acquiring a taxi always seemed an impossible task when one was in a hurry.

The bells of St. Dunstan's in the West were just chiming the hour of nine o'clock when Julia stepped down from the cab in front of Aidan's offices in the City. She tossed a full shilling to the driver, not wanting to bother counting out the proper amount of change, and raced into the four-story stone and granite building on the corner of Fleet Street and Chancery Lane.

She halted in the impressive Italianate foyer to get her bearings and spied a clerk seated behind a lavishly carved rosewood secretaire. As she approached him, the tap of her heels echoed off the Siena marble floor and the impressive high ceilings.

Aidan had obviously left instructions that she was to be expected, for upon giving her name to the clerk, she was led to an electric lift and handed over to the liveried young man operating it, who took her to the top floor.

"To your left, ma'am," the boy told her as he opened the wrought-iron gate so that she could her exit the elevator. "Shall I escort you?"

Julia glanced toward a set of tall baize doors and back at him with a smile. "That won't be necessary."

"Very good, ma'am." Tipping his cap, the boy slid

the gate closed between them, then pressed the electric button and sank out of sight.

Julia went through the doors and found herself in another office suite, this one far more masculine and far more English in its decor than the lavish foyer downstairs. In fact, she reflected as she glanced around, it suited Aidan so perfectly, he might have decorated it himself.

Everywhere was solid practicality combined with comfort, everything understated, nothing too lavish. There was oak paneling, hunter-green wallpaper, a thick, muted Persian carpet, and sporting prints and English landscapes on the walls. Everything was tasteful but subdued, the lighting was electric, the pictures hung perfectly straight on the walls, and there was no sign of frivolity or absurdity in sight.

Before her reposed a massive desk of dark cherrywood, and behind it, a sandy-haired young man with pince-nez rose from his chair.

"Lady Yardley?" At her nod, he bowed. "I am Mr. Lambert, His Grace's secretary. The duke is expecting you, if you will come this way."

She followed him to the door, pausing as he opened it and announced her. Aidan rose from the chair behind his desk as she entered, and once she had passed into his office, his secretary started to depart. Aidan's voice, however, made him pause.

"Mr. Lambert, close the door behind you, if you please."

Both Julia and the secretary looked at him in surprise. Mr. Lambert didn't question him, but Julia did so the moment the door clicked shut.

"The two of us alone behind closed doors, Aidan?" she teased as she approached his desk.

"You came to discuss a topic that last night seemed private to you, expressing the desire that no one overhear. I assumed you would feel the same today. Am I wrong?"

"No, but it's not really proper, is it?"

"With you, Julia, propriety always seems to go out the window anyway. I've rather given up on it."

She chuckled. "I always knew there was hope for you."

"I'm glad to hear it." He gestured to a chair opposite his desk. "Shall we sit down?"

He waited until she had taken the offered chair, then he resumed his own seat and came straight to the point. "You said last night you need employment because you are in debt?"

"Yes. I want to clear those obligations and start my life fresh. The most logical course seems to be a profession."

"Unfortunately, there is really only one well-paying profession open to women." He paused, looking at her. "As we discussed last night."

His reminder of what he'd said the night before about having a mistress brought all her nervousness rushing back, along with a new, different sort of agitation, and Julia realized to her horror that she was actually blushing. Heavens, she thought, feeling the heat flood her face, what was wrong with her? She hadn't blushed since she was a girl of sixteen.

She appreciated that something was different, but she couldn't pinpoint just what it was or the reason for it. Acutely aware of the heat in her cheeks, she forced herself to say something. "But you already have a mistress," she reminded, taking refuge in flirtation. "Such a shame, too," she added, slanting him a naughty look. "We could have had so much fun."

"Yes." His expression didn't change. His gaze flicked down, then back up. "I agree."

Her blush deepened. Heavens, what was wrong with her? Never before had she felt this way with Aidan—so off-balance and unsure. She didn't like the feeling, and she strove to regain her usual careless assurance. "It would have been amusing for both of us, I daresay, but c'est la vie." She gave an exaggerated sigh. "You want to get married, and I want to rebuild my reputation, for my family's sake."

"Not for your own?"

She shrugged. "I was prepared for losing my reputation when I—"

Seduced you.

The words hung in the air for a split second before she went on, "When Yardley divorced me."

"I see." He leaned forward in his chair. "I don't know how much you owe, of course, but it seems to me there is a very simple and honorable way to resolve your difficulties, at least in part. Why do you not sell your jewels?"

"Jewels? I don't have . . ." She paused, realizing which jewels he was talking about, remembering the glittering three-strand necklace and drop earrings she'd taken to wearing for formal engagements. "Ah, you mean the diamonds I wore last night. I can't sell those."

"Why not? Selling them would surely bring enough to pay at least some of your debt."

She stirred uneasily, not wanting to explain. "Heavens, Aidan," she drawled instead, laughing. "Women never sell their jewels! That's almost sacrilegious."

He didn't smile. He didn't even change expression. But when he spoke, there was a hint of reproof in his voice. "Don't do that, Julia."

She looked at him, wide-eyed. "Do what?"

"Joke and deflect and make light of something because you don't want to discuss it. If you can manage to be straightforward with me, I might have some helpful suggestions to offer. Is it sentiment that stops you from selling your jewelry? Jewels are often passed down in a family, but—"

"It's not sentiment. It's—" She stopped, biting her lip, cursing silently. Why was being straightforward so damned difficult? Perhaps because what he wanted to know involved talking about her life when it had been so awful, when she had lived with things that were sordid and a marriage that was a nightmare, and now that the nightmare was over, she didn't want to relive it. Or perhaps it was telling the truth itself that was hard; she'd been lying for so many years to so many people that it had become second nature to her. Lying to Yardley, lying to the family, lying to friends—out of fear or shame or her damnable pride. God knew, lying was all she had ever seemed to do with Aidan. But right now, when he was looking at her with those steady, searching eyes of his, she wondered if maybe it was time to try simple honesty. After all, wasn't that part of the fresh start she wanted?

Julia lifted her chin. "I tried to sell my jewels seven years ago, after Yardley cut off my income. He'd already been reducing my allowance every year until by that point it was almost nothing. He knew I was already in debt, and he was trying to bring me to heel, you see, force me home to Yardley Grange."

Aidan frowned, uncomprehending. "Why didn't you go? If you had, he probably would have reinstated your income."

"No."

"But surely it wasn't unreasonable of him to expect you to live part of your year at home. You were his wife."

She shook her head, struggling not to let an easy lie come tripping off her tongue. "You don't understand."

"You were unhappy. You must have been, I know, but—"

"No, you don't know!" she said fiercely, and slammed down the lid on the topic. "I don't want to talk about Yardley. Please don't ask me to do so."

"All right."

The reply was mild, agreeable, but she still felt

prickly as a chestnut, and she had to take a few deep breaths before going on.

"When Yardley cut me off completely, creditors began coming to him for payment of my bills," she resumed, "and when he realized his refusal to pay my quarterly allowance wouldn't be enough to force me to come home, he announced in the newspapers that he would not honor any of my debts, past, present, or future. I knew my only choice was to sell my jewels. My husband had already taken back the pieces that belonged to his family, but I did have jewels of my own. When I removed them from the bank and took them to a pawnbroker, that's when I found out."

"Found out what?"

"They're paste. All of them. Yardley had removed them from the bank at some point, and replaced the jewels with paste replicas. He had the right. Under the terms of the marriage settlement, all my jewels came into his family. They were . . ." She paused, choking up a little from anger and a hint of pain. "I was too young and naive to realize it, but that was what Yardley wanted—to make sure I didn't have money of my own. It was a way to control me. Yardley likes control. I wasn't—" She stopped. Her hands curled into fists. "I wasn't very cooperative in that regard, I'm afraid."

"I see."

He didn't see at all. He couldn't. He was a man, and an honorable one. How could he see? Men like Aidan didn't have any understanding of men like Yardley. Or perhaps he did see, and he pitied her. What a ghastly thought. She tore her gaze away and took a deep breath. "Anyway, that's all water under the bridge," she said, striving to regain the light, I-don't-give-a-damn demeanor it had taken her years to perfect and which had chosen a most inconvenient time to disappear.

"It's a bit rough, you know," she went on, giving him an aggrieved look. "Explaining all one's past mistakes and bad decisions and talking about that dreadful former husband of mine. Can we talk about my present difficulties, rather than my past ones?" When he didn't answer, she began to feel a bit desperate. "Please."

"Very well." He gave an indifferent shrug, putting aside his curiosity without a qualm, seeming in no frame of mind to offer the pity she dreaded. "Another way to raise funds would be to sell your motorcar."

She shook her head. "I won't sell the Mercedes. It's very dear to me, and I can't bear to let go of it. I fought tooth and nail to keep Yardley from taking it. Don't ask me why it's important to me, for I can't explain, but I cannot bear to sell it."

"Do you have any other salable assets? Property? Investment funds? Shares?"

She shook her head with each question. "I have my cottage, but I can't sell that. It's entailed to me, and my eldest daughter after me, should I have any children. If not, it goes to my closest female relation upon my death. None of that matters, though, because I would never sell Dovecotes. It's my home. At least . . ." Her throat went dry and she swallowed hard. "It's the closest thing I have to a home of my own. The cottage and the motorcar are the only things of value that I have. Control of all my other property, including my jewels and what I inherited from my parents upon their death, went to Yardley. That was agreed in the marriage settlement."

Aidan made a sound—exasperation or surprise, she couldn't tell. "For heaven's sake, what sort of marriage settlement did your father lay down upon your engagement? Your jewels became Yardley's. Your inheritance became Yardley's. Was there no protection of your assets at all? Not even a guarantee of pin money?"

"I wasn't really in a position to bargain. The point is," she hastened on, afraid he would ask more questions, "I know I have very few options, but I so badly want to pay my debts."

"Why? Does it matter? Most people have debts. And although those to whom you are indebted can press you, they can't do much else to you, really, unless—" He broke off, frowning at her. "Julia, you've not entangled yourself with any riffraff, have you? The sort who'd threaten you if you don't pay?"

"No, no, nothing like that. Heavens, give me a little credit for my intelligence!"

He looked relieved, and she felt oddly touched. "Why, Aidan," she said, half joking, "are you worried about me?"

His chin lifted a notch. "I would be worried for any woman in distress of that kind."

Of course he would. "Well, let me put your mind at ease, petal. No riffraff."

"My mind is never at ease with you in the vicinity. Chalk it up to past experience. And don't call me petal."

"If I'd been involved with that sort of crowd, I'd have become some man's mistress and paid the moneylender long ago. But it's not like that. I just want a fresh start, and I've already put my family through so much, I don't want to be a burden to them or a worry any longer. And I want . . ." She paused, struggling for a way to explain. "I want to be useful somehow. I daresay that sounds silly to you."

"On the contrary, I don't think it's silly at all. Why would you think I should?"

"I'm a woman, that's why. Men do have the most irritating tendency to pat us on the head and say things like, 'There, there, my dear, you're pretty, and that's enough for a woman. No need for you to be useful.'"

He grinned at her mimicry of the typical British male.

"It makes us want to kick you," she added in a normal voice. "Since you are looking to marry, that's something you should know."

"I'll keep it in mind." He paused, thinking a moment. "Are you certain Paul can't honor your debt?"

She shook her head. "I won't ask him to. He's already paid my debts twice. Besides, though he's been reasonably well-off in the past, his wife's income is gone now, and without that—" She broke off, for it wasn't right to be revealing Paul's troubles. "Anyway, that's not the point. I told you, I don't want to have to go to him again."

"Fair enough, but you could at least have gone to him for advice. But you've come to me instead." He paused, studying her. "Why?"

"Isn't it obvious? You're rich! You could employ me."

"And in exchange for my money, what skills could you offer me?"

Though he was looking at her with nothing more than polite disinterest, she felt a wave of heat run through her body at the question, and she wanted to fire off a flirtatious rejoinder, but for the life of her, she couldn't think of one. "I don't know," she admitted. "I also thought that since you're a man with vast business interests, you might see another alternative, something I hadn't thought of, some clever way I could make money."

"Thank you for the compliment, but even I am having trouble finding a solution for you. As you've said, a profession seems your only option, although any post you took up would not be likely to pay enough in wages to reduce your debt much. At least not in the short term. It depends on the interest rate and how much you owe." He shot her a look of inquiry.

She hesitated. "It's a lot."

"How much?"

"Too much." She gave him a disarming smile, but it didn't work. He continued to look at her, waiting, and her smile faded into a sigh. "Twenty thousand pounds," she answered, readying herself for a lecture about extravagance.

He didn't bother. He didn't even seem surprised. "I

see. And the interest? Or is it all tradesmen's bills?"

She shook her head. "No, I borrowed from a money-lender last year to pay off all the tradesmen I owed. I've accumulated more bills since, but the bulk of my debt is to a moneylender."

"You'd have been wiser to leave it with the trades-men. They would never charge a baroness interest."

"I know, I know, but people in trade can't afford such largesse. They have bills of their own to pay, families to feed. It might not have been the wisest decision from a business standpoint, but it's done. No undoing it now."

"And the interest rate for this moneylender?"

"Eleven."

He shook his head with a sound of exasperation. "That's robbery. Julia, since part of why you came to me for is my advice, let me say don't ever handle money matters yourself. You're hopeless at it."

She was prepared to take that criticism on the chin. She wholly deserved it. "I know. But what do I do now? As you said, a profession would have to pay enough to be worth the bother. And what would I be qualified enough to do? I'm not really accomplished at anything. I'm a social butterfly, with no talents to speak of, and though I'm quite amusing to have at parties, I daresay, that's hardly a profession!"

"No," he agreed. He paused a moment as if consid-ering. "You could marry again, of course."

She stared, looking straight through Aidan, out of London, into Dorset, back into the past, back to Yardley Grange. She could see her former husband's brooding face across the drawing room, watch his hands toying in seeming idleness with that damnable silk cravat he always carried, observe how his black eyes covertly followed the maids who brought the tea or made up the fire—maids who were always very young and very pretty.

She suddenly felt sick.

"Julia?"

The sound of Aidan's voice jerked her out of the past, and she returned her attention to the present and the man before her, a man whose face was agreeably handsome and whose eyes were warm and steady, a man as different from her husband as chalk was from cheese, a man who probably didn't even know men like Yardley existed.

Aidan was looking at her with a frown of concern. "Are you all right? You look quite ill all of a sudden."

She felt ill, and she could only imagine what sort of expression was on her face. She pasted on a smile. "Sorry. I was woolgathering, I'm afraid. I didn't have breakfast, and that always makes me terribly absent-minded. What were you saying?" She fixed an expectant stare on him, giving herself time to curb the nausea in her stomach and regain her usual careless air.

He was frowning slightly, looking puzzled. "I was saying you could remarry."

"Remarry?" She injected just the right amount of amused surprise in her voice. "Heavens, no! Why on earth would I want to do that?"

"It's a way out of your present difficulty."

"A way out?" She laughed, but she couldn't quite hide the bitter tinge in it. "A way in, you mean. A way into prison."

He was staring at her, his eyes searching . . . seeing . . . what? She didn't know, but she wanted to run away from whatever it was he saw.

"Many women remarry, Julia," he said gently. She didn't reply, and the silence seemed interminable before he spoke again. "I might have one idea for you."

"Oh?" Relief flooded through her. "What would that be?"

"I'll explain, but first, I'd like to talk about something else for a moment." He paused again as if considering his words carefully before he went on. "You are not the only one who finds it difficult to talk about mistakes, Julia. The other night at the ball, you told me certain things about myself which I have been forced, reluctantly, to admit were correct."

This seemed rather an odd turn in the conversation. "Indeed?" She'd said a lot of things the other night, and she was unsure which pearls of her cheeky wisdom he was referring to. "Just what was I right about?"

"In the past I have not exercised particularly good judgment in choosing a wife. I can hardly deny it, having two broken engagements to my credit."

"You weren't in those engagements alone, Aidan. Trix and Lady Rosalind bear some responsibility, too. As do I," she forced herself to add, "at least in regard to the second one."

"Yes," he agreed. "You do."

She grimaced at that uncompromising reply.

"The point is," he went on, "I am reconsidering my approach to the entire business of finding a wife."

She chuckled. "You mean you've discovered at last that you can't order a bride as if she's a meal at Claridge's?" she asked, grinning at him across the desk. "You've realized it isn't as simple as, 'I'll have the daughter of a marquess, please, with pretty face, agreeable temperament, pristine character, intelligent mind, and, of course, brown eyes.'"

"If you like to put it that way, although, brown eyes aside, I still maintain that things like suitable backgrounds, mutual respect, and compatible temperaments are important, Julia. More important than a romantic feeling, surely?"

She thought of Stephen, and she wondered—if she had married him, if fate had not stepped in, would they have been happy? Possibly. For a lifetime? Possibly not. There was no way to know. Was anyone ever happy with marriage for an entire lifetime? That didn't matter now, not for her, but for Aidan, it might be different. "I suppose it's at least as important," she conceded. "But really, Aidan, you have a way of making love sound dry as dust."

"I'm not talking about love. I'm talking about marriage. And for me, marriage is—must be—an alliance, a union of like minds and compatible souls. I must choose my bride carefully, for I don't think either my reputation or my pride would withstand a third mistake. That is where you come in."

"Me?" She blinked, startled. "But what have I to do with it? Good Lord!" She jerked upright in her chair, staring at him in horror. "You're not proposing marriage to me, are you?"

"God, no!" He stared back at her, seeming just as appalled. "Marrying you would be utterly inappropriate for a man of my position!"

She leaned back again, relieved. "Thank heavens. I thought for a moment you'd gone completely off your onion. Heavens, if you married me, you'd never take your seat in the House of Lords again. Besides, I was a terrible baroness, and I should be even worse as a duchess. Although," she went on, unable to resist teasing him now that the ghastly idea of marrying her was off the table, "you might have been a little less vehement about it." For good measure, she gave an injured sniff. "I may be a scandal, but I do have my feelings, you know."

His lips twitched. "Sorry if I hurt your feelings," he said solemnly.

She pretended to relent. "So if you're not wanting to marry me, then what is this talk of marriage leading to?"

"It's leading exactly where you hoped it would," he answered. "I'm offering you a job."

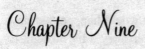

Chapter Nine

A job?" Julia echoed, and she couldn't help laughing. "As what, your marriage broker?"

Aidan grinned. "A novel idea, but no."

"What then?"

Instead of answering, he gestured to a stack of papers that lay on one corner of his desk. "These are all the unanswered social invitations I have received since my appearance at the May Day Ball. About three dozen more arrive each day."

She gave a chuckle. "Told you so."

"Don't gloat, Julia."

"Sorry."

"In choosing to attend a public ball, I was fully aware that I was communicating a message not only to those within my own social sphere, but also to many outside of it, the message being—as you so accurately pointed out—that I was ready to again begin my search for a wife. Nonetheless, many of these invitations are from people with whom I have only the slightest acquaintance."

"Well, of course. That's why they sent them. They want to deepen their acquaintance with you, forge connections."

"Just so, and I realized that would happen, but now that it has, I am finding this territory a bit difficult to navigate."

"What's wrong, Aidan? Afraid there are more Felicia Vales lurking in the shrubbery?"

"Something like that. You, Julia, are a social creature. Even after your divorce, even after six months in exile, you are still holding your own, and you still have powerful friends when most other women in your place would be universally shunned. People like you. You're always staying with one friend or another."

She didn't point out that part of the reason for that was twelve years of refusing to live with her spouse.

"You hear all the gossip," Aidan went on. "And you are a very shrewd judge of character."

Was she? She'd been given cause to wonder about that often during her marriage, for though she'd always sensed Yardley possessed a dark, troubled streak, she'd had no idea before marrying him just how deep that streak had run. Still, she did like to think she had a particular knack for sizing up people. "Thank you for the compliments, Aidan, but I still don't quite understand you. Is it my advice you're wanting? If so, that's hardly a job, and even if it were, my advice would be don't marry at all."

"I don't have that particular option. I have a duty to marry, and it is a duty I genuinely want to fulfill. I would value your opinion of any new social connections I might make along the way."

She'd have thought the last thing Aidan would welcome would be her judgment about anything. "As you well know, I am always happy to offer my opinions! And I must admit," she added with a wink, "I adore showing off how clever I am, so I'd be happy to give you any insight I can. But I'm still a bit at sea about how you intend to employ me for it."

"I want you to act as my social secretary."

"Ah. But surely you could find anyone to do that, so I can only assume it is my skill as a judge of character you are most interested in?"

"Yes." He paused a long moment before answering. "Most men in my position would rely on the opinions of their female relations to assist them with vetting potential marriage partners. My Aunt Caroline is the only close female relation I have, and she cannot be relied upon in that regard. And I am not inclined to trust my own judgment much these days either. Twice my choice of whom to marry has proved a mistake, and I am wary of doing so again."

"Are you sure you want to employ me, though?" she asked. "After all, you did deem me a female Iago."

A pained expression crossed his face. "That was an unforgivable thing to say. Again, I must apologize."

She relented. "Don't. As I told you at the ball, never apologize for telling the truth, at least to me. I have very little regard for the truth, you see," she added lightly, "so it's refreshing for me to find someone who values it."

"I value it highly enough to pay you for it. I am aware that I cannot take forever to choose my duchess, but I do intend to take enough time to make a considered choice. This might take several seasons, and many social events, and Lambert has enough to do without the added burden of an extensive social calendar. Therefore, a social secretary is needed, and I believe you would be the perfect person for the post. I will pay you a salary of sixty pounds per month—the same wages I pay Mr. Lambert—to arrange my social calendar, handle my invitations, and see that any engagements I accept are suitable ones for a man of my position. Sixty pounds a month won't pay your debt, I realize, but I would be happy to take over your loan from that moneylender and apply your salary toward payment of the principal."

"All twenty thousand pounds?" She laughed, unable to quite believe it, even when he nodded in confirmation. If this were anyone else, she'd suspect this whole thing to be a tissue of lies, or a great practical joke, but Aidan neither lied nor joked. "At what rate of interest?"

"I would not charge you interest, Julia. I'm no moneylender."

"That's very generous."

"It's not generosity. I want to employ your unique talents. I'm using you, if you like that description better."

Her eyes narrowed with suspicion, for this sounded

just too good to be true. "Do you have something else up your sleeve?"

He looked back at her, his handsome face the picture of affronted dignity. "I don't know what you mean. What could I possibly have 'up my sleeve,' as you put it?"

"I don't know, but I have the uneasy feeling this is a chess game, and you are planning out some devilishly clever move that shall take me completely by surprise."

He grinned at that, and she straightened in her chair, leaning forward to squint at him across the desk as if trying to see something that was hazy and indistinct. "Why, Aidan, is that . . . is that a smile on your face, a smile directed at me? And they say miracles don't happen anymore."

His grin widened. "I have been known to smile on occasion, even at you."

Julia tilted her head, studying him. "Well, do it more often, would you? You've a nice smile, and it doesn't do any harm to show it off."

"Thank you for the advice. An excellent beginning, I think. However, before you decide whether or not to accept my offer, I must tell you that I have certain conditions for your employment."

"I knew it! You do have something up your sleeve."

"You make me sound quite devious, and as you've already said, deviousness is not my strong suit."

That might be true, but somehow she didn't find it particularly reassuring.

"Julia, I do not want any additional scandal associated with my name. Given our past associations, if you are to act as my social secretary, I believe it is necessary to establish some ground rules."

"Ground rules?" she echoed and made a face at him. "I'm not sure I like the sound of this. Rules and I," she added in mock apology, "don't muddle along together very well."

"Why doesn't that surprise me? Nonetheless, if you are to assist me and I am to pay you for it, I must insist that you comply."

She heaved an exaggerated sigh. "Oh, very well. What are these rules?"

"One, you will never, at any time, do to me what you did to Marlowe last night. He might not care about such things, but I do. You will not issue invitations to others on my behalf without my express consent. We shall be in consultation every step of the way. I want no surprises."

"I agree," she said with dignity. "But you'd enjoy life more if you allowed yourself to be surprised once in a while."

"Two," he went on without admitting anything of the kind, "I am employing you for your advice and your opinions, but once I make a decision about something, you will accept that decision without argument, as any other person in my employ would be expected to do."

"But—"

"When I give you instructions, you will carry them out. When I have questions, you will answer them honestly and directly, without your usual inclination to prevaricate or evade. Can you do that?"

Julia wasn't sure she could, but she'd be mad not to accept this offer. "I suppose I can manage that. Anything else?"

"Yes. You will desist from smoking."

She sat up straighter in her chair. "What, you mean in your company?"

"No, I mean you will abandon the practice altogether."

"Of all the highhanded nonsense! What do you care if I smoke as long as it isn't around you?"

"Because even if you don't actually smoke in my company, I can discern that you have from the smell on your clothes, and you know I hate that smell. Besides, you should be glad I'm insisting on this. You said you were trying to stop the habit, and this rule can only give you additional incentive in that regard."

That might be true, but it was still quite highhanded. She folded her arms, feeling a bit mutinous. "Do men in your employ smoke?"

"Not the ones with whom I spend significant amounts of time. And all people in my employ are expected to conduct themselves within acceptable social parameters. Smoking, for women, is not acceptable."

"But it's tolerated."

"Not by me." He met her eyes across the desk. "This rule is nonnegotiable, Julia."

"Oh, all right," she grumbled, unfolding her arms and capitulating to his demand. "I have been wanting to stop, it's true. And I only took up the silly habit all those years ago in the dire, desperate, last-minute hope it would make Yardley call off the wedding."

"What?" He frowned in surprise. "You only took up smoking because you didn't want to marry Yardley?"

"Oops." She grimaced. "Cat's out of the bag now, isn't it? But it was all for naught. Yardley didn't care two pins about my smoking."

"I know you didn't want to marry him; your family wanted it. But you're so independent. Why didn't you defy them?"

"That's the question, isn't it?" she said, keeping her voice light, not liking this turn in the conversation one bit.

"Without prevarication or evasion, Julia."

"Oh, for heaven's sake!" She wriggled in her chair. "These rules of yours surely don't demand I bare my innermost secrets. It would be most unchivalrous of you if they did."

"Ah, so you disapprove of my chivalrous nature until you can use it against me?"

There was unmistakable chagrin in his voice, but also a hint of amusement, and she decided to offer a counter before he resumed delving into her past. "Let's compromise, shall we?" she suggested. "I promise to answer any questions pertaining to my work for you. Others, I'll answer or not as I choose. And I promise to make every effort to stop my smoking habit. Is that satisfactory?"

He was looking at her as if it wasn't, but to her relief, he nodded. "Very well."

"Goodness, do you give a set of rules to all the people who work for you?"

"Only the people who seem to need them."

She wanted to stick out her tongue at him, but she quelled it. "I accept your offer, even with all its silly rules." She laughed. "I'd be insane not to."

"Good." He shoved the enormous pile of invitations toward her across the desk. "You may start by handling these."

She nodded, but as she took the sheaf of papers from him, she wondered again if there was more to this than met the eye. "Are you sure you don't have some ulterior motive?" she asked. "You're not . . ." She hesitated, struck by a sudden thought. "You're not doing this for me, are you? To be kind?"

"Kind?" He looked back at her as if astonished. "Believe me, Julia, being kind to you is the last thing on my mind."

She didn't know if that statement made her feel better or not. "Thank you, Aidan."

"Don't thank me," he said with a touch of humor. "You may come to regret this, for I am not an easy employer. But I am a fair one."

Julia couldn't imagine him otherwise. "I shall go through these invitations immediately."

"Excellent. There is one other thing I think we should discuss before you go, and that's discretion. I don't think we can avoid gossip altogether, but I think it's best if we don't encourage it. I think we should keep the fact that you are working for me a secret."

She nodded. "That's probably wise. No one would believe it's innocent."

"Quite," he said, and shifted in his chair, looking so terribly proper and uncomfortable all of a sudden that she had to bite her lip to stop a smile.

"Don't worry," she assured him. "No one in society should ever have occasion to meet your social secretary, so that's not a problem, but I shall need to write letters on your behalf, and I can hardly sign them with my own name."

"Are you suggesting you should assume an alternate identity for this post?"

"I am." She paused, smiling, for the idea appealed to her mischievous side. "You have now hired . . . Mrs. Boodle to manage your social engagements."

"Mr. Boodle," he corrected, "otherwise people will assume my social secretary is my mistress."

"Nonsense. You already have a mistress. Besides Mrs. Boodle is a very stout, very respectable widow."

"Is she?" He paused and his gaze slid downward. "She doesn't look very stout."

Julia felt warm inside suddenly, as if she'd downed a swallow of brandy. "She's wearing a corset."

"Indeed?" He tilted his head to one side, his gaze traveling slowly back up to her face, and though his expression was impassive, the warmth inside her began to spread throughout her body. "It doesn't seem to have made any difference," he murmured. "Not from what I remember, at least."

By the time his gaze once again met hers, Julia felt she must be pink as a peony. Aidan, however, didn't seem to notice her discomfiture, nor did he seem to feel anything similar. The desire she was used to seeing in

his eyes wasn't there now, and his voice was indifferent, his manner scrupulously businesslike.

"All invitations shall continue to be directed here,"
he went on, "but I shall inform Lambert to expect many
pieces of correspondence directed to Mrs. Boodle, and
to have each day's social invitations delivered to you for
your perusal. I believe you and I should meet several
times each week to go through them, and to coordinate
my social calendar with my business engagements.
We'll meet in my offices on Mondays, Wednesdays,
and Fridays at nine o'clock. I hope that is acceptable
to you?"

Without waiting for an answer, he reached for a
leather-bound volume on his desk and opened it. "I am
already engaged at nine on Monday, but I am free at
four, so we shall meet then." He reached for a pencil
and noted that appointment in the book, then set the
pencil aside and began flipping through the pages al-
located to future dates. "From then on, however, nine
o'clock appears to be a convenient hour, so that shall
be our customary time to meet for the remainder of the
season."

As she listened to him outlining his expectations and
preferences, Julia began to appreciate what working
for him would entail, of how it would bring them into
close, repeated contact, and she suddenly wondered if
she ought to call the whole thing off. There were things
about that day in Cornwall she never wanted him to
know, and if she worked for him any length of time, her
secrets might come spilling out.

Aidan closed the book and stood up, indicating their

meeting was at an end, but when she didn't move, he gave her a quizzical little smile across the desk. "Was there anything else?" he asked.

She told herself to stop being silly and jerked to her feet. "No, nothing else."

"Excellent." He nodded to the sheaf of papers in her hand. "Go through those, and be prepared to advise me on which ones I should accept. And Julia," he added as she started to turn away, "be sure to give Lambert the name of that moneylender on your way out."

"Heavens, what will he think of me?"

"Does it matter? Lambert is discretion itself."

"Of course." She smiled, working to regain her wits, which seemed to have scattered to the four winds. "I shall see you Monday, then."

"Yes." He bowed. "Good day."

She departed, pausing to speak with Aidan's secretary on her way out. But as she left his offices, Julia still felt stunned, and a bit uneasy. In coming this morning, she'd been seeking Aidan's advice and hoped for a post of some sort, but she'd never really thought he would hire her. But he had, providing her with a way to build a future for herself. Perhaps this was a chance to heal the breach between them as well, as long as she kept her mouth shut about what had really happened that afternoon at her cottage.

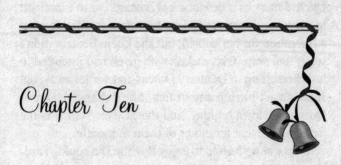

Chapter Ten

St. Ives, Cornwall
1901

By the time Julia met Aidan Carr, the Duke of Trathen, fate had already tied her to Yardley. Ten years later, when she encountered the duke again, she decided fate needed to make up for that ghastly mistake.

She was at the St. Ives Ball, a charity event held in the Cornish seaside town of St. Ives every year. Aware that Yardley had just gone chasing off to France after her, Julia had managed to slip back into England, and was spending a few blissful weeks at her beloved Dovecotes, the cottage in Cornwall she'd inherited from her grandmother.

She'd brought her cousin Beatrix along for company. Beatrix's father had died in the spring, and Trix was still mourning his death. Julia, who'd always regarded her Uncle James as a despotic old bastard, wasn't inclined to view his departure for the hereafter as anything but a liberation for her cousin, but she knew Beatrix didn't see it that way. Trix, racked with grief, had intended to hole herself up in Danbury Downs and wither away, but Julia wasn't having any of that. She'd dragged Trix to Dovecotes for a holiday, and the St. Ives Ball was the first social event for either of them in months.

Julia knew she had to enjoy it while she could. Yardley would learn she was here soon enough and come after her again, but she was going to savor every minute of this holiday. Tapping her foot in time to a rousing polka, she was studying the crowd when she spied Trathen standing near the door.

"Hell's bells!" she exclaimed in surprise. "It's him!"

Trathen's ducal seat was here in Cornwall, but she'd never known him to attend the St. Ives Ball, and if she recalled the gossip she'd heard about him over the years, he didn't like to dance. Despite all that and the fact that it had been ten years since she'd met him that day in Dorset, there was no mistaking his tall, splendid body across the ballroom.

"Who are you looking at?" Beatrix, shorter than she, craned her neck, trying to determine who it was that had caught Julia's eye. "See someone we know?"

"Someone I know."

She was given no chance to explain, for at that moment the polka ended, and Beatrix's company was commandeered for a reel by the next gentleman on her dance card.

Beatrix took the floor with her partner, and Julia continued to study Trathen, feeling a bit chagrined by the realization that the attractive youth she'd met ten years ago was even handsomer at twenty-seven than he'd been at seventeen. What a pity she hadn't met him before she'd agreed to marry Yardley.

Aidan had wanted her. That fact had been plain as a pikestaff that day on the footbridge, though he'd tried so desperately to hide it. He might—just might—have wanted her enough to marry her, if she'd been given time to win him over. But it wasn't meant to be. After the botched elopement with Stephen, her father had insisted on marrying her off, and hadn't given her any time to be choosy about the groom.

If only things could have been different, she thought, feeling a queer and unexpected pang of longing as she watched Aidan move with athletic grace toward the refreshment table across the room.

The feeling surprised her. She wasn't the sort for wishful thinking, and indulging in romantic contemplations about Aidan Carr and what might have been did her no good, especially since she doubted she could muster a smidgen of sensual feeling anymore. Most of the time, she felt like a dried up widow.

Aidan vanished from sight, merging into the crowd, and Julia's attention returned to her own troubles. She might feel like a dried-up widow, but unfortunately, the man responsible for this complete lack of passion on her part showed no signs of making her a widow in the literal sense. He'd had a bad bout of fever the previous spring, but that brush with death hadn't carried him off.

It had only served to remind him that he had no heir and make him resolved to beget a son with her before she was past her childbearing years.

Julia was equally determined not to let that happen, but she knew she was running out of options. She was also running out of time.

Yardley was rushing around France looking for her, but it wouldn't take him much longer to realize she wasn't there. A few mentions of her were already appearing in the British society pages, and her husband would soon get wind of it. Once he knew she was at Dovecotes, he'd come tearing back, prepared to drag her to Dorset so that he could transform her into a dutiful and pregnant wife.

Julia's hand tightened around her glass of punch and she thought back to the early years of her marriage when she'd submitted to her husband's efforts in that regard, and she knew she'd never return to Yardley Grange again. She'd kill herself before she let that man ever touch her again.

There had to be a way out. Eventually, she'd be too old to become pregnant, but the chance she would be able to evade him that long was close to nil, especially since he was now threatening to use legal means to force her home. She'd tried so many methods of escape already—scandalous behavior, consultations with solicitors, outright defiance. She'd even, God help her, gotten down on her knees and begged him to divorce her. He'd laughed, pleased to see her on her knees, expressing the wish to see her that way more often, and she'd been running away—the only means of escape left to her—ever since. But now, the noose was tightening, and a few short weeks here in Cornwall might be all she had left.

Panic rose up inside her, closing up her throat, making her feel as if she were choking. She closed her eyes, taking deep breaths and striving to keep believing there was a way out if only she could find it.

With that thought, she shoved her panic aside and opened her eyes, scanning the room for a distraction. She didn't see Aidan, but she saw Trix.

Her cousin was laughing as she moved down the center of the reel with her partner, and Julia smiled, for Trix laughing was a welcome sight indeed. Abandoned as a child by her mother, smothered by her overprotective father, jilted at the altar by her childhood sweetheart, the Duke of Sunderland, a man she'd worshipped since childhood, Trix hadn't had much to laugh about in her life. It was good to see.

Julia's gaze moved on, then paused again. Trathen had somehow gotten cornered by Lady Jolette, whose entire life revolved around her prized Sealyham terriers. Julia grinned, imagining Lady Jolette's deep bass voice going on and on about the new bitch she'd acquired from Wales. Poor fellow, she thought with a chuckle, but then, as she thought of how valiantly he'd tried not to look at her legs all those years ago, she realized he was probably the sort of man who was far too nice to women for his own good. Any other chap would have slipped free of Lady Jolette at the first mention of the prized bitch.

Julia watched him, smiling, feeling a sudden rush

of affection, thinking of that day on the footbridge. She'd liked that stuffy, serious young man, she'd liked teasing him and managing to make him smile, and she'd been terribly flattered by his fascination with her legs.

Ah, he was escaping at last, taking refuge at the refreshment table, and Julia decided it was time to renew their acquaintance. The chance to tease him about dog breeding or something equally amusing was too delicious to pass up. She circled the ballroom and sidled up beside him, pretending a fascination with the canapés as she watched him out of the corner of her eye.

She timed her reach for the handle of the punchbowl just as he was doing the same.

"Sorry," he said at once, pulling back his hand and turning toward her with a bow. "Ladies first."

"Why, hullo!" she cried, pretending the liveliest surprise. "I do believe it's my very own handsome prince!"

His face, still gravely beautiful, looked at her without the slightest hint of recognition, which was rather a blow to her feminine pride. His brown brows drew together in puzzlement, trying to place her, and then, just as she was berating herself for her conceit in thinking he'd actually remember her, his brow cleared. "Sleeping Beauty, if I am not mistaken?"

"The very same." She laughed, pleased and relieved to be remembered after all. "But alas, dear prince, I fear I've stumbled into the wrong fairy tale, for it's Cinderella who's supposed to be at the ball. I'm supposed to be malingering in a glass coffin."

His mouth curved at one corner, not quite a smile, but almost. "I don't think strict adherence to a script bothers you overmuch. The play," he added in explanation, noting her bewildered look. "You didn't learn your lines, remember?"

"That's right!" She grinned at him. "Improvisation inevitably follows procrastination, I fear. Still, I flatter myself most people didn't notice."

"Not even your fiancé's mother?"

Julia grimaced. "Oh no, she noticed. Yardley's mother was the sort to notice everything."

His smile faded. "So you are the girl who married Baron Yardley? I had heard that a Miss Julia Hammett, daughter of Squire Hammett . . . that is, I thought it might have been you, but I wasn't sure."

"It was me, yes. Heavens," she added at his expression of distaste, "it's bad enough Yardley makes me sour as a persimmon. He needn't make you so as well!"

The distaste vanished behind a gentlemanly veneer. "Forgive me, Baroness," he said with a bow. "Your husband and I have sometimes chosen to disagree over political matters, that is all. I'm surprised you don't already know of our divergent views."

"Should I? I don't keep up with British politics, and I live on the Continent most of the time. Besides," she added with practiced carelessness, "I'm afraid five minutes' conversation with Yardley is about all either of us can manage. I keep hoping he'll divorce me, but so far, no luck. He's standing by me, right or wrong."

"As a husband should."

Julia, in the act of taking a sip of punch, nearly choked. "You think he's being noble? Oh dear, you do have chivalrous notions, don't you? Sorry to tell you, but he's stood by me all these years because he knows how much I want to be free. It's my punishment."

He frowned. "Punishment for what, in heaven's name?"

"For not wanting him, of course."

"If you didn't want him, why did you ever marry him?"

"I didn't have a choice," she blurted out. "My family—"

She stopped, not wanting to reveal any more.

"They forced you to marry a man you didn't want to marry?"

She watched his frown deepen with anger, anger she realized was on her behalf, and tightness squeezed her chest. Suddenly she felt raw, exposed, far too vulnerable, and she was impelled to take cover. "Well, I couldn't blame them, really. I was such a scapegrace of a girl. My father was quite fed up with me." She winked. "I think it was wanting to elope with a poet that did for me in the end, and my father felt Yardley was better than a poet. Too bad you didn't come along sooner," she added with a smile. "I would rather have married you."

"I didn't know you. If I had—" He stopped, and the anger in his face dissolved. His lashes lowered, as if he were imagining her bare legs.

It was then, at that moment, that she saw her way

out. Her means of escape. She'd considered the possibility of taking a lover several times, but she'd never been able to quite stomach the idea. Until now.

The music stopped, dancers exiting the floor pressed her closer to him, and she didn't feel any tinge of the fear that had always accompanied her previous speculations on this topic. Aidan as a lover?

She felt a ray of hope, faint but unmistakable. Oh, if only he could be the key to her escape from the hell she'd been locked into for so long. Aidan was just the sort of man to jerk Yardley's chain, enrage him enough that he would demand a divorce. Aidan was a duke—handsome, rich, athletic, powerful, already a political enemy. How fitting it would be if this man—he was her prince, after all—should be the one to rescue her. But could she do it? Despite the scandals she'd deliberately attached to her name, she'd only bedded two men in her life. The first had been a man she'd loved and adored, and from him, she had learned passion. The second, a man she despised, had poisoned everything the first had given her. Now, she had none of an ordinary woman's sensuality. She hadn't experienced desire in so long, she hardly remembered how it felt. Inside, as a woman, she felt dead. When it came down to brass tacks, when the clothes were coming off and it was time for Aidan's body on hers, could she do it?

Yardley, she reminded herself, wanted a son.

She looked into Aidan's eyes, warm hazel eyes, and something in their depths made her catch her breath. Yes, she decided. With this man, she could do it.

She stepped a little closer. "If you had . . ." she prompted softly.

She waited, heart in her throat, but he had no chance to answer.

"Julie, so this is where you've got to," Trix's cheerful voice entered the conversation, and Julia almost groaned aloud at the unfortunate timing. Aidan, always polite, gave her a brief, rueful glance before giving his attention to the newcomer and awaiting an introduction.

"Trix," Julia said, turning to her cousin, "may I present His Grace, the Duke of Trathen? Trathen, my cousin, Lady Beatrix Danbury."

Aidan bowed. "Lady Beatrix."

The moment she looked at Trix's face, Julia felt a sickening knot in the pit of her stomach. Trix was smiling up at Aidan, her big, beautiful brown eyes shining with an interest Julia hadn't seen her display for any man since Sunderland had gone away.

No, she wanted to scream, as if she were an adolescent girl. *You can't have him. I saw him first.*

The band began the opening strains of a waltz, and Aidan spoke. Not to her, but to Trix. "Lady Beatrix, if you are not otherwise engaged, may I have this dance?"

Julia watched them go, hope dying inside her as they swirled their way across the floor. They looked so perfect, so well matched, she couldn't bear it. Abruptly, she turned and walked out of the ballroom, shoving down the sick fear and bitter disappointment, telling herself she didn't care. She'd learned long ago it was always better not to care, easier, safer.

Outside, she walked across the terrace of the St. Ives Assembly Rooms and down the short flight of steps to the promenade by the beach. She sank down onto a bench, wanting to deny what she'd seen in Trix's face, wanting it to not be true.

"Damn." She bent down and slid her hand beneath the hem of her ball gown to pull the cigarette and match from her garter. She struck the match, lit the cigarette, and eased back on the bench, exhaling smoke toward the starlit sky. "Damn, damn, damn."

She could fight Trix for Aidan's attention, she supposed. She might win. But she would be the only one who would gain by it. Trix was unmarried, she wanted a husband and children. Aidan was a duke, an unmarried man who no doubt needed to wed and could give Trix what she wanted most. All Julia wanted was a man she could bear to let touch her so that she could rid herself of another. She wasn't like Trix, soft and beautiful and generous. She was brittle, hard, better at hating than loving, with nothing to offer any man except her body.

She didn't know how long she sat there before Trix found her. But the cigarette had long since been ground out beneath her heel and several more waltzes had come and gone.

"I thought I'd find you out here."

She roused herself and sat up. "Well?"

Trix gave her an innocent stare as she sat down beside her. "Well, what?"

"Don't be coy. I saw your face when you were dancing with Trathen."

That was enough. "Oh, Julie!"

"You like him." Julia couldn't keep the flatness out of her voice, but Beatrix, caught in the exciting throes of meeting a gorgeous man, didn't seem to notice.

"Like him? What girl wouldn't? He's a dream."

"What about Sunderland?" the devil in her couldn't help asking.

"Will?" Beatrix bit her lip, wavered just a second. "He's never coming back from Egypt, is he?"

She could have said yes. She could have urged Trix to keep waiting for the man who had left her behind. She could have propped up her cousin's hopes about Will so that she could have Aidan for herself. But she looked into Trix's eyes and she didn't do it. "No, Trix. I don't think Will's ever coming back."

Beatrix nodded, almost as if she hadn't expected any other answer. "And Trathen? Is he a man of good character?"

Julia looked away, squeezing her eyes shut, tempted, so very tempted, to disparage Aidan, to deem him a horrible man and discourage Trix from any romantic notions about him. "Trathen—" She stopped and took a deep breath, opening her eyes. "Trathen's a very good man. At least, I think he is. A bit stiff and very old-fashioned, but top drawer. One of the best."

Trix nodded. "I like him. And I think . . . oh, Julie, I think he likes me, too."

Of course he did. How could he not? Beatrix was bright as the sun, radiant, beautiful, and warm. Born the daughter of an earl, she'd be a perfect duchess, having been preparing for just such a role all her life.

And surely Aidan wanted to marry. They were a match made in heaven, a golden god and a golden goddess.

And it might be true love in the making. Trix deserved true love—and everything that was supposed to go with it—the romantic courtship, the wedding of the season, the big brood of children, the happy ending. How could Julia, who'd done so much to mess up her own life, who couldn't even fall in love anymore, who only wanted to use one man to get away from another— how could she stand in the way of Trix's happiness?

She couldn't. Not even to save herself from Yardley. Not even if Aidan was the perfect choice for her purposes. She forced herself to speak with the air of carefree *joie de vivre* she'd spent so many years perfecting.

"Well, you've a clear field, darling. He's not entangled with any other woman, so far as I know." She managed a perfect laugh as she waved her free hand toward the ballroom. "So don't stand out here, talking to me. Go back inside and dance with the prince."

Beatrix laughed and went back in, and as Julia watched her go, she also watched her chance for freedom crumbling into dust.

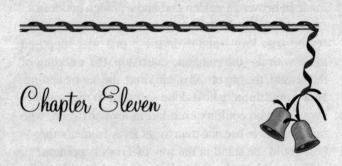

Chapter Eleven

*J*t didn't take long for Julia to appreciate Aidan's astuteness in giving her a job so well suited to her abilities and temperament. As she spent the weekend sorting through the correspondence he'd given her, as she met with Lambert on Saturday morning to discuss the transition of Aidan's engagements to her purview, as she began deciding which invitations would be worth his time, she realized being a social secretary was the one job in the world at which she could truly excel.

Though he'd denied it, she still suspected that in giving her this post, Aidan had been partly motivated by his innate chivalry, but since he'd offered to take over her loan interest-free and was paying her sixty pounds each month on top of it, she wasn't going to quibble about his motives. She didn't even tease him about it.

In fact, Monday afternoon when they met again, she made no mention of his susceptibility to women in distress. Instead, she strove to get straight down to business, assuming he preferred that sort of businesslike demeanor from those in his employ.

Within an hour, they had successfully dealt with most of the invitations. Only a few remained to be discussed when the door to Aidan's office opened and Lambert came in, carefully balancing a laden tray on one forearm as he pushed the door wide with his free hand. "Afternoon tea, sir?" he inquired, pausing by the door as he secured the tray firmly in a two-handed grip.

"Tea already?" Aidan asked, sounding surprised.

"It is five o'clock," Mr. Lambert pointed out. "But if you would prefer to wait . . ." He let his voice trail off, and Aidan looked at her.

"Tea?" he asked, and when she hesitated, he glanced again at the man by the door. "You did bring enough for two, didn't you, Lambert?"

The secretary didn't even blink. "Of course, sir. I assumed Her Ladyship would be in need of refreshment also."

"Excellent." Aidan beckoned the secretary forward and began clearing space for the tea tray on his desk.

Julia watched Lambert lay out the tea things, and she noted there were only two teacups. "You prepared tea for yourself as well, I hope, Mr. Lambert?" she asked, fully conscious that both of them were Aidan's secretaries and hoping she was not incurring the young man's ill will by being the only one taking tea with their employer. "Shall you join us?"

Lambert smiled. "Oh no, ma'am, thank you for asking, but I always have my afternoon tea at my desk." He turned to Aidan. "Will that be all, sir?"

"Yes, thank you, Lambert. You may go."

The young man departed, closing the door behind him, and Aidan leaned toward her across the desk. "Lambert always reads during his tea," he told her in a confidential voice. "Books by lady novelists."

She laughed, for a more unlikely reader of romantic fiction than Mr. Lambert she could not imagine. "You're having me on," she accused.

He shook his head as he reached for the teapot. "I'm not," he assured as he poured for both of them. "Lambert adores novels, and the more romantic they are, the better he likes them. You take milk in your tea, I believe?" he asked, setting aside the teapot and picking up the milk jug. "And sugar?"

"I do. How on earth did you know that?"

"I saw you take tea every day at Marlowe's house party."

"But that was two years ago!" She felt a sudden rush of pleasure, flattered that he remembered such a thing. "I can't believe you remember how I prefer my tea."

He shrugged as if it was inconsequential, added sugar to her tea, stirred it, and handed the cup and saucer to her across the desk. "What food would you like?"

She glanced over the various refreshments Lambert had brought them. "A scone, please, with cream and jam. Oh, and one of those cucumber sandwiches. I love those."

"Do you, really?" he asked as he filled her plate.

"You seem surprised," she said, a bit puzzled, setting aside her teacup to take the plate of food he offered. "Is there a reason I shouldn't like cucumber sandwiches?"

"We had them in Cornwall." He paused, then added, "In hindsight, I thought all the food on that picnic was for my benefit, that you picked my favorite things only because . . ." He paused again and met her eyes across the desk. "Only because you wanted to entice me."

"Well, that was the main reason," she confessed, wincing a little at her own mercenary motives that day. "I mainly chose foods you would prefer, I admit, but I certainly wasn't going to pick foods I *don't* like. Pâté, for example. You love the stuff, but I didn't include it in the picnic basket. Sorry, Aidan, but even you aren't worth choking down goose liver."

He chuckled at that. "Hate pâté, do you?"

She shuddered, an indication of her soul-deep loathing for that particular food, and reached for a knife, putting any revolting thoughts of liver out of her mind by slathering cream and strawberry jam on her scone and taking a hefty bite. As she did so, she glanced at him from beneath her lashes to find he was smiling at her. "What are you smiling about?" she asked around a mouthful of scone.

"You have cream on your face." He leaned forward, reaching across the desk to slide his thumb over one corner of her lips. "Right there."

At the contact, Julia's stomach dipped with a strange weightless sensation, and she didn't know quite what to do. A minute ago she'd have thought Aidan touching her was about as likely as unicorns cavorting in Trafalgar Square.

He pulled back, taking the dab of cream with him, sucking it from his thumb as he lowered his gaze to the desk and picked up an invitation. His manner seemed so natural, so nonchalant, but she felt all at sixes and sevens.

Her face felt as if it burned where he'd touched her so casually, and she looked away as memories of that day at her cottage came roaring back to her, memories of how they'd stood in her kitchen, of how he'd unbuttoned her dress and caressed her bare skin. It was all so vivid in her mind it might have happened yesterday— his fingers pushing tendrils of hair out of her face, skimming across her cheekbones, caressing the nape of her neck. His warm palms cupping her cheeks, gliding down her arms, toying with her breasts. She lifted her gaze to his face, and when she did, she remembered his mouth on hers.

Suddenly, it was there: desire, flowing over her like warm honey, physical and fleshly and luscious. Desire was something she never thought to feel again, and she was stunned by the unexpected sensations suddenly flowing through her.

Had she felt this way that day with him at her cottage? she wondered. Probably not, she was forced to conclude. That day, she'd been in the grip of other, darker emotions. But now, there was no desperation or panic to stifle desire, and as it spread slowly through her limbs, it felt so gloriously warm, she actually leaned closer to him, like a plant in a window leaned toward sunlight.

He looked up, and she jerked back in her seat, lowering her gaze to the papers in her lap, her body flushed with heat. Oh God, she thought, chagrined, agitated, and thoroughly embarrassed.

"About the Horbury dinner party on the fourteenth," he said, tapping the invitation in his hand with one finger, not seeming to notice her discomfiture. "Would that be the Hertfordshire Horburys or the Derbyshire Horburys?"

Julia could not answer his question. In fact, she couldn't even think. "Umm . . . that would be . . . umm . . ." She paused, staring down into her lap, not daring to look at him as she struggled to come to her senses. For the life of her, she could not recall which set of Horburys had sent him the blasted invitation. She took a deep breath and guessed. "Hertfordshire."

She lifted her gaze a notch, but he wasn't even looking at her. His attention was on the invitation in his hand, and she let out her breath in a silent sigh of relief. Aidan needed a wife, not a mistress. And she needed an honorable job, not a lover. Harboring any feelings of desire for him or any notions of picking up where they'd left off last August was idiotic. She didn't want to awaken things inside her that were better left asleep.

In any case, she doubted he was interested in bedding her now. He'd wanted her then, but there was no reason for him to want her now. And if all that wasn't enough to discourage her suddenly amorous inclinations, becoming his lover would make the truth of what had really happened last August much more likely to come tumbling out of her mouth. If that happened, not only would she be out of a job, but any chance to gain his respect would be irretrievably lost. In fact, if he ever discovered the truth, he would hate her.

Just why the possibility of losing what little respect Aidan might have for her bothered Julia, she couldn't say, for she'd never been the sort who set much store by other people's opinions of her. Strangely though, she cared what Aidan thought of her. The idea of losing the rapport that was beginning between them, of never having a chance at the friendship she'd told him all those years ago they would have one day, was something she didn't want to contemplate. Besides, the last thing she needed now was an amorous intrigue. Desire and romance were about as useful to her as wings were to a fish. Julia picked up her pencil and brought her mind back to what was important.

"I was mistaken," she told him. "It was the Derbyshire Horburys. Lady Susan Horbury is a lovely girl," she added, pushing aside all the delicious, tingly feelings of a moment before. "Do you wish to meet her?"

Giving Julia a position in his employ, Aidan knew, was akin to bringing matches into proximity with gunpowder. Spending time with her, having her close to him, would be torture, a delicious but agonizing torture that could explode into chaos if he didn't keep tight rein over his desire.

Ah, but that was what he wanted, wasn't it? Aidan leaned back in his chair, staring at the now-empty chair opposite. Wasn't that how he intended to conquer this? By once again pitting his will against his desire, by testing the discipline of mind and body he'd always been so proud of against the lust Julia always managed to evoke in him was the only way to conquer this and put it behind him.

He'd known that all along. He'd known it last August, which was why he'd gone to her cottage that day. The last time he'd tested himself this way, he'd failed. This time, he was determined that the outcome would be different.

If all he'd wanted was to satiate his desire, he could have offered to make her his mistress. He almost had. Standing there with her at the Savoy the other night, he'd imagined what it would be like to have her again, and again, any time he wanted, anywhere he wanted, over and over, until this mad desire fizzled and died of its own accord and he was free of her spell. He'd imagined it again in his office as she'd sat across from him, fighting the base and wholly dishonorable notion to suggest she pay off her debts to him with her body.

He didn't know if she would have agreed to such an arrangement, but if she had, it would not have been because she wanted him. And despite his indulgence in a fantasy or two about her as his mistress, he couldn't act on it. A woman who had already chosen the profession of being a courtesan was one thing; a woman made into a courtesan because of him was another. However much he wanted her, that was a line he just couldn't cross. And the only thing about his own character it would prove was that despite all his strong moral principles, he was a cad. So, instead of making her his mistress, he'd offered her a job.

If he were a hypocritical sort of man, he'd have told himself it was the chivalry she insisted upon imposing on his character that inspired his action. He'd have flattered himself that he'd been noble to offer her respectable employment—the hero rescuing the beauty in distress. But though Julia had suspected him of that motive, he was not so self-deceiving as that.

No, he was being completely selfish. Every bit of his cooperation in her efforts to rebuild her life were for one purpose: helping him conquer his lust for her. Asking about her financial situation to determine how desperate she was and what other options she might have, offering to take her loan, keeping cool and hiding what he felt—all meant to prove to him and to her that he was master of his emotions. Even his requirement that she stop smoking was part of it, for it would make her even more luscious and tempting than ever, raising the stakes even higher, testing him to the maximum degree. When he stopped being tempted, he would be over her.

He was playing a dangerous game, he knew, one that

would put his character, his honor, and his self-control to the ultimate test, a test he had already failed with disastrous results. This time, he was resolved to succeed, but however it unfolded, one thing was clear. Having her in his employ would either make him stronger or break him utterly. Just now, Aidan didn't know which was a more likely possibility.

Despite her misgivings about working for Aidan, during the two weeks that followed, Julia discovered that although being the social secretary to a duke was a post that suited her down to the ground, it was no walk in the park.

It was quite a challenge to manage a duke's engagements, for there were many rules of etiquette and social nuances to consider. Every choice made for every hour of the day was a snub or an indication of favor to someone, one wrong word in a letter she wrote on his behalf could have serious repercussions, and during her first fortnight in his employ, Julia often felt so exasperated by the complicated juggling, she wanted to give it all up in despair, a feeling compounded by the fact that she did not have cigarette smoking as an outlet for her tension. She'd never realized how dependent—addicted, really—she'd become to smoking until she made a true and serious effort to give it up, and the pangs of withdrawal from the habit proved difficult to conquer. Painful as it was, however, Julia persevered.

She met with Aidan three times each week as they had arranged, going over his social calendar, reviewing his correspondence, and discussing which connections were worth his time and which were not. He listened to her assessments and usually accepted her conclusions. He was courteous, polite, and seemed thoroughly indifferent to her as anything but his employee.

Julia, adept by this point at shielding herself from unwanted feelings, was able to shut out any silly twinges of desire she might have felt for Aidan that first day on the job. When he asked her opinion about various young ladies of the *ton*, she was able to give it honestly and without a qualm. Though her private opinion was that not a single one of the young ladies he asked her about was worthy of him, she kept that opinion to herself. He met many women during the two weeks that followed, and though she told herself she shouldn't care either way, she couldn't help feeling a bit relieved that none seemed to garner his particular interest.

Mrs. Boodle began to be mentioned in the society columns as the Duke of Trathen's secretary, and it was Aidan's turn to tease her for a change when he commented on the perspicacity of the press, who seemed to know the Duke of Trathen's secretary was a stout, middle-aged widow, and therefore seemed to take no further interest in her. Julia, who had conveyed that bit of information about Mrs. Boodle to the various society columns via the Marchioness of Kayne, merely gave him an innocent look in reply and moved on to the next invitation that had come in the post the previous afternoon.

"Do you wish to attend Lady Rathbone's house party over Whitsuntide?"

"Should I attend?" He leaned back in his chair. "What is Mrs. Boodle's opinion?"

Julia shrugged. "Lady Rathbone's all right. She can't help being a perfect fool."

He chuckled. "I cannot tell you, Julia, how much I appreciate your razor-sharp opinions. They spare me no end of trouble."

She looked back at him with tongue-in-cheek sincerity. "I consider fielding the Felicia Vales and their matchmaking mamas as one of my most important responsibilities," she told him gravely.

"Is Lady Rathbone a matchmaking mama? If so, that means she has an unmarried daughter, I take it?"

Julia, in the act of putting the invitation of Lady Rathbone on the pile of refusals, paused as she remembered that Flora Rathbone was a stunningly beautiful, intelligent, and charming young woman whose only reason for not being married was her justifiable discernment regarding her many suitors. Aidan, Julia realized, would be just the man to meet all of Flora's high expectations, and vice versa. Before she could stop it, Julia felt a queer and unwarranted stab of pure jealousy.

"Well, Julia?" he prompted as she didn't speak. "Do Lord and Lady Rathbone have an unmarried daughter?"

"I don't know," she lied, and then could have bitten her tongue off. What did it matter to her if Aidan chose to court Flora Rathbone? "That is," she amended at once, "I believe the daughter is unmarried, but I don't know very much about her. Would you . . . would you like to attend the house party and meet her?"

She made a great show of turning to the proper page

in his appointment book, and then she looked up at him expectantly, pencil poised.

He was frowning. "The Rathbone house party is during the Whitsuntide recess, I believe you said?" When she nodded, his frown deepened. "I seem to remember I have another invitation during that fortnight."

"Do you?" She was careful to sound wholly indifferent and keep any hint of relief out of her voice. "Mr. Lambert has nothing written down," she added as she flipped through the pages of his appointment book. "And I know I have not confirmed any invitations for you during Whitsuntide."

"I've got it," he said, snapping his fingers. "I was invited to your Aunt Gennie's house party."

Julia stared at him, thoroughly taken aback. Her Aunt Eugenia would have loved Aidan to attend her house party, for the status accorded to those who entertained dukes was enormous, but with Julia there as well, decorum had precluded issuing an invitation. "Aunt Gennie invited you to our house party at Danbury Downs?"

"Not Eugenia," he said, shaking his head. "Paul invited me the day we played tennis."

This was becoming more surprising by the moment. "You and Paul played tennis?"

Aidan smiled a bit ruefully. "I think he was holding out the olive branch."

"Possibly, but surely you didn't accept? The invitation to the house party, I mean?"

"Not yet, but I should like to. I know it would raise

a few eyebrows—you're going, I assume?" When she nodded, he continued, "There will be gossip, of course, I realize that, but I'm willing to risk it. I've missed my friendship with Paul. We used to be good friends, you know."

She bit her lip, feeling a pang of guilt, appreciating in the sudden, stilted silence that in addition to everything else he'd lost as a result of last August, he'd lost a friend. "So you wish to come to Danbury Downs, then?"

"That rather depends on you. I wouldn't want you to feel awkward because I'm there. Would you rather I didn't go?"

"It's not up to me," she said at once, forcing a laugh. "Why should I care?" She paused, but a mischievous imp inside her impelled her to add, "I'm not sure it'll be your cup of tea, though. We always have silly games at our parties, and you don't seem the sort for charades and blindman's bluff."

"If the parlor games are not to my liking, I can always play chess with Paul or find a foursome for whist or bridge."

"There will be dancing, too," she warned, "and since you're unattached, Aunt Gennie will be forever urging you to dance with the wallflowers because she knows you're too nice to say no."

"I'm not particularly fond of dancing, as you are aware, but I have come to accept the fact that a man looking for a wife has to dance with many women. I don't mind the wallflowers, because that's usually just shyness, and I'm a rather reserved fellow myself. But I leave it to you, Julia, to keep any Lady Felicias at bay, and their mamas, too."

"That's all very well, but I don't know how we'll keep Aunt Cora away from you." When he looked at her without understanding, she went on, "Our Aunt Cora, Lady Esterhazy, is quite a character. Because of precedence, you'll escort Aunt Gennie into dinner and sit next to her, but on your other side, you're sure to have Aunt Cora."

"So? Is she dull?"

"Dull? Quite the contrary. She's eighty-two, and terribly naughty. She'll rub your thigh under the table in a most licentious manner."

Aidan actually laughed at that. "I think I can hold my own with Aunt Cora."

"You really want to go?"

"Yes, I do. That is," he added, "as long as you don't play that god-awful ragtime music you're so inexplicably fond of just to provoke me."

That reference to the Marlowes' house party two years earlier when she'd flicked him on the raw by playing bawdy music on the piano impelled her to give him a look of mock apology. "Sorry about that."

"You're not the least bit sorry," he accused, but he was smiling as he said it. "You relished every minute of tormenting me with that music."

"Well, yes," she admitted, laughing, but then she remembered what else had occurred at the Marlowes' party, and she sobered at once. "I'm glad you can smile about the time you spent at Pixy Cove, Aidan. It must have been awful for you, what with Sunderland there and Trix breaking your engagement and all. And I ragged you endlessly, I know. It's just that I find teasing you almost irresistible. You were so scrupulously polite to me, and yet underneath, I could feel your disapproval like the heat from a radiator."

"Disapproval?" He gave her an odd, thoughtful look. "Yes, I suppose you could call it that."

"What else would I call it? You were practically glowering."

"I wasn't glowering."

"Oh yes, you were, and it was like waving a red flag to a bull, I'm afraid."

"Ah, so being forced to listen to that awful ragtime music was my own fault?"

"Yes," she answered at once with her most charming smile. "Yes, it was."

He grinned back at her. "Then thank God this time I have something to hold over your head."

"You do?"

His grin widened. "Play that ragtime next week, Julia, and I'll sack you."

She laughed merrily. "How unfair! And unchivalrous."

"It's born of desperation."

"All right, all right. I promise not to play ragtime. But," she added, "I can't promise not to find other ways to tease you. Are you sure you really want to come?"

He nodded. "I'm looking forward to it. And who knows?" he added, "I might meet a smashing girl and fall madly in love, just like you wanted me to."

Once again, she felt an inexplicable pang, but she again set it aside. "Well, that's the rub, isn't it?" she said lightly, pasting on a smile. "I fear our definitions of suitable are very different."

"No actresses, Julia," he said with a stern look of warning. "No music hall singers, no can-can dancers."

She sighed. "Really, Aidan, must you spoil all my fun?"

One week later, Aidan arrived at Danbury Downs, and as his hired carriage, open to a warm May afternoon, pulled into the tree-lined drive, he couldn't help remembering all the times he'd visited Beatrix here during their courtship and engagement. He didn't feel any sting at the memory, perhaps because his feelings for Beatrix had always been fond and affectionate, agreeable but not earth-shattering—a combination he'd deemed the perfect recipe for domestic bliss. His feelings about her cousin, however, had always been vastly different—primal and volcanic and not likely to incite anything but chaos. Out of that chaos, however, he intended to bring order back to his life.

It was teatime when he arrived, and about a dozen people were gathered for that afternoon ritual around a wrought-iron table beneath one of the enormous elms that shaded the south lawn. Other guests strolled the grounds or played croquet, and in the distance, more

were gathered around the tennis lawn. His upbring-
ing dictated being taken to the front entrance of any
home where he'd been invited to stay, but when he saw
that Julia and Paul were among those having tea on the
lawn, he abandoned his usual preference for formality. Reaching up, he tapped his driver's shoulder. "Stop
here, Mr. Robinson," he directed, and the gnarled
old man, who'd brought him to Danbury many times
before, pulled the carriage to a halt.

Aidan stepped down from the landau, and Mr. Robinson carried on, taking Dawes and the luggage on
to the servants' entrance, as a series of loud, staccato
barks issued from the vicinity of the tea table.

Spike, he realized, remembering too late Julia's ill-
mannered, belligerent bulldog. As he approached the
group on the lawn, Spike jumped up from his place
beside Julia on the grass and came toward him a few
paces, barking furiously, causing him to pause.

"Spike!" Julia admonished, and the dog stopped
barking, but as Aidan circled around Julia to greet
Paul, Eugenia, and several other guests, the animal
continued to watch him with a malevolent eye, shifting
position to remain between his mistress and this new
interloper at all times.

As he approached the tea table, Paul came forward
to shake hands with him. "Glad you came, Trathen.
I expect you know everyone," he added, gesturing to
those in the immediate vicinity.

"Not everyone, Paul," Julia corrected. "Honestly,
you are terrible about social introductions. Sorry, Tra-

then," she added with a glance at him and then at the red-haired girl seated beside Paul at the table. "Sorry, Eileen. If it were up to my cousin, I fear no one would ever learn anyone's name. "Eileen, may I present His Grace, the Duke of Trathen? Trathen, Miss Eileen DeWitt McGill."

Aidan bowed, noting without interest an agreeably pretty freckled face and a pair of green eyes below an enormous straw hat before he returned his gaze to the woman on the blanket. Weight on her arms, Julia tilted her head back to look at him from beneath the narrow brim of her straw boater hat, and he could see both amusement and a spark of challenge in those big violet eyes. "You remember Spike, of course."

"I do." His only previous encounter with Julia's dog had been brief, for that day at Gwithian, she'd had the animal tied, but he did remember that Spike had been equally ill-mannered on that occasion. "I didn't realize he was to be a member of the house party."

"Did Paul fail to mention that when he invited you?" She grinned. "I supposed he took it for granted that you knew. Spike goes everywhere with me, and I couldn't have left the poor boy behind in London while I went to the country, could I?"

"I suppose that would have been too much to hope for," he acknowledged, eying the animal with chagrin.

"Don't you like dogs, Your Grace?" Miss McGill asked.

"In this case, it's really more the other way about," he told her. "This particular dog does not like me."

"That's not true," Julia protested. "He adores you, really."

Spike chose that moment to give a low, menacing growl.

"You mustn't feel too badly about it, old chap," Paul advised him as everyone laughed. "It's not personal. Spike hates me, too. And Geoff, and any other man who comes within ten feet of Julie."

Ah, he thought, glancing at the dog again with a new appreciation. Spike was the guardian at the gate. The question was why Julia felt she needed one.

"Spike is impossible, my dear Aidan," Eugenia told him as she lifted the teapot. "Shall you have tea?"

At his nod, she proceeded to pour him a cup, and Aidan, defying a possible bite in the leg, passed Spike and his mistress and sat down in the empty chair beside Miss McGill.

"Not only does Spike growl at all the gentlemen," Eugenia added as she stirred lemon and sugar into his cup, "he frightens the chickens down at the farm and chases my poor cat at every possible opportunity."

"Perhaps he needs training," Aidan suggested with a meaningful glance at Julia.

"Hear, hear," Paul endorsed, lifting his teacup in salute.

"But Spike doesn't chase the cat anymore," Geoff put in, laughing. "Mama's wrong about that. He's grown too fat. Perhaps that's the ticket, Trathen. Feed him crumpets under the table until he's too stout to jump. That way, he can't clamp his beastly jowls around a chap's arm."

"Won't matter," Paul put in. "We all have ankles."

"I think you're all very cruel to my poor Spike!" Julia cried. "He is trained, at least well enough to suit me. He's my guard dog." She looked at the animal, smiling fondly, and the bulldog bounded up to a sitting position at this sign of encouragement from his beloved mistress. He placed his forepaws on her thigh, and though his tail had been docked, his backside wiggled against the grass beneath his bum with ecstatic happiness as she patted his broad, wrinkled head. "He protects me, don't you, boy?"

"Protects you?" Aidan echoed, surprised by her choice of words. "Protects you from what?"

There was a sudden, awkward silence. Aidan was watching Julia, saw her hand go still on the back of Spike's neck and her fingers curl into the deep creases of the animal's fur. He could feel her sudden tension, though he did not know its cause. "Are you in danger, Lady Yardley?" he asked.

"In danger?" Julia laughed. "How dramatic that sounds, rather like a gothic novel."

Her voice was light, but her smile seemed artificial and her laughter forced, and though the others laughed with her, Aidan did not. He continued to study her thoughtfully, and she looked away, flushing slightly beneath his scrutiny. "You mustn't take what I say so literally, Aidan," she said after a moment. "Of course I'm not in danger. What an idea! But Spike is a loyal fellow, and he feels duty bound to look after me." She resumed petting the dog. "Don't you, sweetums?"

That particular nickname seemed singularly inappropriate for a man-hating, teeth-bearing beast, but Aidan kept that opinion to himself.

Conversation eddied around him, and though Julia participated, he did not. Instead, he wondered why a woman might choose to own a dog that possessed a particular animosity toward men. But as he looked at Julia, as he studied her artificial smile, he wasn't sure he wanted to know what her reasons might be.

Chapter Twelve

A large house party was a somewhat informal affair, particularly on the first day. Guests arrived by various means at various times, and the hosts were compelled to rush about at a frantic pace to make sure everyone was comfortably situated. Julia dashed off with her aunt just after Aidan's arrival to see to other guests, he was shown to his room by the butler, Groves, and it was not until just before dinner that he saw Julia again.

When Groves sounded the Chinese gong in the staircase hall to signal that the evening meal would commence in fifteen minutes' time, Aidan was already downstairs. Because he'd forgotten about the gong ritual at Danbury, and because he was in the library, which was within twenty feet of the immense Oriental instrument, and because Groves always sounded the gong with particular relish, Aidan dropped the book of Henley's poetry he'd just pulled from the shelf and clamped his hands over his ears with a grimace the moment Groves put hammer to brass.

By the time Groves reappeared to sound the second gong announcing five remaining minutes, Aidan was more prepared. Open book in hand, he was leaning against one of the marble columns that flanked the gong's enormous black lacquer frame. The moment Groves had done his duty, Aidan stretched out his arm and clamped his fingers around the edge of the four-foot disk to stop the resonation, looking up from Henley's "When I Was a King in Babylon" to meet the butler's puzzled stare with a meaningful glance of his own. Groves gently hung the hammer back on its dragon-head hook without a word and departed.

Aidan let go of the now blissfully silent gong, and vowed to talk with Paul before the end of this visit about that useful modern device, the electric bell. He then returned to the library as hurried footsteps sounded along corridors overhead and various voices echoed down the staircase.

"Was that the second gong or did I imagine it?"

"It can't be eight o'clock already."

"I do believe it was the second gong."

"It sounded so queer, not at all like the first."

Smiling a little, Aidan returned to the library as members of the house party began pouring into the staircase hall from various other parts of the house. Uncaring that he'd been the cause of uncertainty among other, less punctual guests, he began searching for the place on the shelf to return the book he'd pulled out before joining the gathering throng in the staircase hall.

He was about to slide the book back into its place on the shelf when the French doors nearest him were suddenly flung back. He paused, looking up as Julia, dressed for dinner in ice-blue silk and long white gloves, stopped in the doorway. She didn't see him, for she was looking back over her shoulder. "Spike," she called, and gave a whistle, patting her hip. "C'mon, boy."

She turned to come inside and stopped again at the sight of him standing only a few feet away. The bull-dog waddled up to the doorway and stopped beside her, giving a low growl at the sight of Aidan, and then sitting back on his haunches as if quite satisfied he'd put this evil man in his place.

"Julia." Ignoring the animal, Aidan turned to her with a bow.

"Did the second gong go?" she asked, coming in.

"It did." He paused and glanced over her, frowning in pretended bewilderment. "But I fear Groves must be running late."

"Groves? Never! I'm the one who's always late."

"Exactly." He reached into his waistcoat pocket and pulled out his pocket watch. "But not tonight, for there are still three minutes until dinner." He shook his head, looking at her again as he tucked the watch back into place. "Yet you are already downstairs. You are even dressed."

Her lips twitched. "Well, I should hope so! I don't mind being the last one to the table, but as much as I adore scandalizing people, even I haven't the nerve to come down to dinner *naked*."

"That would certainly make the meal more interesting." He glanced down at the shadowy cleft of her low, heart-shaped neckline. "And more delicious."

She blushed. He watched it happen, a soft wash of delicate pink that started beneath her gown and spread upward. He followed it with his eyes—over her clavicle and across her shoulders, along her throat, and into her cheeks. Her lips parted, but no words came out. Her enormous eyes stared back at him, and their violet-blue color seemed even more vivid now in the dusky twilight of evening than it had in the bright light of the afternoon. As Aidan looked at her, he saw something in her startled expression and wide, pretty eyes, something that took him utterly by surprise, something he realized, to his chagrin, that he'd never seen in her face before.

Desire.

His body responded at once—a tensing in his muscles, a quickening of his pulses, but then she was giving him a wink and a smile, and he thought perhaps he'd been mistaken.

"Why, Aidan," she drawled, her voice light and teasing, "I do believe you are flirting with me."

"No," he denied gravely. "I don't flirt, Julia. You know that. I always say what I honestly mean."

She stirred, lifting a gloved hand to touch the side

of her neck in a self-conscious gesture, and her blush deepened, but before she could reply, Phoebe Marlowe appeared behind her in the doorway, Geoff Danbury on her heels. "Are we late?" Phoebe asked, sounding a bit out of breath, pressing a hand to her ribs.

Aidan saw Julia smile, but as earlier today, there was an artificial quality about it—reminding him of a marionette whose strings had just been pulled.

"Not yet!" she answered her friend, turning her head with a laugh, "but we will be if you two keep dawdling."

"This from the person who never arrives anywhere on time." Phoebe looked past Julia and spied him standing by the bookshelves. "Oh!" she exclaimed, and dipped a curtsy. "Your Grace. I didn't see you. My apologies."

He bowed. "Miss Phoebe."

"Aidan," Julia said, nudging Spike aside with her foot and turning sideways as she gestured her friend into the library, "will you escort Phoebe into the hall?"

"Of course." Reluctantly, knowing it was far better for both their reputations if he walked to the staircase hall with another woman on his arm, he turned to Phoebe. "Shall we?"

She moved to his side, and Geoff entered through the French doors, earning himself a growl from Spike as Julia pulled him to her side. "And Geoff can escort me," she told him, hooking her arm through his.

"What?" Geoff scoffed, for at nineteen, he was somewhat inclined to be cavalier about social niceties.

"That's just silly. We're only twenty feet away. You girls hardly need escorting that far, and it's not as if we'll be paired this way to go into dinner."

"That doesn't matter, Geoff," Aidan told the younger man over his shoulder as he started with Phoebe toward the door. "A lady's request is reason enough."

They joined the other two dozen people gathered to go in to dinner, and he parted from Phoebe to join Eugenia, for as the gentleman of highest rank present, he was duty-bound to escort his hostess into the dining room. As he waited beside her at the table, he watched the other guests file in, and Julia passed him on the arm of Sir George Debenham. She took her place on the other side of the table, and though she was not directly across from him, he could see her face plainly. When she glanced in his direction, he saw none of the desire he thought he'd seen earlier, and he could only conclude that he'd imagined it.

That was probably just as well. He was here to stop wanting her, and if she started wanting him, that resolution would become far harder to keep.

As Julia had predicted, he was groped beneath the dining table by Lady Esterhazy, who sat on his other side, but once she'd been allowed an appreciative feel of his thigh and knee, the elderly lady proved a surprisingly interesting dinner companion. Her late husband had been a diplomatic attaché in Ceylon, and their conversation centered on her life there with her husband. He was grateful for the distraction. If his dinner companion had been dull, he doubted he could have managed to keep up a pretense of disinterest in the violet-eyed woman across the table.

After dinner, however, when he and the other gentlemen joined the ladies in the music room for entertainments, Julia became harder to ignore.

She was standing by the open doorway onto the terrace when he came in, talking to Eugenia, Phoebe, and Phoebe's older sister, Vivian, but when she caught sight of him entering the room, she murmured something to her aunt, and a moment later, he found himself at Eugenia's mercy. She bustled over to his side, issued a fervent promise to make his stay at Danbury as enjoyable as possible, and ushered him at once to a tête-à-tête sofa and a blushing Miss McGill. "There, my dears," Eugenia said, thrusting him toward Miss McGill with all the delicacy of a freight train. "Now, do enjoy yourselves."

With that, she departed in a flutter of ecru lace, leaving Aidan and the girl facing each other on the S-shaped settee. They both stared for a moment, seeming equally disconcerted, and then they both laughed.

"That was deuced awkward, was it not, Miss McGill?" he murmured.

"I should say. I feel like a card forced at bridge!"

"An apt description. Lady Danbury is not the most subtle hostess, I fear."

Again they looked at each other, and there was a long, rather awkward pause. She glanced around the room and so did he, but when his gaze came to rest on Julia, who still stood by the terrace door with her friends, Aidan knew this wouldn't do. He took a deep breath and forced his attention back to his companion.

"Is your family near here, Miss McGill?" he asked.

"Yes, at South Brent. My father has an estate there."

"He is a man of property, then?"

"Yes, he is a squire." At his urging, she began to tell him about her family, much to his relief, but it wasn't long before his relief began to evaporate into dismay, for within half an hour, he found himself on the receiving end of a dissertation that could have been titled, "The Pranks of the Family McGill."

All of them, he learned, had an inordinate fondness for practical jokes, including Miss McGill herself. Her initial awkwardness having evaporated, she confessed with relish to turning drawers filled with clothes upside down, slipping garden snakes between bedsheets, and putting salt in the jam pot, and despite his best intentions, Aidan's attention soon drifted, sliding eventually back to the terrace door. Julia was no longer there, but a quick glance around located her on the other side of the room beside Paul at the fireplace.

He bent his head as if looking down at the glass of port in his hand, trying to be subtle as his glance slid sideways to the woman by the fireplace, even as he tried to resist, even as he reminded himself she'd never really wanted him, not even when she'd stood in front of him in a soaking wet dress. But such reminders were useless, for what kept coming to the forefront of his mind was how she'd looked earlier in the dusky shadows of the library, her lips parted and her cheeks flushed with color, and he wanted to believe she wanted him as much as he wanted her. For that, Aidan knew he ought to give himself a good swift kick in the head.

Once again he forced his attention to his companion. "Your family sounds quite mischievous," he murmured.

"Oh yes, we're all terrible, Your Grace, just too terrible for words! Particularly my niece."

Desperate, Aidan grasped at that. "Ah, you have a niece. How old?"

"Ten. And when it comes to mischief, that child puts the rest of us to shame."

Aidan did not point out just what a feat that truly was. His restraint, however, was rewarded with yet another story. "Let me tell you what Sally did only a few weeks ago," Miss McGill offered, and, with the occasional murmured query from him, she proceeded to give him a detailed account of little Sally's most recent prank, a long story that somehow involved the vicar of her village, a cuckoo clock, and a frog.

Aidan tried, he really did, to give her his full, undivided attention, but when Julia once more moved directly into his line of vision, sitting down at the piano, she was perfectly visible to him past Miss McGill's right shoulder. Spike, never far from her heels, settled beneath the instrument, and Phoebe moved to her side to turn the pages for her.

"She vowed, most convincingly, that she'd put the frog back in the pond," Miss McGill was saying as

Julia ran her hands over the piano keys, "but one can't ever believe a word out of that child's mouth. She'd hidden it, the little imp."

"Play 'Maple Leaf Rag,' Julie, do," Geoff entreated from the card table, where he was playing bridge with three of his friends, but she shook her head. Beside her, Phoebe pointed to the sheet music on the stand and asked a question, but again she shook her head and Phoebe drifted away, obviously unneeded to turn the pages. She started to play, but then stopped, her gaze meeting his over the long, polished top of the grand piano. She glanced at Miss McGill, then back at him, and the corners of her mouth curved in an unmistakable smile, one he suspected was at his expense.

Recalling that Miss McGill had fallen silent, he jerked to attention again, striving to remember where their conversation about Sally's frog had got to. "But where did she put it?" he asked, and feeling Julia's amused gaze on him, he gave his companion his most charming smile. "You mustn't keep me in suspense, Miss McGill."

"Well, that's where the vicar comes into it, Your Grace. You see, he was supposed to come to tea . . ."

Julia began to play, and the beautiful notes of Beethoven's Moonlight Sonata poured from her instrument in a delicate stream. Aidan managed to last about fifteen seconds before looking up again, and when he did, he lost all hope of keeping track of where little Sally McGill might have put her frog.

Julia's head was tilted slightly in a pensive pose,

and the dreamy, faraway look on her face riveted him. He wondered if she was even reading the notes, or if she was playing the entire piece from memory. When she closed her eyes, he had his answer.

Her lips parted and her head fell back, exposing fully the bare, luscious column of her throat, and it was so enticing, so erotic, that the arousal he'd been trying to keep at bay all evening flared up inside him at once, as quick and hot as the flare of a match.

Some things were just too much for any man, and Aidan gave up the fight. That night at Covent Garden a few weeks ago, he'd striven to remember the details of what had happened in Cornwall, but now, he didn't even try. Instead, he imagined it, recreating in the space of a few heartbeats what might have been, conjuring luscious images that spread the arousal through his body like wildfire.

He had to keep it contained lest what he felt became evident to the girl opposite him, who had done nothing to deserve his wayward thoughts and lack of attention. He jerked in his seat, took a hefty swallow of port, and forced his gaze back to his companion.

"And what," Miss McGill was saying, "do you think happened next?"

"I can't imagine," he answered truthfully.

"The clock struck five!"

Aidan stared at her blankly, and she was forced to explain. "That's where she'd hidden the frog! It popped out of the clock along with the cuckoo, and landed with a splat right on top of the vicar's head!" Miss

McGill laughed at the memory evoked by her own story, laughed so hard, in fact, that she began snorting through her nose.

Aidan laughed, too, forcing a polite chuckle, which was all he could manage in the circumstances. "Charming," he said, and took another swallow of port. "Absolutely charming."

With the snorting laughter of Miss McGill still echoing in his ears and lust for Julia flooding through his body, Aidan realized this house party was going to be a very long fortnight. If he managed to get through it with his honor intact, he wouldn't just be cured of Julia. He'd be a candidate for sainthood.

Breakfast at large country house parties usually consisted of warming dishes on the sideboard from eight o'clock until eleven, and the Danbury household kept to this custom. Julia wasn't in the dining room when Aidan came down at nine, and since he'd spent most of the night engaged in erotic dreams about her, he was rather glad of her absence from the table.

Miss McGill was there, however, and when she gave him a big, beaming smile, Aidan made short work of his bacon and kidneys, gulped down his tea, and beat a quick retreat to the outdoors, thinking a walk in the cool morning air would do him good.

He skirted the edge of the long south lawn where some of the guests were playing croquet, passed the tennis courts where a footman was chalking the lines for later in the day, and strolled through the rose garden. When he reached the millpond at the edge of the woods, he started to turn around and go back, but then he saw Julia, and he stopped.

She was walking along the edge of the pond, Spike at her side, and when she circled the water, she saw him and also came to a halt.

He took a step toward her, and she turned as if she hadn't seen him, veering off the main path, away from the pond. A moment later, she ducked into a thicket of rhododendrons, and disappeared.

She was avoiding him, he realized in surprise. But why?

Perhaps she'd spent a restless night, too. Perhaps she'd had some erotic dreams about him. Perhaps she'd tossed and turned and felt the same hot, desperate need he'd spent the night feeling. It was unlikely, he knew. Julia always seemed cool and polished, always ready with a witty remark, always in complete command of herself. He couldn't imagine her hot and desperate.

Looking back, he realized it had always been that way. Unavailable to him from the very first, she had always been the forbidden fruit he craved, and though he had always tried to deny it or suppress it, it had always been there, ever since that day on the footbridge. She knew that, she'd always known. And even now, after she'd used that knowledge for her own purposes, he still burned for her, while she still remained aloof, cool, and polished. Even without a husband, she seemed curiously unobtainable and untouchable, almost as if there was a wall of glass around her. But what was beneath that polished surface?

He thought about that day in Cornwall, of how brazenly seductive she'd been. What had she felt that day? Had she wanted him at all? When he'd woken up and seen Yardley standing in the doorway, when he'd realized how thoroughly he'd been used, he'd concluded that all the seduction was an act by a woman with a cold heart and a ruthless purpose, but the woman in the library had not seemed cold and ruthless at all. She'd looked soft, and warm, and vulnerable. And then she'd shoved Phoebe Marlowe in his face. And then Eileen McGill. And now she was avoiding him.

Aidan stared at the break in the rhododendrons where she'd pushed through them to get away, and he took a step forward, but then he stopped.

He ought to let her go. He ought to go back to the house, join the others on the lawn, challenge Paul to a chess game—anything but go after her. And yet the idea that she might have spent the night feeling some of what he felt, that underneath her cool veneer she might want him as much as he wanted her, was too irresistible to ignore.

He retreated back amid the trees and came around from another path, one that intersected with the one she was now walking. This was a chance to get closer to the truth, to see again the soft, vulnerable woman he'd seen in the library, and he wasn't going to waste it.

Spike, however, appeared to have different ideas about the matter. As Aidan approached where they had stopped by a fountain, his footsteps on the gravel alerted the animal, who looked up from the clump of thyme he was sniffing and gave a low growl of warning.

Julia turned as well, and the moment she saw him, she gave a glance around as if seeking a means of escape or a diversion. Finding none, she returned her attention to him with a charming smile, but he saw the artificial quality of it. She did not seem glad to see him, but he was undeterred.

Spike growled again, and Julia's hand tightened on the leash in her gloved fingers. "Spike," she admonished, and the animal quieted.

"Good morning," Aidan greeted her, coming closer, keeping a wary eye on the animal. "You really should do something about that dog," he said, halting in front of her. "He's a menace."

"You only say that because you don't like him," she said, reaching down to pat Spike's flank before turning to continue down the path.

"I'm not the one who growls every time we meet, Julia," Aidan pointed out as he fell in step beside her. "Still, one of these days, I shall be forced to show your dog that I am not only bigger than he is, but also far more ferocious when I choose to be."

"Are you?" She shot a sideways glance at him. "I've never seen your ferocious side."

"If that animal growls at me again, you will."

Today, however, Spike deigned to be gracious. He allowed this interloper to walk with them, although he did keep his short, stout body firmly planted between Aidan and his mistress.

"Have you been out walking long this morning?" she asked as they merged into the thickly planted grove of beech trees.

"I only came down about twenty minutes ago."

"How terribly indolent of you, Aidan, to stay abed so long."

He didn't tell her his indolence was the result of a very restless night.

"I've been down for over an hour," she added.

"You have?" He shot her a dubious look that made her laugh. "You, up and about at eight o'clock in the morning?"

"I am capable of it, you know," she assured him with a smile.

"Well, you can't really blame me for having doubts. I seem to recall that at Pixy Cove, you were nearly always the last one down to the beach."

"Are you saying I'm lazy?" she demanded, but the humor in her voice told him she wasn't insulted. "Pixy Cove's different. When I'm there, I'm on holiday. Here, I have things to do and no time to laze the day away. I've been hard at work on your behalf, I'll have you know."

"My behalf?"

"Yes. I've been through all the new invitations your secretary forwarded. What with helping Aunt Gennie prepare for the house party, this morning's the first chance I've had to set to, and there are some definite possibilities. Shall we discuss them after dinner?"

Somehow, he couldn't muster much enthusiasm, but he nodded.

"Also there are several young ladies who live nearby with whom you should become acquainted. We may want to involve Aunt Gennie in that. She knows the local gentry hereabouts far better than I do."

"Eugenia?" He groaned. "No. Her matchmaking efforts I can well do without. She ushered me over to Miss McGill last night with so much eagerness, you'd have thought the girl was her own daughter."

She made a choked sound, but when she spoke, her voice was bland. "Yes, so I saw."

"It was not amusing, Julia."

"Yes, it was. Just not to you." She gestured to another path. "As to Aunt Gennie," Julia went on as they turned in that direction, "you can't really blame her. She feels some responsibility for you still being a bachelor. She was chaperoning Beatrix at Pixy Cove, you know, and to her mind, if she'd been a more diligent chaperone, you never would have caught Trix and Will in a compromising situation. And she finds it reassuring to know that you are considering matrimony again, proving that her negligence caused no permanent damage."

"I can understand that. Just don't let her labor under any misapprehensions that I harbor a romantic interest in Miss McGill."

"What, you didn't like Eileen?" Julia asked, actually sounding surprised. But as they stopped to let Spike investigate an intriguing smell amid the rhododendrons along the path, Aidan shot a sideways glance at her and saw that upward curve at the edges of her lips. "But I don't understand. She's a very sweet girl."

"Yes, she is," he agreed, "and I'm not the least bit interested in her. But I suspect you knew I wouldn't be."

Her smile faded, and suddenly, she seemed just as interested in the flowers bordering the path as Spike was. "I don't know what you're talking about," she said, leaning forward to pluck off a few spent blossoms.

"Don't you? Hmm . . . amazing that someone who was so perceptive about what I would think of Felicia Vale should be so obtuse when it comes to Eileen McGill."

She still didn't look at him. "Attraction is sometimes an inexplicable thing, and Eileen is a remarkably pretty girl. How was I to know she wouldn't attract you?"

"Oh, I don't know. Perhaps the fact that she snorts when she laughs might have been a clue?"

"What does that have to do with anything? Really, Aidan, it's a bit shallow of you, isn't it, to judge a woman by her laugh? For all I knew, you might have been captivated enough to overlook it, or perhaps even find it endearing. You might have decided on the spot you want to spend your life with her."

He thought of a life of upside-down drawers and frogs popping out of clocks, and he shuddered. "While I'm sure Miss McGill will make some man an excellent wife, I can safely say I will never be that man."

She shrugged. "All right, then. You don't want Eileen. Now I know."

"I think you knew it all along." He leaned sideways,

easing closer to her while allowing Spike to remain between them. He studied her profile, appreciating with pure masculine pleasure the luminous flush of pink that spread across her cheek, liking the finely molded line of her chin and the delicate shape of her ear. He imagined the velvety softness of her earlobe against his mouth and the satiny texture of her inky black hair sliding through his fingers. "I think you were perfectly aware of Miss McGill's fondness for practical jokes, and you knew what my reaction to that sort of woman would be. So you engineered a little practical joke of your own."

She made a smothered sound, trying for all she was worth not to laugh and give the show away. "Why on earth would I do such a thing?"

"To bedevil me, perhaps? You seem quite fond of that particular sport." He paused, and as he studied her, he thought again of how she'd looked in the library, and a deeper revelation occurred to him, one that was even more intriguing and dangerous than the desire he thought he'd seen in her face. "But bedeviling me isn't really the reason you had Eugenia shove Miss McGill in my direction, is it?" he added softly.

Her amusement vanished. "I don't know what you mean."

"Don't you? Eileen McGill was the first unmarried girl you could use to block my path." He moved closer. "My path to you."

"You hired me to introduce you to potential brides."

"Not precisely. I hired you to assist me with forming a wider circle of acquaintance."

"With a view to matrimony. And anyway," she added, her voice rising a notch in obvious agitation, "I didn't shove Eileen at you!" With a tug on Spike's leash, she continued down the path.

"No," he agreed, easily keeping pace with her hurried steps. "You introduced us. Your aunt did the shoving, at your instigation. But Eileen aside, you can't deny that you were the one who practically threw Phoebe Marlowe into my arms in the library yesterday."

"What?" She stopped again, causing him to stop as well. "I did not—"

"Another woman you know I have no interest in," he added, interrupting her outraged protest, "and who is not the least bit interested in me. That's why you felt safe in using her to keep me at bay."

"I don't know what you're talking about. Being that you are a gentleman, you should have offered to escort Phoebe into the hall, and you didn't." She paused, then added in a lofty tone, "I covered your lapse of good manners."

"My lapse?" He laughed. "That's the lamest thing I've ever heard. Really, Julia, your clever brain can't come up with something better than that?"

"I don't see what's so amusing. And I don't understand why you are attributing me with all these secret motives. I'm your social secretary, aren't I? You want to marry, don't you? You wanted a wider social circle, didn't you? Well, I'm helping you along. That's just the plain truth."

"The truth?" He smiled, more convinced his theory was correct with each defensive, indignant word she uttered. "You're right to say the truth is plain. At least, it is to me. I'm wondering, however, if it's equally plain to you. I don't think it is."

"I wish you'd stop speaking in riddles!" she burst out. "If you have something to say, then say it."

"All right. I think you're shoving all these other women at me because you're afraid."

"Afraid of what, in heaven's name?"

He leaned closer. His gaze lowered to her lips, watched them part, watched her tongue dart out to lick them in nervous agitation. "You're afraid of being attracted to me yourself."

"What? Of all the conceited, asinine . . ." She spluttered, her voice trailing away, as if she just didn't have words to articulate how absurd his conclusion was. From Julia, who was always ready with a clever quip, spluttering was a sure sign he was on the right track.

"Strange, isn't it," he went on. "You're so damned perceptive about everyone else, but you don't understand the first thing about your own feelings. No wonder I didn't see it sooner—you're superb at hiding how you truly feel, even from yourself."

"How I feel? I don't feel anything, not for you."

He leaned even closer, so close he could smell the scent of lilacs on her skin, so close his lips almost brushed her ear, and when he spoke, his breath stirred the dark tendril of hair at her cheek. "I don't believe you."

She jerked, stepping back and folding her arms as if to erect another barrier between them. "I was never attracted to you," she said in a hard voice. "You said it yourself the night of the May Day Ball. I used you, it's done, and though I seduced you, I didn't care two straws for you. I never did."

He already knew that, but after yesterday in the library, he also knew it might not be true anymore. "I like the forbidden fruit," he murmured. "What can I say?"

She made a sound of exasperation. "For heaven's sake, if I wanted you myself, why would I ever agree to introduce you to other women? Hmm?" She nodded, as if she'd scored a point or something.

"A child could see why. You're using those women to keep me at a distance because you're afraid of having me—or any other man, for that matter—get close to you."

Her chin quivered, showing that under the surface bravado, he was the one scoring points. He kept going. "That's why you have Spike. That's why you lost no time shoving other women at me. Yet at the same time, you can't bear the thought of introducing me to a woman I might actually desire. Hence, Eileen. And Phoebe, too. We've known each other for years, and if I wanted her, I'd have made a move in that direction long before now. You know that, so it's safe to throw her at me. Face it, Julia." His smile widened with a complacence he was far from feeling. "You want me."

"This is nonsense, complete and utter nonsense! And . . . and . . . I can prove it!"

"Really? How?"

"By doing what you hired me for! During the next two weeks, I'll introduce you to women so beautiful, it'll make your head spin; women so charming, you'll be enchanted; women so desirable, it'll drive you mad. Before this house party is over, you'll be lusting after one of those women like a randy sailor on shore leave!"

She turned on her heel, jerked Spike's leash, and marched away with the bulldog in tow.

"Too late, Julie," he murmured under his breath. "I met that woman thirteen years ago."

Chapter Thirteen

During the years of her marriage, Julia had developed a talent for evasion and avoidance, and during the days that followed her conversation with Aidan in the gardens, she made good use of that talent, but though she managed to keep well away from him, his words to her proved harder to avoid. They had the irritating tendency to come back to her again and again.

Face it, Julia. You want me.

"Of all the conceit," she muttered, not for the first time, and rolled her eyes.

"Pardon, madame?" Giselle paused in the act of placing a spray of lilacs in her hair, and met her gaze in the mirror of the dressing table.

"Nothing, Giselle," Julia said hastily, waving a hand in the air. "Carry on."

The maid resumed dressing her hair, and Julia's

thoughts returned to Aidan's contentions, contentions that she knew were absurd. Of course he was a terribly attractive man, she'd always known that. And of course any normal, healthy woman with an ounce of sensual feeling would find him desirable. Those facts weren't in dispute. But Julia didn't fall into that category. Any sensual feeling she had within her was long gone.

And even if what he said was the truth, even if she did feel a certain attraction to him herself, what difference could it make? He wanted to marry, and that was the last thing in the world she wanted.

No, best all around if she diverted his attention to some other woman, a woman who had some chance of making him happy.

She knew his type well enough, and over the past few days, she had determined that there were several young ladies here who might suit him, right down to their brown eyes, sweet dispositions, and perfect pedigrees. Tonight, she intended to steer them in his direction. One of them was bound to catch his eye and make him forget any silly ideas he might have about her.

Two hours later, however, Julia was forced to admit her confident prediction might have been a bit premature.

After dinner when everyone was milling about the drawing room and its connecting music room, she ascertained the locations of her first two choices, and then sidled up alongside Aidan at the table of fruits, cheeses, and cordials.

"Are you ready to take the plunge back into courtship?" she asked him, nibbling a grape as he poured himself a glass of port.

"Plunge into courtship?" he echoed, frowning in bewilderment.

"What," she countered, opening her eyes ingenuously wide, giving him her most mischievous smile, "did you think I'd forgotten my vow from the other day?"

Julia would not have been human if she didn't find his expression of dismay a bit gratifying. But it took him only one or two seconds to recover.

"I suppose I'm as ready as I'll ever be," he said and shrugged. "I mean, if you don't want me, what other choice do I have?"

His voice was suspiciously bland, but she chose to take those words at face value.

"See the girl in pink standing by Sir George and Lady Debenham? Dark brown hair? Pearls around her neck? That's Lady Frances Mowbray. She's—"

"No," he interrupted, shaking his head. "I've already met Lady Frances. She won't do."

"Oh." She felt a bit disconcerted by this immediate and unequivocal refusal to consider Lady Frances. "Didn't you like her?"

"I thought she was charming. I didn't like her father."

"What's wrong with her father? Lord Mowbray is a viscount, with substantial lands."

"He's a lout. Far too fond of music hall dancers, if the gossip is to be believed. He's a heavy drinker, and an even heavier gambler, and he's deeply in debt from these dissolute habits."

"That has nothing to do with her," Julia pointed out reasonably. "She can't be blamed for her father's dissolute habits."

"Agreed, but it doesn't change the fact that I don't want to be paying my wife's father's gambling debts. That's a bottomless well if ever there was one. Not to mention the possibilities of scandal associated with a skirt-chasing gambler. No."

"All right then," Julia said, rallying with another glance around. "There's a slender, willowy blond standing by the piano with Vivian Marlowe. See her? White lace dress, with pink rosebuds in her hair? That's Jane Heyer."

Aidan gave Miss Heyer a considering glance. "She's lovely," he was forced to concede.

"Jane is the daughter of Sir Alfred Heyer, the famous botanist, and she's the granddaughter of Earl Cavanaugh. As you see, she's an exceptional beauty. She even has brown eyes, your favorite."

"This notion of yours that I have a preference for brown-eyed women is nonsense," he objected.

"If you say so. Jane's mother, Lady Margaret, was the daughter of Henry Albemarle, Second Baronet Oxmoor, but she died when her daughter was a baby. Miss Heyer assisted her father extensively with his work in Africa, but came home four years ago to pursue a university education. She attended Girton College, graduating with honors."

"No." He shook his head again. "I couldn't possibly consider marrying her."

Julia was beginning to feel a bit frustrated. "How can you say that? You haven't even met her."

"I don't have to. She attended Girton College, you said?"

"Yes. Why should that matter?" She frowned. "Oh, I see. You want a woman of keen intelligence, but heaven forbid she should actually put her keen mind to good use by obtaining a university education. Is that it?"

"Not at all. I take no issue with a woman attending university. I find it laudable, in fact." He took a sip of port. "You're missing the point."

She lifted her hands in a gesture of futility as he paused again. "What is the point?"

"She went to *Girton*." When she still continued to stare at him blankly, he added, "Girton is a Cambridge school."

Julia made a sound of disbelief at such an absurd excuse. "You would refuse to consider marrying a woman because she went to a Cambridge school?"

He pointed a finger to his chest. "Oxford," he said, then nodded at the girl. "Cambridge. It would never work. Who's next?"

She opened her mouth as if to argue, but closed it again. She knew Aidan well enough to know that if he'd made up his mind, there was no changing it, not about things like school ties. She might as well argue with him about the merits of bohemians and divorce. Not Jane Heyer.

Julia took a glance around, searching for the third candidate on her list, and when she spied Peggy Bourne-

West, she breathed a little sigh of relief. "There's a girl in blue silk standing by Paul at the fireplace. Light brown hair."

"Very pretty," he said, and Julia couldn't help noting his lack of enthusiasm.

She persevered. "Her name is Miss Margaret Bourne-West," she said. "Her family—" She stopped, eyeing him doubtfully. "I don't think I'll provide any more information about her background. If I do, you'll find a reason to be prejudiced against her."

"Too late," he said, smiling. "I know her mother. Loathsome woman. I can't tolerate Mrs. Bourne-West, and if she were my mother-in-law, I'd have to shoot myself. Do you have any other candidates for me to consider?"

He made short shrift of the remaining three young ladies on her list as quickly as he had the first three, and she gave a sigh, thoroughly exasperated. Despite that, she was also just a little, tiny bit relieved. Knowing that was absurd, she tried to shut down.

"You've now dismissed half a dozen perfectly acceptable young ladies without even talking to them," she pointed out. "Don't you think you're being just a little too picky?"

He shrugged, unperturbed. "I'm a duke. I'm allowed to be picky."

"For all you know, one of those six young ladies could be the perfect duchess for you. Don't you want to at least become better acquainted with them before you dismiss them?"

"Not particularly."

"You might regret it later," she said. "Other men will sweep them up, and you'll meet one of them years later and regret that you didn't take the chance when you had it."

He looked steadily at her. "Yes," he agreed with emphasis. "That's quite possible."

Julia's heart slammed against her ribs. "Meeting them takes just a few minutes of your time," she murmured as she looked away. He couldn't mean it. He couldn't mean he felt regret over not pursuing her that day on the footbridge. That was a lifetime ago. She swallowed hard, striving to gather her scattered wits. "A few minutes seems a small price to pay," she said, sliding a sidelong look at him, "for the chance to fall in love."

"Perhaps, but as we've discussed before, Julia, love is not my most important concern at present." He paused, looking steadily at her. "Lovemaking, on the other hand, is always important."

"Ah, but you have a mistress for that," she said, striving for blasé sophistication, chagrined when her voice came out in a breathless rush.

Her words caused him to laugh under his breath. "Ah, yes, my mistress," he murmured. "I'd forgotten all about her."

"Forgotten her?" Julia sniffed, trying to recover her poise. "A fine thing indeed. Poor woman. She must be plain, then, or not very accomplished at her profession, if you forget her so easily." She paused, but her curiosity was too much to bear. "Who is she? Do I know her?"

"I doubt it. And," he added giving her a reproving look, "I hardly think my mistress is an appropriate topic while you are telling me about women I might wish to marry."

"No need to worry about that," she said with a sigh. "You've eliminated all the viable candidates in the room."

He smiled at her. "What a shame."

"There will be others at the ball on Friday. Would you like me to tell you about them now?" she added wryly. "That way, you'll have five full days to come up with your excuses not to meet them."

His smile widened into a grin. "I'll wait."

She gave a huff of exasperation and turned away, studying the young women in the crowd that milled about the room, although she knew it was a waste of time, and she wondered if perhaps she should bow out of working for him altogether. "I know love isn't your primary concern, but given these excuses you keep offering, I'm wondering if I'm wasting my time. I am beginning to suspect that I could line up a thousand suitable women, and you'd find something wrong with every single one of them. Why?"

"You know why." He glanced around, then leaned closer to her. "These days I'm far too preoccupied with one particular woman to work up an interest in any others."

Her lips parted, but for the life of her, she couldn't

think of anything to say. "I—" She stopped, cleared her throat, and it was a full five seconds before she tried again. "Really?" she finally managed. "Do tell. Which woman do you mean?"

He laughed, and she knew her pose of dry sophistication wasn't fooling him for a second. "I think you know," he said, his gaze sliding down to her mouth. "I think you've always known."

"Oh no," she denied, shaking her head, laughing in disbelief, even though panic flooded through her, though she couldn't say what, precisely, was causing it. All she knew was that her heart was racing and she couldn't seem to catch her breath. "Oh no, no. You can't possibly mean me."

His gaze met hers, steady, purposeful, utterly sincere. "I do mean you, Julia. Why do you think I hired you?"

"I don't know." Her voice was so low, she barely heard it herself.

"I wanted to be near you," he said simply. "Is it so astonishing?" he added, watching her face. "Given what happened between us last summer?"

She licked her dry lips, took a frantic glance around. "But that was different!" she whispered, although no one was within earshot. "That was . . ." She stared at him helplessly. "That was an anomaly, a once-in-a-lifetime thing."

"I wouldn't know. I don't remember most of it." He looked at her mouth again. "But I'd like to."

Her lips started to tingle, and she forced them into a

blasé smile. "Why, Aidan, you're still carrying a torch for me? I'm flattered. You want to pick up where we left off, I daresay, but really, it's a bit late for that, isn't it? We had our fling, darling," she added with a laugh that she suspected didn't fool him for a second. "And now it's over."

"Not for me."

"But it is for me, despite all your arrogant assumptions to the contrary."

"I don't believe you. Being the arrogant fellow that I am," he added, assuming an air of mock apology, "I think you'll have to prove it."

"That's what I'm trying to do, you impossible man, but you are being singularly uncooperative with my efforts!"

He grinned. "Really, Julia, what would introducing me to other women, beautiful or otherwise, prove at this point? That you're a hypocrite?"

She made a sound of outrage, but he ignored it. "Still, there is a way to prove you don't want me."

She turned toward the refreshment table, reaching for a crystal flute and the bottle reposing in a bucket of ice, feeling in need of a drink. "What way?"

"Meet me in the maze at midnight."

"And what?" she scoffed, taking a gulp of champagne. But though the wine was ice-cold, it did nothing to cool her blood. "Allow you to make love to me in the moonlight while I valiantly attempt to resist your considerable charms?"

"Something like that." He was still smiling, but

in his eyes was unmistakable challenge. "If you *can* resist."

"And if I do manage that monumental feat, what do I receive in return?"

"Crowing rights?"

She smiled sweetly. "Not good enough. You will agree to dance at least one waltz with each of the beautiful, charming, potential duchesses I've selected for you to meet. All six of them, including Lady Frances and Miss Heyer. And you'll promise me, on your word of honor, to keep an open mind about them."

He didn't even hesitate. "Done." He downed the last of his port and set the glass on the table. "Midnight," he reminded, turning away. "Don't be late."

Aidan waited for her in the center of the maze, trying not to pace amid the ornamental pieces of Danbury's medieval lawn chess set. It was a glorious night, warm for May, and the strains of piano music and the sound of laughter drifted through the open windows of the house and down to where he sat. The moon was full and bright, and the knee-high granite sculptures scattered around him cast distorted shadows of knights and castles across a chessboard of turf and flagstone squares. He studied the chess pieces as he waited, feeling rather at a loss regarding his own next move.

It was a strange thing, but though he was thirty years old, he'd never actually had to seduce a woman before, and he had absolutely no idea how he was going to set about it. Worse, challenging her to meet him for a midnight rendezvous had been a spur of the moment impulse, and he was not a man given to impulsive things. And just the thought of seducing her, of being able to relive at least some of those tantalizing moments last year, was sending renewed lust through his body that he wasn't absolutely certain he could contain.

She would come. He knew that. It wasn't the arrogance of which she had accused him that made him confident. Julia, he felt certain, would never run away from a challenge like the one he'd thrown down a few hours ago. She might laugh in his face or act cold as a stone, but she'd come. He knew that as surely as he knew anything.

What he didn't know, and what he should have had the wits to foresee, was that she would not come without reinforcements.

"Spike?" He stared in disbelief at the fat bulldog that trotted into the center of the maze with Julia several minutes past midnight. "You brought Spike with you?"

She laughed, flashing an impudent smile at him in the moonlight. "You didn't say I couldn't."

"No," he conceded wryly, "I didn't. I should have, but I'm afraid I wasn't thinking that far ahead. You've outwitted me there. I admit it."

What he didn't say was that he had no intention of allowing something as inconsequential as an overfed bulldog with delusions of grandeur to stop him now, but when he took a step toward her, the overfed bulldog in question growled in a very menacing fashion.

"This is hardly fair," he said as he took another step and earned another warning from the animal by her side.

"If fairness were on your mind, you wouldn't be trying to seduce your secretary," she pointed out, her smile widening. "You'd have allowed her to perform the duties you hired her for and never suggested a midnight rendezvous in the maze."

"Point taken, and you needn't smirk, Julia. You haven't won yet. In fact, with Spike here, how do you expect to prove anything? Best if you tie him."

"Not a chance." But she glanced at the dog, and seemed to decide on a compromise. "Sit," she ordered.

Spike planted his bum on the turf at once, but his square head moved watchfully back and forth between her and the distrusted man nearby.

"Satisfied?" she asked, looking at him again.

"Not nearly." Aidan resumed walking toward her, but he kept one eye on Spike, well aware that a protective dog was not a thing to take lightly. Still, as he came closer, he noted that Spike wasn't baring teeth, and when faced with his direct stare, the animal looked away. Those, he knew, were very good indications that he could gain the upper hand.

He halted in front of her. He leaned closer, but once again, he was stopped by a growl of warning from Spike. "Are you going to do something about this animal of yours?" he murmured, his lips an inch from hers.

She smiled, seeming confident she was the one with the upper hand just now. "What would you suggest?"

"Shooting's out of the question, I suppose?" His gaze slid down for another quick look at the bulldog as he leaned even closer to Julia, and when Spike growled again, he was ready.

With a savage sound that caused Julia to jump back in alarm, Aidan moved. Within the blink of an eye, he'd taken Spike by the muzzle and hip and pushed him down onto his side in the grass, and using his superior body weight, he kept the animal firmly pinned. "No," he said in a calm, firm voice. "No, Spike."

The dog whined in protest at this unexpected challenge and wriggled fiercely, trying to extricate himself from Aidan's hold. Aidan, however, didn't move and didn't relax, and after several minutes of futile struggle, Spike's whines lessened, and his efforts to get away became halfhearted. At last, he went completely quiet and still. Aidan waited a bit longer to be sure he'd established his dominance, and then he relented.

"Good boy," Aidan said and stood up, letting go of the animal, but holding on to the leash and watching for any sign of aggression.

There was none. The dog stood there, quiet and calm, looking at him, then looking away. When Aidan gave the leash a gentle tug and started walking, the animal followed him. He glanced around at the chess pieces scattered about and looped the handle of the leash around one of the crenellations along the top edge of a rook. "Now," he murmured, returning his attention to her, "where were we?"

Chapter Fourteen

*J*ulia's confidence that this midnight rendezvous was within her control went from reasonably high to dismally low in about three seconds, the exact amount of time it had taken Aidan to make a snarling sound meaner than any dog she'd ever heard and toss her beloved Spike down to the turf.

A few minutes later, the dog she'd bought because it hated men—her loathsome former husband in particular—was docile as a lamb and safely leashed, and she was beginning to fear she'd made a big mistake in coming here at all. When Aidan began walking back toward her, she had to fight the impulse to run away.

She'd been prepared to let him kiss her. She'd come expecting that, knowing the only way she could put an end to this idea he had in his head was to prove she didn't want him by being unaffected by his attempts at seduction. Bringing Spike with her had been a whim, the sort of joke that appealed to her mischievous side, and the look on his face, a rather charming combination of humor and chagrin, had made the joke worthwhile. He did know how to make her laugh, she had to admit, usually when he wasn't trying. But now, with Spike leashed to a granite sculpture and Aidan walking toward her, his expression much more serious and purposeful than before, she wasn't laughing, and the closer he came, the more her confidence deteriorated.

She tried to remind herself that she was on familiar ground here. She'd kissed him before, quite a few times, in fact, that afternoon last August, so it wasn't as if there were any surprises in store.

But she couldn't deny that she'd developed a strange, most inconvenient nervousness around him during the past few days. As he halted in front of her, as she saw his thick brown lashes lower a fraction, as she realized he was thinking erotic things about her and what they had done that afternoon ten months ago, that nervousness flared up, and she forced herself to speak.

"Where did you learn to do that?" she asked. "What you did with Spike. I've never seen anyone do that to a dog before."

"My father had mastiffs and Alsatians, and I learned as a boy how to deal with aggressive dogs. The best thing, of course, is to steer clear, since a dog bite can be quite serious. But in this case, I felt establishing my dominance was a better course of action."

He took another step closer, and she reacted without thinking, stepping back, but when she hit the tall boxwood hedge behind her and she could retreat no further, panic rose up, panic that was vastly out of proportion to the circumstances. "Is that what this is about then?" she asked, giving him a challenging look. "Shall you be attempting to exert dominance over me?"

"Over you?" He laughed, seeming genuinely amused by the notion. "That would be like trying to hold on to a running stream of water."

Something in her relaxed, and she let out a long, slow breath. "Oh."

He caught that faint sigh of relief, and he tilted his head to one side, seeming puzzled by it. "I did what I did with Spike simply because I didn't want him to sink his teeth into my leg at an inopportune moment." He leaned down as if to take her hand, his puzzlement deepening when she stupidly jerked away. He straightened. "Are you nervous?"

"Me?" The question came out in a squeak—worthy of Felicia Vale, she thought in disgust. Her hands curled into fists, but she strove to speak in a natural way. "I'm not nervous at all. Why do you ask?"

He leaned down again, and this time, she let him clasp his hand round her wrist. "I only ask," he said, as he lifted her hand in the air, "because you're clenching your fists, and that's usually a sign of either anger or nervousness. I hope it's nervousness, because anger, I fear, would put a damper on our evening."

"I'm not angry," she said, and made a concerted effort to relax her hands. "And I'm not nervous. What do I have to be nervous about?"

He met her eyes. "Nothing," he said, entwining their fingers, "unless you don't know how to waltz."

She blinked. "I beg your pardon?"

"Waltz." He nodded in the direction of the house. "Can't you hear it? Strauss's Blue Danube. I'm asking you to dance."

"Oh." She cocked her head and heard the sound of the piano. "It's not very impressive without the violins, is it?"

"A bit tinny, perhaps," he agreed, "but good enough." He put his right hand on her waist and began to sway. "And one and two and three."

As they began to waltz, he said, "I want you to know that this is a very unusual situation for me. I don't usually like to dance. Most of the time, I'd prefer to be stuffed with nails and rolled down a hill."

She laughed at his wry tone, but she couldn't help noticing that he guided her across the grass in perfect steps. "But you dance beautifully! Why don't you like it?"

"Too many boyhood sessions of practice with my mother. Every step had to be perfect, you see, every move exactly proper, every figure executed just right. Over and over and over. Had she not been a duchess, my mother could have been an army general."

"Your mother taught you to dance?"

"Well, my tutor couldn't do it," he answered with a touch of humor. "Herr Brunner was this old German fellow, very stout. He always trod on my feet."

"You couldn't take lessons with the other local children?"

"God, no! My mother and father would have been horrified by such a prospect. Future dukes," he told her, "don't associate with the lesser mortals unless and until absolutely necessary. No, until I was twelve and sent away to school, I was taught at home, in splendid, ducal isolation."

She caught the bitter undertone of his voice. "That must have been lonely."

His mouth tightened and he looked away. "It was hell."

She studied his profile in the moonlight as he swirled her around the fountain, their footsteps swishing on the grass in time with the faint, tinny notes, his body leading hers with effortless ease. She imagined what life must have been like for him, a boy prevented from having either friends or amusements, for whom even dancing was turned into an exercise in discipline. "Going away to school must have been a godsend."

He chuckled. "Not at first. I felt terribly awkward, and I was shy, to boot. I was teased without mercy that first year, and harassed, even beaten. Because I had no siblings, I never learned how to fight back, you see, and it was a miserable year. I came home for the summer holidays, and I knew I had to do something or my second year at Eton would be as horrific as the first. And there was no way I could avoid going back."

Julia remembered their first meeting on that bridge, and how he'd pokered up so stiff when she'd teased him. Now she knew why. "What did you do? Go to your father?"

"God, no. My father would have cuffed me on the side of the head and told me to be a man, and stop bothering him with schoolboy trifles."

Listening to him, Julia felt a fierce wave of outrage rising up within her on his behalf. "Bastard."

He shrugged as if it didn't matter. "I hired the local blacksmith—who was quite a sound pugilist—to teach me to fight. The day after I returned for fall term, one of the upperclassmen tried to have a go at me, and I gave him the thrashing of his life. Afterward, I stood over him, fists clenched, blood running down my face, and I dared any other boy who had issue with me to come forward and demonstrate it now."

She smiled, picturing it. "My head is bloody but unbowed," she murmured.

He stopped abruptly, bringing her to a halt as well. " 'Invictus,' " he murmured, staring at her in the moonlight. "That is one of my favorite poems."

"Is it? Mine too." In a rush, she blurted, "It's rather how I always think of you. That is, when I think of you. I mean—"

She stopped, agonizingly self-conscious all of a sudden.

"Do you know how I always think of you?" he asked. "With your legs over the side of the bridge and your pretty feet in the water."

Warmth washed over her like the sun coming out between clouds, chasing away shadows and darkness.

"You see?" he added, smiling a little, "you've been bedeviling me since we were seventeen."

"I thought so," she admitted, "but then, that night in St. Ives, you met Trix, and I thought I was wrong. I—" She stopped, too proud to confess how keen her disappointment had been. "You paid your addresses to her."

"You were married. I don't enter dalliances with other men's wives." He grimaced. "At least, I've always believed that it was morally wrong to do so."

I'm sorry, Aidan, she thought. *I'm sorry.*

"Still," he went on in a lighter voice, "you're no longer married, I have you in my sights again, and I can't bear the thought of walking away now, not if there's the slightest chance you want me as much as I still want you."

She opened her mouth to tell him there was no chance, but other words came out of her mouth instead. "I thought I was here to prove I don't want you."

His gaze was unblinking, steady, looking into hers. "I'm hoping you fail."

I won't fail because I don't feel. "And if I can prove I don't want you?" she asked, her whisper sounding harsh to her own ears. "What then?"

"I suppose I shall be dancing about half a dozen waltzes on Friday with your idea of suitable duchesses, which, now that you know I don't like to dance, should prove quite entertaining for you, given your wicked sense of humor. But—" He paused, and slowly, ever so slowly, he eased his body closer to hers. "You can save me from that fate, Julia. When I kiss you, all you have to do is kiss me back."

How could he want her now, after everything that

had happened? After she'd used him and exploited him? He didn't remember most of it, but he knew he'd been manipulated, the knight she'd used to checkmate Yardley. She'd never have thought he could want her now, but he did. It was in his eyes when he looked at her. It was in his voice. He wasn't like her, she knew, for he could still want and need and make love and not be afraid of it all.

Pull away, she told herself, but she could not seem to make her body comply with the demand of her mind. She stood as if paralyzed, afraid tonight would only prove he knew more about her innermost feelings than she did.

Aidan's eyes, dark in the moonlight, were locked with hers, and in their depths was not only desire, but also the question they were here to answer. His fingers entwined with hers, and his other hand pressed against the small of her back, bringing her closer. Her heartbeat, already quick and fast, began to beat even harder in her chest.

His fingers slid up her spine, a light, delicate caress that was like the rekindling of a fire amid the ashes, and when his palm cupped her cheek, warmth flared within her.

"Why are you doing this?" she whispered as he tilted her head back.

"Isn't it obvious? I'm turning the tables. This time, I'm seducing you."

"But why?" she cried, growing desperate. "I'm a female Iago, remember? How can you want me now?"

"How can I not?" His gaze roamed her upturned face. "You started this, you know. Ten months ago. But I don't remember how we finished it."

She licked her dry lips. "Yes, you do. We finished it that day in the divorce court."

He shook his head. "No. That afternoon in Cornwall still holds some very vague but tantalizing blank spaces for me. Things I don't remember. Things I want to remember very badly. They echo back to me again and again, and the more I see you, the more I imagine filling in those blank places." He gave a caustic chuckle. "The details become more erotic each time my imagination sets to work, I'm afraid."

Julia stared up at him in dismay. He didn't know, not really, just why and how she'd done what she'd done. And when he found out, when he learned the extent of her duplicity, when he figured out that she was dry as dust and as erotic as a fence post, he wouldn't want her anymore.

Best if she just called a halt now and let him think whatever he liked, imagine whatever he wanted, as long as he never learned the truth. And yet, as he lowered his head, she just couldn't find the will to turn her face away. If she was cold and dead, why did she feel so warm inside?

He paused, his mouth only a hairsbreadth from hers. "C'mon, Julia," he whispered, his lips brushing hers in a feather-light caress. "Refresh my memory."

He kissed her, and it was like sunshine, bringing heat and light and radiant glow, lighting her up from the inside, sending heat to her fingertips, to her toes, to the ends of her hair and the tip of her nose. And it was like rain, drenching a parched soul, and like food for a starving body.

There was no conscious thought; she was aware of only the most primitive sensations—hunger and pleasure—as she rose up on her toes, seeking more. And when his lips opened against hers, the hunger in her became need, and the pleasure deepened into lust.

He felt it, too. His hand let go of hers, and his arms slid around her waist, pulling her even closer. She came willingly, pressing her body to his, and when his tongue entered her mouth, she welcomed it, tasting, savoring, surrendering to a luscious carnality she hadn't felt in years.

With that surrender, something seemed to unfold inside her. Like leaves unfurling, tight-budded roses spiraling open, shoots pushing up through dark soil to reach the light. It began to hurt, this pleasure, but not like any pain she'd ever felt; it was a pain that came from deep inside her and spread through her body, sharp, acute, and sweet. It was joy. The blissful sting.

Suddenly, it was all too overwhelming to bear, and she tore her lips from his. Panting, she stared up at him in shock, for she'd never felt this when she'd kissed him that day in Cornwall. She'd been too driven, too focused on her goal, too detached. But now, she felt vibrant, alive, raw, and afraid. So terribly afraid.

She shook her head, trying to deny what had just happened, but there was no possibility of denial. She strove to think, but she couldn't form coherent thought. She wanted to hide, but there was no refuge. Suddenly, his arms around her felt like chains, binding her to him, and all her deepest fears came roaring up, like the snarl of a cornered, wounded animal.

"I don't want this!" she cried, hardly knowing what she was saying, her palms flattening against his chest to push him away, her body twisting out of his embrace. "I don't want it, damn you!"

Overwhelmed, she did the only thing she could. She bolted.

Whirling around, pulling folds of her gown up in her fists, she ran out of the maze, guided only by the vaguest memory of how she'd come in, her panic growing with each wrong turn, until at last, her heart racing and her breath coming in shuddering gasps, she found the exit. Free, she raced like a mad thing across a wide expanse of lawn to seek refuge in the woods beyond, and she ignored the sound of Aidan's voice calling her name.

Aidan didn't go after her. He might not have Julia's exceptional perception when it came to people, but in this case, he didn't need it. Her face and her body had told him everything a man needed to know.

He shut his eyes, envisioning her in that split second before she'd turned and fled. Her eyes, silvery gray in the moonlight, wide with shock. Her lips, puffy from his kiss. Her cheeks flushed, and her breasts heaving from her uneven breathing. Her hands, shaking, as she'd grasped folds of her skirt. She'd been stunned by that kiss, and confused, and unmistakably aroused, giving him the confirmation he'd been seeking. She wanted him as much as he wanted her.

But he also recognized fear when he saw it, and that was something he didn't understand at all.

That kiss had terrified her.

Aidan opened his eyes, confounded. What on earth was she afraid of? Him? Surely not, or she never would have come tonight. Kissing? Not that, either, for she'd kissed him plenty of times that afternoon in Cornwall, and there had been no sign of fear in her then. Still, he had no intention of running after her, asking questions and seeking explanations. That would only agitate her more, and he doubted she would answer him anyway.

Still, he now had the answer to one question, but though it was a gratifying answer to be sure, he feared it was only drawing him into a deeper mystery, the mystery of Julia's soul. And that, he reflected, thinking of her frightened face, was a place she did not want him to go.

A whine brought him out of his reverie and he turned to find Spike sitting by the carved granite rook where he'd been leashed. The bulldog was looking at him, head cocked to one side in a quizzical fashion, as if trying to understand what had just taken place.

"I know how you feel, old chap," Aidan said with a sigh. "I don't really understand, either. But we are talking about Julia, so that's no surprise."

Chapter Fifteen

Gwithian, Cornwall
1903

Dovecotes, the Cornish cottage Julia had inherited from her grandmother, was a small, square, stone farmhouse north of St. Ives. Tucked into the isolated eastern side of a little promontory above the beaches at Gwithian, Dovecotes had a pretty little beach of its own, a few caves, a few acres of empty, overgrown pasture, and a sadly neglected garden of herbs, roses, and, of course, a dovecote. It was Julia's favorite haven, the place to which she often escaped when Yardley didn't feel inclined to chase after her.

But in the summer of 1903, Yardley was always chasing after her. The work to stay one step ahead of him was becoming exhausting, and she was running

out of time. For most of August, she'd been hiding at
Pixy Cove, Lord Marlowe's villa at Torquay, but when
she received her husband's final ultimatum, a letter in-
forming her that he was in Torquay and would call the
following afternoon to fetch her and take her home to
Yardley Grange, she knew she couldn't hide any longer.
Yardley's letter assured her that he had the proper legal
decree granting constables the authority to drag her
from Marlowe's villa, or any other residence to which
she decided to flee, by force.

Julia, who didn't give a damn about legal decrees,
had promptly put petrol in the Mercedes and fled to
Cornwall. If she was to be dragged anywhere by constables, it wasn't going to be done in front of her family
and friends, who would have to stand by helpless,
unable to come to her aid.

Spike and a small valise were the only things she'd
brought with her, for she hadn't wanted to linger long
enough to pack her things. Giselle, along with her husband, Pierre, were packing up the rest of her belong-
ings and following her by train.

She didn't mind making the journey alone. She was
used to this sort of thing, and she knew that on this long
stretch of Cornish road, with only Spike for company,
she would have time to think. The problem was, six
hours later, she was nearly to Dovecotes, and she had
no solution to her problem.

What was she going to do? Even before her husband
had laid down his ultimatum two summers earlier that
she was to come home to Yardley Grange for good,

be a proper wife, and give him a son, Julia had been determined to free herself from her marriage, but she'd never been able to gain a way out.

Yardley had given her no grounds for divorce, according to the various legal minds she had consulted on the subject.

Nor would any adultery on his part be considered proper grounds. Divorcing one's spouse for adultery alone was a privilege reserved for men. Women had to charge adultery with some other pertinent offense, such as desertion or impotence. And since the letters from his attorneys demonstrated that Yardley was willing to take up residence with her again, desertion as a secondary cause was not possible, nor was impotence. Yardley had at least four bastard children that she knew of.

No, she'd been over this a thousand times, and she knew there were only two ways to be free of her husband. Murder was one, and though by the summer of 1903, Julia's numbed soul ought to have become hardened enough for homicide, she couldn't ever quite bring herself to contemplate that course, partly because of conscience, and partly because being locked in prison until she died was hardly the sort of freedom she was looking for. Making Yardley divorce her was the only option she had.

Yardley, however, wasn't cooperating with that plan. She'd staged a few affairs over the years, but she couldn't seem to bring herself to actually have one. She'd flirted with the idea two years earlier when she'd seen Aidan at the St. Ives Ball, but with that exception the thought of having a man touch her in a sexual way had the unfortunate tendency to make her physically sick. And none of her staged affairs had ever been convincing enough to inspire her husband to a divorce suit.

As she drove the road to St. Ives, Julia couldn't help remembering the last time she'd been here, when a means of escape had danced before her eyes. But then Aidan had met Trix, and she had stepped aside, fleeing to Biarritz. It was from there that she'd received Trix's letter announcing their engagement. But now, two years later, Trix was married, not to Aidan, but to Will, her childhood sweetheart, the Duke of Sunderland, and Julia's sacrifice had been for naught.

It wasn't Trix's fault. She'd always loved Will, probably from the day she'd first laid eyes on him, and she was ecstatically happy digging up relics with him in the Egyptian desert. Her world was opening up to include all sorts of new experiences and adventures. Julia's life, on the other hand, was narrowing, thinning down with each option that was taken away.

She tried to look on the bright side. At least she was going home. The Mercedes sped through the Cornish countryside amid green pastures and hedgerows, and the salty tang of the sea was in her nostrils. She smiled, breathing deep. No matter what tragedies befell her, the smell of the sea could always lift her spirits.

Spike was happy, too, she noted, glancing sideways at the bulldog. He loved riding in the motorcar. He sat in the passenger seat, his square head lifted into the wind that rushed past his wrinkled face and flapped his heavy jowls, an expression of canine ecstasy on his face.

Julia returned her attention to the road ahead, and her smile faded, for she was nearly home, and she had no idea what she was going to do after that. She down-shifted, slowing the vehicle, and turned onto the rutted lane that led to Dovecotes. At the end of the lane, she guided the motorcar into the narrow drive, came to a stop in front of the seventeenth-century farmhouse, and set the brake. She hopped down, circled to the back of the Mercedes, and pulled her small valise from the open boot. Whistling for Spike, she walked to the front door and unlocked it, and the bulldog she'd acquired two years ago jumped down from the vehicle and fol-lowed her into the house.

Blinking at the dim interior after the bright sunshine outside, she set down her valise by the stairs. Almost two years to the day since she'd been here with Trix. What a grand time they'd had that summer.

Julia stood in the foyer for several minutes, looking around. Against the far wall of her tiny parlor, swathed in white sheeting, was her grandmother's pianoforte, and she thought of how she and Trix had sat here with the windows open to the summer breeze, drinking champagne and playing comic songs. Just as when they were children, they'd toasted bread and cheese over the fire and walked barefoot on the small stretch of beach down below, explored the tide pools and taken midnight swims, and it was the freest, most glorious time she'd had since she was a girl.

Julia swallowed past the lump in her throat. There was no point in standing here mooning about the times when she'd been happy. She had to think, to plan, to decide what to do. But first things first. Spike at her heels, she walked through the tiny foyer past the parlor and dining room, making for the kitchen at the back, where she took stock of what supplies she needed for the larder. Tea, of course, milk, sugar, bread, butter, perhaps a few eggs, and some fish paste for sandwiches. She didn't need much, she knew, for she wouldn't be staying long.

Yardley would arrive at Marlowe's villa tomorrow and discover she'd fled. No one at Pixy Cove would tell him where she'd gone, but he would simply have to go into Torquay and make a few inquiries. He would learn she had filled the Mercedes with petrol—for motorcars and their need for fuel were not a commonplace thing in the West Country, even in the seaside resort of Torquay. He would also discover that Giselle and Pierre had taken the early train to St. Ives, which meant they were following her to Dovecotes. He would follow on the first train he could, the afternoon one that would bring him to her doorstep about five o'clock tomorrow evening. Julia, pulling her little pocket watch from her skirt pocket, saw that she had thirty hours left. If she didn't come up with a plan before then, she would have to catch a ship for the Continent out of St. Ives or Plymouth, as she had done so many times before, but really, what was the point?

She didn't want to run anymore. She just wanted to come home. Once Yardley had her imprisoned at Yardley Grange, it wasn't likely she'd ever be able to return here. Wasn't that why she'd come? Wasn't that why she really hadn't bothered to cover her tracks this time? Because she knew it was over, and she'd wanted to see her beloved home one last time before the end.

She didn't know what the end was, precisely, but she felt it coming. She could sense it, like a change in the air just before a thunderstorm. On the one hand, she didn't think she could bear what she knew Yardley had in store, and yet, on the other, she was so tired of trying to stop the inevitable. So, so tired.

She walked to the window and looked out at the rocky cliffs that jutted out into the sea. She could escape that way. She felt the hair on the back of her neck stand up, and she turned away from the window. *Maybe tomorrow*, she thought, not without a touch of humor. She was such a terrible procrastinator.

Leaving Spike at the house, she once again jumped into the Mercedes, but she drove only the few miles around St. Ives Bay, where she stopped at the grocer and bought tea, sugar, a pot of jam, and a pot of fish paste. She would stop by the dairy at Gwithian for milk, butter, and eggs, she decided as she placed her purchases in the boot of the Mercedes. She then circled to the front of the vehicle and cranked the engine, but before she could drive away, she spied a tall, wide-shouldered, and very familiar figure coming out of Grammercy's Bookshop across the street.

One hand on the steering wheel, one foot on the running board, Julia froze, giving a gasp of surprise. Was it really him? She stared, watching as he caught sight of her and stopped, seeming as astonished to see her as she was to see him.

The last time they'd met had been last year at Pixy Cove, when they'd both seen Sunderland haul Trix into his arms and lay an absolutely ripping kiss on her. As Trix's fiancé, Aidan probably wouldn't have deemed it ripping, but Julia wondered if he'd really been all that surprised by it. She herself had been able to perceive within a day of her arrival at Pixy Cove that Trix's feelings for Will were anything but gone, even though her wedding to Aidan had been a mere six weeks away.

Julia studied his face across the street that separated them. He didn't look happy to see her, but she couldn't really blame him. She'd been rather awful to him at Marlowe's house party, playing ragtime when she knew he hated it, teasing him mercilessly, and wondering how long his manners would hold out before he told her to sod off. She had no excuse, except that she'd been aggravated to know her selfless sacrifice at the St. Ives Ball seemed to have gone utterly to waste. Of course, there was also the fact that she'd always found chaffing Aidan deuced good sport.

But no matter how she'd teased him during that house party, he hadn't ever been anything but polite to her, and perhaps it was time she made amends. Odd, she reflected, how when one's day of judgment loomed, one began to feel contrite about one's past sins.

Still, a girl couldn't change her entire character because of one newfound resolution to be good, and when he glanced away, clearly uncomfortable, she couldn't resist being a bit—just a bit—of a tease. When he looked at her again, she flashed him a grin and waved. "How now, my prince has come!" she called across the street. "Hail, sweet prince."

He smiled, trying not to by pressing his lips together. He looked away again, and she thought perhaps he was seeking a means of escape. But then she realized he was only looking away to verify there was no traffic coming up the street before he crossed to her side.

"Baroness," he said with a bow as she hopped off the Mercedes' running board to land in front of him on the sidewalk. "Have you come to St. Ives for the summer?"

"No, winter," she answered at once.

Her unerring tendency to tease him over obvious statements made his pressed smile widen a little. "You're early," he pointed out.

She laughed. "So I am. Are you staying at Trathen Leagh?"

He nodded at the mention of his Cornish estate twelve miles down the coast, but then he tilted his head to one side, studying her. "You look tired, Baroness," he said unexpectedly. "Are you all right?"

"Of course," she said at once. "I'm right as rain."

"Why are you not at Torquay for August? I thought you would be."

"You did? Why, Aidan, I'm touched to know you've been thinking of me."

He shifted his weight a bit, embarrassed at having been caught doing such a thing, and she relented. "I was at Torquay, actually," she said, "but I decided to come home for a bit."

"Home?" His brows drew together quizzically. "I didn't know Yardley had property here."

"He doesn't. I mean my home. I own a cottage above Gwithian."

"Ah. I didn't know that. By the lighthouse?"

She shook her head. "The other side. It's called Dovecotes."

He frowned as if trying to place it. "I can't seem to recall an estate of that name."

"Estate?" She laughed at such a grand description. "Heavens, Dovecotes isn't an estate, by any means! It's just a little farmhouse, quite isolated, very spartan, but I do adore it. It's at the end of the Churchdown Road, although you can't see it from there. You have to turn down the lane to the sea at the point the road ends in order to find it. It's on the promontory there."

"So it has a sea view?"

"One of the best on the coast. And," she added proudly, "there's a pretty little cove below it, with a nice scrap of beach and some caves. But since you're a duke, it wouldn't seem like much to you. You're used to much grander places, I daresay."

"Not at all. It sounds lovely. I believe I know which cove you mean, for I've sailed around that promontory many times. There's a stone farmhouse up above it. Is that yours?" When she nodded, he went on, "It looks a very fine cove for bathing. Do you swim there, then?"

His gaze slid downward, and with that look, Julia saw her second chance, and hope flared to life.

"I do swim there," she answered his question, her brain working feverishly. "Nearly every day. In fact, I was going tomorrow afternoon. Yes," she added, improvising, fleshing out details even as she spoke, "with a picnic. But I wanted it to be a . . . umm . . . nice picnic. I fancied something very stylish and upper crust, you know, with linen and silver. And caviar," she added, knowing he loved the stuff, striving to remember Marlowe's house party the previous year and what other foods they both might like. "Ham, chicken, cucumber sandwiches, various cheeses. Blackberries."

Did he like blackberries? she wondered a little wildly. She couldn't remember.

He was looking at her, frowning a bit, looking dubious as she listed off the foods for this supposed picnic. "All that food for yourself?" he asked, and she felt a stab of fear that she'd overdone it and he would guess what she was up to.

"I always buy too much, I know, but they are particular favorites of mine."

"Indeed?" He sounded surprised, but not suspicious, bless the man. "I'm very fond of those things, as well."

"Really?" Wide-eyed, she looked at him, thanking God she was such a damned good liar. "What a coincidence."

It was now or never, she decided. "Would you like to come along?" she asked, tossing all her chips onto the table with that careless question.

It took him aback. He glanced away, then back at her. "On your picnic?"

"Why not? You can come see the view at Dovecotes, which is a splendid one, truly. I'm not merely boasting. If you come to call around eleven, we could have a walk down to the beach, have a picnic, perhaps play some chess. Do say you'll come. I'll bring the Victrola, and we'll play music while we eat. Mozart," she assured, "not ragtime. And we could have a bathe," she added, throwing that out there as casually as possible. "You would be back in St. Ives by six o'clock, with plenty of time to change into evening clothes and go off to whatever dinner party you're no doubt invited to."

He paused, and she could tell he was tempted. She waited, striving to look as if she didn't give a damn either way, as if her life didn't depend on this one thing. She could almost hear the click of the wheel of fortune spinning around. Red or black, yes or no, whichever came up, she was—as the gamblers were wont to say— all in.

He looked at her, and she saw in his eyes what she'd seen that day on the footbridge when he'd looked at her legs. She saw his desire, she knew what he was imagining, and her heart gave a leap of exhilaration with a hint of panic in it. How queer, she thought, to feel so exhilarated when one's entire future hung by a thread.

"I'm engaged," he said. "To be married."

That brief flash of exhilaration died, snuffed out like a candle, and Julia felt herself falling back into despair. Down, she went, down, down, down, straight into the pit of hell. If Aidan was engaged, his damnable sense of morality would never allow him to be seduced. Unless . . .

Champagne. She'd need champagne. That was the ticket. But first, she had to get him to change his mind. Already the refusal was on his lips. She spoke first.

"It's just a picnic, darling," she drawled, laughing. "I hadn't intended to seduce you." With that, she hopped into the Mercedes and gave him her naughtiest smile over one shoulder. "Not unless you want me to."

She blew him a kiss, released the brake lever, and drove away, knowing he wanted to come, hoping he would, vowing that if he did, she would put aside the distaste for lovemaking she'd acquired at Yardley's hand and make it the most wondrous fuck he'd ever had, and a long one, too, long enough for Yardley to arrive from the train station.

So much for feeling contrite about past sins.

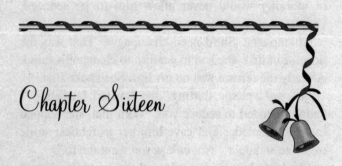

Chapter Sixteen

*J*ulia didn't know how far she ran. She just put one leg in front of the other and kept moving, guided only by her instincts, which at this moment were telling her to get as far away from Aidan as possible. Yet no matter how far she ran, she couldn't escape the lush taste of his kiss.

How could this happen? Why him? Why now? She'd kissed him that afternoon at Dovecotes and it hadn't been like this. She'd kissed him and touched him and lain naked with him asleep beside her, and there had been none of this sweet, hot passion inside her.

She'd taken up his challenge tonight to prove to him what she already thought she knew about herself—that she was dead to feelings like this. She'd gone to meet him knowing he would kiss her, believing the press of his lips to hers would evoke nothing, sure that it would all be like that day at Dovecotes. But tonight hadn't been like that at all, and she did not understand why. Where was the difference?

Her heart began to thump hard in her chest and her lungs began to burn, but she didn't stop. Impelled by panic and fear, though she didn't really know what she was afraid of, she kept running. But at last, the tightness of her corset and the burning rasp of her lungs and the hard pounding of her heart forced her to a stumbling halt.

She sank to her knees in the grass, sucking in deep, shuddering gasps of air, everything in her still rebelling against what had just happened, her mind still denying what was undeniable.

"No!" she panted, shaking her head back and forth with violent force, sending the spray of lilacs flying and bringing her loosened hair tumbling down around her face. "I don't want this!"

She might not want it, but it was there, all the sweet tenderness only a lover could evoke. Try as she might, she could not deny reality. Her lips still tingled from Aidan's kiss, her skin burned from his touch, and every cell and nerve ending in her body seemed charged with sensation. Suddenly she understood why this kiss was different from the ones at Dovecotes.

Because she was different. She was no longer the driven, desperate creature who wanted to trap one man to free herself from another.

All this time, all these years, she'd thought she was dead to feelings like this. But she hadn't been dead, she realized; she'd only been sleeping. Now she was awake from that long, cold, frigid sleep, and she was a woman again, vibrant and alive. She could feel lust again, rich and carnal and overpowering. She could feel joy and she could feel pain.

It scared the hell out of her.

Something tickled her face. She pressed her hands to her cheeks, and then stared at the tears on her fingertips, disbelieving and horrified.

She didn't cry anymore.

She'd learned to shut off tears a long time ago. Crying meant one could still feel, and she'd wanted to be numb. Crying meant one was vulnerable, and she'd needed to be invincible. Crying meant one felt pain, and she was crying because what Aidan made her feel also made her hurt. It burned her chest in racking sobs and smothering gasps for air. This was the pain of being happy, something she hadn't felt since she was a girl, when the future had been full of hope and the world had been wonderful and all life's possibilities lay ahead.

This was the pain of light and beauty and a man's tender kiss. It was the burn in your eyes when you looked into the bright, shining sun, and the pinch in your chest when you saw the first green shoots of springtime, and the lump in your throat when you heard the sound of a newborn baby's cry. It was life, life, life.

She didn't want it. She didn't want to feel like this, raw and open and laid bare. Not because of a man. Not because of his kiss. Not because of anything.

Julia put her face in her hands and sobbed like a

child, sure she must be broken beyond repair, because only someone broken could feel pain over something as beautiful as that kiss.

During the next few days, Julia did whatever she could to avoid Aidan. In the mornings, she breakfasted in her room. In the afternoons, she took the Mercedes for long drives or went with Spike for long walks, and being that she was so independent and her actions were often quite incomprehensible to her family, they didn't think her long absences from the house the least bit odd. In the evenings, she glued herself to Eileen like a limpet on a rock to keep Aidan at bay, but it didn't seem to matter, for much to her relief, he didn't seem any more inclined than she for a discussion of that kiss or a repetition of it.

But three mornings after that extraordinary kiss, Julia witnessed something so insufferable, so intolerable, that avoiding Aidan went to the wall.

She had just finished dressing, and the maids had brought her breakfast on a tray as usual. While sipping her morning tea, she walked to the window to discern what the weather might be. It had rained the day before, and if it rained again today, the roads might become too muddy for an afternoon drive in the Mercedes.

The day, however, seemed to be shaping up as quite fine, and Julia was relieved, but her relief was short-lived, for when she looked down over the south lawn, she caught sight of the very man she was trying to avoid, and with him was her beloved Spike.

Aidan was tossing a ball for the dog, and Spike was actually fetching it. Julia blinked, not quite able to believe what she was seeing, for despite his excellent guarding capabilities, Spike was probably the laziest dog in England. Yet he didn't look the least bit unhappy about fetching the ball for Aidan. Even more surprising, he didn't seem unhappy about being in the company of a male human being. Quite the opposite, Julia noted with growing alarm as the animal brought the ball to Aidan, laid it at his feet, and sat down in front of him, looking thoroughly pleased with himself as he waited for the requisite praise.

When Julia saw Aidan pat the dog, she couldn't stand it. She set down her tea with a clatter and flung up the window sash to stick her head out. "What in blazes are you doing with my dog?" she shouted down to him.

Aidan, in the act of throwing the ball again, stopped and glanced up. "Good morning," he called without answering her question, and tossed the ball. "Fetch," he commanded, sending poor Spike bounding across the grass again before turning to her. "I'm exercising your dog. God knows, he needs it."

"He does not! And I never said you could—" She broke off, too angry to continue as Spike once again trotted slavishly over to Aidan and deposited the ball at his feet. "Don't you dare move, either of you!" she commanded. "I'm coming down there at once!"

She slammed down the window. What gave him the right to do anything with her dog? She marched downstairs and out to the south lawn, glad it was too early for most of the other guests to be up and about as she strode across the grass toward Aidan, who had just thrown the ball again.

"Leave my dog alone," she ordered as she approached. "He hates you."

Spike, in seeming defiance of this assertion, walked right up to Aidan and deposited the ball at his feet.

"He doesn't hate me. In fact, we've become fast friends." He opened his left hand to reveal a handful of sliced bangers. "It's amazing what can be accomplished with a few sausages," he added as he gave one to the dog. "Good boy."

"You've been training my dog."

He laughed. "You say that as if I've been torturing him."

His laughter only fueled Julia's anger. "You have no right."

"Well, someone has to do it." He picked up the ball with his free hand and tossed it. "Fetch," he ordered, and as the dog ran after it, he turned to her. "Spike wouldn't be a menace to men if you didn't allow it."

"That doesn't justify your interference. Isn't this sort of thing too presumptuous for a gentleman?"

He shrugged, not seeming to care overmuch. "I'm tired of being growled at. I'm doing something about it."

She didn't want him to do something about it. Spike was her guardian, her knight at arms. "You're ruining everything, damn you," she said as Spike traded the ball for another sausage. "I bought him because he doesn't like men!"

"I think he might be over that particular aversion," Aidan said as he patted the dog's head.

"But you can't do this! Spike is a guard dog!"

He looked at her thoughtfully. "Against who? Yardley?"

She pressed her lips together and looked away, but she could feel his gaze watching her. "Yardley hated my dog," she said after a moment. "The dog hated him. I found that . . . convenient."

"I realize you bought him to keep Yardley at bay, Julia. I appreciate how unhappy you were in your marriage. How could I not after what you did to end it?"

You don't know the half of it, she thought.

"Julia," he said, his voice gentle, "I won't pry, but—"

"Thank God for that!"

"But Yardley's gone now," Aidan reminded, moving closer, bending his head, forcing her to look at him. "So why do you care if Spike no longer hates men? Why should it bother you if your dog and I become friends? What are you afraid of?"

Afraid? God, she was a mass of fears, too many fears to name. She looked at him, helpless to explain. "I'm not afraid of anything."

Aidan turned to the dog. "Sit," he ordered.

Spike did so, and so quickly it was like a military snap to attention. Aidan held up his hand, palm toward the animal's snout. "Stay."

When he returned his attention to her, Aidan was smiling a little. "Shall I tell you what I think?" He didn't wait for an answer, but went on, "If Spike and

I become friends, that's a barrier down, isn't it? Spike is a line of defense. Like a witty remark. Like a lie. Like running away. I just wish I knew why you need defenses. Perhaps it's simply to avoid being vulnerable. To prevent other people from seeing what you really feel."

His gaze, tender and warm, was too much to bear. "And just what," she said through clenched teeth, "do you think I feel for you?"

"After the other night, I think we both know the answer to that question, Julia."

Her toes curled inside her shoes and she felt that brandylike warmth seeping into her. She tried to speak, but what could she say? She ducked her head instead, staring at the ground.

He leaned closer. "What I wonder is why you can't admit it. Is it that you want me to go first, is that it? I will."

He bent down, ducking his head to look into her face. "I want you. I've always wanted you. I want you so much, I can't think about anything or anyone else." He smiled, and the tenderness in it pierced her defenses like a knife through butter. "Your turn."

"I don't want you," she lied, her voice so unconvincing to her own ears that she winced. Impossible to be cold and numb when she felt so warm and alive. She struggled to say something that would drive him away, wondering why she wanted that so much, fearing it was impossible anyway. "I had enough of you in Cornwall."

His smile widened. "That's a lie."

Don't. Don't see inside me. She looked at him with

a pretense of scorn. "That's what every man believes when a woman spurns his advances."

"Spurns?" He was grinning now, the impossible man. "So that's why you wrapped your arms around my neck and kissed me back. You were *spurning* me. I didn't realize."

Her face grew hot with embarrassment. She didn't remember doing that. "I did no such thing."

"Oh yes, you did. You also raked your hands through my hair and put your tongue in my mouth. Forgive me if I didn't interpret those things as a spurning of my advances."

She stared at him, unable to remember these wanton actions on her part. She'd done them in Cornwall, of course, but they had been deliberate, calculated, and the idea that she'd done them the other night in a passionate daze made it all even more unbearable.

The taste of him the other night came back to her—a full-bodied, lush, and fleshly taste—like port-soaked strawberries. And the warmth in her deepened and spread, arousing her.

You're numb. You're numb.

Such a lie. She wasn't numb at all.

"I don't want you," she repeated. Another lie.

He continued to look at her, still smiling, but he didn't say anything, and the silence goaded her on.

"All right, all right!" she cried, furious that he was so sure of himself, when she was the one used to feeling that way. Furious that he seemed to know her feelings better than she knew them herself. "I don't want to want you! I want you to leave me alone. Is that better?"

"Yes, it is better," he murmured. "At least you're being honest. Can we keep that honesty going for a bit?"

"What do you mean?"

"There are things about that day in Cornwall that I don't remember, things I don't know, things I think you can tell me about what happened."

She licked her suddenly dry lips. "You know what happened."

"I told you, I don't remember most of it. I'd like you to tell me about it."

"Tell you about it?" She forced a laugh. "Darling, what's to tell? We got drunk and had a tumble. It isn't particularly complex, you know. People do it every day."

"Don't." He reached out to cup her cheek. "Don't prop up those defenses. Don't put on the sophisticated façade you seem able to don at will. Don't deflect. Don't give me a charming smile and a glib, witty reply. I'd just like to know certain things about that day that only you can tell me."

"There's nothing to tell!" she said, and jerked free. Cursing herself for ever having come out here, she decided a retreat was in order.

She bent down and grasped Spike's leash, then stepped around Aidan. "From now on, leave my dog alone," she said, and started across the lawn toward the gardens, but she'd barely taken three steps before she was halted by resistance at the other end of the leash, and she turned to find Spike had not moved to follow her.

"Come, Spike," she said, and patted her thigh in an encouraging fashion, but the dog still did not move.

"I ordered him to stay," Aidan reminded, as if that should matter.

She didn't give a damn what her dog had been commanded to do by Aidan, or anyone else. "Spike, come," she said, her voice more commanding than before.

The bulldog whined and looked at Aidan as if uncertain what to do and expecting him to provide new instructions. When Aidan did not do so, he whined again and returned his gaze to her with something like apology in his droopy brown eyes. To Julia, that was the last straw.

"Traitor!" she burst out, and to her mortification, tears stung her eyes, tears of anger and frustration, hurt and fear, tears she knew were all out of proportion to a dog's disobedience. She felt vulnerable, fragile, and she knew she had to escape before she let Aidan see it.

"Be damned to both of you," she muttered, and turned, walking away, leaving her formerly faithful friend in the hands of the man who had suddenly become her nemesis.

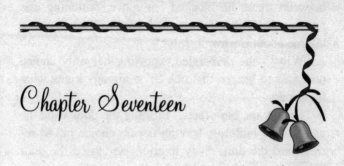

idan was following her. With a pang of alarm, Julia quickened her steps across the turf, but she was headed in the wrong direction to escape him. In order to return to the house, she'd have to face him, and that was the last thing she wanted right now.

In the distance, she spied the lavender house, and deeming that her best option, she hurried toward it. When she reached the small stone building, she jerked the door open, and stepped inside, but the moment she started to shut the door behind her, she realized that there was no latch or bolt on the inside to keep out the man who was coming toward her with a very determined expression on his face. "I want to be alone," she said, hoping his innate chivalry would impel him to withdraw. "Please go away."

Aidan's sense of chivalry, however, didn't seem to

extend quite that far. When she started to shut the door between them, he blocked her move, flattening one palm against the splintering oak panels. "I want you to tell me about Cornwall, Julia."

"Why?" she demanded, knowing her only choice now was to brazen this out. "You already know what happened."

"I know the bare facts." Pushing the door wide, he entered the building, leaving her no choice but to retreat into the dim, dusty interior. He closed the door behind him and leaned back against it. "I want more than that."

Her throat went dry. She glanced around, but the lavender house, used for drying herbs, had only tiny windows to let in a minimum of light and no other doors. Cornered, she raised her chin. "I don't owe you any explanations."

"I think you do. I think I'm entitled to have my questions answered. You were right that I went to your cottage because I wanted to. And although I don't remember it, I have a pretty clear picture of what happened later."

She tried not to grimace at the certainty in his voice as he made that statement.

"And God knows," he went on, "if it was anything like that kiss the other night, I can understand why I lost my head so completely and bedded a married woman."

Julia looked away so he wouldn't see the truth in her eyes.

"And," he went on, "it was obvious to me all along

what your intentions were that day, putting together a picnic of foods I like, seducing me. I was flattered. I didn't know then that I was being used." He paused. "I applaud your timing," he said, his voice suddenly tight. "It was flawless. Yardley arrived at just the right moment."

Don't do this. Don't relive it. Just forget it. She forced herself to look at him, and she smiled, a wide, artificial smile that made her jaw ache. "Well, it seems you already know everything," she said brightly. "I don't know what I can tell you."

"I want to know what you *felt*."

Her smile vanished, and she stared at him in dismay, her throat tight. "What did you say?" she whispered.

"I want to know what you felt."

"What does it matter what I felt? Good God," she added, striking out in self-defense, "is it praise for your lovemaking prowess you're after? You were wonderful, darling, the best lover I've ever had. And considering all my previous affairs, that's saying something, isn't it? There," she added with the air of one patting a child on the head. "Feel better?"

It didn't. It made him angry. She could tell by the press of his lips and the muscle that worked in his jaw. She didn't blame him. She was being awful, she knew, but she couldn't help it, not when he was pressing her for things she did not want to tell him, things she never wanted him to find out. When he stepped forward, she stepped back.

"Why should being so obviously patronized make

me feel better?" he demanded, stepping forward, forcing her backward until she hit the cool stone wall of the lavender house. "Another time, I might be curious, I admit, to know how my lovemaking ability stacks up against what must be—if the society pages are true—a significant amount of competition, but no. I want to know what you thought, what you felt. I want to know why you chose me." He took a deep breath and reached out, cupping her face in his hands, his fingers tangling in the hair at her temples, tilting her head back and forcing her to look at him.

"Did you want me at all?" he demanded. "Or was I just the mug who happened to be standing on the street that day? You knew Yardley was coming on the five o'clock train. You must have done. So, why did you choose me? If not me, if I hadn't happened along, would you have just seduced someone else?"

Admitting he'd been the only man she'd ever considered as a lover was impossible; she could never allow herself to be that vulnerable. And yet, try as she might, she couldn't seem to prop up her defenses. If tearing them down was his goal, he seemed to be succeeding admirably.

"So you're refusing to tell me what I want to know, hmm?" he asked as she remained silent. "How about if I tell you what I remember, then?" He eased his body closer, and his breath was warm against her mouth. "You smelled like lilacs. And when you held out that glass of champagne to me, I remember just how you smiled, and the thought went through my mind to leave, leave now, this is a mistake, that if I drink this champagne, I'll never be able to be this close to you and not have you. And I remember thinking I'm such a fool because I came that day, proud bastard that I am, to prove I could resist you, to prove I could live up to my principles."

He laughed under his breath as he kissed her lips, her cheek, her jaw. She began to shake, deep down, on the edge of feeling. "Damn me a fool for thinking I could ever resist you."

He pulled back a little to look into her face. "I drank that champagne. And then you offered me another, and another, as you told me all the things I wanted to hear. That it wouldn't hurt me to live a little before settling down to matrimony, that a few drinks wouldn't hurt. I told myself you were right, I reveled in it. Another petty rebellion, just like when I was sixteen years old. But then you knew that's how I would feel, didn't you?"

"Yes," she said, feeling wretched.

"I remember that white dress you wore," he murmured, "and how you gathered it up around your knees, and how I watched your legs as you waded into the water. But you knew I'd watch, didn't you?"

Guilt slid through her at his recitation of how thoroughly she'd played him. "Yes. I knew."

He closed his eyes. "You dove underwater, and when you came up and started walking back toward me, that dress was plastered to your body. God," he added in a hoarse whisper, his lips brushing hers as he spoke, "it was so transparent, I could see your skin underneath. No doubt that was why you wore it."

Aidan opened his eyes, and somehow, looking into their warm depths hurt her, like an exposed wound in her chest. "And then," he went on, his voice hardening, "you sank down on the sand in front of me, running your fingers along your neckline just above your breasts. 'Go on,' you said, tilting your head back and leaning toward me. 'Take it. You know you want to.' And I did want it. God, I wanted it all, right there in the sand."

Julia didn't reply. She didn't like this, hearing from his point of view just how relentless she'd been, and yet, his words were stirring arousal inside her, arousal she'd been unable to feel that day, that she didn't want to feel now, that she never wanted to feel again.

"I remember your lips were full and soft when I touched them." His thumbs brushed over her mouth, making her shiver, and she tried to be numb.

"I remember kissing your throat." He ducked his head to press his lips to the pulse in her neck. "And I thought your skin was like warm satin. And then I kissed your mouth . . ." He lifted his head, and his lips brushed hers, a light tease. "You tasted like the blackberries we'd eaten. And I felt as if I was drowning, and I didn't give a damn if it was wrong. I felt as if I could go on kissing you forever."

His words made it all seem so tender, so intimate, when the whole time, she'd been striving against intimacy, striving to feel no tenderness, striving to seem warm on the outside and be ice cold on the inside, so that when the moment came, she wouldn't lose her nerve. "Aidan, I—"

"I just couldn't say no to what you were offering. Hell," he added, with a laugh, "if you'd stopped at that point, I might even have begged."

"Don't." She didn't want to hear any more. She didn't want to hear what he thought, how he felt, that she'd hurt him. She couldn't bear it. "Why are you doing this?" She tried to duck past him, but he was quicker, wrapping one arm around her waist, pulling her hard against him.

"I don't remember anything clearly after the kissing part," he said, his voice hardening to a ruthless tone she'd never heard before. "Somehow, we ended up in the kitchen, I know that. I remember you unbuttoned my trousers, and I pulled down your dress, but other than that, it's all a blur. An erotic, delicious blur. So you'll have to fill in those missing parts for me. Did we make love right there on the kitchen floor, and then go upstairs? Or did you take me upstairs first? How did we do it? Were you on top, or was I?"

Desperate, she tried to free herself, but he would not let her go. "I want the truth. These questions have been tormenting me since August, and I want some answers, Julia. Did you want me? Did you? At any point, did you feel what I felt? When our bodies were pressed together and I was inside you, did you want it? Like it? Did it feel good? Or did you stare at the ceiling and wonder if Yardley had gotten off the train yet?"

She couldn't take any more. "Stop it!" she shouted, slamming her fists against the hard wall of his chest. "I can't tell you what you want to know! I can't!"

"You mean you won't."

"I mean I can't," she shot back, at the end of her tether, "because it didn't happen!"

The moment the words were out of her mouth, she wanted to take them back, but it was too late.

"What do you mean?" he asked tightly, and let her go only long enough to grip her by the arms. "What do you mean it didn't happen? Of course it bloody well happened. I remember pulling down your dress and your hands on my groin. I remember—" He paused, for everything after that was blank.

"And that's as far as we got. You stopped." She laughed, a laugh without humor, for she felt the same disbelief now that she'd felt then, the same disbelief that she saw on his face now. "You said no, it was wrong, I was married and you were engaged, and it was wrong for us to do this."

"I stopped?" He shook his head. "I had my tongue in your mouth and your naked breasts in my hands. Your hands were wrapped around my—" He broke off and shook his head again. "There's no way I could have stopped. No man could stop at that point."

"You did," she said, hearing the acerbic note of her own voice. "You said you couldn't do this to Rosalind, you couldn't cuckold another man, you couldn't dishonor me. Even drunk, even randy as a stallion, you had to uphold your principles. I couldn't believe it. We were standing in the kitchen of my cottage, sweaty, breathing hard, and nearly naked, and you were calling a halt."

"Nearly naked?" he echoed. "Julia, we were naked! I woke up in your bed without a stitch on and your damned husband standing in the doorway! I don't need you to refresh my memory about that part. And you were naked, too. I sure as hell didn't dream it."

She sagged in his hold, feeling all the fight go out of her. "You insisted on going home, and I said you were too drunk to ride a horse until you'd sobered up a little, so I made coffee. And in your cup, I put a dollop of laudanum."

"Laudanum?" His voice rose instantly to a shout. "You drugged me?"

"I had to. Yardley was coming for me, and I couldn't let you leave. You passed out from the laudanum, and my manservant, my maid, and I carried you upstairs and put you in my bed. I took off the rest of our clothes and waited for Yardley to come. I remembered all those years ago, when you told me how drink affects your memory, and I could only hope you wouldn't remember calling a halt or realize afterward what I'd done with the coffee or remember that nothing really happened. When Yardley came, you had just woken up, and after he stalked out, you looked at me and said, 'Oh, my God, I bedded another man's wife.' That confirmed what I'd hoped you would believe, and I let you continue to think it. So, even though kissing was as far as we got, all the rest of my plan worked like a charm. My luck finally changed, and things went right."

"Right?" He let go of her and rubbed his hands over his face. "*Merde*," he muttered.

Despite the awful circumstances, she almost laughed at that. "Only you, Aidan, would say obscene words in French because it's more civilized."

He didn't seem to find that amusing. He lowered his hands and glared at her. "I refused you, so you drugged me?" He said it as if he still couldn't quite believe it. "Of all the low-down, conniving—" He broke off, as if trying to regain his temper. "I wrote a statement that we were intimate that afternoon! I swore to its veracity in court! And it was a lie? I don't suppose it ever occurred to you to tell me any of this sooner?"

"I couldn't take the chance, not until my divorce decree was final. You're so noble and honorable. I couldn't risk that you would go to Yardley and confess the truth. He'd have had the divorce decree reversed. And as for telling you beforehand, that would never have worked. You have this hopelessly old-fashioned idea that marriage bonds are sacred and infidelity is wrong and truth is noble. You'd never have agreed to any sort of charade if you knew it was a charade."

Tight-lipped, he looked away. "I'd like to think I could have found an honorable way to help you."

"How? There were no honorable ways. Would you have colluded with a woman you barely knew and certainly didn't like to stage an affair? Collusion is against the law. Would you have knowingly helped me stage a love nest and then lied about it in court?"

"I did lie about it in court!"

"You didn't know you were lying."

"And you think that justifies what you did?"

"I don't give a damn about justifying anything!" she shouted, her own anger rising up. "Not to you, or a judge, or even before God!" Now it was her turn to be angry. "My husband was going to drag me back and force me to live with him again. I did what I did because I had no choice!"

"No choice? He was your husband, the man you married, the man you swore to honor and obey, the man with whom you were supposed to have sons."

"Sons?" She spat the word. "I'd have spawned sons of the devil before I'd have given that man a son." Now she didn't have to be cold. Coldness was flowing through her veins like ice water. "I told you, I hated my husband, and there was no way in hell I was going back to him. You asked me a minute ago what I'd have done if you turned me down, and the answer is anything. I would have done anything! I'd have shot him with a gun, jumped off a cliff, or fucked the Archbishop of Canterbury, as long as it meant I didn't have to go back to that man!"

He shook his head, staring at her in appalled bewilderment. "Why? What did he do to make you hate him so?"

Her anger melted into fear. Her throat closed up, and she couldn't speak, couldn't force words out. She could only stare back at him, helpless to explain.

Still, something of what she felt must have shown in her face—the sickening fear, the panic and dismay.

Aidan's expression changed, first to shock, then a dawning awareness. "My God," he muttered. "I never understood. I thought your marriage was unhappy. I thought it was because you were having affairs and running away from your husband. But it wasn't that at all, was it?"

She jerked her chin, looking away from the compassion in his eyes. "No."

"Julia." His hands cupped her cheeks, lifting her face so that she had to look at him again. "God, Julia, what did he do to you?"

How could she answer that question? How could she tell him the things Yardley had done to her? She hadn't even been able to tell her own family. "What does it matter?" she cried. "Why should you care?"

"Because I do," he said simply, his thumbs caressing her cheeks. "I care."

She'd hurt him. Until this moment, she hadn't appreciated that fact. Julia froze, staring up at him, dismayed. Most men wouldn't have been hurt by her actions. Angry, yes, humiliated, perhaps. But she had not only roused Aidan's anger and caused him humiliation, she had also inflicted pain. She hadn't known she had the power to truly hurt him, not until now.

Yet, despite that, he was looking at her with tenderness, so much tenderness, she couldn't bear it. "Don't!" she said fiercely, bringing her hands up between his upraised arms, shoving his hands aside. "Don't touch me! Don't care about me. Don't want me. Just leave me alone, Aidan. For God's sake, leave me alone."

She ducked past him, but his words followed her to the door. "That's rather difficult now, Julia. You work for me."

Work for him? Did he think she could continue that now? Manage his social engagements and guide him toward a suitable wife? Her hands were shaking, she realized. She clenched them at her sides and took a deep breath before she answered. "Considering what happened the other night, I think we both see that my continuing to work for you is impossible. Consider this Mrs. Boodle's resignation."

With that, she left, and this time he didn't try to stop her. She ran out of the lavender house, away from the nightmare of her past, away from him, and most of all, away from the tenderness in his face when he looked at her. Running away, after all, was the thing she did best.

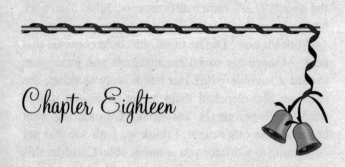

Chapter Eighteen

Aidan stared at the closed door Julia had slammed behind her, but it was not the door's peeling paint that he saw, for fixed in his mind's eye was the image of Julia's face. Julia had a face that was expressive, vivid, and mobile, and he'd seen many emotions there before—mischief, reticence, disdain, amusement, desire, to name a few—but he'd never before seen fear.

She'd tried to hide it by running away, but it was too late for hiding. She had not only hated her husband, she'd been afraid of him, and the possible reasons for her fear sickened and enraged him. He wanted to find Yardley and kill the bastard for making her look like that.

What had he done to her? Had he beat her? Beatings would have given her grounds for divorce by cruelty, but proving that sort of thing was difficult. Still, he had the feeling this went far beyond purely physical abuse.

In fact, he had the gut-wrenching feeling that it was even worse.

What sickened him almost as much as contemplating what she'd been through was his own willful blindness about it. Whatever her husband had done, it had made her life enough of a nightmare that she was driven to the most desperate measures to end it. He should have understood that long before now, but he had refused to see. He'd wanted to blame her for the collapse of her marriage, he'd wanted to paint her the villainess, the seductress, the adulteress. Putting her into that role made his lust for a married woman and his subsequent behavior easier for his conscience to live with.

Despite the fact that it was making him take a long, hard look in the mirror, Aidan was glad he'd caught the truth in her face. He was glad.

He thought about the other things she'd revealed to him. She'd drugged him, but strangely enough, he didn't care. She'd lied to him, and to everyone, and he didn't care about that either. Her actions had been compelled by her need to save herself, and though he didn't know precisely why, he didn't need to. The fear in her face had told him her reasons had been good ones. Perhaps he was hopelessly skirt-smitten, but he meant what he'd said earlier. Her reasons didn't matter because he cared about her.

He wanted to help her overcome this. He wanted to help her heal.

That was such a chivalrous-sounding notion. Aidan's mouth curved with both self-disparagement and a touch of humor. Julia had called him chivalrous, and he'd always liked to believe that about himself, but he knew now that his chivalry toward her was, and always had been, self-serving. If he helped her, he might be able to bed her. It was that simple.

No, Aidan was forced to admit, when it came to Julia, he wasn't chivalrous at all.

Julia didn't come down to dinner, pleading a headache, and Aidan was rather glad of it, for he didn't think he could bear having her so tantalizingly close, not when she'd surely put on that witty, aloof mask she seemed able to don at will.

Everyone else gathered as usual in the drawing room for entertainments, but Aidan wanted to spare himself any conversations with Eileen McGill about her dear niece, or from any conversation at all, for that matter. Nor did he want to engage in the game of charades being organized by Geoff and Vivian. He took his single glass of port and walked over to Paul, who was reading a book. The other man looked up as Aidan halted by his chair.

"Feel up to a game of chess?"

Paul set the book aside at once, and the two men excused themselves from the others in the drawing room and went into Paul's study, where the chessboard was always kept ready.

Paul opened the windows that gave onto the terrace to let in the cool, evening air, then they both sat down, and Paul reached for two of the pawns, one of each color.

"Are you sure you want to play?" he asked, grinning at Aidan as he held the pawns behind his back. "I've been playing chess with Colonel Westholm all winter," he added as he held out his closed fists, "because Westholm is one of the few men I know who can defeat you."

Aidan chose the left one, and Paul began to laugh. "Black," he said, opening his hand. "I start."

Aidan shrugged, seeming unperturbed, and leaned back in his chair as his friend returned the chess pieces to their places on the board. "Having the opening move won't help you, Paul. Nor will all your practicing with Westholm."

Paul slid a pawn forward. "This could be just like our tennis game last month."

"We'll see."

The game started at a rapid clip, but after two hours, it slowed to a crawl, and though Paul was an excellent player, the game wasn't challenging enough to keep his mind away from the most fascinating woman he'd ever met. He studied her cousin across the chessboard, wondering how he might broach the topic, and he knew there was no civil, polite, gentlemanly way. "Paul?"

The other man slid his rook forward and looked up. "Hmm?"

"What happened to Julia?"

Reticence entered the other man's expression, quite a proper reaction under the circumstances. "What do you mean?"

"This isn't a time for discretion, Paul. If you know anything—"

"I don't. Julie is a law unto herself, and she reveals only what she chooses to."

Not always, he thought, remembering the way she'd blurted out the truth about Cornwall to him this afternoon. He suspected she'd never intended to tell him about it, that she'd meant to take the secret to her grave, along with the truth about her husband.

"It's your move," Paul prompted.

Aidan glanced at the board, and moved his knight, uninterested in thinking out chess strategy. "Did he beat her? Did he—" Aidan paused for a deep breath, rage flaring up in him as he forced himself to ask the question. "Did he rape her?"

Paul's face revealed nothing. "A man can't rape his wife," he said coldly. "Don't you know the law?"

"So he did rape her." As he spoke, Aidan's rage deepened. "That bastard."

Paul moved his bishop, then leaned back, studying Aidan with a thoughtful frown. "Why all these questions about Julia? Why should it matter to you, now?"

His eyes met Paul's across the chessboard. "It matters."

Paul's gaze raked over his face. "So it's like that, is it?"

He knew what his friend meant. "Yes. It's like that."

Paul nodded slowly. "I wondered, after . . . Cornwall." He paused, lowering his gaze to the board. "Her divorce is final now," he reminded.

"I know. Why did she need one? That's what I'm trying to understand."

The other man rubbed four fingers across his forehead. "Look, Aidan, I don't know what happened. I know Yardley was a bastard, I know Julia hated him. Beyond that, I can't go because I genuinely don't know. I do know it was all a nightmare for her, and I have certain theories, of course, but I have no intention of sharing them with you or anyone else. If you want to know about her marriage to Yardley, you'll have to ask her."

"I did. She wouldn't tell me."

Paul nodded, not looking surprised. "She's never told any of us about Yardley, either, if that makes you feel better, except to say he was a brute. What that entailed, I can only imagine."

"Couldn't you have done something?" But even as Aidan asked it, he knew it was an unfair question.

"I tried, but—" Paul swallowed hard and looked away. "There's not many ways out of a bad marriage."

"No," Aidan muttered, wretched. "I suppose not."

He let it go at that. He supposed he didn't need to know the sordid details; in fact, a part of him would rather never hear whatever awful secrets had impelled her to the actions she'd taken. What he really wanted, he realized, was for Julia to trust him enough to tell him. And he wanted her, damn it all, more than ever before.

She wanted him, too. He knew that. But he wanted more from her than just her desire. He wanted her to welcome it, revel in it, be made happy by it. That, he knew, was too much to expect of her right now, and that meant he had to do what she wanted and leave. If he stayed, he wouldn't be able to resist pursuing her, and instead of bringing her closer to him, that might push her even further away.

"Checkmate," he said, moving his bishop.

"Damn." Paul fell back in his chair. "I didn't even see that one coming."

"You never see that one coming. It's the one move you never see."

With that, Aidan stood up. "I'm leaving in the morning, Paul. But," he added, "if you think there's any chance she might want to see me, I'll be at Trathen Leagh."

Paul nodded in understanding. "If you still want her, and she still wants you, all well and good. God knows she deserves some happiness, and you do as well. But she's fragile, Aidan. She doesn't see it, of course. If you hurt her in any way—I don't mean physically," he hastened to add. "I just mean in general, if you hurt her, she might break apart completely."

"I know what you meant. Before I let that happen, I would kill myself."

With that, Aidan left the study. He went upstairs and instructed Dawes to pack his things, then he went to the library, pulled out a current Bradshaw, and began looking up trains to St. Ives. She'd told him to leave her alone, and he was going to respect her wishes, but only for now. He wasn't giving up, by any means. There were times, however, when a man had to make a strategic retreat to win the game.

* * *

Julia spent a restless night. She'd eaten dinner in her room, occupying her time and her mind by writing letters to friends, but once she'd crawled into bed, she'd done nothing but toss and turn, unable to sleep. Every time she closed her eyes, she'd seen Aidan standing before her in the lavender house, his eyes filled with desire and tenderness and anger on her behalf, and it was a combination she'd never seen in any man's eyes before.

Stephen had desired her, and he'd loved her, but it had never been tender. It had been giddying and breathless and wrenching, a passionate, desperate, immature love, a love doomed, she saw now, to eventually end. The fact that Stephen had died had only ended it sooner.

As for Yardley, the only other basis for her experience of men—well, tenderness was something he'd never displayed, not to her, not to his mother, not to anyone. She doubted he even knew what tenderness was.

Aidan, looking at her yesterday, had been so different. It hurt, yes, and it made her afraid, but that was because it was genuine and real, and it asked her to reciprocate, something she was terribly afraid she would never be able to do. She was brittle and hard—too hard for tenderness, too cold for lovemaking, too afraid of pain. And there would be pain. When it was over, when passion was sated and died, there was no future for her with him. She'd had enough pain already; she didn't want the pain of heartbreak.

At last, Julia fell into a troubled sleep, but she woke

before eight, unfreshened by her few hours of rest. But by the time she had bathed and dressed, she felt more like herself, more sure of her ground. She had done the right thing by resigning her post and ending any chance for a love affair with him before it could begin.

Still, she couldn't spend the remainder of the week avoiding him. Deciding she had to face him sometime, she went downstairs for breakfast, but when she entered the dining room, she learned she wouldn't have to face him at all.

"Trathen's gone?" She stilled, one hand holding the cup of tea she'd just poured from the pot on the sideboard, her other hand on the back of the chair she'd just pulled out at the table. She stared at Paul, who had imparted this news quite casually between bites of kidneys and bacon. "Gone where?"

Her cousin shrugged and took a sip of his tea. "Trathen Leagh, I expect. There's an early train to St. Ives."

"But—" She broke off, for there was no point in asking why. Aidan had clearly seen, as she did, the futility of the two of them continuing any sort of association. Best all around that he'd left. "Right," she said, nodding, and forced a little laugh, shaking her head, trying to shake off the absurd disappointment she felt at his departure. "Trathen Leagh. His estate in Cornwall. Of course."

Well aware of the curious gazes of the other guests at the table, she shrugged and pasted on an indifferent expression, careful to hide the stinging disappointment. Eileen, Jane Heyer, Peggy Bourne-West—all of them were looking at her, frowning, their gazes curious, speculative. They were wondering, no doubt, if she was carrying on with Trathen even now. Eugenia was also looking at her, dubious of her earlier assurances that there was nothing between Trathen and her, that, of course, any young unmarried ladies coming to the house party had a clear field for his attention.

Under their stares, Julia felt like such a hypocrite.

She stood up again. "I think I'll take my tea outside on the terrace," she mumbled. "It's so nice this morning."

Cup and saucer in hand, she walked out of the dining room and out to the terrace. Sitting down at one of the wrought-iron tables that overlooked the south lawn, she stared at the lavender house in the distance. Safe now from any prying eyes, she thought of him, of yesterday, of how she'd finally told him the truth, and how the truth had driven him away. But then she'd known it would. That was why she hadn't told him sooner, why she'd never wanted him to know. Despite all her protestations to the contrary, despite all her assurances that she didn't care, Aidan's opinion of her mattered. Aidan's opinion had always mattered.

Footsteps on the terrace interrupted her, and she straightened with a little jerk as Paul joined her.

"Lovely morning," he said, pausing beside her chair and pulling out his cigarette case. "Nice for a drive."

"Yes," she agreed. "Quite."

He opened the case, extracted a cigarette and a match, then slid the case back into his breast pocket.

"There's a good supply of petrol in the stables," he went on as he bent to strike the match on the stone railing nearby.

Julia looked at him, frowning as she watched him light his cigarette, baffled as to why he'd feel it necessary to remind her of such a well-established fact. He always kept a supply of petrol in the stables, had for years now. Beatrix's Daimler was stored there while she was in Egypt, and Paul sometimes drove it. Also, Julia often stayed at Danbury, and extra petrol had always been available in case Yardley had decided to make himself a nuisance and she had needed to fuel the motorcar and flee. "Yes, I know," she answered. "I used a bit of it the other day."

"Plenty left, though, I expect." Cigarette in hand, he moved to sit opposite her, tossing the match into the ash canister on the table.

"Thinking of taking a drive, are you?"

"I'm not, but I thought you might." He met her gaze across the table. "Cornwall's what, five hours away?"

She stared back at him. "I'm not going to Cornwall."

"Why not? Plenty of time to arrive at Dovecotes before dark."

"I'm not going to Cornwall!"

"Sorry, my mistake." He got up and turned to look out over the garden. "It's just that when you found out Trathen was gone, you looked like a little girl who wasn't going to get any Christmas."

"Oh, I did not."

"Julie." It was a sigh on his lips. He turned. "You

spent years getting away from Yardley, and yet here you are, still running from him even after he's long gone. Don't you think it's time for you to run toward something for a change, instead of away?"

Julia's mind went back to that afternoon with Aidan at Dovecotes last year, then she thought of his kisses a few days ago, and she suddenly wondered what it would be like to meld the two. Could it be like that? she wondered with a flash of hope. Could she have that afternoon at Dovecotes again, but without the desperation and panic she'd felt? Could she be again as she'd been a few days ago—vibrant and alive, not numb and cold? Could she be kissed and caressed and filled with desire? Could she cease to be what Yardley had made her?

"Paul?" She jumped up. "You're absolutely right. Have Warren fill the Mercedes, would you?" She started back into the house. "I have to find Giselle and pack."

Half an hour later, valise in one hand, Spike's leash in the other, she stood on the front steps at Danbury, watching as the chauffeur brought the Mercedes around. When Warren stopped the vehicle beside the drive, and stepped aside for her, she slid into the driver's seat. Warren put her valise in the back beside the jug of additional petrol and Spike hopped happily into the passenger seat. As Julia drove down the lane, she glanced over her shoulder at Danbury Downs. It was a familiar view, for she'd left Danbury this way many times before, but this time, the view seemed completely different. She was running again, but this time, she wasn't running away from a man. She was running to him, and that was a ripping miracle.

The drive from Danbury to Gwithian was a bit under five hours in the Mercedes, for in Cornwall, the roads weren't always smooth, and a motorcar couldn't ever really travel above twenty miles an hour. As always when she drove, Spike was sitting in the passenger seat with his muzzle lifted to the breeze, and Julia was thinking.

Not of escape or railway schedules or which ships left which harbor towns or if detectives were following her. She was thinking about Aidan, and as she did, she felt a rush of breathless exhilaration and giddy excitement she hadn't felt since she was a girl. In fact, she felt more joy now than she'd felt then, perhaps because it took suffering to truly appreciate sweetness. It took pain to savor bliss. As a girl of seventeen, she hadn't understood that. She understood it now.

At first, she thought she would go straight to Trathen Leagh, but she changed her mind and stopped in the town of Liskeard, where she sent Aidan a cable. In Redruth, she bought supplies, and in Hayle, she bought chipped ice. By half past two o'clock, she was turning off the Churchdown Road and onto the lane to Dovecotes, feeling nervous as a cat on hot bricks.

Would he come? she wondered, her heart pounding as she drove down the rutted lane. When she saw a gig with his coat of arms standing in front of her cottage and him sitting on the seat, her heart twisted in her breast with a joy that she didn't even try to extinguish, and she lifted one hand from the wheel to wave. When she halted the motorcar in front of the cottage and saw him smiling at her, she laughed out loud.

Spike saw him, too, and jumped down from the passenger seat, not with low, warning growls, but with eager, happy barks. He ran to Aidan, who stepped down from the gig and immediately reminded the animal who was in charge. "Sit."

Spike obeyed and was immediately rewarded with a pat on the head, a rub behind the ears, and a bit of praise. "Good boy."

Julia secured the brake lever and stepped down from the motorcar. "You received my message, I see, asking you to meet me here."

"Asking? It was more in the nature of a command than a request."

"Oh, it was not a command."

He pulled a folded sheet of paper from his pocket. 'ARRIVING GWITHIAN ABOUT TWO O'CLOCK STOP,'" he read. "'MEET ME THERE STOP HAVE PICNIC STOP WANT SECOND CHANCE WITH BETTER ENDING JULIA STOP STOP.' He looked at her, shoving the note back in his pocket and walking to the back of the Mercedes to remove her valise from the boot. "That doesn't sound like asking to me."

She laughed, tucking her handbag under her arm and grabbing her hatbox as he reached for her valise and the picnic hamper. That was when he saw the bottle of Laurent-Perrier reposing in a bucket of ice chips. "You brought champagne, too?"

"Of course! I brought all the exact same things. We are restaging this play and giving it a different ending."

"Are you sure that's a good idea? The champagne, I mean." His eyes looked into hers. "I might lose my head."

She looked back at him, seeing into the depths of those warm, steady eyes, and she suddenly realized why she liked them so much, why she'd turned to him as her means of escape from Yardley. She liked that steadiness, she savored that warmth, she turned instinctively toward those things she saw in his eyes.

"You won't lose your head," she assured him. "This time, I only brought one bottle of champagne, and you are only allowed one glass." She smiled her most seductive smile. "This time, I want you to remember everything."

Chapter Nineteen

idan fully appreciated what the eminent French philosopher Émile Boirac called déjà vu. He'd experienced that particular phenomenon several times since Julia had walked back into his life, but this particular occasion had to be the most delicious. For the second time, Julia was propositioning him, something that only yesterday had been about as likely as Queen Alexandra allowing him once again into the Royal Enclosure at Ascot. Nonetheless, Julia had asked him on a picnic. She'd brought champagne. And she was giving him the same seductive smile she'd given him last August.

He took a deep breath. "One glass," he agreed. "But what if I stop you at the crucial moment, and cite codes of honor and moral responsibility?"

Her smile widened. "I'll kill you."

He laughed. "All right then. But couldn't we skip

over the picnic and champagne part and go straight to the dessert?"

Her eyes widened in pretended innocence. "That's right! I remember how much you love blackberries."

"Love them. Especially *after* dessert," he murmured, his gaze sliding down her legs. Not that there was much to see beneath the long motoring coat she wore.

She laughed again, but shook her head as she wrapped her free arm around the champagne bucket, grabbed her hat box, and started for the door of the cottage. "No, no. This all has to be done in the proper order. C'mon, bring my things up."

He reached for the valise and picnic basket and followed her. "Proper order?"

"Yes." Her arm wrapped tight around the ice bucket so as not to drop it, she set down her hatbox, thrust a hand in her coat pocket, and extracted a key. "What that means," she explained as she unlocked the door, shoved the key in the pocket of her motoring coat, and pushed the door wide, "is that you have to steer clear until I'm ready."

"What?"

Ignoring his groan, she grabbed her suitcase out of his hand, shoved the ice bucket at him, and picked up her hatbox. "I was hoping to arrive before you because I have preparations to make so that we can do this right, but the road out of St. Dennis was too muddy and I had to go around, so we have to delay our picnic about half an hour. C'mon, Spike," she added, moving farther into the foyer to allow the bulldog to enter the cottage. Aidan kicked the door shut behind them.

She nodded to the refreshments he carried as she started up the stairs with her valise. "Take the picnic things to the kitchen, would you, and put the kettle on? Well's outside the back door, and there should be coal in the scuttle."

"You are a devil, Julia," he accused as she started up the stairs, "making me cool my heels like this."

"It's good for you," she called back. "Dukes are far too accustomed to having things their way."

"I'm not," he muttered. "Not with you anyway."

There was the tap of her heels on the stairs as she came back down far enough to peek at him. "And stable your horse," she said, giving him that smile again. "This time, you're staying all night."

With that delicious promise, she vanished, and he spent the next half hour thinking it was an eternity. He stoked up the fire in the stove and put the kettle on as she'd requested, and the knowledge that she wanted the hot water for a bath sent his desire ratcheting upward.

Not that he needed much incentive in that regard. In leaving Danbury Downs, he'd tried to put her out of his mind, knowing it might be weeks or even months before he would see her again. But from the moment he'd received her telegram this morning, he'd begun imagining all the ways he wanted to make love to her, and the intervening hours had given him plenty of time to reawaken every fantasy he'd ever had about her and invent several new ones. Waiting was become harder, his anticipation keener, with each excruciating moment that passed.

He drove his carriage into the stables, unhitched the gelding, gave it water from a rain-filled trough outside, and led it to a stall. Grooming supplies hung along one wall, and he currycombed the animal as well. These mundane tasks kept his body preoccupied, but could not preoccupy his mind or prevent his thoughts from returning to the erotic possibilities that lay ahead. He could only hope when the time came, he had the will and the discipline to make them as pleasurable for her in reality as they were in his imagination.

When he returned to the house, he knew she was ready the moment he opened the back door. He could smell lilacs, the scent of her perfume, even before he saw her dark head peeking around the corner of the doorway from the corridor.

"You have to come to the front door," she told him. "Just like last time."

"Your wish is my command," he said, backed out of the kitchen, and went around to the front of the cottage. She didn't even wait for him to knock, and as she opened the door to him, he knew that drunk or not, he must have been a complete idiot last August to say no to this woman.

She was wearing that dress, a muslin affair of snowy white with a wide navy-blue sash that looked just as he remembered. It was the sort of simple daytime frock ladies wore to the balloon races at Ranelagh or the Henley Regatta every year, only without the necktie, gloves, or straw boater hat. He also knew, now, that beneath that dress was absolutely nothing. Just as before, her black curls were caught up in a loose chignon, secured with nothing more than a pair of pearl-edged combs. Her feet were encased in the same shoes she'd worn before, he noticed, looking down to see the white leather toes peeking from beneath her hem. It was the sort of shoe most women wore to the seaside. Most other women, however, wore stockings.

"I'm glad you came," she said, pointing to the picnic hamper she had waiting just by the door. "Would you carry that?"

Spike was beside his mistress again, but this time, there was no barking and no growling to warn away the distrusted man at the door. She looked into the animal's eager, wrinkly face and shook her head. "Sorry, old chap. I know you like Aidan now, but you still have to stay here."

Leaving a dejected Spike tied to a fencepost outside, they started along the same path they had walked before, a well-worn path carved into the steep, winding hillside that led down to the same small, isolated cove and pretty little beach where they had picnicked last time. There, spread on the grassy turf at the edge of the sand, was the same blanket, and at one corner were the same two neatly folded towels. On another corner of the blanket was the Victrola, with its enormous horn and mahogany casing, and on top of it was a phonograph—Mozart, he suspected. When she sank down on the blanket, turned the handle of the machine, and placed the arm of the Victrola on the recording, his suspicion was confirmed as the lively notes of *Eine Kleine Nachtmusik* filled the air.

The champagne was there, too, but this time, there was only one bottle in the silver bucket. This time, he waged no internal battle about how many glasses he was going to have. As she'd said, only one was allowed.

"What did you think when you saw all this before?" she asked. "You must have known what I was doing."

"I suspected. When I saw the trouble you'd gone to, I was flattered that you . . ." He paused and swallowed hard, finding the admission hard to make. "I was flattered that you wanted me that much."

"I'm sorry," she whispered. "I never meant to hurt you or humiliate you."

He sank down beside her on the blanket, then he took up her hand, lifted it to his lips, and kissed it. "I know."

She laughed a little, entwining their fingers. "Yet you came that day. I didn't really think you would."

"I convinced myself that it was harmless because I could resist you." He gave a hoarse chuckle. "Amazing how many ways a man can fool himself when he wants something he knows isn't very honorable. You were right about me and the whole notion of forbidden fruit."

"Still, I thought sure my motives were plain as day, and there was no way you'd fall into that trap."

"I tried not to. I saw all this, and I thought of what was *not* going to happen on that blanket. I thought about how I was *not* going to touch you and kiss you and unbutton your dress. I thought about not doing those things over and over again."

She laughed, and led him by the hand to where she'd arranged the picnic things. "Perhaps you should have a more positive outlook this time?" she suggested, sinking down on the blanket. Hitching up the hem of her skirt a bit, she pulled off her shoes.

His breath caught at the sight of her bare feet, and he knew if this was going to go the way he wanted it to, the way he wanted it to be for her, he had to keep his desire in check. That meant not staring at her pretty feet, and when she wiggled her toes, he jerked his gaze away. He opened the picnic hamper and rummaged inside for glasses. He found them, wrapped in linen napkins. "Pass the champagne, would you?"

"Not yet. You're too buttoned up." She lifted one hand, waving it in an up and down gesture. "This is a picnic in Cornwall, not afternoon tea with an archbishop," she went on as he moved to comply. "And," she added as he tossed his navy-blue jacket to an unoccupied corner of the blanket, "remove that necktie. And undo a button or two of that shirt."

"Did I take these off last time?" He didn't remember doing that.

"Yes. Well," she added, laughing, "with a little help from me. And only after two and a half bottles of champagne."

"Ah." He considered a moment, then gave in. "Well, we are rewriting the ending, aren't we? I suppose I could loosen my tie a bit earlier this time." His tie joined his jacket and he undid the three buttons of his shirt. Only then did Julia comply with his request, pulling the bottle from its now-slushy ice bath and handing it to him. He popped the cork and poured for both of them, then lifting his glass, he proposed a toast. "To second chances."

"And better endings," she added. They clinked glasses and looked into each other's eyes, and as they drank, Aidan vowed this ending wasn't just going to be better, it was going to be the best he could make it for her.

They set aside their glasses and began pulling foodstuffs out of the picnic hamper. He opened jars of caviar, mustard, and pickles as she unfastened plates and silver from beneath the lid of the hamper. He sliced bread, ham, chicken, and various cheeses as she pulled out tins of savory biscuits and shortbread, and a basket of blackberries.

"How long have you had this place?" he asked as they ate.

"About seven years. I inherited it from my grandmother. She died after my parents, and it came to me. It's one of those quirky entailed properties that comes down through the female line, and since I have no older sisters—no siblings at all, in fact—it came to me. I'm glad, too. I love it here."

"But you didn't grow up here?" When she shook her head, he added, "If you had, we would have met much sooner, I suppose, since Trathen Leagh is so close."

"I spent a few summers here as a girl, though I always went to Pixy Cove for August. Like my cousins, I grew up in Devonshire, not by Danbury, but further east, closer to Dorset."

"Since you have no brothers or sisters, we have something in common, then. I, too, am an only child. My mother died shortly after I began at Eton, and my father only a year later. That's so frequently the way, isn't it?" he added thoughtfully. "When one spouse dies, the other often follows shortly after. Why do you suppose that is?"

She shrugged. "Loneliness, perhaps. I wouldn't know. My parents died together, in a carriage accident when I was twenty-two. I'm glad they never knew how unhappy my marriage was. It would have grieved them."

"Would it?" Aidan paused over his sandwich, thinking it over. "That surprises me."

"Really?" She reached for a hunk of chicken. "Why should it?"

"I don't know. Perhaps because I gathered your parents knew you didn't love him, even though they had pushed for the marriage."

"I think they hoped it would all turn out well. They did love me, and they wanted what they thought was best for me."

"Why was Yardley their choice? His rank?"

"Partly. My father had a prosperous farm, but no title. More important, Yardley wanted to marry me. His family often spent the summer just this side of

Dorset, near our farm. We'd known each other most of our lives, but I never liked him. I don't know quite why he wanted me." She paused, considering, as she ate another bite of chicken. "Probably because he knew I didn't want him," she said at last. "He was . . . perverse like that. But my parents believed he had genuine affection for me, and they felt that my becoming a baroness was an excellent match that would give me a secure future. They assumed I would grow to love him."

"It does often happen that way."

"Does it?" She seemed doubtful, but she didn't debate the point. "I'm glad they never knew my aversion to Yardley became loathing. It would have grieved them. Their marriage was a contented one. They liked each other and were fairly happy. No real passion, though I suppose they may have had that once."

"Well, I'm glad that at least one of us had parents with a contented marriage. My parents' marriage was an emotional tumult."

"What do you mean?"

He shook his head. "They were madly in love when they met, and suitable to marry, but my father simply could not resist other women. It was a source of great unhappiness to my mother, always."

"I see." She paused, and he could feel her gaze on him, studying him. "That's why you feel fidelity is important, don't you?" she asked. "Because infidelity made your mother unhappy?"

"Not just my mother. My father, too, in a strange way. None of his mistresses ever made him happier than my mother did, and he knew his infidelities grieved her, and he had terrible guilt over it. There were constant quarrels, but my father never stopped his philandering. He was in bed with his current mistress when he died. I could never understand that, and I vowed that if I ever married, I would not stray. I would not dishonor my wife nor make her so unhappy."

She reached out, touched his hair. "You didn't even betray the woman you were going to marry. You must have gotten your mistress after Rosalind broke your engagement, then."

"My mistress?" Puzzled, he turned his head and looked at her, and then he remembered. "Oh, her."

He lifted his fist to his mouth and gave a slightly guilty cough. "I . . . umm . . . I don't have a mistress. She doesn't exist."

"What?" Julia sat up, setting aside her plate.

"I have had mistresses over the years. I mean, I'm no saint. But I gave up my most recent mistress when I decided to find a wife."

"What, before you met Beatrix?"

"Yes."

"And you haven't had a mistress since then?"

"No." He tugged at his collar, a bit embarrassed by this admission. "A courtesan every now and again. Between engagements," he added with a touch of wry humor. "But nothing else."

"But you don't have a mistress now? Aidan, you lied," she added when he shook his head, staring at him in disbelief. "You lied to me."

"Yes, I did. Sorry, but it just came out. I couldn't resist. A man has his pride, you know. And I—"

He was stopped by her fingers against his lips. "It's not a lie, really, not now," she said, a smile spreading across her face, a wide, happy smile that made him feel as if he were the king of the earth.

Aidan, though he liked that smile, liked it a lot, was puzzled by her cryptic remark. "I don't quite understand what you mean."

Still smiling a little, she moved to sit on her knees, facing him. "You have a mistress now. If you want her." Being Julia, she just had to add irrepressibly, "You don't even have to pay me. How's that for a bargain?"

"So we are lovers, then?" he said, and reached out to rake his fingers through her hair. Pulling her close, he kissed her.

She nodded. "Lovers, it is. Aidan?"

"Hmm?"

She lifted her hand, fingering his collar. "Before this goes any further, there are certain things I want you to know about me."

To his surprise, her tone had become quite serious. He was even more surprised when she took his plate off his lap and then reached for one of his hands to hold it in her own. "When we were here before, I was ready to give you my body, and I was acting the part of the sultry seductress, but the truth is that every second of it, I was afraid I'd lose my nerve." She gave a laugh, but she didn't sound amused. "I'm no innocent girl, God knows, and I've done more carousing than most women ever will, and I know I was as brazen as I could be that day, but Aidan, I want you to know that despite all the talk about me and what a scandal I am, and the blatant way I seduced you, the truth is, I've only bedded two men in my entire life."

He stared at her. "What?"

"It's true. The first was Stephen Graham, a Scotsman who'd rented a cottage on my father's estate the summer I turned seventeen. He wrote poetry and read Marx. I was violently in love with him, as only a girl that age can be. He became my lover. When he proposed that we elope, I agreed, ecstatically. We made plans, he went ahead to Glasgow, his home, to arrange things. I was to follow him."

Aidan remembered her words about why she'd married Yardley, because her family insisted, and he began to get a picture of where this was going. "And did you go to Scotland?"

"Yes." She paused, her face working, her lips trying to form a smile, as if even now, she was fighting for a mask to put on. "But he was dead. They had an outbreak of scarlet fever and he died."

She reached for the champagne. "My father wanted me to marry Yardley," she said as she poured herself another glass. "Their fathers had been friends. He thought it would be a good match for me. Yardley wanted me, but until that business with Stephen, I had refused to consider him. As early as that, I sensed something . . . wrong about him."

She paused to set aside the bottle and take a swallow of champagne, and he wanted to ask what she meant, but as he opened his mouth to raise the question, she spoke quickly, forestalling him. "When I came home from Scotland," she said, setting her glass down again, "I was disgraced, no longer an innocent girl, with my reputation at risk. There was gossip already about Stephen and me, which is how my father found out. I don't know how it happens, but somehow, these secret affairs never stay secret, particularly in small villages. Servants, prying spinsters with too much time on their hands—someone always knows, and the gossip spreads, and before long, a girl is ruined. Anyway, Yardley was known to our family, my parents wanted the match, he wanted me, so it was all arranged. As I said, I didn't want to do it. I didn't love him, but I'd made so many mistakes. I had always been a rebel, you see. A disobedient, willful, independent girl."

"You?" He pretended to be surprised. "Not possible."

"I had already caused my parents more than enough grief. I wanted to do something right for a change, make good for all the stupid things I'd done wrong. How ironic that in trying to do something right, I was to make the biggest mistake of my life." She shook her head and swallowed hard, squeezing his hand. "That's not what I wanted to say."

She sat back, facing him, wriggling and pulling at her skirt so that she could sit cross-legged on the blanket. It exposed her lower legs, reminding him of that day on the bridge, causing arousal to flicker up within his body.

"In the lavender house," she said, her voice bringing his gaze back up to her face, "you asked me if I felt anything when we . . . when we almost . . . the last time we were here. You asked if I wanted you, and I said I would have done anything, but that wasn't quite true. I had been trying to work up the nerve for an affair because I hoped it would impel Yardley to divorce me, but I never could take a lover, because . . . well, I just couldn't. But then I saw you again at the St. Ives Ball, and I remembered how much I liked you that day on the footbridge, and how you had the divine good taste to appreciate my legs—"

"They are the finest pair of legs on God's earth," he said fervently, and once again he glanced down, sliding his gaze along her calf.

"Anyway," she said, jerking firmly at her skirt to conceal her legs and giving him what she assumed was meant to be a look of reproof. But he wasn't fooled, for there was a mischievous curve to one corner of her mouth. "When I saw you again at the St. Ives Ball, that's when I decided to have a go at seducing you."

"That night?"

She nodded. "When I saw you, I noticed you were even better-looking than you'd been all those years ago. And when we talked, you were so . . . well . . . so *nice*."

"Nice?" He pretended to be affronted. "Nice? Woman, I am a duke. I have been involved in politics, the most ruthless occupation there is. I have vast business interests. There are men who shake in their boots when I walk into a room."

"I'm sure there are," she said, her smile widening, "but I think you're terribly nice. And," she added before he could protest again, "nice is a very good thing. So, I was thinking about throwing myself at you in a most shameless and wanton manner, but then you met Trix, and she sort of fell for you, and you seemed to like her, and I . . . well . . ." She paused, giving a deep sigh and looked away. "I gave up my chance."

He thought of that night in St. Ives when he'd met Beatrix, and he didn't know what to say. The idea that even then, only the second time they'd ever met, she'd been thinking of seducing him was rather astonishing. "Julie, from the moment we met, I've always had a deep desire for you. You know that. But you were married. When I met Beatrix, I was looking to marry as well. I never dreamed—"

"I know. And Trix was trying to put Sunderland behind her. I love Trix dearly, and I knew she would be a fine choice as a wife for you, while I had nothing to offer you but an affair. So I stepped aside." She laughed with a hint of chagrin. "So many times afterward, I thought, 'Oh, if only I'd danced with him first!' But it wasn't meant to be, and I put any plans to seduce you out of my head. Then you and Trix became engaged, and when I came home that summer for the Marlowes' house party at Pixy Cove, I tried to be happy for you both. But, oh, it was hard!"

"It was?"

She gave him a rueful look. "Yes, it was awful— seeing you with Trix, wanting to be happy for the two of you. I tried to put on a good show, laughing with Will and playing comic songs on the piano. That's why I kept trying to aggravate you. I felt so resentful, and so sorry for myself, though I was trying not to." She sighed. "You have no idea what I was going through."

"You?" he echoed with a wry chuckle. "Put yourself in my place. There I was, about to marry your cousin, my fiancée, a woman I wouldn't hurt for the world, and across from me was her old love sitting with you, you, the woman I had desired from the time I was seventeen, a woman I could never have. I was striving to be a gentleman, but the whole time, I kept imagining those amazing, beautiful legs of yours. It drove me mad. And I hated myself for it."

"And me as well, I imagine."

"Well, yes, in a way. You wouldn't stop playing that damnable ragtime."

She laughed. "I was so awful to you during that entire house party! I'm so sorry."

He considered a moment, then he said, "As long as we are telling truths here, I have something to tell you as well. Later that night at Pixy Cove, I walked Beatrix to the stairs, and I kissed her just to reassure myself I was doing the right thing by marrying her, but the whole time my lips were on hers, I was thinking of you."

"You were?"

"Yes."

"If Sunderland hadn't come back, you would still have married Trix, though, wouldn't you?"

He leaned back on his arms, looking into her eyes. "Yes. A gentleman does not break an engagement except for the most egregious behavior on the part of his fiancée, and until she kissed Sunderland, Trix had done nothing to deserve being jilted by me. And I would have spent my whole life striving to be the best husband I could be to her."

Unexpectedly, she chuckled. "You are such a *pukka sahib*."

"A good thing to be, in my opinion, though you tease me for it."

"It is a good thing," she agreed. "Men like you, who believe in honor and don't just talk about it, are rare as a hen's teeth. I ought to know. Anyway," she added, "the point I'm trying to get to, in a most rambling, round-about way, is that I . . . I'm . . . not very experienced at this lovemaking business. All those supposed affairs I've had? They're bunkum. I staged them, hoping Yardley would be so disgusted that he'd divorce me."

Aidan thought of all the times he'd disapproved of her behavior, her disregard for fidelity and her scandalous, party-loving lifestyle and restless, constant living off her friends, and he wanted to kick himself for being such an ass.

"I finally learned that every time a new affair was supposedly in the wind, Yardley would send private detectives after me to verify it. That's why he never brought a divorce suit. He knew it was all a hum. I realized if I was ever going to rid myself of him, he'd have to catch me in the act, or as close to it as possible."

"And you chose me for this. Why me?"

She looked at him steadily. "Because after what Yardley had done to me, you were the only man I ever thought I could allow to touch me."

Aidan stared at her, stunned, flattered, and pleased beyond words. But then, a second later, the sickening, sinister implications about her former husband began snaking back into his consciousness. He forced himself to speak. "You felt nothing that day with me, did you? There was no pleasure in it for you."

"It wasn't quite nothing," she admitted, "but it probably wasn't anything like what you were feeling."

"And you've never taken a lover, because of him and what . . ." He could barely get the words out. "Because of what he did to you."

"Yes. I was so used to being numb, and cold, feeling hate rather than any sort of desire, so used to not wanting to be kissed or touched. It's more than that, but I don't know how else to explain it to you. The point is, I couldn't give myself to you fully that day. I wanted to, but I just couldn't. It wasn't in me to give of myself that way." She paused, then added softly, staring out at the sea, "It may never be."

"I don't believe that."

"You don't know." She swerved, looked at him again. "You don't know how he made me feel. It was like the pit of hell to me. Anyway, I thought you should know all that." She tried to smile. "I don't want you to be too disappointed."

"I won't be disappointed at all. You must believe me

about that." He brushed a tendril of hair back from her face. "Julia, do you—" He stopped, knowing this question could ruin everything today. But he also knew he had to ask it. "Do you want to tell me about him?"

She shook her head. "No. Maybe one day I'll tell you, but not today."

"All right," he said, unable to suppress a tiny hint of relief. He didn't want any talk of that bastard to spoil their day.

"The reason, of course," she went on, a lightness coming into her voice that he knew was forced, "is that I have far more important things to do right now." With that, she picked up her glass, drained it of the last swallow of its contents, and tossed it onto the grass as she stood up. "Like dip my feet in the water, for example. It's deuced hot today."

It wasn't—not like last August. But he was relieved by her pretext to change the subject. And though it might be selfish of him to so easily postpone hearing what her husband had done to her, wrong to want her to seduce him again when the first time had been an act of desperation, he couldn't help it. He watched her pull the combs from her hair and toss them into the picnic hamper, and he loved the way her loosened black curls swirled across her face in the ocean breeze. He loved the easy grace with which she moved as she turned away and walked toward the shore. He loved the way she didn't just dip her feet in, but gathered up the folds of her skirt around her knees and waded into the water. And he loved those long, gorgeous legs of hers.

Unlike last time, he wasn't shocked by her brazen display. Instead, he grinned with pure, unadulterated pleasure. He wasn't shocked when she dove underwater and came up facing him in folds of clinging, transparent muslin. No, he thought as she came out of the water and back across the sand toward him, he wasn't shocked at all. But just as before, by the time she sank to her knees in front of him, he was fully, flagrantly aroused. He could see her breasts, small, perfect breasts, her nipples jutting against the wet fabric like hard pebbles, and just as before, he felt his wits slipping, along with his moral code.

"Go on," she breathed, tilting her head back and leaning toward him just as she had done before, her fingertips trailing along her throat between the unbuttoned edges of her dress. "Take it. You know you want to."

He stared, riveted, his throat dry, as her fingertip grazed the hardened nipple of her breast. One second, and then two, and he was grabbing her by the arms, just as before, and falling back onto the blanket, pulling her with him.

She sank onto him, her hair falling in wet spirals around his face. She kissed him, her mouth open and lush, tasting of sweet blackberries and salty sea. Her hips moved against his in a slow, lascivious slide, and he tore his mouth from hers with a groan.

God, had it felt this good last time? he wondered, lost in an erotic, sensuous haze.

She lifted up, resting her weight on her arms as she looked at him, her breath coming in soft huffs between her parted pink lips. "I think it's time to move this picnic indoors. Don't you?"

Just as before, he didn't even hesitate before he answered. "Yes," he breathed, and stood up, pulling her with him. "God, yes."

It was déjà vu all over again.

Chapter Twenty

When Julia took him by the hand and led him back up the path, Aidan had no intention of arguing with her. "Your wish is my command," he told her, and followed her into the house. He closed the kitchen door behind them, and when he turned around, she was in his arms. Her mouth opened over his, warm and lush and willing. Her arms slid up around his neck.

He tilted his head, his hands came up to cradle her cheeks, then tangled in her wet hair. But when she entwined her arms around his neck and pressed her body closer, tasting him with her tongue, the desire he'd been holding back all afternoon threatened to flame out of control, and he fought to contain it. Pulling back, he gentled the kiss, suckling her lower lip between both of his, tasting her as if she were a piece of candy.

Slowly, he eased back, thinking how he was going to

take his time with this, but she seemed to have different ideas on the matter. She grasped his hands and lifted them, bringing them to her breasts. "This is what you did last time."

"I did?" He opened his palms, embracing the small, perfect shape of her breasts through the thin layer of her dress. Arousal was once again banked to an aching heat inside him, but he knew that it could flare up again quick as lighting a match, and he wasn't going to let that happen. Not yet.

He jerked his hands back, ignoring her protest. "I don't care if I did that last time. This time, I'm sober, and I want to do it differently. We are composing a different scene."

"Different ending," she corrected.

He shrugged, refusing to quibble about it. Instead, he lifted his hands to her bodice and began undressing her, slipping the pearl buttons free one by one from her collarbone to her waist. Then he pulled her dress apart, off her shoulders and down her arms. It caught at the sash tied around her waist, and for now he left it there to trace his fingers in light caresses across her bare shoulders. He didn't dare look any lower, for he wanted to keep lust under tight rein as long as possible, and a view of her bare breasts was not going to help him do that right now. He kept all his attention on her pretty white shoulders, watching his fingertips trace light caresses over her skin from her neck to her arms, then back across her collarbone, then over her shoulders and down her spine to her waist. He worked to untie the sash of her dress, easing the knot loose as he pressed kisses to her throat.

"I should have done a bow," she said, laughing, a bit nervously, he judged. Somehow, that made him feel better; he was nervous, too. Not only because last time he'd consumed a great deal more champagne, but also because back then he hadn't known anything about her past, her husband, or the lack of tenderness in her life. Now he did, and he was nervous as hell.

The knot came loose, the sash came off, and the sodden dress fell to the floor around her ankles. He looked away, waiting until she'd stepped out of it and shoved it out from under her feet. Then he allowed his gaze to travel slowly upward from her pretty feet over what seemed miles of gorgeous legs, catching his breath as he passed a soft triangle of black curls.

"My God," he breathed, as his gaze moved up, up over slim hips and a tiny waist. "Did I have this splendid view last time?"

"Yes."

He paused at her breasts for just a second. *Not yet*, he reminded himself, and lifted his gaze higher, to her long, slender neck. He tilted his head, pressing a kiss to the pulse at the base of her throat.

"Did I do that before?" he murmured against her silken skin.

"Yes."

"What about this?" He trailed more kisses along the side of her throat and across her shoulder, using his tongue and making her shiver.

"Yes."

"What about this?" He drew her close, slid one arm around her waist, and kissed her again, full and open on the mouth as his free hand finally embraced her breast. He pulled back, lowered his hand to his side, and looked into her eyes. "Did I do that?"

"Yes. And then you pushed me away."

"I—" He paused and looked down, his throat going dry at the sight of her erect, rosy pink nipples. "I was an idiot."

Her throaty chuckle lifted his gaze to her face. "Yes," she agreed, that unmistakable glimmer of mischief in her eyes. "That's just what I thought."

He laughed with her, but then her laughter stopped and she frowned. "Wait," she said, and pulled his hands down. "This isn't quite right."

He glanced down. "It looks quite all right to me."

"That isn't what I mean." She reached up to finger his unfastened collar. "At this point last time, you were half undressed."

"Ah." Enlightened, he spread his arms. "Well, then you'd best get busy, hmm?"

"I should say so." She unbuttoned his waistcoat and slid the vest of yellow silk back from his shoulders, and it fell behind him to the floor. Then she undid the last button of his shirt, and unbuttoned his cuffs. "You had cuff links last time."

"I did? You probably thought I was overdressed for the occasion."

She smiled. "I thought you were adorable."

"I'm not sure that's a compliment to a man," he complained as she pulled his braces down and tugged his shirt out of his waistband.

She stepped back a little as he pulled his shirt over his head and tossed it aside. "You want a compliment?" she asked, glancing down, and even though she already knew what his bare chest looked like, her breath still caught at the perfection of it.

"You have the most ripping chest." She fanned her hands over his pectoral muscles, down his flat, hard abdomen, up along his strong, sinewy arms and across his powerful shoulders, ending where she began, her palms over the flat, brown disks of his nipples. "Damn," she added, laughing, "when I pick a lover, I do it right."

She leaned in, pressing a kiss to his chest right over his heart, and something hot and tight twisted there, something that had nothing to do with the lust in his body. Something in her hushed voice when she whispered, "I want this to be right, Aidan," that awed him and scared him and made him randy as a dog.

"Anything you do will be right, Julia. Do what you want." He cupped her cheeks, nibbled gently at her lips. "Do what you feel."

She rose on her toes to kiss him deeply again, but this time there was a tender sweetness in it, a vulnerability, that hadn't been there before. The touch of her tongue wasn't driving or desperate. It was tentative, exploring slowly, almost as a child might stick her toes experimentally into the cool water of the sea before plunging in. But the contact, soft and tentative as it was, sent shudders of pleasure through his body nonetheless.

When she unbuttoned his trousers for more explorations, he gritted his teeth and bore the agonizing suspense, but when she slid her hand into the opening of his linen to touch his penis, he groaned, unable to take any more. "I can't," he muttered.

She froze, her hand around him. "Please tell me you're not stopping."

"No, no. That's not what I meant." Gently, he extricated her hand. "I can't hold back if you go that fast."

"But why should you hold back?"

"Because I want you not to." He didn't explain. Instead, he pushed the hair back from her shoulders, cupped her cheeks, and kissed her—long, slow kisses that went to his head in a more powerful rush than any champagne. He slid his hands down to cup her breasts, and broke the kiss to ask her, "How does this feel? Do you like it when I caress you like this?"

"Aidan!" It was a shocked laugh with a hint of embarrassment. "Now who's being seductive?"

"I'm a quick study." Resting her breast against his palm, he toyed with her nipple, rolling it slowly in his fingers. "So you do like this?"

She nodded, tilting her head back, closing her eyes. As he watched, her skin took on a rosy hue in the late afternoon sunlight.

He bent his head. "What about this?" he asked, and took her nipple into his mouth, suckling softly at first, then harder until she was shivering, until she gasped a little affirmative answer against his hair.

Suckling one breast, he caressed the other as his free hand slipped around behind her to cup one of her buttocks. He pulled back long enough to ask, "This?" before returning his attention to playing with her breasts. He caressed them, shaped them. He toyed with her pretty nipples, brushing his thumbs back and forth across them and rolling them between his fingers. As he played with her, she began to moan, soft and low, and he could feel the quivers running through her body, the tension in her taut like harp strings. Gently, ever so gently, he scored her nipple with his teeth. She cried out with pleasure, and her knees gave way. He wrapped an arm around her to hold her upright, his tongue still licking her nipple. "Like that, do you?"

She made a smothered sound, and he laughed, nipping playfully at her breast. "Was that a yes I heard?"

She nodded, making a strangled sound that was definitely positive. Her hands slid into his hair, cradling his head, and he could feel her arousal growing hotter. Her body began to move against his in little jerks, but the sounds she made were hushed, as if she was still holding a part of herself back. That, Aidan decided, wasn't enough. Perhaps he was selfish, but he wanted it all, with no holding back.

He sank to his knees, gliding his palms along the sides of her waist to her hips, and then behind to cup her buttocks. He pulled her closer, pressing a hot kiss to her navel that made her stomach muscles quiver in response. "Do you like that?" he asked, breathing the question against her skin.

"Yes." A sigh. "Oh, yes."

"How about this?" Pressing slow, hot kisses to her stomach, he moved lower and lower, until his lips touched the midnight-black curls at the apex of her thighs.

She sucked in a deep gasp of shock at the contact, and pressed her thighs tight together. "Aidan, what are you doing?"

"Do you like it?" he asked, the brush of his lips as he spoke making her body jerk in response.

"I don't know!" She sounded a bit frantic.

Good, he thought, and kissed her again. "You haven't ever had a man do this? Kiss you here?"

"God, no! I told you, I've only had—oh God," she moaned as he tasted her. Her legs parted a little, and he nuzzled her warmth. "Aidan," she wailed. "Don't. It's . . . it's indecent!"

He chuckled, blowing warm air against dark curls.

"What are you laughing at?" she demanded, sounding aroused and embarrassed, excited and angry all at once.

"You," he answered, "turning missish on me all of a sudden."

"I am not missish!" she shot back, then immediately gasped as his tongue dipped for a second taste. "Oh, you mustn't do that!"

"But do you like it, Julia?" He stroked her with his tongue. "How does it feel?"

She cried out, a sharper cry this time. "I can't explain how it feels! I can't."

"Is it good?"

"Good? It's wicked, that's what it is. Oh God!" she moaned as he licked her again, and her knees sagged beneath her.

Wicked? He laughed as he cupped her bum and rose, lifting her onto the kitchen table that was against the wall behind her. Sliding his hands out from beneath her buttocks, he knelt to taste her, savoring how her body quivered with each stroke. She was soft, and slick, and lusciously warm. And he wanted to keep kissing her like this forever. Though she wouldn't say it in words, he knew these carnal kisses pleased her. As his tongue slid along her silken folds, her body began to move in little jerks, and her breath began to come faster, until each breath was a gasp. When he touched her clitoris with his tongue, she cried out, but then immediately smothered the sound with her hand.

"Don't, Julia, don't." Reaching up, he pulled her hand away from her mouth, took both her hands in both of his. "Don't hold back how you feel, not with me. Show me what you want and how you feel, or I won't know how to please you." He moved up a bit, licking her stomach. "Did you like what I just did?"

"Yes." She ground out the word.

"Was it good? Do you want more?"

"Yes!"

"Then just say so. Tell me you want me to kiss you there."

"I—" She tilted her head back, laughing in chagrin as she stared at the ceiling. This was the hardest thing she'd ever done. "Kiss me," she mumbled.

He did, on her stomach. "There?"

Julia shook her head, frantic, scared, so aroused she couldn't think. "Lower." She forced the word out through clenched teeth. "Lower."

He did as she bid, his tongue lashing her with the softest, most incredible caresses she'd ever experienced. From a distance, she heard his voice, tender yet insistent, demanding an answer.

"How does it feel, Julia?"

Impossible, she thought. He wanted her to describe it?

She felt him release her hands, and she didn't bother to cover her mouth again, but she bit her lip instead, trying hard not to give way, fighting with him, and not even knowing why. She wasn't afraid; she was long past fear. There was no pain, only tenderness, and lush, hot, blissful kisses. There was no shame, not even naked in her sunlit kitchen with her legs spread apart and Aidan doing this naughty, naughty thing to her. Aidan? Never could she have imagined it. Aidan licking her . . . her quim? Good God. Where had he learned to do this?

She couldn't think, she was lost in a maelstrom that prevented coherent thought. She had only instincts, and those were at war—lust against self-preservation. And he wanted her to describe all this? *Luscious*, she thought and clamped down harder on her lip. *Glorious. Oh God.*

"Julie, Julie, let go," he coaxed, his lips brushing her curls. "You don't have to fight it with me. You can show it. You can feel it. It's all right."

He kissed her and licked her, and slowly, she allowed tension to slide away and the arousal she felt to take freer and freer rein. She began to move her hips. She began to find a rhythm in this, and he took his cue from her, pleasuring her at the pace her body demanded, until she was trembling all over and arching into him, her body moving with frantic little jerks that thumped the table on which she lay against the wall behind her. The tension built, higher, higher, and she strained to reach it, gritting her teeth. And then she felt it, a white-hot flood of sensation that tore a wail of pure pleasure from her throat and throbbed through every part of her body. Her hips thrust toward his mouth, her heels pressing against his back, waves of climax washing over her like tides and finally ebbing away into a dreamy bliss.

She collapsed against the table and heard her own sigh, a soft sound of rapture that floated on the warm hush of afternoon.

She'd known about this carnal kissing, but she'd never experienced it. Stephen had never done this to her, and Yardley certainly hadn't. When she felt Aidan stand up and she opened her eyes, she could only stare into his face, a handsome, boyish, serious face that she now knew only looked innocent.

And the release. She'd forgotten that. Not since she was seventeen had she experienced that rush of pleasure from a man's caresses and kisses. Yardley's brutality seemed very far away now, a lifetime ago, and she wondered how she could have ever forgotten the pleasure of climax. That building sweetness, layer upon layer, higher and higher, and the ecstatic, blissful explosions? How could she have ever forgotten that?

But this was different from what she'd felt thirteen years ago. She'd been a girl, awkward and inexperienced, with no real knowledge of what it all meant. Stephen's kisses hadn't been like this. He hadn't pleasured her with his *mouth*. He hadn't insisted upon knowing how she felt when he kissed her and touched her.

That was why this man, a genuine, good, honorable man, strong in mind as well as in body, was such a balm to her soul. And what a ripping fine body he had, too. She smiled as she stared at his splendid chest, enjoying the view for several moments. Finally, she looked into his eyes again, and she grinned. "Told you so." At his puzzled look, she added, "You do have a bit of the devil in you."

His lips curved just a little, but his expression remained grave as he reached out and touched her face. "You bit your lip." His thumb brushed her mouth, she felt a sting at the contact, and when his hand pulled back, there was a smear of blood on the pad of his thumb.

It startled her, the sight of that, a sign of how tightly she'd held back, how much she'd tried to withhold herself from him. "I—" She stopped, for she didn't know what on earth she'd intended to say. "What are you thinking?"

He didn't even hesitate. "I'm thinking how beautiful you are."

A whole different kind of pleasure washed over her.

"Funny," she choked, "I was thinking the same about you."

"And," he added, leaning forward to press a kiss to her hair, "I was thinking that I really prefer women with eyes the color of lilacs."

That made her smile, and he liked that. In the late afternoon sun that streamed through the window, she was rosy and tousled, her hair falling all around her, her breasts peeking out between long ebony curls. In those gorgeous violet-blue eyes, he saw pleasure, and a little bit of astonishment. She didn't have to say what she was feeling. He saw it in her eyes.

Then, suddenly, her thick black lashes came down as she slanted a glance down to his hips, and what must be flagrantly obvious, especially since his trousers were unbuttoned. "Do you know what I want now?" she asked.

He shook his head.

"I want to go upstairs. I want . . ." She paused, then added, "More."

He laughed and stepped around the end of the table to lift her into his arms. She wrapped her arms around his neck, and he carried her up the stairs, bending to duck them both beneath the low beams at the landing.

He reached the top of the stairs and glanced to the corridors that branched left and right. Glimpsing a brass bedstead and white linens through a doorway at the end of a corridor, he started that way even as he asked, "To the right?"

"Yes."

Her room was sparsely furnished with a wrought-iron bedstead, a marble-topped washstand, and an armoire. A carpet of Turkish design in blue, green, and red covered the plank floor, and sheer curtains of white chiffon fluttered at the open windows that overlooked the sea. Opposite them was a primitive stone fireplace.

He'd banked his own desires, holding back as much as he could so that she could let go, but as he laid Julia on the bed, as he looked at her, naked and so lovely against the white linens behind her, he feared his self-discipline was coming to an end.

His eyes locked with hers, he yanked off his shoes. He unfastened the remaining buttons of his trousers and pulled them down, along with his linen, and stepped out of them.

"What do you want now, Julia?" he asked, joining her on the bed, stretching his naked body out beside hers.

"You," she answered, her voice a soft sigh on the sea breeze.

But he didn't move to enter her. Instead, his hand slid between their bodies, and his fingers eased between her folds to caress her, to spread the moisture of her arousal.

"Oh," she moaned, and this time, she relished the sound of her own voice, for it seemed to enhance and deepen the pleasure. "Oh God. You are such a tease."

"Does that feel good?" he asked, the tip of his finger sliding up and down, in and out, teasing her.

"Yes," she said, shivering with wicked excitement.

"Do you want me?" he asked. "Inside you?"

"Yes," she said again, her hips pushing toward him. "Yes."

His hand withdrew, and then she could feel the tip of his penis stroking her where his hand had stroked her before. He flexed his hips, his cock sliding, hard and hot, along the folds of her opening, bringing renewed pleasure to her with each tiny move. "Sure?"

She was panting now, feeling desperate, but in a way that was amazing and wonderful. "Yes, I want you inside me. Yes, inside me. Now. Do it, damn you, and stop teasing me!"

He laughed, but as he eased into her, as he moved on top of her, pushing slowly in, pulling slowly back, she knew it was time to get revenge. If he wanted her to say what she wanted, she was going to do just that.

"I want you to come," she panted, her hips jerking against his, trying to speed the pace, wanting him to have the release she'd already had. "C'mon," she added, only half teasing. "You know you want to. Just give in."

He shook his head. "Shan't," he said, breathing hard and fast. "You first."

She clenched tight around him, pushing with her hips, urging, feeling a bit frantic. "Aidan, for God's sake, faster, please."

Again, he shook his head. Lifting his weight on his arms, he tilted his head back, and his mouth made a grimace of both pleasure and agony as he moved inside her, holding back. "I want you to come first."

Despite his words, his movements were quickening, his thrusts against her stronger and deeper. This was what it all meant, a shared pleasure. When she pushed upward, he groaned, torturing her, too. When his hips thrust hard, she matched his pace, reveling in it. His breathing was harsh and ragged, and so was hers; her frantic urgency became his. And with each thrust, the pleasure built, hotter, stronger, deeper.

Aidan got his way in the end. She climaxed first, a rush of feeling so intense, she cried out, a cry of surprise that became a keening wail of ecstasy and ended in panting, glorious oblivion.

His cry came right behind hers, and the shudders of both their climaxes rocked the bed. This, she realized, was something she'd never really had. This was far beyond the quick, intense couplings she'd managed to sneak with Stephen, and not at all like anything she'd experienced with her former husband. No, this was something else—this was lovemaking, and it filled her with wonder. Aidan thrust against her one more time, and then he stilled, his body heavy on top of her, his breath coming hard, his face buried against her neck, his fingers tangled in her hair.

She stroked him, liking the hard, smooth muscles of his back and the sleek curves of his bum. She liked the thick, curling tendrils of his hair, and when he said her name in a low, satisfied groan, a grin of pure happiness and satisfaction spread over her face. She turned her head and kissed his temple, feeling an overpowering wave of tenderness that was like nothing she'd ever felt in her life before.

She was no longer the love-struck, rebellious girl

who'd gone running up to Scotland to elope, nor the guilt-laden child who wanted to make good for her mistakes. And, thank God, she was not the numb doll who couldn't feel sexual desire, or the driven, desperate, panicked creature who'd seduced a man against his will, or the flippant, witty socialite who deflected pain like a mirror refracted light.

No, she was just a woman. And that meant she could feel, she could need, she could give, and she could receive. Happiness bloomed within her, an incredible, overpowering wave of joy that made tears sting her eyes.

This time, she didn't fight those tears. Crying meant she wasn't numb, she wasn't cold and lifeless. She wasn't a Sleeping Beauty. She was awake and alive, and the world was full of new beginnings and glorious possibilities. She still felt raw, she still had wounds. She was still a bit wobbly and weak, like a colt trying to walk on shaky legs. But with Aidan's arms around her, she didn't mind any of that, because for the first time in over twelve years, she was truly free. She was free, she was beautiful, and she'd just made love with a man for the very first time.

Julia let the tears fall.

Chapter Twenty-one

She was crying. He felt the tears, wet against his cheek. He lifted his head, filled with alarm. "Julia? God, are you all right? I didn't hurt you?"

"No," she choked out, shaking her head. "You didn't hurt me. Quite the opposite." She touched his cheek, smiling. "I'm crying because I can, my darling. I welcome it, I want it."

He rolled away from her and sat up, staring at her, unable to comprehend her words or her radiant smile. "That makes no sense. I've made you cry and you want me to?" He lifted a hand to cup her wet face, his thumb catching on tears.

She also sat up, facing him. "For twelve years I wouldn't cry. It became a point of pride with me, a badge of honor, a sign that I didn't feel anything. Remember that night you kissed me in the maze, when I ran away? I cried. Because of what you made me feel, you see. I was happy, and it hurt. I didn't want to be happy, and I was frightened, and I could feel myself falling apart, unraveling, and—" She started to laugh, looking at his face. "You don't know what I'm talking about, do you?"

"I haven't the least idea," he admitted. "I'm still trying to accept that I made you cry and you think that's a good thing. But," he added, weaving his way carefully, "I have the feeling it has something to do with your former husband."

She paused, and her smile faded. She nodded and looked down at her hands in her lap. "Shall I tell you about him?"

He felt a knot of dread forming in his stomach, but what he felt didn't matter. "If you want to, Julia."

She considered for a moment, then she nodded. "I'd like to, but I don't . . . I don't know if I can. I've never been able to tell anyone what it was like."

Aidan waited, and she sat there silent for a long time before she spoke again. "He had this cravat, of ivory silk, that he kept in his pocket. He always carried it. He was always playing with it, idly, you know, the way some people drum their fingers. I asked him about it once, and he just smiled and said, 'It's my favorite cravat.' It was on our wedding night that I learned why."

Aidan felt the hairs on his neck stand up. "Why?" he asked, his voice a strange, harsh whisper, but the question was moot. He was already beginning to perceive the sickening picture, and it appalled and angered him as much as the realization that Yardley had hit her.

"He uses it to tie women up. He has a riding crop, too, and he enjoys using it. He likes inflicting pain on women, it . . . arouses him. And if the woman is afraid of him, so much the better."

Aidan wanted to press his fingers to her lips, tell her to stop, to hush, but wounds healed over with poisons inside didn't ever truly heal. He clenched his jaw, caressed her cheek, and forced himself to listen.

"Needless to say, I was shocked and revolted. One might say Stephen was a rake for seducing a girl to whom he was not married, but Stephen loved me. What Yardley did was all so outside my experience. I didn't know what to do, what it meant, why he did it. I had just turned eighteen when I married him, and I was scared out of my wits. I knew it wasn't healthy; I knew it was twisted, wrong. But I soon learned that if I begged him to stop, or if I showed any fear, it only increased his pleasure. If I defied him, if I fought, he struck me back harder, and he enjoyed that, too. He wanted me to fight, so he could inflict more pain. If I ran away, he eventually dragged me back. But then I figured out how to defend myself."

"How?"

"I discovered that if I just lay there, if I pretended to be lifeless, like a doll or a corpse—if I didn't lift my arms so he could tie my hands, but just let them flop like dead weight . . . if I lolled my head or just stared through him as if I didn't even see him . . . if every time

he lifted my hips and maneuvered me onto my knees,
I sank back down . . . if I didn't cry or speak or make
a sound . . . if I did those things, his arousal just died."
She laughed, a harsh sound in the hushed room. "Like
a collapsed balloon."

Aidan didn't know what to say. He knew, in his conscious, reasoning mind, that there were men like that,
but he'd never dwelled on such an abhorrent fact of
life. He didn't want to do it now, but now, he had to
do it.

"So," she went on, "I learned to be numb, to be lifeless, to say nothing, do nothing. I would chant it in my
mind again and again. 'You're numb,' I'd say. 'You're
dead, and he can't hurt you.' I wouldn't cry or show
fear or show . . . well . . . anything."

"Julia." He wanted to comfort her, to say something
that could be a balm for such wounds, but there were no
words capable of that. "Julia, my dear."

"The trick worked, Aidan. He became bored with
me, and eventually, he stopped coming to my room, and
the next time I ran away, I hoped he would let me go."

"Did he?" He held his breath, even though he knew
from her subsequent actions that the answer would be
negative.

"No."

Aidan let out the breath he'd been holding, and drew
another, wishing to hell he could hold his drink, for he
could do with a stiff whiskey and soda right about now.
"What happened?"

"He tracked me down where I was living in Paris,

and he proposed a compromise. I should spend three months a year at Yardley Grange for the sake of appearances, and the rest of the year I was free to do as I liked."

"And you agreed to that?" It was more a statement than a question.

She nodded. "I didn't have many options. Did you know that tying up your unwilling wife and whipping her buttocks with a riding crop and then fucking her from behind like a dog is not grounds for divorce?"

She spoke matter-of-factly, without emotion, but listening to her, Aidan was feeling anything but matter-of-fact. Rage seethed within him like a boiling corrosive. "No," he said, taking a deep breath, "I didn't know that."

She nodded. "As long as the riding crop doesn't slice the woman's skin open, it's not considered cruelty. I didn't know it, either, not until I consulted lawyers about a divorce. One of them," she choked, "even laughed a little and informed me that many wives found 'naughty things' in the marriage bed quite pleasurable and suggested I learn to like it. They all agreed I had to endure it. So when Yardley wanted to compromise, I consented. Part of the bargain was my silence about his proclivities."

"If you'd spoken out, gone to the press . . ." But his voice trailed off, for he realized the futility of that even before she spoke.

"To what end? It still wouldn't have given me grounds for divorce. Besides, I couldn't bear to tell anyone. I couldn't even tell my own family. I was too ashamed."

"You have nothing to be ashamed of!"

"It's easy to say that, and I know it's true, but to reveal those things publicly? Tell people what he did? Describe it openly?" Her voice wobbled, and she shook her head. "I couldn't do it. As I said, it would have served no purpose. And I had my family to consider. They would have had to stand by, helpless, knowing we had no legal redress. Yardley was careful to never give me provable grounds for divorce by cruelty, and my family would have been in agony on my behalf. Not to mention being fodder for the scandal sheets. And what about my mother and father? For them to know the hell they sent me to for what they thought were good reasons and then being unable to do anything to help me? No. I couldn't. Until they died eight years ago in a carriage accident, neither of them ever knew, and I'm glad of it."

He nodded, respecting that, hating that the present legal system gave her no options.

"And I would have had all of society looking at me, some of them with pity, and some with scorn. After all," she added in a hard voice, "it's widely understood that lots of women don't want their husbands to exercise conjugal rights, and those husbands are entitled to punish their recalcitrant wives. It's also understood that quite a few, like Yardley, have even more twisted inclinations, but wives aren't supposed to go about airing that dirty linen in public. I would have been condemned for my lack of discretion more than Yardley for his perversion."

That, he feared, was all too true, a sickening testament to the shallow, callous views of society. "So you compromised with him. But what changed? Something must have, or you wouldn't have done what you did with me."

"Well, for one thing, I reneged. I couldn't keep the agreement," she confessed. "I tried, but even though he didn't touch me, I knew he was gratifying himself by using the servant girls. When he had been occupied with me, he'd left them in peace. I couldn't keep coming back year after year to Yardley Grange, knowing what had happened to me was happening to other women under the same roof, knowing that as long as I was there, I could have prevented it." Her voice broke, and she paused. "I couldn't bear it. Those girls—"

"Julia, Julia." He caressed her cheeks, smoothed her hair. "It wasn't your fault."

"I tried for several years, but it was so unbearable. One year, I just refused to go back. I was a coward, I daresay."

Something snapped inside him. "You are not a coward," he said in a savage whisper, reaching for her, pulling her into his arms, holding her tight. "I've never met a braver woman. It's true," he insisted when she shook her head. He pressed a kiss to her hair, then leaned back against the headboard, pulling her with him. "I won't have you disparaging yourself this way. And servants are not slaves. They are free, at least to an extent. They can leave his employ."

"Without letters of character? For those who stay, it says a great deal about their options, doesn't it?"

"It's not your fault," he repeated. "You can't save the world, Julia."

"I know. When I first began to refuse to come home, Yardley was wild with rage. But then he acquired a mistress, and was preoccupied enough with her to accept my refusal to come home. I heard through a mutual acquaintance that she shared his kinky inclinations, so everything rather leveled off for a few years. But I knew it couldn't last forever. She left him, finally, and he began coming after me again. I would be at a ball in London, and he'd pop up. Or I'd be at the spas of Biarritz or at a salon in Paris, and he'd arrive. I think it became a new form of pleasure for him, tormenting me by following me, making me always afraid of where and when he would turn up. Sometimes, he let days go by, weeks, or even months, but I always had to be on my guard, ready to run. I found the most ingenious methods of escaping from him."

"Motorcars?" he guessed.

"Among other things. I'd always be sure the Mercedes had a supply of petrol if I had it with me. I always obtained a train schedule wherever I went. Yardley cut off my allowance, and my debts kept accumulating. Even though Paul gave me some money, the whole situation was becoming intolerable. But then Yardley caught a bout of flu. He nearly died, and that must have put the wind up him."

Aidan frowned, thinking it out. "You mean he realized he could have died without an heir. He wanted a son." When she nodded, Aidan swallowed hard, knowing he had to hear it all. "What did he do, Julia?" he asked, forcing the words out.

"The next time he saw me, he proposed a new compromise. He said once I'd fulfilled my duty and given him an heir, he would grant me a legal separation, but I knew I couldn't agree to that. I couldn't let him do that to me, or to the child. Once the child was seven, he would have had full custody under the law, and if I ever wanted a divorce, I'd have to obtain it by committing adultery, but if I did that, and he did divorce me, I'd never have custody of any children. And what sort of perversions would my children see in Yardley's household? It gave me nightmares, thinking about it. I couldn't do it, Aidan. I couldn't bring a child into that nightmare."

He heard her rising panic in her rising voice and began pressing kisses to her forehead, her cheeks, her hair. "I know, darling, I know." He sighed, and pulled back to look at her. "I wish I had known about this long ago."

That made her smile. "My gallant prince! What would you have done?"

"My mind is entertaining various possibilities right now." He cupped her face in his hands, and he looked into her eyes. "Would you like me to employ them? Tarnished reputation or not, I am a duke. I have more money and more influence than Yardley will ever have. There are ways I can make his life a living hell, believe me. I'd enjoy doing them, too."

She bit her lip, tempted, then shook her head. "He's sick and he's twisted, and his life is already a living hell. It doesn't matter anyway. I'm free now, and I'm afraid revenge would only prove he still has a hold over me. If I don't care what happens to him, I'm truly free of him at last, and that is what I wanted more than anything."

He nodded, forced to accept her decision. "All right, but I think there are things that I can do. For example, I can make certain that every woman in his employ becomes aware that should they choose to leave him, there is work to be had elsewhere. I'm sure Lady Weston could assist us there. She owns an employment agency, does she not?"

"Aidan," she said with a rather wicked laugh. "You would lie in a character reference?"

"Certainly not. But I think with a wink and a nod from me, Lady Weston could find those women suitable employment."

"He'll only find other maids to take their place."

"I'm afraid that's true. Tides such as that never ebb. As I said, we can't save the world. But we can do our part to make it better." He paused, smiling a little. "We can also warn off any potential brides he might consider. If certain rumors begin circulating about him, about his . . . ahem . . . tastes, don't be surprised. If the rumors don't come from you, you can't be blamed."

"Be careful, darling. He could sue you for slander."

"There are ways and means, Julia. By the time I've finished with him, London society will be reeling with shock over his perversions, but he will never, ever be able to prove the rumors came from me. Trust me. When it comes to this sort of game, I've got Yardley checkmated before we even start to play."

She grinned, reaching up to take a lock of his hair in her fingers. "Oh yes," she murmured, "there's definitely devil horns peeking out from under that halo of yours."

He felt compelled to protest. "Julia, that is a most unfounded accusation. I attend church services every Sunday. I was a choirboy as a child."

"Hmm." She looked at him in a considering fashion, her head tilted to one side. Her grin widened, and an unmistakably wicked gleam came into her eyes as her hand lowered to his chest and slid down his abdomen, making him catch his breath. Smiling, she eased him back down onto the bed and moved on top of him, spreading those glorious legs of hers over his as she moved her hand lower and began to caress his penis. Feeling it come erect in her hand, she began to laugh. "Choirboy, my arse."

They made love again, and this time, she took the lead, making it last. First, by using her hand, and then—as he had done to her—by using her mouth. It was a sweet revenge for all the delicious, agonizing, beautiful torture he'd given her earlier, and she savored it. She stroked him and licked him and teased him, until his hips were thrusting upward and his breath was coming in ragged pants.

"All right," he said, giving in before she could even demand it, "I want to be inside you. I want it, Julia, I want it now."

Straddling him, she rose on her knees. "Gentlemen," she said as she eased her body over his hips and pressed the tip of his cock to her opening, "say please."

"Please," he said at once, and she laughed, feeling wicked, and aroused, and yet awed by the sheer beauty of the sexual act when it was with him. When he pushed upward, entering her with a hard push, she came at once, crying out in surprise at the sensation, and as he thrust into her again and again, she rode him, clenching around him, savoring each wave of pleasure he gave her. And when he climaxed, she watched his face, delighting in his expression, glorying in the sound when he cried out her name.

After it was over, she leaned down and kissed him. "Now that's the sort of 'naughty things' in bed I can always take pleasure in. At least, if it's with you."

When Aidan woke at dawn, Julia was still asleep. He took Spike outside for a walk, and when he returned, he eased gently back into bed so as not to wake her.

Watching her made him smile, for she slept like a child, on her side, palms together beneath her cheek. If this were any other female, he'd think of a little girl who'd fallen asleep while saying her prayers, but in Julia's case, that was doubtful. Her lip was swollen, he noted, and marked where her teeth had drawn blood yesterday. Her lashes were like tiny black fans across her cheeks, and in the pale, gray, early morning light, her skin was luminous.

He thought of that day on the footbridge, and how she looked now, of how in the thirteen years he'd known her she'd gone from being a pretty, pixyish hoyden of a girl to a beautiful, strong, and terribly vulnerable woman, a woman who had suffered much and come out stronger on the other side. A woman who needed rest and tranquillity and security more than even she understood. He could give her all those things.

He thought back over the past few years, of his search for a wife, and all the requirements he'd thought made a particular woman suited to be a duchess. He realized there were really only a few necessary qualities, and all of them stemmed from character, and character was something Julia definitely had. The strength, the resiliency, and the courage in her took his breath away.

He wanted this impossible, incorrigible, invincible woman and no other. He loved her. He supposed he always had, from the very first moment, through all the intervening years, though he'd never been able to admit it until now. He loved her. He always would. He'd never be able to control her, or bend her to his will, or force her into society's conventions, but he'd always known that. Julia was an unconquerable soul.

Suddenly, her eyes opened, vivid lavender eyes in the dawn. She blinked, giving him a sleepy smile. "You look terribly serious," she murmured. "What are you thinking?"

He smiled a little. "I'm thinking of our favorite

poem, and how you are the first person I've ever met who truly has an unconquerable soul."

"Me?" She frowned, looking a little taken aback. "But I'm not Invictus. You are. I always see you as you were that day in the courtroom, your head bloody from the scandal, yet unbowed."

"No, darling." He shook his head. "That's you. I live by the rules and play the hand I'm dealt. You are far more likely than I to shake a fist at fate and say, 'Fuck you.'"

She laughed. "Such language, Aidan! I fear I'm having a very bad influence on you. Still," she added, considering what he'd said, "you are right, I suppose, although I've never thought of myself that way, as unconquerable."

He pressed a kiss to her injured mouth. "I love you. I want to spend my life loving you." He pulled back and looked into her beautiful eyes again. "Marry me."

He hadn't meant to propose, and the moment the words were out of his mouth, Aidan knew he'd made a serious, perhaps fatal, mistake.

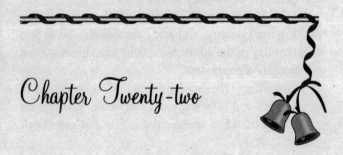

Chapter Twenty-two

Fear. Julia felt it like an enormous weight pressing on her chest, holding her down, pinning her to the bed. She laughed, trying to shake it off. "Aidan, you can't possibly want to marry me."

"Why not?"

She sat up. "I'm a scandal, that's why."

"So am I."

Julia couldn't believe what she was hearing. Shoving back the covers, she got out of bed to put some distance between them, to give herself time to think, but the moment she was out of bed, she realized she was naked, a fact which made her feel even more vulnerable than before. She walked to the armoire, pulled out a wrapper, and slipped it on, wishing she could also reach for a cigarette. Curbing that impulse, she settled for being dressed, more or less, to calm the fear that was sinking into her bones like a cold winter wind.

She took a deep breath, and resumed the conversation. "You are only a scandal because of me. Besides, being considered a scandal is different for a man."

"In the eyes of society, perhaps. Not in my eyes. And I don't care what society thinks anyway."

"That's love's blind eye talking, darling. You've always cared what society thinks."

"I care about you more. I love you." He got out of bed, crossed the room to retrieve his trousers and linen. Any other time, she might have enjoyed such a splendid view of his body, but not at the moment. He was serious, she could tell by the steadiness in those eyes and the determination in that boyishly handsome face, and panic wavered at the back of her throat until she almost couldn't breathe.

She forced herself to wait until he had put his trousers on before she tried again. "I'm divorced, Aidan. My reputation might—only might—be salvageable. And it might not. If not, you'd still be stuck with me."

"Are you saying I would be ashamed of you?" he asked, buttoning his trousers. "I wouldn't, I shouldn't, and I'm not. I won't ever be."

She could see from the level stare he gave her and the grave earnestness in his voice that he meant that, too. But though he might mean it now, would he still mean it five years from now, if society still threw his choice of duchess in his teeth? Ten years from now, if their son was not accepted into Eton because of her? Twenty years from now, if their daughter wanted to marry a man who rejected her because of her mother? Would

Aidan still feel as he did now? Julia didn't know. She didn't want to find out.

Still, she could tell there was no reasoning him out of his noble-hearted vow to stand by her no matter what, so she tried a different tack. "I should make a terrible duchess. Awful. I hate opening fetes and doing good works." She shuddered.

He laughed and came to stand in front of her. "Darling," he said, brushing back her tangled hair with one hand as his other arm wrapped around her waist to draw her close. "I'd never make you do anything you didn't want to do."

Make her. She felt dread creeping in, adding to fear. "But you could," she said, pulling back out of his arms, easing her way slowly, afraid he'd tighten his hold and hang on to her. "It's in the wedding vows. Obey. I'd have to swear to obey you. Making me do things is your legal right." She heard the way her voice had gone suddenly faint and far away.

She saw him frown. "But I wouldn't," he said slowly.

"But you could." She glanced around, wanting, illogically to run. "Why?" she cried, the panic she felt edging into her voice. "Why do we have to marry? Can't we simply go on this way?"

"You mean a love affair?"

"Yes. There's nothing wrong with a love affair!"

"Yes, there is. I love you. I'm in love with you. I want us to be married. I want children." He tried to take her hands, but she didn't want to touch, not until they settled the fact that she was not marrying him, or anyone else, ever.

"You mean you want an heir to the dukedom."

"No, Julia," he said patiently, his hands falling to his sides. "I mean children. A family."

Her gaze slid away. "I don't even know if I can have children. I'm inclined to doubt it. I'm thirty, after all, and I've never been pregnant. What if it's not possible?"

"Then I suppose my cousin will be the next duke, and you and I will be our family."

Her fear grew and deepened as she felt his love wrapping around her like chains, tying her to the ground and to a future from which she could never escape. "You won't want that. You'll want children, and if you're tied to me, you'll come to resent our lack of them. We'll grow apart, as married couples always do, or we shall fight and quarrel and make each other miserable, and . . . and . . ." Her voice trailed off as she tried to find the right words to explain the deterioration that would eventually occur. She gave up. "Oh, marriage will just be awful and ruin everything!"

He heaved a heavy sigh and bent to put on his socks and shoes.

"What was that for?" she asked. "The big sigh?"

"If you really want to know," he said, "I feel you're making a child's argument."

Anger blazed up within her. "I am not being childish!"

"I didn't say you were," he said, and the very reasonableness in his voice made her even angrier.

"Don't patronize me."

"I'm not!" Shoes on, he faced her, hands on his hips. "I said you were making a child's argument. You talk as if marriage would be the end of everything beautiful between us, as if marriage destroys passion with domestic dullness, or passion destroys marriage because the people can't live together amicably."

Relieved that he'd put it just right, she nodded. "Yes, yes, that is exactly what I'm saying."

"You see no in-between, no ebb and flow over the years, no gray areas, no compromises?" When she shook her head, he went on, "You've just made my point. That's a child's thinking—full of absolutes and either-ors."

"Childish or not, it's the truth!" she shot back, resentful, trapped, desperate to keep her freedom, freedom she'd barely had the chance to savor. "Marriage, whether it was a nightmare like mine, or contented and dull like my parents, or filled with passionate, lurid quarrels like your parents, marriage is never what it ought to be!"

"And what is that?"

"Passionate *and* happy *and* content."

"I see no reason why we can't have all of that."

"We can! If we're not married."

He made a sound through his teeth, derision and impatience. "What is the difference? Do you think posting banns and saying vows and plighting troth is what makes love die?"

"No. Love always dies."

"God, how cynical you are."

"I have the right to be. Love always dies," she repeated to emphasize the point. "It's a question of when and how. And if we're married, we'll be stuck with each other after it's dead."

"How terrible for you," he shot back.

Now it was her turn to sigh, for she knew the more they discussed this, the more she was hurting him. "Why can't we simply have an affair? You used that word to describe what we were engaging in only yesterday."

"But everything is different today." He raked a hand through his hair, seeming thoroughly exasperated with her, which only added to her fears. "I love you. I think I always have. Watching you sleep, I knew I want us to spend our lives together. Not just hours, not just Friday-to-Mondays at a little love nest in the country. I want us to be together every day of our lives. To grow older together. Is it that you don't love me?"

That was the perfect way out. She could give a little laugh, don the blasé, worldly, woman-of-experience veneer, and say the perfect words to drive him away.

Love? Oh, Aidan, my darling petal, you didn't really think this was about love, did you?

She couldn't say those words. They stuck in her throat because they would be a lie. In this, at least, she could not lie, though it seemed a damned inconvenient time to lose that particular ability. "I do love you," she said, the admission making her feel heartsick and miserable, bruised instead of glad. "But," she went on at once, "what I want for us is what lovers have. Passion and excitement, not staid, dull domesticity. Why can't we just be lovers and enjoy each other? Continue on as we are for as long as it lasts?" Even as she said it, she watched him shaking his head, intractable in his old-fashioned, hopelessly Victorian view of matrimony. "There is nothing wrong with an affair. If we have that, we have everything we need, and we have it without the chains."

"Chains? Is that what you think I offer you when I offer you my hand, when I ask you to be my duchess, share my life, and have my children? Chains?"

"Yes!" she shouted. "I want to be free! Free, damn it all! I spent twelve years enslaved by marriage, and I won't do it again. How could you think I would?"

His head moved as if she'd slapped him. "What are you saying? That I am like Yardley?" Now his voice was cold, cold with anger. "That I would tie you up?"

"Not physically, of course not!"

"But metaphorically, yes?" He drew a deep breath. "God, that you think so little of me, it's no wonder you don't love me."

"I do love you."

He shook his head. "No, you say you do, but I don't think you really do. Love implies trust."

"That's not fair," she whispered. "You can't ask that of me, not after—"

"Yes, I can, and I do. Because I am not him! I am not even remotely like him! And that I should even have to state that fact baffles me. We are not strangers to each other, Julia. You have known me for thirteen years. Do you believe I am capable of anything like what your husband inflicted on you?"

"No, of course not. What I'm saying is that I do not want to marry again. Ever. I will never tie myself down like that again."

"I love you. I would never tie you or trap you."

"Marriage is a trap, even if it is velvet-lined!"

"God, Julia, marriage is not prison."

"It is to me."

He spread his arms in a gesture of futility. "So what is our alternative? To meet here, snatch weekends whenever our separate lives permit so that we can fuck?"

She winced. "I didn't think what we did was fucking. I thought it was making love."

He shrugged, as if she were splitting hairs. "You're saying you want to be my mistress. Is that it? Do I give you money, I take care of your needs, and you belong to me because I paid for you? If so, how is that less of a prison for you, exactly?"

"I'm not saying I should be your paid whore! I want us to be together as much as you do. I just don't want to marry. Why can't we live just as married people do, but without the legal formality?"

"You are suggesting we live together openly without marriage?" He sounded shocked, bless his upright, honorable nature.

"Why not? People do it every day."

"I don't!" His expression hardened. "What about children?"

She swallowed hard, looked down at the floor. "There might not be any. As I said, I might be barren."

"And if you're not?"

"There are ways to prevent pregnancy—sponges, condoms . . ."

"Such methods don't always work. If they fail, my child will be a bastard."

He said the word with loathing, and her panic grew, for she could feel each of them digging in their heels, becoming more intractable, and she tried to stop it. Desperate, her mind raced, working to find that gray area, that compromise, a way that they could both have as much as possible of what they both wanted, grasping at the straws of love and bliss before they slipped through her fingers and vanished forever.

She drew a deep breath and lifted her head, looking into his eyes. "You could marry someone else. That way, you would at least . . . have a legitimate heir."

Even as she said it, she was already wretched from the idea, not only because it would mean he would be making love with another woman as well as her, at least until he had a son and heir, but also because she was asking him to enter the same sort of marriage his parents had suffered. But it was the only tenable idea she had left.

His eyes narrowed, he leaned back from her, a tiny movement that seemed like repulsion. "I can't believe you would suggest such a thing."

Because it's the only other choice we have.

"You were intending to marry without love anyway," she reminded, the devil in her trying to use his own notions about love and marriage against him.

Of course it didn't work. "Only because I thought

love might not come first, only because I wanted a woman that even if I didn't love her passionately, I would grow to love her over time. I never intended to become the faithless husband my father was!"

"But if you married a woman who didn't care about our affair, who knew about us and married you anyway . . ." Her voice trailed off as she watched him violently shaking his head, and she began to realize the impossibility of any future for them.

"I can't believe you would suggest such a thing," he ground out between clenched teeth as if the words were torn from him. "It goes against everything I believe in. Marriage is the only honorable option we have."

And an impossible one. "Now who's speaking in absolutes?"

"Be damned to you." He turned away, walked to the window that looked north, toward Trathen Leagh. He fell silent, he was silent for a long time. "I love you, Julia," he finally said and turned from the window. "I love you with all my heart, my body, and my soul, but even that is not enough to sacrifice my honor as a man."

She felt a violent surge of resentment, anger, and fear, hatred even; she hated his moral code and his honor and his damnably old-fashioned ideas about marriage, and she hated him for expecting what she could not give him. But even more, she hated herself, for not having the courage to give him what he wanted most.

"Why do you want this so much?" she cried, watching him as he started toward the door. "Because I won't give it to you?"

"In a way, yes." He stopped as he passed and turned to look at her, and the tenderness in his face ripped her heart into shreds. "I love you, and I want you to love me in return."

"I do love you! Why do I need marriage lines to prove it?"

"Because I want you to love me enough to commit your life to me. Yes, I want you to love me *that* much, and no less. I want you to love me enough to let go of your fears, because if you don't, you'll never truly be free of Yardley, and I love you so much that I want you to be free of him forever. And I want you to love me enough to understand that you don't have to run away when you're afraid, because you will always have me by your side to protect and defend you. I want you to love me enough to believe in me, and us, and to always know that whatever happens, we are in our lives together. I want you to love me enough to trust me, knowing without a shred of doubt that I will always love you, and take care of you, and cherish you until the moment of my death. Because I will, Julia."

She wanted to believe him. But, oh, God, what if she was wrong?

"For me," he went on, "all that means marriage. Vows made in a church, in front of our friends and families, vows made before God until death do us part. All that and nothing less."

"Aidan—" She stopped, fear trembling in her breast. It was an irrational fear, for she knew Aidan was not Yardley, and yet it was still fear, able to paralyze her, trap her.

"It's too much!" she cried, knowing that from what he was asking of her, there was no escape. If the love died, if they made each other unhappy, if they grew apart, there would be no divorce, for he would never, ever, ever agree to that, and he would never provide her with grounds to divorce him. "You want too much!"

"I won't take less." Once again, he started for the door, walking away, walking out of her life.

"You want the impossible," she cried after him. "I want to be free, and you want to chain me down with promises that I would have to destroy our lives to break!"

"No, but if that's how you see it, then there's nothing more to say. I'll be at Trathen Leagh for the summer."

"Why tell me that?" she asked, dismayed that he would be only a few miles away for at least another two months, so close, and yet so impossibly far. "Because you think I might change my mind?"

He stopped in the doorway, but he didn't turn to look at her. "No. I'm telling you because I want you to know where I'll be, if—" He broke off and bent his head as if struggling to get the words out. "After last night, there might be a child," he muttered, lifting his head, "and if there is, I bloody well want to know about it."

With that, he walked out, and Julia's tears of heartbreak were falling before she even heard his footsteps descending the stairs.

Aidan strode down the stairs, stepped over Spike, and entered her tiny kitchen—a room he suspected he'd now remember all his life. He put on his shirt and his waistcoat, putting his attire back together even as he felt his life coming apart.

She demanded something he could not live in, something his duty and his position could not allow, something he did not want.

He left the house, so frustrated he wanted to slam the door behind him. He was so in love that it hurt like dying to know he couldn't see her beside him every morning the way he'd seen her today. Most of all, he was so angry with himself that he wanted to smash his head into a wall. Why had he told her he'd stay two more months? Why should he stay? And if there was a child, what could he do about it? Nothing. He could not even give his child his name.

He flung back the stable doors, desperate, his only thought to hitch the gig and drive away. But then he remembered her Mercedes was still in the drive, and the Victrola was still down at the cove, and it looked as if it might rain, and . . . oh, hell. Damn it all to hell.

He strode down to the cove to retrieve the things they'd left from their picnic, and packing them up was like torture. The blanket where he'd sat with her, his jacket and necktie, the champagne glasses, the bottle, the bucket, the foods she'd chosen—twice—because he liked them, the Victrola. Each was like another cut slicing him open.

It took two trips up and down the path to bring everything up. He tossed his jacket and tie into the carriage. Everything else he took into the kitchen, but if he'd had any hope she would be downstairs and he would see her again, that she would melt at the sight of him and change her mind, he was disappointed.

He doubted she would ever change her mind. He had no illusions about Julia's aversion to matrimony. He'd seen the horror and fear in her face the moment he'd proposed, and he couldn't blame her for it. At the same time, however, it angered him beyond words that she could think even for a moment there would be anything about committing herself to a life with him that would give her cause for fear. He now understood the nightmare she'd lived in, at least as well as anyone could hope to, but the comparison to Yardley wounded and insulted him in more ways than he could name. As a gentleman, as a man, as a human being.

He went back out to put the Mercedes in the stable but paused beside the motorcar to look up at the cottage. He wanted to shout up at her window, *I am not Yardley, damn it all! I am not Yardley!*

But what good would it do? She obviously thought he was, at least to the extent that marriage to him was a chain, and she wanted to be free of chains.

He released the brake lever and pushed the motorcar to the stable. After opening the second set of stable doors, he guided the vehicle inside and again secured the brake. He then began to hitch the carriage, and as he did, the mindless task gave him even more time to think, to berate himself for deciding to stay in Cornwall for the summer, but he knew the reason for his decision.

Not because he had any illusion she'd change her mind. Not because he hoped his proximity would soften her resolve. No, he'd decided to stay only because he wanted to be near her. To perhaps run into her in town. To perhaps sail by the cove and see her bathing there. To perhaps even come quietly here to Gwithian and just . . . watch her from a distance.

God, he was deranged. Aidan looped the harness collar around the horse's chest with a sound of derision. Or if he wasn't, he soon would be with torture like that. He'd barely managed the self-control to leave her upstairs. How long could he stay in the area before he gave in, before he told her he'd take whatever crumbs she was able to give and tell himself it was enough? Already, he could feel his resolve weakening, and he felt a sudden despair.

How, he wondered, would he ever be able to resist her?

He desired her as much now as he ever had, yet she was as remote and unavailable to him divorced as she'd been to him married. And he was long past just wanting her. What was he going to do now that he was in love with her?

"Aidan?"

He lifted his head, stiffening at the sound of her voice behind him. He tightened the harness and began to secure the traces, and nodded to the motorcar nearby. "I brought your Mercedes inside."

"I see that. I didn't know you knew how to drive."

"I don't. I pushed it in. It looks like rain later, and I didn't think it ought to be out in the rain. I brought the picnic things up, too."

"Yes, I saw them in the kitchen. Thank you."

He wanted to ask her what she wanted, why she'd come out here. If it was just to say good-bye, he wished she'd have it over and go. She spoke before he did.

"That was quite a speech," she said. "Very eloquent."

"Not eloquent enough, it seems. It didn't persuade you." He didn't look at her. Instead, he focused all his attention on finishing his task so he could get the hell out of here.

She entered the stables, moving to stand beside him, but he still couldn't look at her. It hurt too much. He secured the trace, then turned, stepped around her, and circled to the gelding's other side, but she moved to again stand beside him. He could smell the scent of lilacs on her clothes, but at least she was fully dressed now. He could thank God for that small blessing.

"What do you want, Julia?"

"I thought we could talk a bit more." When she put her hand on his arm, his fingers fumbled with the harness. Damn it.

"Talk?" He jerked his arm away. The pain of her refusal was already like a knife in his heart. Did she have to come out here and twist it? "I don't see what there is to talk about. I asked you to marry me. You said no. Seems to me it's all been said."

"Then you'd be wrong." She paused, then said, "Aidan, please look at me."

He closed his eyes, marshaling all the discipline he had before he opened them and turned to face her. "What do you want to talk about?"

She took a deep breath. "Matrimony."

Hope rose up inside him like sunrise peeking over the horizon, but he reminded himself not to get carried away. He said nothing, he simply waited.

"When you first brought it up," she went on, "I was stunned. I suppose I shouldn't have been. I mean, if I'd had time to think it out, I would have seen that you could never tolerate for any length of time the sort of free love arrangement I was suggesting. But I wasn't able to assimilate what it would be like to be married to you. I didn't have time to become accustomed to the idea, to think it over, and I just reacted with instinctive aversion. But in the hour or so that you've been out here, I've had the chance to do the thinking I needed to do."

She paused, and he waited for her to go on, although each second of silence seemed an eternity.

"I kept feeling this fear at the back of my throat at the idea of marriage, but I've never felt fear at being with you, Aidan. Quite the opposite, in fact. As I sat upstairs just now, I thought of all the times I've seen you over the years, and my mind kept going back to that night at the St. Ives Ball, when I wanted you, but I gave you up to Beatrix. I realized I gave you up to her, not only because I wanted her to be happy, but because I wanted you to be happy. And I knew, even then, when I barely knew you at all, that you could never be happy with a woman married to another man. And now, I have also realized you could never be happy living in sin with a woman. And more than anything in the world, my darling, I want your happiness."

His hopes dared to rise a little higher. "What are you saying, Julia?"

She gave a laugh that he probably only thought sounded a bit shaky. "I'm saying yes. I will marry you."

"You will?" Hope flared into jubilation, but he tamped it down, not daring to be convinced. "Are you sure about this?"

"Yes, Aidan. I'm sure." She smiled a little. "You see, you were right when you said I'd never be free of Yardley if I remained afraid. And you were right that people who have children ought to be married, and I realized how much I wanted children. I never let myself believe in that possibility, for every time I was with Yardley, I spent a lot of time praying I was not pregnant. I don't know if I can have children, Aidan, but if I do, I don't want them to be bastards. I want them to be yours, in name as well as in fact. And . . ."

She paused, and he caught his breath, waiting, still not quite daring to believe she meant it yet. "And I love you," she said. "That night at the St. Ives Ball was the night I fell in love with you," she added softly, in a musing sort of way. "I looked into your eyes that night, and they were so reliable and so steady and strong, and I felt as if I'd landed on a rock in a very stormy sea. I turned it down, but now, I would be a fool to turn it down again. Because it's what I need more than anything else in the world. I need you, Aidan, not to be chains that weigh me down, but to be the rock I can cling to when the waves are too high."

"I can do that." His chest hurt, but not with pain.

He felt awed, suddenly, by the responsibility of holding this woman's free-spirited heart, but he'd always been a responsible sort of man. And he couldn't imagine life without her. "I love you," he said, and bent his head to kiss her. "I love you more than my life."

He pressed his lips to hers, but he could feel her lips smiling against his and he pulled back a little, smiling, too. "What's amusing you?"

"I wasn't finished. I have more reasons."

"Oh, sorry." He kissed the tip of her nose. "Go on."

"I thought about what would happen to you if I don't marry you."

He cradled her face in his hands. "Which is?"

"You'll eventually marry someone else, someone—I have no doubt—who is completely and utterly wrong for you, and I love you too much to see you in an unhappy marriage. I have to save you from it."

"I didn't know the prince in the story was the one who needed saving, but thank you."

Once again, he started to kiss her, but just before their lips met, she added, "Oh, and one last thing. Spike would hate me if I let you get away."

He smiled tenderly. "All your defenses are down now, my darling. How do you feel?"

"Free, Aidan." She wrapped her arms around his neck and laughed. "I feel free."

It was terribly old-fashioned to post banns, but Aidan insisted it was the only practical way to go about marriage with a woman like Julia, joking that posting banns gave her three full weeks to change her mind, jump in that motorcar of hers, and dash off for parts unknown.

Still, when the vicar expressed concerns about holding the wedding of a divorcee in his church, Aidan laid all joking aside. After several long talks on the subject, during which Julia tried her best to look sincerely penitent about her past behavior, and both she and Aidan offered many assurances that this particular marriage was not going to end up in the divorce court like her last one, the vicar agreed to perform the ceremony in the St. Ives Church, and the banns were duly posted.

An announcement was made to the press that the Duke of Trathen was engaged for the third time, and this time, his choice of bride caused quite a sensation. Some people thought their engagement the height of bad taste, while others thought it was only fitting, but no one thought the wedding would actually happen, particularly not Julia's astonished family, who, though happy at the news of her engagement, were doubtful she'd make it to the church.

The public was also skeptical. Bets were laid at White's, with odds five-to-one against, and society pages assured the public that the scandal-ridden divorcee who'd been so cold and indifferent to her first husband was sure to jilt the unlucky duke at the altar, making them the scandal of the year twice in a row.

But Julia proved them all wrong. One month after she nearly broke his heart by refusing to marry him, and wearing a white—yes, white—wedding dress, the notorious Lady Yardley, née Miss Julia Hammett, stood up with Aidan Thomas Carr, the Duke of Trathen, at St. Ives Church in Cornwall and said her marriage vows for the second time, but it was the first time she said them with the conviction of her heart.

Her voice never faltered as she promised before her friends, her family, and God to take Aidan as her wedded husband, to have and to hold him from that day forward, for better, for worse, for richer, for poorer, in sickness and in health and all the rest, right out of the Book of Common Prayer, word for word.

Well, not quite word for word. She did leave out the word *obey.*

She must have forgotten that part.

If you loved SCANDAL OF THE YEAR
and are looking for another
sensual, emotionally rich romance,
try the latest in Julie Anne Long's
sparkling Pennyroyal Green Series . . .

Turn the page for a sneak peek of
WHAT I DID FOR A DUKE
Available March 2011
From Avon Books

After discovering his fiancée in another man's bed, the Duke of Falconbridge—a notorious noble with a reputation for sin—plans a most suitable revenge: he will seduce his rival's innocent sister, Genevieve—the only Eversea as yet untouched by scandal. But he's unprepared for the passion simmering beneath Genevieve's meek and self-controlled surface. And though Genevieve has heard the whispers about the Duke's dark past, she is shocked and exhilarated to discover what a woman is capable of in the arms of a wickedly irresistible man . . .

I t was decided—no one knew where or when the idea originated, but it had been taken up with enthusiasm—that a walk would be undertaken to enjoy the weather while it lasted. The ladies would bring their sketchbooks and embroidery and the men would bring their cricket bats out to perfect their swings ahead of cricket season, and presumably to impress the women.

Since Genevieve could conceive of no place where she would be happy, outside was as good as inside, and it hardly seemed likely that Harry would propose to Millicent whilst surrounded by friends and holding a cricket bat.

And so walk out they did.

The day had remained insultingly bright and clear. It hardly seemed fair to her that Autumn had divested the trees of their leaves and left them to stand embarrassingly nude in a relentlessly lemony sun, let alone the fact that made the world seem cheerfully indifferent to her internal chaos.

Everyone seemed to be oblivious. Chase, if he were here, might have noticed. Chase was seeing to business in London; he'd sent a brother and a sister, Liam and Meggy Plum, to live in Pennyroyal Green. And Colin could be very observant, but Colin was generally a rascal before he was sensitive, and Colin was at home with his wife a few miles away. Olivia assumed her head hurt.

Ian *had* asked her if her head hurt, which seemed to be the extent of male knowledge of female complaints. She'd asked Ian if his head hurt, as he'd looked a little wobbly, too.

They both denied a thing was wrong.

She drifted away and found a place on the scrupulously barbered lawn far enough away from the cricket horseplay to spread out an old shawl. She sat down, tucked her dress neatly over her knees and leaned back on her hands and she watched the men, and ached, and thought.

Harry was all but glowing in the autumn sun. It was both soothing and bittersweet to watch him. A painter could create an entire palette and call it "Harry's hair," and include in it gold and wheat and flaxen and—

A shadow blotted her view before she could add another color to the palette in her mind.

The shadow turned out to be the Duke of Falconbridge.

He settled down next to her on the grass. His pose almost mimicked hers. He stretched out his legs and leaned back on his hands. He plucked off his hat and gently laid it alongside him.

He said nothing at all for a time.

Merely shaded his eyes and followed the direction of hers.

She wondered again if she'd imagined him walking through the garden. So sodden and exhausted had she been she somehow doubted it. And yet . . .

She wasn't going to trouble to be polite.

She was certain he would find something to say that she would object to or be uncomfortably fascinated by.

"He's handsome." The duke gestured with his chin toward Harry. "Osborne is. No *lines*."

She froze.

And then slowly, slowly turned toward him and fixed him with what she hoped was a subject-quelling incredulous stare.

"I suppose," she agreed warily. When one looked from Harry to the duke, the duke certainly suffered by comparison. And it wasn't as though sunlight wouldn't have anything to do with him. But he was certainly Harry's chiaroscuro opposite. He didn't *glow*. His hair was . . . his hair was black. Apart from that frost of gray at the temples, that was. And it was straight and just a bit too rakishly long, just in case anyone should forget his reputation for being dangerous. His skin was so fair that his dark eyes and brows were like punctuation on a page.

She turned away again, her body tensed against any further insights he might volunteer. Olivia and Millicent and Louisa looked like an autumn bouquet in their walking dresses. She focused on that soothing sight instead, deliberately blurring her vision until they were only color, rather than people, one of whom Harry wanted to marry.

"And you're in love with him?"

Holy—!

She actually yelped. It was as much his tone as the observation: conversational. She turned away again and looked straight ahead, her vision blurring in shock. I am a glacier, she told herself. I am a slippery ice wall against which his insights can gain no purchase. He will stop talking. He will stop talking.

"And he's . . . somehow broken your heart?"

He said this almost brightly, as though they'd set out to play a guessing game.

Oh, God. *Pain.* She made a short involuntary sound. As though a wasp had sunk a stinger in.

She whirled furiously on him again, eyes burning with outrage.

So much for glacial control.

Oddly, he didn't look triumphant. He looked almost sympathetic.

"I'm afraid it's evident, Miss Eversea. To me, anyhow. If I'm not mistaken, no one else seems to have bothered to notice, if that's any comfort. Unless you've confided in anyone? Your sister, perhaps?"

Rather than claw him in fury, she curled her fingers into the grass, and would have yanked it up by the roots if she wouldn't have felt guilty about killing innocent plant life and creating more work for the groundskeeper.

And no. Olivia was the last person she would burden with the news of hopeless love.

"No," she said shortly. Thereby admitting her deepest, darkest secret.

"And has he kissed you?" he asked, lightly.

Each impertinent question shocked her anew and flayed fresh welts over raw and newly exposed secrets. All of her muscles contracted, as if colluding to shrink away from him.

Why was he doing this? How did he *know*?

"He's a *gentleman*," she said tightly.

How quickly could she spring up and bolt away? Could she pretend she was being chased by a wasp? If she ran screaming from the duke surely a scandal would ensue. If this was his idea of courtship then she had no doubt his fiancée had abandoned *him*.

"And has he *kissed* you?" he repeated in precisely the same inflection apart from a fresh and maddening hint of amusement.

Her heart rabbited away in her chest, kicking, kicking painfully. This kind of misery was entirely new, and she hadn't yet learned to accommodate it. Her stomach was roiling, her cheeks were flushed, and she wondered if she ought to go have a lengthy heartfelt chat with her handsome cousin, the vicar, to ask if there was any particular penance she could do to stop the unprecedented variety of suffering raining down upon her this week.

"He has kissed me," she confirmed coldly.

What made her say it? It wasn't entirely a lie. Perhaps pride had made her say it. Perhaps the very notion of another man kissing her would drive him away.

But Harry *had* kissed her hand once, lingeringly, as though her hand was a precious thing. It had surprised her; in her mind it had cemented their attachment.

"*Has* he?" Amused and clearly disbelieving. "Point to the part of your body he kissed."

She stared rigidly across the expanse of green, eyeing her brother's cricket bat and contemplating other more satisfying uses for it. Ian was demonstrating a swing for Harry. And for Olivia and Millicent, of course, so Olivia and Millicent could admire his form.

As if they knew or cared anything about form. The things we do for men, Genevieve thought.

She was silent. She could simply refuse to say another word to the man.

"Was *this* the part?" the duke tapped the back of her hand with one long finger.

She snatched it away from him and cupped it in her other hand as though comforting it and glared daggers at him.

"If you *please*, Lord Moncrieffe."

The anguished embarrassment and her glare deterred him not at all. He raised his brows, waiting with infinite, infinite, downright *evil* patience, unruffled. His eyes were dark and deep, as reflective in the sunlight as the polished toes of his boots. Like a body of water, where one couldn't tell whether you could wade safely through or step in and be swallowed whole by depth. She had the strangest sense he could absorb anything with those eyes and reflect back the same irony: a glare, a smile, a tragedy, a comedy.

But there was something about him . . . She was tempted to wade in. Just a little. it was the same temptation she'd succumbed to when he'd discussed—just as deliberately—Venus and Mars. Because he wasn't wrong. Because he was honest, and she liked it. Because he was relentless, and she admired it. Because she half-hated him, but he didn't bore her.

Because he spoke to her the way no one else had ever spoken to her, which meant he saw her in a way no one else saw her.

"Very well. He has kissed my hand, yes. Surely there's nothing untoward about that."

"I suppose whether it was *untoward* depends on his intent and the circumstances and how much you enjoyed it."

"It was an excellent kiss," she all but whispered.

"Oh, I'm certain it was." The bloody man was amused. "A real man would have kissed you on the mouth, Miss Eversea. 'Gentleman' or no. And it's a very good mouth you have." He volunteered this as though offering advice on Harry's cricket form.

She stared at him, shock dropping open her mouth.

Her *very good* mouth.

Damn him for inciting curiosity about what constituted a *good mouth*.

She nearly raised her hand to touch it. Stopped herself. And then she did, surreptitiously, rest the back of her hand against it.

They were soft, her lips, barely pink. Shaped neatly and elegantly.

But what made it *good?*

She'd no vocabulary at all for this type of conversation. For the types of compliments he produced. They were very adult, and he presented them to her as though she ought to know what to do with them.

She didn't. But speaking with him reminded her of the first time she'd taken a sip of coffee. A bitter, foreign black brew, that grew more appealing, more rich and complex, the more necessary, the more she sipped.

He casually, deliberately removed his coat, folded it neatly, laid it next to him. The wind took the opportunity to play in his hair, lifting it a bit, tossing it about, letting it drop, satisfied at having mussed a duke.

He leaned back on his hands. And then idly turned to her. He inhaled, and exhaled an almost long-suffering sigh.

And he began in a patient, almost leisurely fashion, in a voice fashioned from dark velvet, a voice that stroked over her senses until they were lulled, to lecture directly to her as she was a girl in the schoolroom.

"A proper kiss, Miss Eversea, should turn you inside out. It should . . . touch places in you that you didn't know existed, set them ablaze, until your entire being is hungry and wild. It should . . . hold a moment, I want to explain this as clearly as possible . . ." he tipped his head back, paused to consider, as though he were envisioning this and wanted to relate every detail correctly. "It should slice right down through you like a cutlass with a pleasure so devastating it's very nearly pain."

He waited, watching her face, allowing her to accommodate the potent words.

Her mouth was parted. Her breathing short. She couldn't look away. His eyes and voice held her as fast as if he'd cradled her face with his hands.

And as he said them, an echo of sensation sounded in her, like a remembered dream, an instinct awakened.

She thought about Mars getting ready to give Venus a good pleasuring.

Stop, she should say.

"And . . . ?" she whispered.

"It should make you do battle for control of your senses and your will. It should make you want to do things you'd never dreamed you'd want to do, and in that moment all of those things will make perfect sense. And it should herald, or at least promise, the most intense physical pleasure you've ever known, regardless of whether that promise is ever, ever fulfilled. It should, in fact . . ." he paused for effect ". . . haunt you for the rest of your life."

She sat wordlessly when he was done. As though waiting for the last notes of a stormy, discordant symphony to echo into silence.

The most intense physical pleasure.

His words reverberated in her. As if her body contained the ancient wisdom of what that meant, and now, having been reminded, craved it.

She should have gotten up to leave and not looked back.

"So you've had this kiss? Or is it something you aspire to?" Her voice was a low rasp.

For a moment he said nothing at all. And then a faint, slow, satisfied smile.

She had the oddest impression she'd passed a test. And that she'd surprised him yet again.

"I'll leave you to wonder about that, as well, Miss Eversea. I'm a man who cherishes my mystique."

She gave a little snort. But she was undoubtedly shaken.

She turned back to watch Harry, who was now making a great show of balancing the cricket bat on his palm. It was jarringly the opposite of the conversation she was in the midst of.

Does *Harry* know about those sorts of kisses? Does he have those kinds of *thoughts*? Did he have any idea what one kiss of my hand would do to me? Of what dreams I would unfurl from it?

Is it only me, or do all women think this way?

Would a real man have kissed my mouth?

She was tempted to touch her mouth again, and to imagine.

She gripped the grass again, more tightly, needing to feel solid ground. She was dizzy, more confused than she'd been yesterday. As though the land around her was sea and she'd just been cast adrift in an ocean of sensual knowledge she would never now partake of if Harry married Millicent.

Damn the Duke. She was devastatingly clever, but he'd just made it very, very clear that *she* knew nothing, nothing at all about . . . anything.

"Did he make you a promise on the heels of this 'kiss,' Miss Eversea?"

She was never going to enjoy the mocking way he referred to that *kiss*.

She said nothing.

But he seemed to take this as a confirmation.

"Are you spoken for? Did he back away from a promise?" he asked hurriedly. He sounded tense. Oddly as though he intended to deal unkindly with Harry if this was the case.

"Not . . . not as much. No. But everything was . . . implied. Or so I thought. We've been so close for so long, you see, and . . . there was no reason at all not to believe . . . especially not after yesterday . . ."

"And yet he is preparing to launch a proposal at your dear friend Millicent."

He might as well have shot an arrow straight into her solar plexus. Hearing those words spoken aloud by another human were just that pleasant.

She covered her eyes with her hand, sucked in a jagged breath. "Yes. He told me so. Yes."

She took her hand away and bravely looked back at him.

The duke took this in with raised eyebrows. And gave his head a little wondering shake, whether at Harry's or her expense, she could not be certain.

"Has *he* ever sent flowers to you?"

"He once presented me with a bouquet of wildflowers he'd just picked," she confessed dismally.

The duke thought this was amusing, judging from what his eyebrows did.

"Has he kissed *her*? Any of her parts? Or sent flowers to her?"

Argh. The misery. "I don't know. She hasn't told me. *He* hasn't told me. And usually . . . well, Millicent and

I tell each other everything. And I thought Harry told me everything, too."

"If you haven't told Millicent how you feel about Lord Harry, then you haven't told Millicent everything, have you?"

Well, then. She was generally assumed to be clever, but in that moment she felt a fool. He had an excellent point. She hadn't *dreamed* Harry harbored a tendre for Millicent; she'd floated along in the comfortable certainty of friendship.

"I'm afraid all of this is rather evident. To me. Otherwise, you are exceptionally inscrutable and I'm certain not a soul suspects," he humored. Suppressed laughter in his voice.

She scowled darkly at him. "And isn't that *just* my good fortune that *you* should notice and choose to torment me with it."

He laughed. Admittedly, he had a fine laugh, deep and genuine. She sensed he didn't do it easily. She liked the sense that she'd surprised it from him.

And therein lay his vulnerability. She could make him laugh.

She had another surprise for him. "Lord Moncrieffe, do tell me, since we're speaking so frankly. What is your game?"

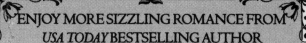

Unforgettable, enthralling love stories,
sparkling with passion and adventure
from Romance's bestselling authors